WHATEVER
— THE —
COST

TAVIAN BRACK

Copyright © 2023 Tavian Brack
All Rights Reserved

Writing this novel was particularly personal for me. I wrote this with my grandmother in mind. As a little girl who grew up in London, she was forced to leave school at fourteen when the Blitz began and never returned to finish. Growing up I remember her always talking about the shelters, the underground where Londoners would congregate, and of course, Mister Churchill: that calm voice at the other end of the BBC broadcast. I dedicate this book to my grandmother, and to all of the grandmothers and grandfathers who suffered through those dark days.

I'd like to thank Jessica for all of her hard work in helping me with this book, the previous one, and everything still to come. Your talents are amazing, and I can't wait for the next project.

PROLOGUE

Manchuria
May 1st, 1941

"Your move," the Japanese Foreign Minister said after putting his white stone down on the Go board. He then filled up his own small teacup and that of his guest. The rooftop pavilion of his private residence inside the Japanese Administrative Center in Manchukuo was a quiet enough environment and provided him with an ideal place to host important guests when the weather cooperated.

It also came with a splendid view of Manchuria's central valley. The lush green valley with its gently rolling landscape and distant mountains was an impressive sight to any that saw it. The spring bloom was in its full glory, and the trees were a fascinating mix of white and pink on this fine spring morning. Birds nested in tiny coves all over the rooftops of the wide-open Japanese compound.

Heinrich Stahmer stared down at the board before him. His fingertips gently rubbed the small, black stone between them. Go was an ancient Chinese game of strategy that he'd recently been introduced to by his Japanese host. Far superior to Chess by any means. The German had found an instant love for the game.

"Thank you," he softly spoke. He took his teacup, never taking his eyes off the board, and sipped slowly on the green beverage. Japanese tea was another thing he'd been introduced to recently that he enjoyed. His trip from Germany had been long, and tiring. But his Japanese hosts understood how to rest and recuperate after such stressful ordeals, and had provided him with all the comforts that anyone could possibly desire.

Across the table from him, Foreign Minister Matsuoka took his eyes off the game board as he quietly started to thumb through the green paperbacks that his guest had brought with him from Berlin. The information within those pages was as precious to him as gold or diamonds. Matsuoka's face was expressionless but inside he was elated. He had promised Emperor Hirohito that he would deliver such valuable information, and now he could say that he'd succeeded.

"And the information contained here is accurate you say?" he asked Stahmer without once taking his attention from the pages.

"Highly accurate," the German special envoy answered, sparing only a moment to look back at Matsuoka. "Directly from a highly reliable source." He then turned his attention back to the Go board. He had no less than four good moves open to him. He'd taken quickly to the game since his arrival only two days before, and he'd always been a swift learner. But he was, after all, only an amateur compared to his host.

The Japanese minister continued to peruse through the pages. He was tempted to ask whether that source was in the Kremlin but decided against it. He knew the German wouldn't give up that information. Had their roles been reversed he wouldn't have either. But it really didn't matter. So long as the information contained in these pages was reliable, the source was irrelevant. Besides, who in their right mind would think that such information could possibly be so valuable outside of a geologist's office. But it was. At least to the

Japanese High Command, and the Emperor. After all, it was the guarantee of such information that he had decided on the Japanese Army's proposal.

There had long been two trains of thought that concerned Japan and its future as an imperial power. Most military and political planners back in Tokyo were quite sure that war with another major power was all but inevitable. Most of them believed that the United States of America and the Empire of Japan would eventually clash, as the Japanese need for more and more material resources would compel it to expand into the southern oceans and the wealth of the East Indies. However, another school of thought, pushed mostly by the Imperial Army, wished to take a different approach. The wide-open lands of Siberia had offered the empire a tempting target for expansion. Past conflicts with the Soviet Union had ended those hopes. But that was before Tokyo had a solid alliance with another major European power.

"I think," Stahmer began, "that you will find these reports to be highly interesting." His Japanese was rusty but conversational. "Useful?"

Foreign Minister Matsuoka slowly nodded his head as he continued to absorb the information. "Quite."

"Then I trust that your government will make good use of it." He put his hand out as if he were about to put his stone down then thought better of the move.

The Germans had indeed come through with the information, just as they'd promised. The volumes were full of highly detailed pages. Mineralogical surveys, maps of mines, oil refinery output reports, the list went on and on. It would take the Imperial Army weeks just to digest what Stahmer had brought them. But the best had come as a surprise to the Japanese. Included with the volumes of earthly records, was a rundown of Soviet military formations that guarded the eastern borders of that country.

"Provided it's accurate information. Some of the maps are twenty years old. Hard to believe that the Russians could not have exploited such important resources by now." He shook his head disapprovingly. "But if these reports are correct..."

"Then your empire stands to gain a treasure trove of mineral wealth," the Nazi finished the other man's sentence. The words drew an agreeing nod from Matsuoka. "And in the end, both of our nations stand to gain. To take our rightful positions as world powers."

The pages, filled with thirty years' worth of mineralogy and geological surveys, would be highly valuable, both to his government and to himself personally. Such highly accurate surveys could significantly boost his standing within the government. Siberia was an untapped dream, full of untapped resources. All the things that the Japanese Empire was in desperate need of in order to expand. China be damned. Russia was where the real resources lie. It was unfortunate that their previous campaigns against the Soviet Union had gone so sourly.

Matsuoka gazed up at the German as the other man studiously planned his next move. "And what was the name of the mineral again? The one that your nation wants in exchange?" His eyelids fluttered as he tried to think of the word. "Uran...?"

"Uranium," the Nazi told him.

"Uranium," Matsuoka repeated the word. He'd never heard of it before. But the Germans obviously had some sort of use for it. So far as he was concerned, they could have all they wanted, so long as the intelligence their government was providing them with secured victory. He was quite sure Tokyo would agree with that logic.

"How fortunate that you came across this information when you did. My emperor was quite prepared to grant the Navy its request for a southward approach. Now... the Dutch colonies in the Pacific don't seem so appetizing."

"Good. I'm glad," the Nazi envoy replied. "You can still pick off those islands later if you wish. The Dutch government won't have much they can do about it." He laughed as he said it. His eyes searched the Go board, considered two moves, settled on one, and dropped his black stone next to a white one. He grinned at his host. "Your move now."

CHAPTER ONE

Flight Lieutenant Christopher Sharp sat on the single wooden bench just outside the CO's tent. The sun was warm as it beat down on him and he was tempted to reach into his pocket and light up a smoke while he waited but knew better than that. Crew chiefs tended to frown upon smoking in the open around airfields where flammable material could catch. But even had that not been the case RAF policy forbade it and failure to observe it came with a pretty stiff fine that Sharp really was not interested in paying. He had just returned to active duty after all.

His new posting was RAF Chilbolton, an airfield in the south of England an hour north of Portsmouth. He'd arrived just an hour earlier after catching the only truck heading this way following the approval of his new orders. In truth, he'd been surprised when he'd received confirmation that he was being returned to flight status and had wasted no time in packing up his bag and heading out the door. He'd been almost sure that a mistake had been made and didn't wish to waste any time getting there. At any moment he expected some staff sergeant to come up and inform him of the mistake and reversal of his orders, sending him packing back to the hospital in London.

But for the moment he was just happy to be back on a flight line, having spent six months in a Soviet detention center where it had been no picnic. Miserable weeks spent staring at empty walls, with only minutes a day of outside activity, had nearly driven him mad. Now he understood and sympathized with people in any country confined to any kind of isolation for extended periods.

"Sharp!" a booming baritone voice called out through the wooden office wall. Sharp jumped up, ran his hands down his tunic, quickly made sure his top button was undone, as was customary for fighter pilots, then entered through the door. He'd departed London before being able to get his haircut. His brown hair was shaggy and unkempt, but there was nothing he could do about it now.

His new CO sat behind a single metal desk, scribbling out some notes. His eyes looked up at Sharp as he stepped inside then he returned his gaze down at the report in his hands.

Sharp stepped into the center of the small office and stood at attention. The other man was Group Captain Bushwell, his new commanding officer. A middle-aged man with well-groomed black hair and a thin mustache. Despite his age, he was in remarkable shape, and Sharp could tell that he was a physically active man. Though he'd never met Bushwell before now he'd heard about the man's reputation as an able pilot and administrator. A man who knew how to win in the skies.

"At ease, Sharp," he said, not bothering to avert his eyes from the paperwork he was reading through. Sharp stood silent. The tent was obviously a temporary structure that looked like it was only recently thrown together. It was surprisingly cool inside. A single fan sat atop a score of filing cabinets that lined the walls of the cramped space. A chalkboard with the names of squadron pilots written on it was propped up against the makeshift wall. From outside he could hear the winding sound of a plane flying low overhead.

After a few very silent moments Sharp began to wonder if his new CO was testing his medical status by having him stand so long. Bushwell tossed the report on his desk and leaned back, his wooden office chair squeaking.

"So," he began, "how are you feeling, Lieutenant?"

"Fine, sir," Sharp replied. "Fit for duty."

Bushwell nodded slowly.

"Are you? I wonder." His voice was surprisingly placid.

Sharp didn't respond. Just blinked. No doubt Group Captain Bushwell had a copy of his medical report and knew what he'd been through since Poland last May. He'd been in the service for some time and had been both in the ranks and a commissioned officer. He knew commanders liked short answers. Yes, sir. No, sir. Right away, sir. Sharp felt no need to confuse them anymore with extended replies.

"Flew in Poland," Bushwell went on. "Three confirmed kills. Nasty crash, followed by months spent in some Russian hospital. Is that about right?"

Sharp quirked his head oddly. He was sorely tempted to say that it hadn't quite been a hospital where he'd been while in Russia. But he thought better of it. The first few weeks there had been the absolute worst. After going down in Poland and finding himself in Red Army custody, he'd been carted off to some isolated camp in the center of nowhere. Though not technically a prisoner, since there was no conflict between the USSR and Britain, he certainly had not been treated as a neutral combatant either. In fact, his Red Army captors had treated him, and a few other foreigners captured in Poland, nearly as bad as a POW. Days without food, inadequate water, and medical treatment, eight weeks with his right arm in a sling, and no contact at all with the British embassy had worn him down physically and mentally. Had that not been bad enough, his interrogation by the NKVD, Soviet Secret Police, had been much, much worse.

Days spent in bright cells, sleep-deprived and physically intimidated, he was still appalled by his treatment there. Their fearsome state security agents had treated him as some enemy spy, captured in their territory when in fact he'd gone down in Poland, after narrowly escaping a German squadron. It was only after four months that he'd even heard from the British embassy in Moscow. His conditions had gotten slightly better soon after, but it still took another two months before he'd been released. He'd returned to English soil just before Christmas, forty pounds lighter and spent the next two and a half months on medical absence. So when the doctors had signed off on his paperwork, he'd taken the opportunity to fly the coop as quickly as he could. He was eager to fly again. To get back into the fight.

"Yes, sir."

"Hmm," Bushwell grunted and nodded his head slowly. His eyes looked Sharp up and down. "I see. Have you recovered then, from your wounds?"

"Yes, sir," he replied vigorously. Bushwell nodded again.

"And the other wounds?"

Sharp blinked. He was confused and uncertain as to what to say. "Sir?"

Bushwell bit the inside of his cheek and tapped the paperwork on his desk.

"Do you know what this is, Sharp? It's your record. All of it. I had it sent to me when your assignment here came through. Everything you've done since you enlisted in '32. India, Malta. Flight school in '37. Everything. Interesting reading. You have a good habit of keeping your head down and your mouth shut. But I wonder..." He left the rest of his sentence unfinished and looked Sharp squarely in the eye.

Sharp hesitated for a moment but he knew the group captain was giving him an opening.

"Sir?" he asked innocently.

"Sometimes, Sharp, it's the quiet ones who have the most to say. So my question to you again is this: have you recovered from your wounds?" He crossed his fingers and waited.

Sharp swallowed. His breath ran through his nose and at first, his instinct was to just nod and affirm whatever was written in that report the group captain had in front of him. But the more seconds that went by and the longer he looked the other man in the eye, the more his instincts broke down. What the hell was the worst that could happen?

"My physical condition is fine, sir." He held up his left hand and squeezed slowly. "Little nerve damage here perhaps, but the doctors say I'll be alright."

"Let me tell you something about myself," Bushwell began. "Got my own wings in 1914. Flew in the Great War. Shot down my fair share and saw plenty of my mates get shot down in return. Back in those days, there were no parachutes. Being shot down meant you were dead." He hesitated for a couple of moments, "I understand the other wounds. The ones we don't talk about. The ones up here." He tapped his head with his finger as he finished.

Sharp nodded just slightly but enough that Bushwell could see it and nodded back. There was something about watching helplessly as one's squadron mates were blown out of the sky. His own experiences after his crash landing had been a horrific ordeal. The psychologists who had examined him in London after his return had told him to just forget it. *Don't speak of it and it'll just go away*, they'd tell him. And he hadn't spoken about it, but it hadn't just gone away. He was still haunted by what he'd experienced both in Poland and what had come after.

"You're right, sir," he finally relented. His voice was laced with shame. "I can't say that I haven't been affected by things. I just..." He simply shook his head and looked down at his feet.

"I understand," Bushwell replied compassionately. "I can imagine what the brain doctors said to you. But take it from me, Sharp. Bottling it up is the worst thing you can do to yourself. Doesn't help. It actually makes things worse. I'll leave it at that."

Bushwell adjusted his eyeglasses and flipped through a green folder that he produced from a cabinet. Sharp exhaled a relieving breath and felt a sudden loss of anxiety. Pilot to pilot was one thing.

The men whom he'd flown and fought with in Poland could understand things. It was an unspoken bond. The one that every veteran of every war had spoken about having with his comrades. All you had to do was see it in their eyes. Bushwell struck him as just such a man.

"You're checked out on a wide variety of aircraft. Well, one thing's for sure we're desperately short of fighter pilots, as I'm sure you know."

"Yes, sir."

"Hmm. I need all the qualified pilots I can get." Bushwell opened up his top drawer, produced a pack of cigarettes, and lit one up. Smoking inside was permissible. "Feel free, Sharp," he told him.

"Thank you, sir," he replied then dug into his pocket for his Pall Malls.

"You're assigned to Two Thirty-Nine Squadron, which has seventeen pilots fit for duty," Bushwell went on, reading through his lists. "And twenty-four serviceable aircraft. Hurricanes, mostly with a couple of Spitfires. Out of my seventeen, only six have the minimum number of hours required for status. Eleven came either from flight school directly or flew non-combat planes."

Sharp blinked absently at the news. He inhaled his cigarette and slowly let it back out. Those numbers were pathetic. At least when he'd flown in Poland half the squadron had been checked out on the airplanes they'd flown before the war even began. The other half had the advantage of at least basic training in the weeks before the invasion there.

"The news doesn't get any better I'm afraid," Bushwell added. "Of all my pilots only two have any combat experience. So,"– he closed up the folder and looked back up, – "that makes you a real asset to me here. I'm tasked with a variety of objectives. But first and foremost is to meet the German threat head-on. I don't think I need to tell you what I mean."

"No, sir," Sharp replied. France had fallen and the Germans controlled everything front the Atlantic coast to the North Sea. Dozens of airbases and hundreds of aircraft sat just miles from this position. It hadn't happened yet, but it was generally accepted that sooner or later the Luftwaffe was going to come in force. He drew on his cigarette, taking it nearly down to the halfway mark.

"The Germans are right across a narrow strip of water, and shortly I fully expect that they'll be coming. Hitler isn't going to stop now. I'll boil it down for you even further: the fact is we're desperately outnumbered. Fighter Command is strained to the limit. Jerry outnumbers us by a factor of five, possibly more. I've got children, barely out of flight training, filling the gaps, and squadron leaders are in short supply. So, what that means for you, Sharp, might be something that you're not interested in but you're getting it anyhow. Promotion."

"Sir?" He flinched at the word. A return to flight status was one thing, but promotion meant squadron leadership. After almost a year he wasn't confident that he was ready.

Group Captain Bushwell raised his hand up. "I can't afford a fight with you on it, Sharp, so please spare me any self-conscious rebuff. I'll brevet you the rank, but I can't make it official until headquarters signs off on it. That makes you squadron leader for now. That also puts you in charge. In charge of training. In charge readiness. In short, you'll be responsible for the task of getting these men combat-ready. And then, when the show does start, you'll be the one who has to make the tough calls."

Sharp drew rapidly on the last of his cigarette. Bushwell pointed at the ashtray, and he stamped out the butt and tossed it in the glass bowl. He couldn't say that he liked the sound of that particularly. He'd never trained pilots before, and the ones he'd flown with that couldn't keep up, well... the skies above Poland had a way of separating the weak from the rest. Unfortunately, if that experience had taught him anything it was that RAF pilots were woefully unprepared for what was coming. And after spending months as a guest of Soviet interrogators, he also wasn't sure that he was physically ready to be the leader. But he also knew that the group captain wasn't asking him what he wanted and in the back of his mind, he also knew that his experiences made him the only real candidate.

"Get yourself cleaned up, Sharp," Bushwell instructed. "And pull the proper insignia from supply. I'll have your roster ready for you first thing in the morning. You can start by putting together a basic flight training plan for tomorrow. You're dismissed, Sharp."

"Tomorrow, sir?" Sharp asked him. His eyes nearly bugged out of his head.

Bushwell gave him a hard look.

"How much time do you think we have? Jerry can come across the Channel at any moment. This isn't a boy's club. You have a job to do, and you're expected to do it. You are dismissed."

The group captain picked up a pen and began scribbling down on a pad of paper without paying him any more heed. Sharp stood there for a brief moment stupefied at what had just happened. But he knew better than to say anything.

"Sir," he replied, then did an about-face and walked out of Bushwell's office.

CHAPTER TWO

Mister Edward Bagshaw sank back into his rocking chair and puffed away on his smoking pipe. The aroma of cherry tobacco filled the small living room. Mary, as had become custom these days, was sitting at her secretary, pen in hand, writing out letters. Not everyone in the family had a telephone and writing letters to each of them had become a new daily routine for her. Edward didn't mind. It gave her something to do to fill her time, and it seemed to put her in as good a mood as she was going to be in during these trying times.

Ever since Tommy's funeral, she'd understandably been an emotional wreck. They'd received the news only days after his being killed in France, and it was not anything that either had been prepared for. Though Edward had always known exactly what could very well happen. Mary did too, of course. But for a mother it was different. Bagshaw men had always gone off to war when the country called. He himself had gone off to France when he'd been Tommy's age and seen his own mother break down that day at the train depot, so many years ago. He'd had his own mates back then and many of them had not come home from that war either. But he had. He remembered clearly the day he'd stepped back into his parent's home at the end of it, his mother collapsing on her knees in the door and crying tears of happiness at his return.

His father had gone off to the Zulu War as a young man himself, and before that his grandfather had served in India, putting down the Rebellion of 1857. Yes, the Bagshaw men had gone off to war since the days of Cromwell, and they'd always come home. Until now. The latest addition to the family tradition had been killed in what seemed like a lifetime ago already but in reality, had only been five short weeks earlier.

Mister Bagshaw shifted in his chair, propped his book on his knee, and tried to read. The history of the Stuart Restoration was a favorite subject of his since he was a schoolboy, and he'd looked forward to reading this book. But he'd had it for two months now and barely scratched the surface. Even now he found it nearly impossible to concentrate on it. His thoughts and emotions were elsewhere.

Outside the garden door, he could glimpse Simon, their oldest child and now heir to the family name. Simon was shoveling dirt into a metal bucket and planting a variety of small vegetables in the squared-off corner of the backyard. Edward observed him closely as he watched Simon working the bed of soil and was reminded of just how much like his mother he looked but was headstrong as Thomas had been. He was only now fifteen and full of dreams and ambition. He deserved to have a rich, full life.

Edward brought his thoughts back to the present and tried again to get into his book.

"I'm writing my sister, Caroline," Mary commented, unprompted. She sat behind the small desk, scribbling away on the pad of paper. It would be only one of many letters she'd write today. But he had decided in the past few days that whatever kept her mind occupied was a good thing. It had made the days a little more bearable, and he'd noticed that at night, she was sobbing a little less.

"Oh," Edward casually replied. The end of his pipe bobbed around in his mouth. "And what's happening with Caroline?" Though he already knew the answer.

"Not much. She's getting ready to send the children up to Lancashire for the summer. And Bess is going to go stay at the farm in Maidstone."

Edward looked up at his wife and took the pipe out of his mouth.

"What? Leave her parents alone up there in London?"

Mary turned back to him and gave him a nod and smile.

"But she's the oldest," he told her. "The children, okay I understand. But that house of theirs is quite large, and with Bob's gout, doesn't she have an obligation to help them get along?"

"Dear," Mary began softly. "she's nearly twenty. She's a woman and she has a right to her own life. You know that. Besides, there's no one to take care of the farmhouse, so it makes sense that if anyone should go take care of it, Bess should."

He sighed and shook his head slightly, then put the pipe back in his mouth and went back to his book.

"I suppose," he replied. "Though it's a farmhouse in name only, Mary. It's not like there are any animals up there to tend for. Just a shuttered-up cottage really. Full of rot and termites. I don't know why Bob and your sister don't just sell the damn place off. Seems like more hassle than anything else."

"It was an old family house. Bess is more than capable of putting it back into order." Mary turned back and continued penning her letter.

She'd have it out in today's post and write half a dozen more tomorrow. Writing to everyone from her sister and brother up in London all the way to the distant cousin she hadn't seen since she was five. At first, Edward had been concerned about his wife's mental well-being but then had concluded that Mary had taken her responsibilities as a mother, daughter, and sister very well and that, perhaps, despite her grief, his wife might have been much stronger than he'd previously realized.

"Besides," Mary went on, still writing her letter out. "with the rationing and all having a small working farm might be a good idea.

Perhaps we can send Simon up there to stay. I think he could help her out quite a bit. It would be good for them both. She won't be all alone, and he would have someone a bit closer to his age to bond with."

He eyed her quietly for a moment and a gentle grin graced his features. Simon and Bess were hardly close in age. Bess, or Elizabeth, was Mary's niece and close to twenty. Bess was a young lady who'd spent most of her life in London, and Simon, a fifteen-year-old boy who loved toy soldiers and often re-fought the great Battle of Trafalgar over and over again with model sailing ships. Even as cousins, the two of them had very little in common. But Bess had been close with Thomas, and perhaps his death had also been one of the reasons she was deciding to go to Maidstone. To be alone with her grief.

"Well, I doubt they'd have much in common, but I suppose it's an option," he told her, just to agree with her. But it really wasn't such a terrible idea either, and he knew it. Thomas and Simon had been close as children, and Simon, though he didn't show it, was deeply affected by his brother's loss. The only remaining Bagshaw son had become quiet and reclusive in recent days. Preferring to be alone, he'd often spend hours tilling the new backyard garden.

Edward gave up on trying to get into his book and glanced at the cuckoo clock on the wall, then sat up suddenly.

"Oh. You know I think that French fellow is on the radio," he said as he jumped up and walked over to the radio set. He turned it on, and there was a gentle crackle of static. He fumbled around with the nob until it cleared up. "I'd heard he was going to be giving a speech of some sort."

"Who's that, dear?" Mary asked offhandedly.

"Oh I don't recall the man's name," he replied. "General of the French. I'd read in the paper that he was going to be making an address on the BBC. Ah. There we go."

The radio cleared up, and a single, soft-spoken French voice came over the speaker. His words were at first dry and monotone. Edward turned the volume down just a bit so as not to disturb Mary and listened quietly to the Frenchman speaking. He knew the French language well. He'd been good with it in his studies as a young lad and had gotten fluent in the language during his own time there during the first war.

"Must be very difficult for those people," Mary commented. "The French, I mean. Under the thumbs of that horrible man."

"Aye. We may have had our own difficulties with the French, but they certainly don't deserve this," he agreed. He was fond of the French people. Despite the obvious cultural differences and their lack of some social restraint that he frowned upon, he knew them to be good and sturdy people. Also the thought of them having so quickly been forced to throw in the towel was unnerving to him. The British and French armies had fought side by side for four long years, from 1914 to '18, and had never once broken. The recent peace treaty had been a serious blow to the British people who were now forced to fight the Germans once again. This time all alone.

"...*et sur mon honneur..*" the Frenchman continued, his voice raised only subtlety. Edward sat back down in his chair and rocked back and forth, smoking on his pipe and listening to the other man.

"I wonder how many of them are going to be staying here in England," Mary said. "Mister Smithers, down the road, said thousands are leaving every day out of Dover. It's a wonder those Germans don't just sink the ships they're on. Don't they have boats out there? What do they call them again? Submarines?"

"There's a Swedish vessel in the harbor right now," he told her, somewhat surprised that Mary had spoken this much about the current state of affairs. She'd barely spoken two words about the war in the last few weeks. But it still felt good to hear her speaking again without breaking down. He knew she'd become emotional again tonight when they'd both gone to bed. He'd held her close each and every evening for the last several weeks. Her tears had been understandably overwhelming. "The Germans won't sink a Swedish vessel. They're helping to take those French home. The Jerries won't dare sink one of them. There's only a few countries who'll even trade with Germany these days."

"...*nous nous sommes battus avec acharnement...*"

Mary sighed and shook her head then scribbled her name at the bottom of the letter.

"I can't imagine why anyone would want to," she stated as she began to carefully fold the letter into thirds. "Terrible people," she muttered almost under her breath.

"...*mais nous n'avons pas abandonné...*" the radio uttered. The Frenchman's voice had become much livelier now, with much more passion. "...*le cœur Français est maintenant occupé par nos ennemis...*"

The glass garden door opened, and Simon stepped back inside, wiping his forehead with the back of his sleeve. He barely glanced at his father as he strode by, quiet as a mouse. Edward watched him go by. He wanted to say something to his son. Wanted to get up and tell him that he was going to be okay and get through his grief but then instantly thought better of it. Was it Simon he was looking to comfort, or himself? He wasn't sure right now. He loved both of his boys, and the pain from Tommy's death still clung to him closely. He briefly thought of his father, sitting outside of his bedroom after Edward had returned from France in 1918. He hadn't known it then, but his father had sat quietly outside and listened as Edward fought through the nightmares. The horror of the memory of that war had haunted him for years afterward. His father understood better than anyone the strength it took to not badger his own son but to wait for him to reach out. He wished Simon would speak to him. Wished it more than anything right now. But Edward also knew that Simon had to do the speaking.

"...*notre guerre n'est pas finie...*"

"What's he saying?" Mary asked. She put the letter into an envelope and sealed it with a lick of her tongue.

"Oh. He's saying that the French war is not over. Pleading with his people to resist. He's quite passionate actually. Reminds me a bit of Mister Churchill." *A big improvement from that fool Chamberlain,* he thought. Though he'd not voice that opinion in front of Mary.

"I think you should go speak with him," she whispered to him as Simon's footsteps could be heard going up the wooden staircase.

He grimaced and gave it some thought, then shook his head.

"Simon needs time, Mary," he said to her gently. "I know how he feels. But he needs to have the space and the freedom to say how he feels. We're here to listen, of course. Give him some time."

"I'm going to go to him," she said and began to get up from her chair.

"No!" Edward held up his hand. He didn't mean to snap at her, and his face lightened up when she looked at him. "No, dear. Give him some time. Please. Just give him some time and he'll open up. I don't know. Perhaps you're right. Maybe we should consider sending him to stay with Bess. Just for a little while anyhow."

Mary dropped back down into her chair and frowned. He knew what she wanted to do, what her maternal instincts told her to do. To go upstairs and say something to him, but Edward knew it wouldn't work. Simon might look like his mother, but he drew his traits from his father. No, he'd open up when he was ready to and not a moment before.

The two sat still in the small room together. They sat for a while longer and listened to the Frenchman continue his speech. His tone had become alive and fiery now. All the passion of a man whose homeland he was now dedicated to liberating now thick in his voice.

"*...vive la France, vive la liberté...*"

CHAPTER THREE

President Roosevelt had had enough. Exasperated he took off his round spectacles and rubbed his eyelids. He was tempted to slam his hand down on his desk but restrained himself. He knew such a display was beneath his office and that letting his temper get the best of him would only make matters worse. Besides that, the Resolute Desk was a national treasure, and treating it so dismissively was insulting to the people who'd elected him for an unheard-of third term.

Across the desk from him, Secretary of War Harry Woodring stood red-faced, arms flapping about in the air as the heated argument with his Navy counterpart was getting tenser. Sitting behind the two cabinet secretaries, other advisors and officials sat quietly, watching the tirade take place. What had begun as a simple discussion on national preparedness had quickly devolved into an outright ruckus with Secretary Woodring and Secretary of the Navy Knox taking opening shots at each other. Their opinions and stances could not have been farther apart.

The isolationist Woodring took a stubborn, vocal stance against any proposed expansion of the military, while Secretary Knox was of the mind that the United States couldn't arm itself fast enough. Like Roosevelt himself, he considered the Nazi and Imperial Japanese as threats to the security of America. Woodring's muffled accusations of warmongering were not taken lightly – or kindly.

"Enough!" the president told them both. He naturally had a booming voice, and he knew when to use it. But Roosevelt was also exasperated, and there was frustration in his tone. He was as tired of this dissension between his cabinet as anyone else was.

Both men fell silent. The lanky Woodring let his arms fall to his sides and let out a frustrated sigh. His plump face was flush red, and he was nearly out of breath.

"I've had enough of this bickering, gentlemen," he scolded them. "I called this meeting so that we might air out some of our differences. Smooth things out. Not to get into a boxing match."

Normally a cordial man, there was a blunt seriousness in his voice. Franklin Roosevelt was a man who knew what it took to lead others. Perhaps better than anyone else. His record of bringing two sides of an argument together to find a middle ground had pulled America out of the depths of the Great Depression. His ability to collaborate with the conservatives in both the Republican and Democratic parties alike had molded what many called the greatest cabinet in the history of the country. He went above and beyond to try and coax his political adversaries into working with him. And he was usually very successful. It was only when no middle ground could be reached that he tended to become agitated.

"Mister President," Woodring began slowly and delicately, "I understand the mood of the other people in this room, sir. However, I cannot stay the silent dog lying in the corner."

Roosevelt held up a single hand and gave himself a few brief moments to compose himself. His blood was running hot now, and he silently let out a slow, relieving breath then put his spectacles back on.

"Mister Secretary, no one has asked you to be the silent dog," he told him with as much gentility in his voice as he could muster. Woodring was becoming the proverbial pain in his backside and FDR knew that more than one ranking member of Congress and his cabinet were quietly jockeying to push the old Kansas politician out.

"I must voice my opinion, sir," Woodring said softly.

FDR said nothing. He knew to reply to the comment would only invite the other man's unprompted response and he had absolutely no wish to get into another argument with him. The world was seemingly headed for another conflict, and right now, his focus had to be on getting the nation on the right track. The secretary of war was quickly becoming an obstacle to that goal.

"Let's get back to our original purpose here," Roosevelt said. "Please." He held up an open hand, indicating for the two men to sit on the Oval Office sofas. He flipped back through the stack of papers sitting atop his desk. "I've reviewed the plans the chiefs of staff submitted last month, and I approve of the changes they've requested."

Woodring grimaced ever so slightly, but enough for everyone present to silently take notice of it. The uniformed heads of the Army and Navy both had presented a broad, sweeping plan for the defense of the nation that included massive spending on new armaments and an increase in the size of the forces themselves. Before April such an idea would have had varying levels of support from both the president and Congress. But that was before France. The collapse of the French Republic had shifted public opinion in the United States dramatically since then. Now matters were changing. Gallup recently polled Americans on their feelings toward potential conflict. While more than half of them still said they wanted no part in another conflict, almost forty percent now said they should do something. That was a twenty-point jump from just three months ago.

Roosevelt ignored the war secretary and continued.

"As for Admiral Stark's proposed war plans, I also approve of those as well. I don't know if a war is inevitable. I hope not. I pray to God every day that we can avoid it. But..." – he trailed away for a moment.

– "I also cannot ignore the possibilities. I don't have the luxury. The British are over there, across the Atlantic, with a knife held to their throats even now. Now, I'm going to need each of you in the days and weeks ahead. I believe very firmly that if the Germans pull off a successful invasion of England, then it'll be game over for Europe. Possibly even for us as well." His eyes shifted from person to person, ending with Woodring.

"Now. Where are we? Frank?" His gaze settled on Navy Secretary Knox.

Knox cleared his throat.

"Well, sir. Our position in the Pacific has shifted to focus on meeting the Japanese head-on. The fleet has now consolidated at Naval Station Pearl Harbor in Honolulu. It's a much better place to stage any offensive. Admiral Kimmel is in place out there now. He's confident that they'll be able to react much better – and quicker – from Hawaii. Consensus from the Navy is that the move was good on a strategic level."

"And there's absolutely no chance of a Japanese attack on us there?" asked Secretary of State Cordell Hull.

Knox shook his head.

"In Admiral Kimmel's words, there's 'no chance in hell' the Japanese could possibly hit Pearl Harbor."

Roosevelt shrugged and finally nodded.

"Good. Now what about the other ocean?"

"Yes. We're on schedule to commission half a dozen new destroyers this month. Thirty new coast guard boats are sliding out of drydock by the end of July. Between that and our long-range aerial patrols, we'll see everything running up the coast from Florida to Maine and two hundred miles out to sea. Though I suspect the Germans are a bit busy right now. Consolidating what they've gained these last few months."

Roosevelt had conferred regularly with Prime Minister Churchill in the five weeks since France's capitulation, and the situation there was not good. Not good at all. German submarines were sinking Britain's shipping at a far greater rate than anyone could have expected, and the British populace had been placed on wartime rationing. Everything from tin cans to flour and sugar were being cut back on in order to stockpile. The British were building fortifications all along their southern coast, and there was a foreboding sense by Churchill that a Nazi invasion was all but imminent.

"Very well. But I think we could be doing more. A lot more. Churchill is desperate for whatever aid we can give to him. He's asked for destroyers."

"What?!" Woodring asked, incredulously. He was stunned. "If we arm them with destroyers it would be seen as a flagrant violation of international law."

"As opposed to what?" Knox countered, giving the other man a disgusted face. "Invading neighboring countries? Those Nazis have killed more civilians than there have been military losses."

"So what about the Chinese? Do we go out of our way to arm them too?" Woodring replied. "Who's next after that? The Arabs? Maybe even the Commies? Good God. Does everyone here think this is okay? By arming one side, we risk losing the goodwill of those countries you call belligerent."

"We don't call them belligerent, Harry. Their own actions have done that by itself," Hull told him. "Mister President, I cannot stress enough the severity of the situation. I know you know this, and I may sound a little redundant, but the situation across the Atlantic is growing out of control. No – strike that. It's already out of control. I've heard you say it before, sir, but we should have stepped in at Munich. That was the match that lit the fuse." He paused and let out a frustrated breath. "I apologize if that went too far, sir."

"No apology is necessary," Roosevelt replied. He opened his cigarette case and put a smoke into his cigarette holder and lit up the end. "Going back to your last point, Frank. Securing the Atlantic seaboard."

"Yes. Shipyards from Maine down to Virginia are due to roll out a slew of new ships before the end of the year. I've got some of our older ships in for refit and *Saratoga* out in the Pacific will be putting in for an overhaul. We're sparing no expense getting the brand-new radar systems installed on our ships as fast as possible. You should have my report on your desk."

Roosevelt looked at the rather thick bundle of papers atop his desk. He'd gone through most of it in the past couple of days, and as he'd read the pages, he couldn't help but feel a sense of desperation. That a certain window of time was rapidly shrinking. An omen of things to come, perhaps. Europe was barely occupied by Hitler's armies and already there was word of mass deportations taking place within Germany. Ethnic and religious minorities being rounded up and sent to God only knew. The State Department had been simply overwhelmed by requests for information regarding family members living here in the States. A slew of now-occupied countries had set up governments in exile in London, but even they were finding it all but impossible to get hard information off the continent.

"Hmmm. Cordell, what's the refugee situation like?"

"Right now Europe's flooded with displaced people. The last of those fleeing Eastern Europe just arrived here a couple months ago. Now, we've got Dutch, Norwegians, and everyone else coming in. And, for the most part, they've been welcomed with open arms. But there were those exceptions down south."

Americans were typically sympathetic to the plight of the refugees. But it always seemed to come with a price tag. The more xenophobic elements of society were busy rearing their heads and calling for a strict policy of non-immigration. Some violent confrontations had already broken out in the south, with native-born confronting some of those seeking the safety and refuge of the United States. Attacks on immigrants had been known to happen as well. South Carolina's governor had been forced to deploy units of that state's National Guard to deal with the problem. His own inner New Yorker was happy, however, to know that his home state was as welcoming to new arrivals as they'd ever been.

"Well, keep me updated," Roosevelt told him. "Hopefully, we shouldn't have any more problems like we did. Moving on-"

"Mister President," It was Woodring. Roosevelt lifted his eyes at him and muffled a half-sigh. "If I may."

"Actually, Mister Secretary, I was just about to call this meeting done," Roosevelt told him, an air of authority in his voice. "Why don't we adjourn for this afternoon, ladies and gentlemen? Secretary Woodring and I can take this privately." He waited patiently for the rest of the people to gather their belongings and go. Once the last of them exited the Oval Office and the door clicked shut behind them he turned towards the secretary of war.

"Secretary Woodring. I really am getting at my wits end with this combativeness you've decided to bring to meetings." The tone of the president's voice indicated a finality on the matter. Roosevelt was not reproachful by any means, but he'd simply had enough.

"I'm certainly not trying to be combative, sir," Woodring replied. "I was under the impression that open voices and opinions would be welcome in cabinet settings."

President Roosevelt scoffed and rolled himself back out from behind the Resolute Desk.

"Opinions, yes. But you've repeatedly shown a more disruptive side during our meetings. The treatment you repeatedly give to General Marshall is a prime example. Disagreements and debates are one thing. But you've gone so far out of your way to be condescending, and even outright belittling that now you're just grasping straws. International law? Really, sir? That's the best argument you could have come up with?"

Woodring's forehead creased. He stood up slowly from the sofa he was sitting on and looked down at Roosevelt in his wheelchair.

"It's not an argument, Mister President," he replied, and Roosevelt thought he heard a hint of reproach in his voice. "It's the truth. If we're not a nation of laws then what are we? Sir, if you think I'm the only one who feels the way I do, then I can assure you that you're wrong. More Americans –"

"Yes, yes! More Americans feel the way you do than the way I do. But that raft is sinking more every day. Every single morning more Americans are waking up to the reality of the situation. A nation of laws? What good is a law if it allows chaos to reign? Nazi Germany has laws too. We've watched them time and again pass laws that restrict freedoms, censor the press, give more authority to Hitler, and make war on their neighbor. Laws can be corrupted. They are written by men, after all." He shook his head vigorously. "No. We're not going to sit by and watch as the rest of the world falls into anarchy just so we can thump our chests and say, 'At least we obeyed international law.' Not while I occupy this office."

The Secretary of War stood there half-shocked at what he was hearing. Roosevelt knew he'd become the odd man in the room these days, but his personal relationship with the president had never been anything but functional. At least until now. He adjusted his glasses nervously, looking as if he was about to speak, but Roosevelt got there half a second ahead of him.

"Secretary Woodring, I've allowed you a lot of leeway. Much more than I would otherwise allow. Certainly much longer than I should have let you have. But now I've decided that I cannot bear this any longer." He gave Woodring a cold stare, and the secretary's facial expression betrayed how small he felt at that moment. Roosevelt was weary of the other man. Tired of the constant stream of criticism of his administration. Tired of the combative attitude that he brought into his office.

"Mister President, I would highly urge you to be cautious," he said nervously. "I'm only doing –"

"Oh, I think I've been too cautious for far too long," Roosevelt interrupted. "Mister Woodring, as of right now, I am asking for your full and immediate resignation from your post. I expect one to be drafted and submitted before the end of the day today. Do I make myself clear?"

The other man visibly gulped and ran a finger underneath his shirt collar as if it had suddenly become constrained. His forehead almost instantly beaded up with sweat.

"Congress will not approve of my dismissal," he said. His voice was weak and feeble now. Desperate.

To his surprise, the words drew a lopsided grin from the president. The old New York politician gave him one of his disarming smiles, and the slightest of snorts in reply. Woodring stood there with an expression of mortification as if he were some clownish child who had managed to amuse the adult in the room.

"As I said, *Mister Woodring*," Roosevelt emphasized the last couple words. "today, Under Secretary Patterson will take responsibility until the Senate can confirm your replacement. Good day."

He clenched his cigarette holder between his teeth and gave the man one last grin before grabbing the wheels of his chair and swinging himself back around toward his desk. He barely heard the door click shut behind the other man.

CHAPTER FOUR

Hitler fell into the seat in his personal train car and pinched the bridge of his nose, letting out an exhausted breath. The group of men around him that had let their voices grow too loudly for the Führer came to a sudden silence when he slammed his hand down on the arm of his chair. It was followed instantly by a sharp pain right between his eyes. He said nothing but the excess of people in his train car were rapidly ordered out. A minute later there was a slight jolt as the train began to move forward. The whistle sounded, and the long succession of cars began to pull away from the train station.

Outside the train the famous Führer Battalion stood in a long line down the raised platform, heads craned in the direction of Hitler's car, rifles and sabers raised in salute. A few moments later, the platform was gone from view, and the French countryside was slowly rolling by.

An aide pulled the blinds down to block out the piercing sun and Hitler visibly relaxed, as if the absence of sunlight had taken away the headache.

"Tea. Cold," he piped out.

The past couple of days had been long and exhausting, and he didn't hide his exasperation. There had been a general feeling of relief by the entire entourage when the meeting with Franco had ended. Though still undecided on the course of his country, the Spanish dictator had at least agreed to keep open a formal line of communication on the matter. So much so that he'd allowed his foreign minister, a man named Suñer, to accompany the Führer's train back to Paris before flying home to Madrid. The meeting with Franco had been taxing, and he was looking forward to some rest.

Hitler looked around the compartment at those gathered around him. His top aides and advisors were present, along with Göring and Admiral Otto Schniewind, one of the top officers in the Navy. The last man had no official function during the recently ended diplomacy but had accompanied Hitler on his diplomatic visit to keep him apprised of recent developments at sea.

The compartment door quietly slid open, and a single aide came in with a glass of cold tea on a platter, along with a little white pill. Hitler tossed the pill into his mouth and downed it with some tea. The others stood silently by. Hitler was notorious for his famed mood swings and when he was in pain, like he was now, even the slightest sounds could trigger his anger. Many a politician or general had been dismissed from his sight for just such a small mistake as speaking out of turn.

He gave the pills a minute to set in before speaking. His voice was barely a whisper.

"I'd sooner have three or four of my teeth pulled than to meet with that man again," he said to them, referring to his meeting with the Spanish head of state.

Colonel Friedrich Hossbach, who had been leaning towards Hitler in order to hear his words, nodded in agreement with him. Hossbach was one of Hitler's top aides and knew his Führer probably better than anyone, and knew the best way to handle the man's frantic swings in behavior was silence.

"Yes, Mein Führer," he whispered back. "I've ordered a clear line all the way to Paris. You'll be able to get some rest on the way."

Hitler nodded and gave him a pat on the arm.

"What news from Berlin?"

"Several important updates," Hossbach replied. "Speer cabled this morning. The industrial projects in Poland and the Czech territories are finishing up ahead of schedule. New lines of the Panzer Fours should start to roll out of our Ruhr factories before the end of July. There's a full report on it. I'll have it delivered to you after your evening meal if you'd care to see it."

God bless Albert Speer, Hitler thought. The industrialist was performing nothing short of economic miracles back in Germany. The heir to Fritz Todt had taken full control of the country's war production almost two years earlier and had systematically expanded the nation's industrial base in that time. After being initially reluctant to allow the economy to move to a full wartime one, he'd relented and given Speer what he'd been begging for since Hitler's recovery. At the same time the first soldiers were crossing the Polish frontier, Speer was converting the German state into one giant, centrally controlled experiment in industrialization. And so far that policy was paying off huge dividends. Military production from bombers and heavy tanks to small arms had skyrocketed in that time and were still climbing with each passing day. Factories in the so-called occupied territories were pushing out materiel at a rate not seen before their Germanization.

"Very well. After supper," he replied. "Where is Ribbentrop?"

"Herr Ribbentrop is in his compartment, Mein Führer," Hossbach informed him. "Shall I send for him?"

Hitler thought for a moment, then shook his head. His head was swimming in pain.

"No. He's with the Spaniard," he remembered. "Let him entertain our guest for now."

"As you wish," the colonel replied.

Hitler swished the ice around in his glass, took another sip, then looked at Göring. The other man sat quietly, cooling himself with a paper fan. He'd come along due to his popularity with the Spanish and Franco himself. Luftwaffe pilots were highly respected in Spain after the assistance they'd given during their civil war.

"You seem to be in an unusually quiet mood today, Hermann," Hitler murmured.

The Luftwaffe chief, as usual, was dressed in one of his overdone sky-blue uniforms, adorned with ribbons, medals, and decorations. His reputation for grandiosity was well known, and typically Hitler didn't mind. The man had proved his usefulness many times over. But at times his flair for the dramatic annoyed him.

"I am respectfully quiet," Göring replied. "I know you are not feeling well. But if you wish –"

Hitler stopped him with a single hand, and he fell silent. He sipped again on his glass, the last two cubes of ice melting against his lips.

"What about the preparations?" he asked and looked over at Admiral Schniewind first. "How is everything proceeding?"

"Moving along as planned, Mein Führer," he replied after clearing his throat. "Every port from Wilhelmshaven to Brest are readying things as we designed. Another two weeks, and we will have assembled enough support ships to cover the operation."

"And what about ships for the crossing?" Hitler asked him, and the admiral sighed.

"We're confiscating any and all vessels capable of crossing the English Channel. We have enough civilian boats and barges right now to land two divisions. Our shipyards in Germany are working on piecing together enough craft to land heavy armor. Combined with the landing craft we'd built during the peace, we'll have a carrying capacity of just five divisions at a time. Not enough to secure a large enough beachhead. But we're still working on it."

As Hitler's headache intensified, he shut his eyes and rubbed his brows. The Navy might have been a useful tool in the open ocean; its U-boats were stretched from France to the Labrador coast. But the planned cross-channel invasion would depend upon many more seacrafts being available. Even with the recent capture of so many French warships, they were still coming up short.

"*Gottverdammt!*" Hitler swore. His voice was still hushed, but his displeasure with the news was evident. Not a man who received bad news lightly. "How could you allow this to happen? The Navy should have been better prepared."

Admiral Schniewind said nothing but simply gave an agreeing nod. The truth was that Hitler himself had never given the German Navy the same support that he'd always given the other branches of service. Once the pride of the German Empire, it was now just a shadow of its former self. In the past, when the idea of developing just such a naval force was conceived of, it was Hitler who had swatted the idea down as just a waste of resources, and so one might rightfully claim the führer himself had sabotaged his own plan. But no one would ever say that to him, of course. The Gestapo had a habit of paying unwelcome visits to those who had disappointed or openly criticized Hitler.

"We're still scouring every boat in Europe that's seaworthy," the admiral went on. "Dutch, Belgian, Danish – even our own river barges. We'll have what we need by the time *Sea Lion* commences."

"I trust so." Hitler looked at Göring who was seated across from the admiral, polishing the head of his baton. The reichsmarschall thrived in his rank and was wholly enamored with the symbol of his office. The coveted black-gold baton was the highest badge of the venerable rank. Those who held one were considered the greatest of military commanders. Hitler's brow furrowed. "Göring! Are you listening?"

Göring's head popped up and he gave an awkward grin, putting the baton down in his lap.

"Yes, Mein Führer."

"We were discussing the invasion preparations. Please tell me you were paying attention. That you have better news than the admiral here."

"The Luftwaffe is ready," he answered and shrugged as if it were a trivial matter. "Still solidifying our hold in France, but I fully trust we'll be ready when the time comes. By the end of the month, we'll have replaced all of our losses, and I've got more than enough pilots to accomplish the mission. I have absolute confidence that we shall prevail. The RAF – ha!" he waved a hand dismissively. "We'll simply brush them aside."

Hitler looked at him but said nothing. In truth, the Luftwaffe had done its job splendidly in the last year, and he had little complaints concerning that. Göring had promised victory in Poland and delivered. Then again in the west. His pilots had snuffed the Allies right out of the air, and his bombers had devastated their fortifications and left nothing but rubble and ruin behind, making the job of the Army much easier. Though the man's smugness might at times try his patience, Hitler found Göring to be quite useful.

"I hope so, Hermann. When the time comes, I truly hope so."

The train kept plugging along, the engine now fully open and the tracks ahead clear to run at full speed. Outside the French countryside whipped by. Through the veiled window Hitler saw the rolling hills of the Nouvelle-Aquitaine go by. People here and there, not knowing who was aboard the train, only briefly paying notice as it rolled past. Had his head not been killing him, he'd feel a great sense of joy from watching the pathetic fools.

They got everything that they deserved, he said to himself. *Now if we can bring the British to their senses, we can turn our attention to the true enemy.*

"There is something else that I think you should be aware of, Mein Führer," Colonel Hossbach said to him. He hesitated a little at first, then told Hitler, "We heard from Bormann just before the meeting with the Spaniards concluded. There was a radio broadcast from London. Some French general named Giraud, called for a general resistance to our occupation. It was broadcast just this morning."

Hitler stopped rubbing the pain from his temples and gave the colonel a hard stare. He didn't utter a word, but his eyes said it all. His face went oddly contorted, and the grunt he gave filled the silent passenger car. Göring stopped admiring his baton for a moment and lifted his eyes to the Führer. There was a strange tension that filled the small compartment.

"How far did this broadcast reach?" Hitler asked. His fingernails dug into the wooden arms of his chair.

"It was on the BBC," Hossbach replied after a moment. "It was picked up clearly by our posts in Paris. No doubt most of the occupied zone heard it as well."

"And what is being done?"

"Bormann consulted with Himmler shortly afterward. The Gestapo will be stepping up on crackdowns. Arrests will be made of anyone caught collaborating with or fomenting any resistance. Himmler also suggested locking down the whole city as a precaution. Round up and dispose of any unauthorized radio."

Again Hitler let out an exasperated sigh. He would have raged at the news, but he just didn't have the energy in him, and the painkillers were setting in. His SS chief would no doubt wish to spare no one in a show of force. A reminder to the people of Paris of who was in charge. Himmler was an efficient man but not cautious. Hitler had been to Paris, after the armistice with France. He wished to see that city be an open one. A beacon to Europe and the world that collaboration with the Nazis brought with it a reward of non-violence. But he also could not allow a general resistance movement to form.

"I will consider it," he replied quietly. "Leave me now. I wish to speak with Ribbentrop for a while. Send him in. Then I need to rest."

"Of course." The others gathered their belongings together and began to exit the car. Hitler ordered Hossbach to have another glass of tea delivered. He sat alone and in silence for a while before the attendant returned to fill his glass. The gentleness of the train's movement soothed his headache, and for a moment, he came close to dozing away.

Minutes later there was a gentle rasp at the door, and then it slid open. The foreign minister stepped into the room and slid the door closed behind him then sat down across from Hitler. He gave his Führer a sympathetic look.

"Is there anything that I can do for you?" he asked and Hitler slowly shook his head.

"Talk to me about these Spaniards. What does this man Suñer have to say?"

"What he says to me is that there is a growing movement in Madrid. There are those who are unhappy with Franco's indecisiveness on the matter. Despite his public appearance of supporting us, behind closed doors, he is unsure of himself. Quietly, I think he wishes to appease both sides."

"So he aligns with us but doesn't wish to upset the British. Is that it?" His voice was full of frustration.

Ribbentrop nodded. "That's essentially it. Portugal may not stay neutral if Spain enters into the war. Lisbon and London are very close, and he fears the British may attack him from that country." He shrugged. "He also fears the Americans. Roosevelt is whispering into his ear. The United States supplies Spain with many needed goods."

"Pah! The Americans." Hitler shook his head in dismay. "Playboys. Hypocrites. They segregate their negros from the rest of their population then dare to condemn us from doing the same with our Jews. That wheelchaired man is a fool and a weakling. Leader of a nation of weaklings."

Ribbentrop said nothing. His personal dislike for the Americans was fairly well known, and his concerns had been made clear before. The Americans had nearly limitless reserves of manpower, and their industrial strength could easily outmatch Germany, despite the advancements made in recent years. In 1917 they'd sent four million soldiers to France to fight in only a matter of months. Now they could send many more. Already they were preparing themselves for conflict with the Japanese, and intelligence reports indicated they could very easily draft as many as twenty-five thousand men a day to meet their needs.

"Weaklings, yes," he quickly agreed, "but they are also one of Spain's biggest trading partners. They get most of their oil from the United States. Franco's regime is still precarious. The Republicans still have many sympathizers in Spain. I think that he fears a general revolt."

"And yet every day he placates us with soothing words and talk of a wave of fascism across Europe. I'm the one who brought Europe to heel, not him. So what does he want? Really want? What does this man tell you?"

"That his brother-in-law needs to be made to look strong. I believe him when he tells me that Franco does not fear the British. Not really. But if he fails..." He just shook his head. "His own generals could turn on him very quickly. He believes that if we were to provide him with additional support, his brother-in-law would bring Spain into the war."

Hitler looked incredulous, his eyes wide. "More support? What more can we do that we haven't already?" He sighed loudly, rubbed his brow, and took a slow sip of his tea. "We've given him loans, trainloads of coal, planes, weapons. What more does he wish us to give?" It was a rhetorical question.

Ribbentrop held out his hands. "Between us, Mein Führer, I think Franco would want direct military support for any offensive."

"Pah!" Hitler's hand flew around in agitation. "Send in my armies, you mean. According to the Spaniard, he has a million men. What does he need mine for?"

"Again I think that he fears what the Portuguese may do. Portugal has already reaffirmed their alliance with Britain. If the British landed a force there they could open up a new front against us."

"Enough! My head is hurting me." He paused in agitation. "So, again I ask what has the Spanish minister said? He practically begged us to allow him on the trip back to Paris. My patience with this matter grows very thin."

"He wants us to draw up an agreement. Something such as we did with Molotov in Russia. A treaty. A secret treaty. If they enter into any conflict against our enemies, they'll be guaranteed certain gains. Territorial recognition and such."

"Africa?"

Ribbentrop shrugged his shoulders. "They want to expand their African possessions. Establish themselves once again as a regional power."

"That means giving them lands that belong to France. How can I give them that without alienating Vichy?" Hitler shook his head vigorously. "The French would turn on me. They'd re-enter the war against us. Pétain is already upset that we're even meeting with the Spaniards. No. No. I cannot risk it."

"We may not have to," Ribbentrop told him. "I've had some information come my way that Vichy has been looking the other way concerning guerilla groups operating from their territory. Anti-nationalists who are hiding in France. They cross the border into Spain routinely."

"That's nothing new!"

"No, it isn't. However, Pétain has chosen to turn a blind eye to their activities. New leadership in France might have a different position." He bit his lip and tapped his finger on the arm of his chair.

"Himmler believes that Pétain is not a good choice to lead that country. He doesn't trust the old general. I agree. New leadership in Vichy could be more open to new ways. A reconciliation with Spain would go a long way to getting that country on our side. Pétain may not wish to cooperate but there are others in France who would."

Hitler was silent. His eyes stared blankly back at him. The very thought of what Ribbentrop was suggesting was both unexpected and intriguing. Pétain was not Berlin's favorite choice of people to lead unoccupied France, but his position with the old French Republic made him the obvious choice. But the old marshal of France had suffered a loss of popularity with his people, and others were more closely associated with National Socialism than he was. But anyone who Berlin chose to put in his place would be just as unpopular.

"You have individuals in mind?" he asked Ribbentrop and the other man nodded.

"I do."

Hitler rubbed his jaw in thought. His forefinger ran along the scar on his face. He felt the hideousness on the tip of his finger and drew his hand away. He wasn't opposed to replacing the old Frenchman, and he certainly wouldn't balk at anything that would bring Spain into the fold. Having Franco on Germany's side would certainly be preferable to invading that country.

He nodded gently to Ribbentrop.

"Draw up a proposal. Consult with Himmler. If your friend in the rear car is amiable, and if there is support for this, then I'll sanction the move. But –" he held up a single finger – "I want strict assurances. I would not make such a move lightly. I'm sick of wet nursing Franco. If he wants his empire he can have it. But I'm not going to hand it to him on a platter. Make our position perfectly clear to his foreign minister. Spain is either an ally or she is not."

"I understand."

"Good. Now leave me. I need some rest. Tell the others that I don't wish to be disturbed until we reach Paris."

Ribbentrop stood up and wished Hitler a restful afternoon before exiting the small compartment. In the next car up, in the diplomatic compartment, the Spanish foreign minister sat around a small round table. He was scribbling out some notes as his German counterpart returned, quietly sliding the door shut behind him. Two half glasses of Spanish wine were already poured. He sat down across from Suñer and the other man grinned at him.

"So?" the Spaniard inquired.

"Hitler has instructed me to deal directly with this," he replied and ran his fingers up the stem of his wine glass. "If you're sincere in your interests, and you have the political backing in Madrid..." – he waited for Suñer to nod, – "...then I believe we can come to an understanding."

The Spaniard smiled and raised his glass.

"Then in that case," he said in perfect German, "I have some ideas that I'd like to cover with you."

CHAPTER FIVE

The people of Eastbourne were turning out in droves this morning. The streets were packed with people waiting, watching, hoping to get a glimpse of the man. The crowd gathered became so thick that people began to clamor over each other just trying to get a view. Some climbed trees or street poles. Fathers held their children up so that they could see him. Even over the army of citizens, they could still see his famous bowler hat making its way down the crowded roadway, a group of aides and military men following closely behind. The smoke rings from his cigar could be seen even by those at the back of the crowd.

Prime Minister Churchill strolled down the crowded street, cigar clenched between his fingers, walking cane in hand, and a broad smile on his face. The energy of the crowd was fantastic, and the people cheered with every step that he took. Well, most of them, anyhow. Now and again he'd lock eyes with someone who gave him a scowl or a shake of their head. He just grinned, tipped his hat, and took it in stride. When an elderly woman chided him and told him that had he been her husband she'd have put poison in his drink, even she reluctantly smiled when he'd responded by saying that 'should I have the unfortunate business of being your husband, madame, I would most likely drink it'.

The main avenue through the center of Eastbourne was as packed as any town that he'd ever visited, including London. Nearly the entire town had come out to greet him, and he was better for it. Looking into the eyes of the people that he was devoted to defending from a crazy man gave Winston a humble perspective. Eastbourne was, after all, a sea town in the southeast of England. Just an hour away, across the English Channel, the world's largest air force was waiting. Sooner or later it was going to come, and their planes would fly right overhead. Like it or not, this town was now on the frontline and if any invasion should be launched it could well happen on the very beaches of it.

"Right over here, sir," a voice shouted over the noise of the crowd. It was Jock Colville, one of his aides. He was pointing to a large, circular precipice that was lined with bricks. In the center, flying high, the Union Jack fluttered in the sea breeze. Beyond that were the sandy beaches of southeastern England and the English Channel.

"Thank you, Mister Churchill!" A mother cried, her baby slung in her arms. The woman was little more than a young girl. Churchill smiled back at her and lifted his bowler hat ever so slightly at her.

"Go get 'em, Winston!" an older man in the middle of the crowd yelled. "Let that Bavarian bastard set one foot on English soil, and we'll show him what happens!"

Winston laughed, and the people around laughed with him. Next to him was Brigadier D.G. Stewart, Admiral Bertram Ramsey, who had commanded the evacuation from Boulogne a month earlier, and Jock Colville. An entire entourage of military and civilian aides and bodyguards closely followed them.

He stepped across the pebbled sand beyond the road. Some soldiers had cordoned off the area around the overlook. A hundred feet away, on the beaches below, there were hundreds of workers, military and civilians alike. Anti-tank defenses lined the beach for as far as the eye could see and more were going up. Barbwire, dragons teeth, pillboxes, sandbag redoubts. Anything and everything that could stop an attack from the sea.

Several workers on the beach spotted the prime minister and shook their arms in the air, and he waved back at them. Before long he knew that there'd be hundreds of mines planted along the shore, to be used in the defense of these people. He shuddered to think that some child or townsperson might make their way down onto those beaches and accidentally trigger one of the deadly devices. Such things had happened before. The French countryside was still full of mines that too often claimed the lives of innocents. Leftover souvenirs from the previous war.

"You can see from here our defenses go up," Brigadier Stewart told him, pointing off to the construction going on along the shore. "We're setting up pillboxes for machine guns every hundred meters or so. Each one should be able to cover a wide area."

"We're going to need a lot of them," Churchill muttered as he scanned the beach line. "What a pity. What a pity." During normal times, the beaches would be full of people walking along the shore or swimming in the sea. Children playing and lovers romancing would be a common scene. It felt like such a shame that this was what the world had been reduced to. And worst of all was that war may actually come to British shores. To Britain. The thought was appalling.

"We'll have tank stoppers placed along the water line," the brigadier continued. "Coastal artillery emplacements to support the defenders. Anti-aircraft batteries further back. Home Guard units stretching from Dover all the way to Plymouth are assembling to meet anything that comes. Also, we're establishing. . . "

The general continued, but Churchill barely heard a thing. He knew the situation and didn't need all the details. The trip to Eastbourne had as much to do with public relations and letting the people see him as it did with viewing defensive measures. He'd seen the map a thousand times before and could tell you every nook and every crevasse along England's coastline. All the briefings in the world could only guess what was going to happen from this point on. All he knew was that something was going to happen, and he wasn't going to run from it.

After Brigadier Stewart finished, Admiral Ramsey began to fill in some of the naval details. Winston listened with one ear, nodded his head as the admiral spelled out the defensive plans, and looked around at the seaside village and the people crowded in the streets to see him. Every one of them, he'd noted, had the same look on their face. It was a mixture of both elation and dread.

"... added coastal batteries just to the east of here..." the admiral continued, Winston nodding as he observed the work going on along the coast. Eastbourne sat directly south of London, along the English Channel. The sandy coastline was a perfect place for landing craft, and he could almost hear it, and see it in his mind. The gray uniforms of German soldiers storming across the beach, pouring into the countryside beyond, then pushing on London.

"These are our weakest points, sir," Ramsey went on. "Between Worthing and Dover. If there's any significant German naval activity, it'll be along this stretch. Brighton, Hastings, Folkestone. We'll be at our weakest points here."

Winston tapped his thigh, taking in the view. "Hastings," he whispered aloud. "Hastings." That place where William the Conqueror had come ashore centuries earlier. He repeated the name over and over again.

The PM and his escort toured around the beach for a few minutes longer before heading back toward the gathering. People cheered at his approach.

"Are we going to be alright, Mister Churchill?" a grandmother asked as he walked by.

"Ma'am, we're as safe here as anywhere in Britain," he answered, smiling reassuringly at her. Others peppered him with a variety of questions as he passed through the crowd. 'Was the Navy going to sortie? Would the boys fight on the beaches? What about the rest of the empire?' He tried to answer as many questions as possible. The group parted down the center as he walked. "I will tell you all this," he began gleefully. "if the madman in Berlin comes here, HA! I'll truly pity him. For there is no spirit in this world that I have ever seen that is stronger than that of the British people when we put ourselves to the task. Let the bugger try and cross, and we'll send him packing."

The words sent a cheer up from the people assembled. He grinned as he sucked on his cigar. It was like some surreal dream. He pulled his white handkerchief out of his pin-striped suit pocket and dabbed at his sweating forehead. He took some more questions, shook some people's hands, then began walking again, and for a moment, it looked as if he and those around him were simply going to keep going. But then...

"Are we going to win?" The words brought Churchill to a sudden stop. He looked around for the person who'd asked the question. His eyes locked onto a sandy-haired and trim boy standing in the crowd. The prime minister gazed at him, giving him a curious look.

"What was that?" he asked the young man. He couldn't have been more than fifteen.

"Are we going to win?" the boy repeated without hesitation. The fifteen-year-old seemed totally unphased by the fact that he was speaking to the head of the British government.

Winston looked back at him and considered himself for just a moment, then he placed a single hand on the boy's shoulder. The young man was standing with his hands in his pockets. Behind him, a girl of perhaps twenty, with chestnut-brown hair had her hand on his back.

"My lad, I can assure you that we will neither stop nor tire until we stand victorious." He raised his voice just enough to let those others within earshot hear his words. "We will stand wherever we must to meet our enemy head-on." Many heads in the crowd began to nod in agreement. "What is your name, son?"

"Simon, sir. Simon Bagshaw." He gulped visibly and his eyes reddened "This is my cousin, Bess. My brother Tom was killed in France. He was with the Queen's Own Royal West Kent."

The prime minister scowled slightly and nodded sympathetically at Simon. "The West Kent, you say. The West Kent fought bravely in France, and their courage will not be forgotten. I will say a prayer for your brother's bravery, Simon." He smiled widely, then looked up at Bess. "What about you, my dear? Where are you from?"

"London, sir," she stammered, not believing that she was speaking with the prime minister. "I live in London. But my parents own a country farm. I came down to help out, and to watch over my cousin for a while."

"I see. Well, God bless the both of you."

"When my time comes, sir, I'll fight for you," Simon blurted out, and Bess's eyes widened at the words. Simon was usually such a reserved, introverted young man that to hear him say these words came as a surprise to her ears.

"When the time comes, Simon, we'll fight together," Churchill replied to him. He smiled, and gave Simon a wink of his eye "We'll fight together." He patted him affectionately on the cheek, then continued on his way through the crowd and back toward the black car that he'd arrived in. His escort helped him back into his automobile and the car started off. Motorcycle police officers escorted it around the roundabout and out of town.

Looking behind him, he watched the gathering. The people watched and waved at his car. There were all sorts of talk from the people. The excitement of greeting Mister Churchill was thick in the air. Simon and his cousin Bess were standing in the center. He watched them as the car started to inch forward. The crowd grew smaller and smaller behind him. Eventually, the gathering began to break up and the townsfolk went home.

All along the road out of town, workers were busy pounding signs all along the beach shore.

LANDMINES
BEACH ACCESS RESTRICTED
NO CHILDREN ALLOWED!

CHAPTER SIX

The officer's club at Hickam Field was unusually slow this evening. It was a Friday and the scene at the Pelican Club was barely half of what it would be like on any other typical Friday. Most of the officers here tonight were administrative. Only here and there did Johnny Harkins see any pilots or line officers. He thought that a bit strange. A usual Friday at nine at Pelican's was standing room only. There'd easily be two hundred officers with their spouses or dates pushed into the dance hall alone. But tonight there couldn't be more than a hundred people here, enjoying dinner on the balcony or sipping a drink inside.

As usual, a band played on stage. Some warmup band was playing an old bit of ragtime. It was something that he might have heard his parents listening to back when he was a kid. He took a generous sip of his whiskey sour and shook his head slightly at the scene. There'd been a warmup all evening long, it seemed, at a venue that just wasn't having it this evening. It was too bad too. It was a beautiful evening out and he'd hoped to meet up with some stray dame this evening. But looking around the place, that just didn't seem likely.

His friends let out a burst of laughter and he brought his attention back to the guys he'd come in with.

"Where's your head tonight, Johnny?" It was Artie McDonald. The other pilot was sitting across the small table from Johnny, sipping down some umbrella drink he had in his hand.

"Just wondering where the hell everyone is," Johnny told him, but that really wasn't the truth.

The truth was that there had been something tugging on him for days now. He'd thought that by coming out with his flyboy buddies he might alleviate some of the anxiety he was feeling. Maybe connect with a girl and forget his troubles in a drunken one-night lovefest. That was what he'd hoped would happen anyhow. But now, being here with the boys, he just couldn't shake off the feeling that he only really wanted to be somewhere else. With someone else.

"Well, get your head back in the game, John Boy," Harry Tarkino, upbeat as always, told him and slapped him on the shoulder. Unlike the other guys, Harry was Navy. In the cultural divide between the Army and Navy guys stationed in Honolulu, Harry was the exception to the rule. He flew F4Fs off carriers out of Pearl. While Johnny and the other two were Army pilots, Harry had a strange way of squeezing into any group without causing a stir. Sometimes when too many mixed uniforms were in the same room, things could get dicey.

"Yeah," Johnny replied. He ran his fingers through his wavy, brown hair and took another sip of his drink. "Yeah. You know what? We came out for a fun time, and we should be doing that right?"

The other guys nodded, and Artie raised his flimsy drink. The umbrella bobbed from side to side in the shaped glass.

"Damn right!" he said, and everyone raised their glass to each other. "Here's to us, my friends. Best damn pilots in the Army!" He clinked his glass with the others and drank.

"And the Navy," Harry added, then downed half his drink. He'd fallen in love with a local rum and was working on his fourth glass of it.

"And the Navy," Artie added.

Harry Tarkino was a good guy. He'd been assigned to one of Halsey's carriers when they'd transferred out to Pearl last year from San Diego. He'd found himself in some local tiki bar hangout frequented by Army pilots a few months back. Such an act by itself, depending on the location, often caused friction after working hours. Who the hell knew why such things happened? Boyish vanity perhaps. But Harry had a way of people liking him and had wormed his way into the group. Civilian bars in Honolulu catered to anyone and everyone. But officer's clubs on Army or Navy bases could be a different matter entirely. Some of the officers who frequented them could be a little territorial. Especially after a few drinks.

"Ain't no dames in here tonight," Martin Finch commented, looking around the room. "That one at the bar is eyeballing me. See her?" Finch was the youngest and by far the most virile of the group. A surfer kid from Malibu turned Army pilot. There was a line of girls who seemed to follow him around like he was Clark Gable or something.

Artie craned his head to look then sneered.

"Yeah, I see her. She's old enough to be my mother."

"Hey. So long as it is your mother and not mine," Martin joked. "She's got some legs, though."

"All legs look good in nylons," Artie told him. "Geez. You'd think there was a war on or something. This place is a ghost town tonight. Hey, how 'bout we get a cab down to the waterfront? There's gotta be something going on down there in Waikiki. The women are everywhere."

"Sounds good to me," Harry said. "Mai Tai's should be booming about now."

Artie nodded and then looked over at Johnny.

"Whatcha say, John Boy?" he asked. Johnny thought about it for a minute. That did sound good, and normally he'd be the first to say yes. But he just wasn't feeling it tonight.

"No," he shook his head. "You guys go ahead without me. I'm not sure I'm feeling that well. I might just head home for the night."

"What?" Harry said, astonished at the suggestion. He glanced at his wristwatch. "It's only now half past nine. You're not losing it on us, are you, Harkins?"

Johnny shot him back a friendly grin.

"I'm just not really in the mood, guys."

"Yeah, what's going on with you tonight?" Artie asked him. "You've been moping all day long. You're usually the one who's primed and ready to go. What's going on?"

Johnny shook his head at the question. He was hesitant to talk about what was bothering him. There was a big part of him that said to just go with his boys down to Waikiki and drink the night away – if for no other reason than to just drown his feelings away. But there was another part of him that wanted to go home for the night, pick up a telephone and make that phone call. But he knew that he couldn't do that either. New York was hours ahead of them and it was the very early hours of the morning there. Though right now he would have wanted nothing more than to hear her voice.

"Is there something going on with you?" Artie probed him some more. "It's not that broad in New York, is it? Cause, you know, you just need to shack up with some local to get over that."

Johnny shook his head and gave Artie a serious look.

"No, it's not her. And she's no broad, either." He was silent a moment longer, gave each of his buddies a look, then shrugged. "I've got to tell you guys something. I wasn't gonna, but... I got called into the CO's office this morning."

"Sheffield?" Finch asked, and Johnny nodded.

"Yeah. Some jackass back stateside has asked for volunteers for special assignment. My name came up, and – uh, I don't know. Unless something changes, Sheffield has me pegged for a transport in about a week."

"By volunteer, you mean shanghaied, of course," Finch commented. Johnny nodded and downed the rest of his whiskey sour.

"Yeah. That's what I mean. Anyway. I've had mixed emotions all day."

"Jesus, brother," Artie started to say. "Who's the jackass and what's the assignment? Or can you not talk about it with your pals?"

"Oh, some colonel named Doolittle. Apparently, the Army wants to get ahead of this war business. Not sure exactly how. They're sending a handful of pilots to help train some foreigners on our stuff. Anyhow, like I said, they're sending me stateside next week. I wasn't sure how to bring it up."

The rest of the guys exchanged looks with each other. Everybody was subject to the whims of the service, and they all knew that at any moment they could be told to drop everything and pack up. That was the way things were and what they had signed up for.

"War?" Harry asked. "So what the hell does that mean? You going to China to train those squinties how to fly American planes or something?"

"I've heard that some generals want to head up a mission over there," Martin added. "That must be it. They must want someone to help train the Chinese. Wow. I don't know what to say, John. I'd be in a pretty sour mood too if I got that news."

"Well, I don't know exactly what the destination is yet. But the news shocked the shit out of me this morning when Sheffield told me." He caught the waiter's attention and held up his empty glass, then tapped it with a single finger. "Sorry if I've been in a mood this evening."

"Yeah. You've got yourself a problem there, friend," Artie told him. Artie wasn't just his friend but his squadron mate as well. They had been wingmen for the last six months. The two were practically inseparable both in the air and on the ground. Obviously, Artie hadn't been picked for any special assignment. "Actually, pal, you've got a couple of problems. Don't you?"

Johnny looked back over at his friend and lightly bobbed his head up and down. He didn't need to say it he and Artie both knew: Gwen. He'd spent every waking minute of any leave he had with her, returning to New York whenever he could or meeting her in California a couple of months back. Their casual relationship had taken a different turn, and without asking for it, he'd fallen in love with her. Though they'd never said the words, he knew she loved him too. It had been in her eyes.

Now things had changed. He had no idea where he was going to be sent in the days ahead, but he was doubtful that he would get the chance to see her again before heading off to wherever the Army was about to send him. Besides that, maybe it was for the best that he didn't. If it was China they'd pegged him for then there was a chance he might not return, and if that was the case the last thing he wanted to do was leave behind some grieving girlfriend to pick up the pieces.

"Yeah. I guess I do," he told Artie. The waiter showed back up, a single whiskey sour on his tray, and placed a cocktail napkin in front of him, then switched his empty glass with a full one. "Thanks. So anyway, I've got a lot on my plate. Oh, hell – maybe we should just scram. Head down to Honolulu and pass out on the beach."

The guys sat silently for a minute in the half-empty club. The band on stage stopped playing to take a break, and the atmosphere was suddenly tranquil. The only sound in the club were the muffled conversations going on between the patrons at the tables. The crowd at the bar had thinned out, and at ten o'clock on a Friday night, the whole place seemed like anything other than a hopping establishment, typically patronized by hundreds of people.

"No," Harry Tarkino said. "No. Let's just have another couple of drinks here. Who says we need to leave? Our pal just got the news of his life. I get how you feel. Let's just stay here. We'll have some drinks, toast a few rounds, then head home."

The group nodded their agreement to the idea. Hours went by, and drinks were reordered. Ten o'clock became midnight, and before anyone knew it, two o'clock in the morning came around. The band packed up, and the club staff began to clean up. Johnny must've had half a bottle by himself at that point, and his legs wobbled as he walked. There were always lots of cabs waiting outside of clubs like this one, ready to take home the late-night crowd. Johnny and Artie climbed into the back of one after bidding Finch and Tarkino farewell. It was nearly three in the morning when the cab had reached the officers' housing. By then Johnny had nodded off in the back of the cab.

"You fellas need help?" the cab driver asked them as he came to a stop in front of the small bungalow.

Johnny opened his eyes and nudged Artie in the ribs.

"Nah," he muttered back, then turned the door handle and got out of the cab. Artie was pretty bad off, and Johnny hooked his arm under his friend's torso and propped him up. "What do I owe?"

"Two fifty," the driver replied. He was a native Hawaiian and had a heavy island dialect.

"Two fifty?" Johnny repeated, then reached into his pocket with his free hand. Cab rides in Hawaii were expensive. He pulled out four singles and handed it to the guy. "Keep it," he said.

The driver barely waited for Johnny to pull Artie away from the car before pulling away. Johnny shook his head.

"Shithead," he whispered to his drunken friend as they staggered into their shared bungalow. He tossed Artie onto the futon, then stumbled into the kitchen and poured himself a glass of tap water.

Johnny couldn't believe he was still standing after all that drink. He leaned against the doorway and drank down his glass of water. Across from him, the telephone was mounted to the kitchen wall.

He stared at it for long moments. He really should just go to bed and sleep it off.

Yeah, he thought. *That's what I should do.*

But the phone kept staring at him. Or was he staring at it? His head was swimming with thoughts right now. The clock on the wall said ten after three. *What time did that make it in Brooklyn?*

He staggered over to the phone and picked up the receiver. On the other end an operator answered. Johnny let out a long exhale.

"Yes, can I get – umm..." he tried to think. He was tired and drunk. "I want to make a call to the mainland," he told the operator. "Brooklyn, New York. Uhh... Williamsburg six-two-three-six. Yes, I'll wait."

He was swimming in alcohol right now. If he hadn't been leaning up against the wall he was quite sure that he'd have fallen over by now. He wasn't sure how long he had stood there while the operator connected him. He was aware that it was going to be early in Brooklyn. Very early. But he didn't care anymore.

The operator came back on and informed him that she had an open line. The phone on the other end rang once, and he felt a swell of consternation. On the second ring, he'd hoped that the line would go down. Then on the third ring, someone on the other end picked up.

In a groggy, early-morning voice someone answered. It was her. Gwen. He knew her sweet voice even over the choppy phone line. A single tear welled up in his eye and ran down his face. He wanted more than anything to say something. Anything at all. He wanted to tell her that he loved her and that he wanted to be with her. But as he stood there, he couldn't get a single word out. Couldn't find the courage to say what he wanted – needed – to say. Instead, he hung the phone back up and walked away.

CHAPTER SEVEN

The twin-engine transport plane taxied off the main landing strip toward the hangar. The aircraft came to a halt fifty feet away from the group of Army and Air Force officers assembled, then the pilot cut the engines and the propellers gave out one last winding noise before coming to a stop. The rear hatch opened, and the short ladder dropped to the ground where three Luftwaffe ground crewmen stood rigidly for the transport's occupant.

The heavyset Hermann Göring ducked his head out from under the hatchway and slowly descended the steps, one foot at a time. His bulky frame swung excessively as he stepped down. As usual, he was dressed in his finest uniform, and an absurdly decorated hat custom-made just for him. Medals and ribbons graced his jacket, and his treasured marshal's baton was in his hand. Behind him were half a dozen staff officers.

The knot of officers huddled under the hangar awaiting his arrival began to stir and line up in the proper procession. As senior officer in the region, General Ernst Udet was first in line to greet him. He dropped his cigarette to the ground and crushed it with the toe of his boot. Göring smiled widely as the party of officers approached him.

In addition to Luftwaffe senior officials, there was a handful of German Army officers as well. Though Field Marshall Rundstedt had politely shrugged off the meeting today, he'd sent several of his staff planners to meet with the Reichsmarschall. As an Army officer, Rundstedt was not necessarily required to be here today as he did not answer to the Luftwaffe chief, but his absence was quietly seen as nothing more than an attestation of the animosity that often arose between the two branches of service. There might have also been a note of personal pleasure in it for him. Göring had long been the sole person to hold the title of marshal, and Rundstedt's recent elevation to that rank may have been a signal to Göring that he had no control whatsoever over Army hierarchy.

"Welcome, Herr Reichsmarschall," Udet said warmly and offered his gloved hand to Göring.

The head of the German Air Force was almost childlike in the face. His plump cheeks were rosy red, and his nose wrinkled. He brought his baton up smartly to his hat and snapped off a quick salute before finally shaking hands. To the officers present it was almost like watching two stage actors in front of an audience.

"General," Göring replied. "It pleases me to see you on the front line again. Not sitting behind a desk in Berlin."

"Thank you. You recall my staff don't you?" He gestured to the group behind him.

"Of course." Göring gave another salute with his baton. "You are all to be congratulated. The entire Fatherland is grateful. The capitulation of our enemies might well be the single greatest achievement in German history." He puffed his frame up as he spoke. "Nobody has ever accomplished so much in such a short period of time. And you have all earned the respect and adulation of our people."

Göring went down the line of officers, shaking each hand individually and expressing his congratulations. Luftwaffe officers in particular were eager to shake the hand of their leader, each wanting to endear themselves to the man. His appetite for glory was well known, as was his boastfulness. No doubt it was hoped by many present that their names might reach the ears of Hitler himself. Ingratiating oneself to party officials was seen as the best way to promote a career these days. Udet himself didn't care for the practice. Having come up through the traditional ranks, by way of merit, he was silently disdainful of the practice. But he was realistic enough not to question it. Göring had, after all, recalled him from his unfulfilling administrative desk job at the Ministry of Aviation, and put him in charge of Luftwaffe operations in France. He'd simply been thrilled to be back on the front line again, and out of exile.

"I know that you're probably anxious to oversee our preparations," Udet said to him and gestured toward the open-topped car waiting under an airfield canopy.

Göring looked around curiously. "Field Marshal Rundstedt?"

Udet coughed lightly. "Um. Yes, the field marshal was otherwise ... preoccupied, I'm afraid. General Sodenstern can update you on Army preparations."

Göring sneered. No doubt it had given the German Army's top commander in France some pleasure to be able to sit out this meeting. The newly promoted field marshal's star was on the rise back in Germany, and Hitler could not stop speaking of the man favorably. However, he knew that Hitler's mood could swing as swiftly as the weather changed. Rundstedt's so-called star could just as easily find itself falling out of favor with the Führer, and he was well aware of it. Göring, despite his rank and stature in Berlin, and within the party itself, had fallen out of favor with Hitler more than once.

The two walked toward the car. Its driver held the rear door open and Udet gestured for his superior to sit first. The motorcade started off a minute or two later when all officers had found a car. Beyond the hangar, the fields were lined up with row after row of aircraft. Fighters, bombers, and reconnaissance planes of all sorts were arrayed with their crews standing proudly at attention. The bright-yellow noses of the Messerschmitt 109s were always highly distinguishable. The flamboyant fighter pilots adorned their planes with a variety of artwork, celebrating their victories.

Göring recognized some of their faces as his automobile slowly passed down the rows. Adolf Galland, one of the best pilots in the service, and one of his personal favorites, looked like some model posing for a picture in front of his sleek fighter plane.

"Galland!" Göring propped himself up over the side of the car and waved for the pilot to come over. The car came to a stop. "One of my best pilots here, Udet. Galland, you dog. How are you?"

"Very well, Herr Reichsmarschall. Looking forward to crossing the English Channel." The pilot made a playful smile.

"Good!" Göring replied. "Soon enough, my friend, soon enough. And you'll be marking your plane with a score of Union Jacks." He roared a laugh. "This is the kind of enthusiasm that I like to see in my pilots, Udet."

The car stopped just long enough for Göring and Galland to exchange some brief words about the victory over France before continuing on. The rest of the aircrews watched and saluted as the Reichsmarschall's car drove by. Göring enjoyed the attention and always preferred open-topped automobiles for just such a purpose. He waved back at them as they passed.

"I must say, Ernst, your boys are looking sharp. I'm eager to see how they perform against the British." He smiled and waved some more.

Udet only grinned and nodded. He'd only recently taken command and found it difficult to make any substantial changes. It was hard to improve on what was being praised as a highly efficient military organization. One that had just proven itself to the world as the premier air force of the age. The French and British had taken extraordinary losses in the previous campaign, to Germany's few. His pilots were honed and sharpened weapons of war.

"I'm glad you think so, Reichsmarschall. Morale is certainly high. Though there are some things about the upcoming operation that do give me reason for concern."

Göring looked at him and his grin turned into a slightly dour expression. "Ernst. I can see you haven't changed too much. I would have thought that the last few years spent in charge of aircraft production would have given you a different perspective on things."

Udet said nothing. His time overseeing the development and production of new aircraft could have just as easily been called exile as far as he was concerned. He'd welcomed the assignment back in '36 and had used it to further what he saw as strengthening the service, which was teetering on collapse. And he had succeeded, against all odds, in building up the fledgling force into a formidable one. The fact that they were standing in occupied French territory was proof of it. But his time in Berlin quickly evolved into more of a political role, and he'd found himself constantly battling with others looking to jockey themselves into Hitler's good graces. He'd been a top-notch fighter ace during the Great War; the second-highest scoring ace in German service. He'd felt that his skills as a combat pilot and leader were wasted sitting in an office at the ministry. He had been quite sure that he would have ended his military career sitting in an office, withering away. But just after Germany's crushing victory in the west, Göring had a change of heart and offered him the role of Luftwaffe Commander in France.

"Our adversary is practically crushed," Göring continued. "They're demoralized, and short of pilots. I expect them to be easy targets. Besides, have you seen the new production reports coming out of Speer's office?" He chuckled. "Our new bombers are rolling out of factories at a rate so high that they'll overwhelm the RAF in no time.

In fact"—he chuckled some more—"I fully expect to turn the British Isles into a smoldering ruin in a matter of weeks if not days."

Again General Udet was silent. He'd seen those reports and, yes, he had to admit that bomber production had increased at an impressive rate. But he could read between the lines too. Fighter production had dipped slightly to reach that rate, and worse, the pilots coming out of the schools were untested. On the other side of that coin, the RAF and foreign pilots who'd managed to flee to England were veterans. Even outnumbered he knew that fighting over friendly territory would be a big advantage for the British. This would not be the easy campaign that Göring and others thought it would be.

"I understand that the Führer has yet to settle on an invasion strategy?" Udet inquired.

"It's simply a matter of a wide invasion front or a narrow one. The Army is pushing for a wider landing force. However, much of that will depend upon how well your pilots control the skies. You'll be in charge of all main Luftwaffe forces for this campaign. I'll expect you to cooperate with your Army counterparts to coordinate the landings. Our success in the air will dictate the ground invasion strategy. Timing is vital. The sooner we secure air supremacy, the sooner we can launch Operation Sea Lion."

In other words, I'll be charged if the operation goes sour and you'll be the poster child if it succeeds.

He'd already seen this coming, and fully expected the Luftwaffe commander to abandon him should things not go according to plan. Hermann Göring was his superior, but also an old comrade, and he knew the man well. Knew he'd be willing to throw his own children to the wolves if It meant saving his skin. Udet, on the other hand, was a seasoned combat pilot who was by no means a yes-man. But he'd been brought in to replace those types. A part of him wondered whether he was going to be the sacrificial lamb should the invasion fail, or if Göring was legitimately interested in having someone who cut against the grain leading his forces.

Finally, the car came to a stop in front of a three-story country lodge that served as Udet's headquarters. The driver instantly jumped out to open the rear door. Udet exited first, then waited as Göring forced his body out of the door. It was getting more and more difficult for him to move in tight spaces these days. It was said that his daily diet now consisted of more food than ever and that his personal tastes were for the extreme. Rumors had spread that the fat man had sent orders to have the French countryside scoured for everything from wine and cheese to fine art and antiques. Entire trainloads were being shipped back to Germany as his personal property. Even the famed Louvre museum was not safe from his expensive appetites.

"A fine choice for your headquarters," Göring complimented as he appraised the luxurious-looking building. An honor guard stood at attention just outside of the double front doors.

"I'm glad you think so," the general replied. The interior of the building was just as impressive as the outside. The plush red carpets were immaculately clean, and a small army of civilians was busy dusting and washing the huge double-paned windows that stretched from just above the entranceway nearly to the roof of the cathedral ceiling. The lodge had been known for its luxuriousness before the war; a getaway for rich Parisians looking to escape the bustling city for a while, attended to by one of the most professional staff found anywhere in France. Some of that staff had been allowed to stay on under the German authorities. The ones who could be trusted that was.

"The reason I'm here is to review the preparedness of our forces," Göring told the other man as they strode through the double doors. A staff waiter was standing just inside with a tray of small hand-cut sandwiches. The fat man grinned and licked his lips at the sight of the small delicacies. "But we can enjoy a few well-earned rewards." He snatched one of the small sandwiches and bit into it.

"I've had my staff prepare a formal report for your viewing, Reichsmarschall. At your convenience, I've set aside the observation tower for our use."

The top of the lodge boasted a sizeable roofed platform for its guests. From atop the third story, one could see for kilometers in all directions. The armada of airplanes on the field was far larger than what one saw from the ground. On the runway, a pair of 109s were lifting off with another pair prepping for takeoff. There was the unmistakable smell of petroleum coming from the airfield below. It reminded Göring briefly of his days as a combat pilot.

A large table had been set up under the shade of the canopy, out of the midday sun. Göring instead walked to the edge of the balcony and looked out at the scores of aircraft sitting on the field below. These were *his* planes, and those were *his* pilots out there. He loved nothing more than to bask in his position, and in the power that it brought him. And this was only one of many airfields that he'd visit before returning to Berlin.

With such numbers how can the British stand against us? How can anyone?

"If you'd care for a detailed briefing, sir. I've had a formal presentation—"

"That won't be necessary," Göring said, cutting off General Udet's words. His voice turned harsh. "I've had plenty of formal presentations in the past few weeks. I wish to speak plainly. You all know what the Führer expects. The same thing that I do. Victory." He gestured out to the planes sitting on the grass below. "You've been given the charge of subduing the Royal Air Force. You command the largest percentage of our air forces than anyone. I want to hear from all of you that victory is assured!" The end of his sentence was almost deafening and was followed by moments of silence.

Finally, Udet spoke up. "I believe that victory is very possible, sir. Most likely, in fact. As you say, our numbers alone should see to that."

His head bobbed up and down as he contemplated his next words. Udet was a commander, and a fighting man, not a politician. He did not care to mince words. "But there are some concerns I have that give me pause." The other officers on the balcony remained studiously quiet. "If you wish, I can submit—"

"Just speak frankly, Ernst!" Göring snapped. "I do not wish to upset Hitler with submitted reports." The last words were said in a scathing tone.

"Very well, sir. First and foremost, we must consider our target. We'll be fighting over their territory. Any of our pilots that crosses the Channel will know that they will either be killed or captured, should they be shot down. The British won't have that problem. Then there is their radar. British radar chains all over England will report our advance just as soon as our planes are airborne. That means they'll be able to coordinate a defense accordingly. Those two things alone are enough to worry me. Then there is—"

"I think that you overestimate our enemy, Ernst. Half their aircraft were lost in France! I have intelligence reports that say the RAF commands no more than six hundred fighter planes. We'll roll that out of our factories before the end of the month alone!"

"That's true," Udet agreed. "That is why I said I believe that numbers alone will give us victory. But you asked for my concerns. I'm giving them to you, Herr Reichsmarschall." Göring, having swallowed his words, nodded for Udet to continue. "It was of intelligence that I wished to speak of next." Hesitating momentarily, he resisted the urge to ask the rest of the officers to leave. "It's my belief that our intelligence reports on enemy strength are inaccurate, sir."

Göring's eyes squinted back at him, and he let out a scornful puff. "Inaccurate? How so? Our intelligence has been precise up until now. Colonel Schmid here has personally assured me that our information is highly accurate. Isn't that right, Schmid?"

"Highly accurate," the gray-uniformed Luftwaffe intelligence officer repeated back. The man gave the back of the general's head a stern look. Udet ignored the colonel. Word about the man was that he simply parroted what Göring wanted to hear anyhow. At any rate, the intelligence they'd gathered on Polish and French air strength had been grossly understated before those operations. It was German technological superiority that had won out, not flimsy reports by questionable sources.

"My staff has some reports of their own," Udet went on. "Aerial reconnaissance over Britain has identified several previously unknown bases of operation. Photographs of additional fighter squadrons have been developed. Planes that, forgive me, Luftwaffe intelligence says do not exist." Göring stared back with a look of impatience on his face. Like Hitler, he was notorious for not wanting to hear things that he did not wish to hear. But Udet continued anyhow. "Then there is the quality of the enemy planes we'll be flying against."

"Quality? Yes, we saw many of those qualities blown all over the French countryside. They're out there right now, rusting in fields."

Udet nodded. "Yes. We downed a great many enemy planes. But we had the advantage of a breakthrough on the ground. As our armies advanced, and the Luftwaffe covered them, they forced the Allies to retreat. To move their airbases further and further from the front lines. They couldn't establish quality logistical support. We won't have that advantage here."

"No. You'll have the advantage of having three and a half thousand bombers," Göring told him. "You can bomb them day and night. The advantage of well over a thousand fighter craft, just in the opening stages, to subdue their resistance. Believe me, after the RAF has been reduced to a handful of planes, their cities are on fire, and their population bombed into a state of oblivion, they'll sue for peace."

Udet mentally shook his head. The images of Poland and places like Rotterdam and Liege came to mind. The thought of entire civilian populations being bombed to death was not something that he looked forward to. He'd seen enough of that in two wars and had no desire to see it again. He was only a reluctant Nazi, having joined the party only to further his military career. Underneath, he did not subscribe to the more deranged ideology of National Socialism that some people did.

"Our initial focus is on their airfields," he replied to Göring, trying to move the discussion back to military strategy. "We'll engage with them in the air; we'll pound their airfields over and over until they can't operate. Once we control the skies, and the invasion force lands, hopefully, we can avoid bombing civilian targets."

"That sounds more optimistic," Göring answered. "I have no room for defeatism, Udet. I will give you all that you require to get the job done, but I cannot abide defeatism."

"Not defeatism," Udet replied casually. "I have the responsibility of bringing as many of our good pilots back as possible. However my concerns may come across, they are certainly not defeatist."

The Luftwaffe chief scowled, then nodded his head slowly. He'd known Ernst Udet for many years. He'd flown with him in World War I and knew the type of person he was. He was prepared to let his informality in front of the others go, but only so far.

"I have faith," he told Udet. "Faith in our pilots, in our intelligence reports"—he took two paces forward and put his hand on Udet's shoulder—"and faith in you, General. You will get the job done." He looked the man squarely in the eyes. "You know how much Hitler appreciates those who give him victory."

Udet gave him a half-hearted smile in return. *And what he does to those who bring him defeat. A message, Hermann?* he asked himself.

"Of course, Herr Reichsmarschall. I understand completely."

* * *

Group Commander Balthasar strangely found himself grinning as he lined up the lone British trawler in his sights, and squeezed gently on the trigger. The waters around the small vessel erupted in a flurry of machine gunfire, and a small, smoke-filled explosion balled up from the tiny craft. He pulled his fighter up and away from the vessel two thousand feet below.

Normally he resented the idea of opening fire on a civilian like this, but the hope was that the British would come out from behind their aerial defenses and engage the Luftwaffe in one-on-one combat. Strafing enemy ships in the English Channel seemed like the best way to draw them out. But thus far the British were reluctant to send out any serious numbers of fighters to engage with them.

He smirked as he thought of it. He didn't blame them. Yes, the idea of killing a boat full of defenseless sailors and seamen didn't sit easy with most of the Luftwaffe pilots but orders were orders, and he would much rather try and attract a squadron of RAF Spitfires out over the Channel versus flying over the English countryside where the Tommy's could fight them over their own territory.

After all, this was just the beginning move. Though Luftwaffe Command was mum on the subject, word was that Göring was somewhere in France even now, prepping for an invasion of the British Isles.

Balthasar pulled his fighter around and gazed down at the small little ship quickly sinking beneath the waves. If anybody survived that, then they were going to have a long swim back home. He put his arm out of the cockpit and pointed two fingers back southward, toward the French coast, then swung his craft in that direction, his two flanking companions keeping with him.

He looked in his rearview mirror back at the defiant coast of England. As tempted as he was, they were under strict orders not to exceed the Channel. And as much as he would have liked them to, no RAF craft were coming out to meet them. It didn't matter. Soon enough there'd be a fight.

CHAPTER EIGHT

The newspaper dropped onto Sir David Kelly's desk with a thud. The British ambassador fell into his chair and stared at the front page of the *Gazette* in horror and disbelief. It was a disaster. The only recently formed French government in Vichy had fallen in a late-night coup d'état. Radical elements on the political right had stormed into the city in the late hours of the night and taken control of the French government. The grainy picture on the front page showed an elderly Pétain being escorted out of the Hôtel du Parc by a pair of guards in black uniforms, city-goers, and police watching as the old French general was taken away.

Sir David released the breath that he'd been holding in for several seconds and put his hands on the sides of his head in despair.

"How bad was it?" he managed to ask the room's other occupant.

Roy Keith-Falconer was standing just feet away, holding his fedora in his hand. Though the diplomatic cables had come in early in the morning, Keith-Falconer had been the one to bring the unpublished details of this disaster to the British embassy.

"It was bloodless if that's what you're asking," the Scotsman replied.

"Bloodless." The words were barely audible. Sir David shook his head, pushed the newspaper away, and leaned back into his chair.

In his top drawer, he pulled out a cigarette pack. "How did intelligence not have wind of this?"

Keith-Falconer, tired of standing, sat himself down in the small chair across from Sir David, threw his hat on the chair next to him, and crossed his legs.

"Our intelligence resources in France are limited at the moment. From what I've gathered only a handful of German generals were even aware of the move."

"So this was strictly a French matter?"

"Not exactly, Sir David. The German Sixth Panzer and elements of their parachute division were moved in support. This move seemed to be orchestrated by Himmler's office."

"SS?" Sir David asked dubiously. He leaned forward and touched the shuffle of intelligence reports they'd had on the situation. "I didn't see anything about that."

"I have, uh, other sources that I rely upon," Keith-Falconer told him. He didn't elaborate and Sir David knew better than to press him. "I can tell you this: Some key SS personnel who are known to me were sighted in Vichy this morning. When I got word about it, I put two and two together. Furthermore, this so-called new government is far-right. They have views sympathetic to National Socialism. It makes sense that if Berlin wanted to replace the current—well former—administration with someone, these people would be the likeliest candidates."

"Well, all the same, I'd like to have confirmation of that from MI6. What about the French military? Was there support for this from it?"

Keith-Falconer shrugged. "Probably some. Darlan is an outspoken voice against Pétain but he's no Nazi either. There's a man I know, Darnard. Nasty figure with some muscle. I suspect that he's the one at the heart of it. Pierre Laval, I imagine, will become the figurehead now. He'll have Berlin's support."

"How do you know this?" Sir David asked him. He didn't like being kept in the dark on matters such as this, and right now that's how he felt.

"He's the logical choice. Borderline fascist. He wants to recreate France in Germany's image. He'll appease Berlin to get what he wants. Hitler needs an ally to guard his western flank. This way both sides get what they want."

"You think this new French government will throw in with Germany?" The very thought was ghastly and unthinkable.

"Power does strange things, Sir David. Right now Hitler pulls all the strings. If a new government takes form in Vichy, they could very well find themselves on Hitler's side in order to get back some of their losses. There're still three million French prisoners of war sitting around in German camps. If a person like Laval can negotiate a release, then he'll look like a hero to the people. He has no love for us, that's for certain. To a man like him, a German-French alliance makes sense."

Sir David's expression turned even more sour at the very suggestion. Despite France's defeat it still controlled a formidable navy. The admirals in London were still deathly afraid of that navy, or a portion of it, falling into German hands. Britain's position at sea was precarious enough now. Should France change allegiance it could become impossible for Britain to support its overseas supply lines.

There was a sharp double buzz from the telephone. Sir David picked it up.

"Yes. Very well. Escort him in as soon as he arrives." He hung up the receiver. "Köcher just arrived. He'll be here in moments."

"Köcher?" Keith-Falconer inquired.

"The German ambassador. Surprised you didn't know his name. Don't you know the names of the people you practice your craft on?" His voice was diplomatic, but there was an unmistakable note of disapproval. Sir David and Roy Keith-Falconer had only been acquainted for a short while, but Roy's reputation was fairly well known in the diplomatic service. The dapper Scotsman was a notorious drinker and gambler. His days were short, and his nights were long, often spent in dark rooms. Though his position within the government was a bit unclear, Sir David knew him to be a purveyor of information and minor diplomatic accomplishments.

"I doubt, very much, the ambassador and I run in the same circles. What's he here for?"

"We're at war with them. But we do need to keep some diplomatic channels open. Ambassador Köcher phoned me last night to ask for a meeting."

"Really? And it just so happened to fall on the day when a coup takes place in France?"

Sir David put out his cigarette and stood up, straightening his jacket. "Don't think that fact is lost on me. Our position here is even more dangerous than before. We had some assurances from Pétain before when it came to air travel. I'm not sure we can count on that right now. Should we get cut off from the outside world here, we could find ourselves desperate indeed."

He finished the words just as the door swung open. His secretary escorted the German ambassador into the office. Roy jumped up from his chair. The German was tall and dressed in what looked like very expensive clothing. He had a strange, almost colorless face. As he walked into the office he gave a disregarding look at Keith-Falconer, then turned to Sir David. Roy noted that the two did not shake hands.

"Mr. Ambassador," Sir David greeted him coolly.

"Minister."

"Please come in. My associate Mr. Keith-Falconer." Neither Roy nor Ambassador Köcher gave the other so much as a grin or a nod. "Won't you sit?"

There was a pair of small sofas in the center of the office that they sat in, Roy and Sir David on one and the German on the other.

Ambassador Köcher plopped down on the cushion, his eyes locked on Sir David. Roy studied him for a moment, noticing that the German was going out of his way not to look at him. The door closed behind the secretary.

"So what brings you here, Mr. Ambassador?" Sir David inquired.

"I've come here with a plea from my government. Berlin is hoping that we might begin the process."

"Process of what?"

"Of peace of course," the German puffed. He sighed almost silently. "It is hoped by my Führer that our countries can reach an agreement. I'm hoping that we might begin a dialogue together, Sir David."

"Well, that's an interesting way to begin," Sir David replied. "The British government is always open to the option of peace of course. However, you may find our definitions of peace to be quite different."

Ambassador Köcher raised his right hand up. "We're both practical people. We both understand the political situation. My government is reaching out its hand to you in an effort to secure a peaceful future."

"Peaceful? Peaceful for whom?" Sir David asked, not in a sarcastic way. "I'm genuinely interested to know that. You'll forgive me, but both the British and the French governments have been trying to reach an agreement with Germany for some time now. Since your government reoccupied the Rhineland, in fact. You say we're both practical men and I agree with you. I do understand the political situation. My own government, I thought, had made our position quite clear. We cannot realistically discuss a long-term peace until your military forces are removed from the occupied territories and the governments of such countries are put back in place. I thought Prime Minister Churchill had made himself clear on this."

"Yes. Mr. Churchill's position is well known. That was before. Things have changed now. Your armies barely survived their escape from Boulogne—"

"But they did survive," Sir David quickly retorted.

"And left all of your major equipment in France. Your Air Force has been decimated and the Royal Navy hangs by a thread. Every day the situation for your people grows more desperate. Autumn is coming and with it your last harvest. Your nation has never been able to grow enough food to feed its populace. Do I need to go on?"

Sir David was quiet for a moment, giving no outside appearance of what he was thinking. His finger ran over his lower lip as he contemplated the words. An old veteran of the diplomatic service, he knew the game and how it was played.

"No, we never have. But we're not the only ones in this fight. And you may find out that we're not as crippled as you may think." The German ambassador's eyebrows raised ever so slightly at that. Roy Keith-Falconer, the old card player that he was, observed him quietly. "Unless Berlin is prepared to withdraw its forces, then I'm not sure we can even begin talks for peace."

Köcher smirked. "I was expecting a little bit better than that. The victors don't get dictated to, Minister."

"The war's not over yet, Ambassador," Sir David replied politely and smirked back. "I don't think it's a coincidence that you phoned here yesterday evening for a meeting today; with an apparent French coup that took place just this morning. Interesting coincidence?"

Köcher shrugged. "An internal French matter."

"Supported by two German Army divisions," Keith-Falconer interjected. The German crossed his legs and finally gave Roy the first real glance since coming into the office.

"When I phoned yesterday evening, I did not expect a spy to be in the room with us, Sir David." His words were directed at Sir David, but his eyes were on Keith-Falconer.

"Mr. Keith-Falconer is—" Sir David began.

"With the foreign service," Roy finished. The reply drew a disingenuous smile from the German.

"Yes. With the foreign service. I noticed you when I first entered the room. Your face is known to our own foreign service." The two men locked eyes. "And to the Gestapo."

Roy nodded. "Really? I'm honored."

"I would not be."

"Gentlemen," Sir David intervened in the stare-down. "My colleague was unaware of our meeting this morning. His position with the government is quite official I can assure you, sir. He's no spy."

"Well, it's neither here nor there as you say," Köcher replied. "I came here to discuss a possible pathway to peace. Whoever brings this offer back to your government makes no difference. My Führer is a generous man. He wishes to have peace with Great Britain. He's reaching out his hand to London. Will Mr. Churchill not take it?"

Sir David cleared his throat. "I'm sure he appreciates Hitler's generosity greatly. However, I think I can speak for him when I say no thank you. With all bluntness, Germany has made its intentions quite clear. Every day comes new reports of air raids over the English Channel; civilian ships sunk, having been targeted by your Luftwaffe, the occupation of our allies in Continental Europe, the persecutions of minorities. The list goes on, Mr. Ambassador. If your country wants peace, there must be some concessions by Berlin."

"It's an interesting position you take," Köcher said to him. "Your soldiers garrison huge swaths of Africa, Asia. Do I need to bring up your position in India? Quite hypocritical for the British to demand us to leave the so-called occupied territories. I don't wish to get into a tit-for-tat, but let's review some numbers shall we? There are some two million German troops in the west and nearly five thousand aircraft. I don't feel the need to hide our numbers as I'm sure your intelligence service has already confirmed this. Your forces are in disarray. You have what? Six hundred and fifty fighters, more or less?"

"Why don't you come and find out," Keith-Falconer said to him.

"If we do, I don't think that you'll like the outcome." The German reached into his jacket and pulled out a white envelope. It was sealed, Hitler's signature on the front. "This comes straight from my Führer."

"What is this?" Sir David asked, taking it.

"A guarantee of peace. I think that you'll find the terms he is offering to be very liberal. Prime Minister Churchill would be wise to consider this offer."

Sir David looked at the envelope, and tapped his finger on it. "I shall certainly pass it along, as well as my thoughts on it."

Ambassador Köcher nodded gratefully, then stood back, buttoning his suit.

"One thing please, Mr. Ambassador," Keith-Falconer casually began. He remained seated even as Sir David got back up. "You say you had no knowledge of this morning's coup, that it was a French matter and Germany had no part in it." He lifted his fedora and pulled out a photograph to show the ambassador. "Perhaps you might explain why these men were seen in the vicinity during the takeover?"

Köcher barely glanced at the photo and shrugged. "I don't recognize these men. Sorry."

"They're SS," Keith-Falconer replied. "This one's name is Skorzeny."

"I don't know these men," the ambassador repeated. He looked at Sir David and gave a single nod. "Sir David. I hope to hear from you promptly. Good day."

"Good day," Sir David replied and watched him exit. He waited a moment before turning back to Roy. "You've got a bloody cheek don't you?"

"What do you mean?"

"You knew damn well that the German ambassador was coming here today, didn't you?" He put his hands on his hips and gave Roy a sour look. "Got my phones bugged?"

Roy stood up. "Sir David—"

"You just happened to bring along a photograph of some SS agents in your hat with you today? You knew bloody well he was coming and that's why you raced here this morning. How'd you get the photograph developed so quickly?" He shook his head. "There's a line between diplomacy and espionage and I try not to cross it."

"Minister, all diplomats are spies in a sense. Let's not be naive about how things are. That Nazi cuss didn't just show up here today as a coincidence, as you said before. Whatever French government shakes out from all of this you can bet yer pension that it'll be closely aligned with the Nazis. I needed to see for myself what the ambassador was playing at."

"Playing at?"

"Sir David, please try and see the bigger picture. That man wasn't only 'ere to deliver some piece of paper. That was just part of it. He was sent over to judge our reaction to this morning's events. And to the threat he made about coming in force. He knows damn well how many aircraft we have. He underplayed the numbers to see if we'd correct 'im. And by the way, that little jibe about recognizing me when he came in . . . pah. Bastard knew I was here."

"You don't know that."

"I do know that. The British embassy is constantly under surveillance. Do you think I just walked through the front gate unnoticed? I spotted the little blond bastard scoping this building on my way here. Made sure they saw me, so they'd report to their superiors that I was 'ere."

Sir David's face became alarmed by this news. His hands fell from his hips and his expression turned softer.

"Should we be alarmed?"

"What? That the Germans will breach the embassy?" Roy shook his head. "I don't think so. The Swiss wouldn't allow that to happen. But the situation has just become much, much worse than before.

Besides, I had to get some information of my own from him. Now I have it, and it confirms my suspicions."

The British diplomat's eyes blinked in annoyance, mirroring just how he felt. Embassies were sometimes used for intelligence gathering, but he didn't like the idea of being so directly used in such a way. He certainly did not like that Keith-Falconer had deceived him concerning his visit today and that he had intentionally confronted a fellow diplomat with evidence in the way he had.

"So who was that man in the photograph?" Sir David finally asked him.

"Skorzeny. Nasty character. Special operator for the SS. If Himmler wanted a change in the French government, he's the kind of man he'd send to do the job."

Sir David looked at the photo. Skorzeny was a grim-looking man, with a deep scar on the left side of his face. "Looks like a rough one. How'd he get that scar? Battle?"

Roy chuckled and shook his head. "Dueling scar."

"Dueling. How do you know that?"

"'Cause, I was the one who gave it to 'im," the Scotsman replied.

"Well, Mr. Keith-Falconer, I can't say as I approve of you or your methods, but I suppose someone, somewhere finds your skills most useful. However, in the future, I would very much appreciate it if you didn't play in my backyard without at least letting me know. I don't think that's too much to ask."

"Of course," Roy said apologetically. "Can I ask what you're gonna do with the German's offer?"

"I'm going to review it and pass it along to the prime minister, of course."

"Well ... I think I know what Winston'll do with it."

"Not our job to speculate about such things. So now that you've delivered your news and observed the German ambassador's reaction,

I imagine your job here is finished?" His words sounded hopeful. Roy grinned and put his fedora back on.

"Anxious to see me off, Sir David?" The minister didn't answer him. "That's alright. I understand. By the way, should the situation here become untenable, I'll ensure that you and your staff are relocated to safety. I know you don't much care for me, but should things become sticky, official diplomatic norms may not apply. The Gestapo has arrested foreign diplomats before. And I have avenues available to me better able to secure your person than some diplomatic flight."

"I see. I assume you mean your friend, the American. Shire is his name, isn't it? Smuggler?"

Roy gave the friendliest of smiles. "Impressed, Sir David. Truly impressed. Guess I'm not the only one who's been keeping secrets." He strode toward the door, lifted his hat in gesture, and was gone.

"Strange fellow," Sir David said to himself, sitting back behind his desk. "Strange fellow."

CHAPTER NINE

It had appeared to have gone flawlessly. The pro-fascists had swarmed into the town of Vichy before anyone ever knew what was coming. Hitler laughed at the picture of the French prime minister being escorted away from the building that served as the capitol. Pétain, the old and noble French marshal, was dressed in his best Army uniform. The expression on his face, however, was far from noble. The old man was now locked away in a cottage in the French countryside. Hitler mentally shrugged at the man's outcome. The victor of Verdun deserved whatever punishment awaited him.

"Laval has already openly declared himself head of state," Himmler told him. The two sat in the rear seat of Hitler's bullet-proofed Mercedes-Benz as it made its way through the Berlin streets.

Hitler laughed again as he viewed the rest of the photographs Himmler had brought with him, then handed them back. Germany's victory over France a month earlier, and the occupation since had been highly resented by the French people. Pétain's government, as imperfect as it was short-lived, at least had some provincial support. That was now gone. His successor, as of three thirty-five this morning, was Pierre Laval, a man whose backing came from hard-right supporters and militants. No doubt his ascension to head of state would be highly resented by his people. But that was his problem.

"It was a wise decision, Mein Führer. With someone more closely aligned with us, we ensure ourselves of a stable western flank. We can trust them to police their own. For the foreseeable future anyway."

"I suppose," Hitler replied drearily.

But it'll make Franco very happy. It was the price of alliances.

He didn't regret it, however. He'd made a deal with Stalin over Poland to meet his ends. If a little shakeup in France was needed to do the same, then that's just what would have to happen. The Wehrmacht would like it. Rather than having a potential enemy on its southern flank, it would have the assistance of a friendly neighbor. And it would make the SS very happy indeed. Himmler was already at work setting up a network of offices in the unoccupied zone. In exchange for putting him in power, Laval had agreed, albeit reluctantly, to allow SS security and intelligence personnel a presence in the new regime. And Himmler had wasted no time in putting his people in place, showing the French the ruthless efficiency of his organization.

"I'm trusting you on this," Hitler told him sternly. "You and Ribbentrop seem convinced this would help bring Spain into the fold. The two of you had better be correct."

Himmler gave him a gaze out of the corner of his eye, then looked away. In truth, neither he nor Ribbentrop had made any promises of a Spanish alliance. Should Madrid choose to ally itself with Germany it would be a great triumph, of course. But in Himmler's mind just the act of installing a leader in France who openly aligned with National Socialism was a victory in itself. He didn't put his faith in the belief that Britain would simply come to the bargaining table as Hitler did. But Himmler knew better than to correct the Führer of course.

"I think, Mein Führer, that things could not possibly be going better for the Reich."

* * *

Officer Joseph Portier stood in the center of the four-way intersection, waving the few cars that were still in the city through. His gray and black police uniform had been immaculate when he put it on this morning but was now coated in the same white dust that seemed to cover everything in Liege these days. The bombing of the city weeks earlier had reduced much of the downtown area into rubble, and the stone buildings had thrown up a blanket of limestone powder. Since most of the population had fled during the fighting, there weren't too many around to complain about it. And those who were still around had bigger things to complain about.

A single red-brown automobile slowly maneuvered through the chunks of debris that littered the main street. Joseph waved it forward as it approached him. The single occupant, a middle-aged woman, barely noticed him as she passed. He watched her as she went, wondering for a moment whether or not the woman would be leaving to find some lost family members, or if she would be among those who bravely decided to stay in Liege.

Brave? He inwardly laughed at the thought of the word. Was it brave to remain behind in a town that had been so completely devastated? He mentally shook his head, dusted the white powder off his shoulders, then looked around at the ruins.

The Liege police department, or what was left of it, had reluctantly voted to return to duty. The new mayor, who had been a simple city engineer two months earlier, had begged municipal employees to return to work in order to help bring some form of stability to their desperate situation. It hadn't been an easy decision for many of them, but the alternative was either potentially a city in complete chaos or worse yet, German troops acting as a police force. Rumors and stories of Nazi officials put in charge of towns and cities in Poland would suggest that the Belgians would be far better off policing their own.

He stood in the center of the street for a few empty, quiet minutes. Several dozen people were lining the walkways. Only a small handful of shops were open this morning, and a single café with a husband-wife couple working behind the counter, with a few patrons waiting in line. Such small luxuries, such as tea and coffee, were already becoming valuable commodities.

Another automobile approached slowly. He watched it as it got closer, then waved it through the intersection. The car drove by, and two small children in the rear waved at him as it went.

"Joseph!" a voice called out, and he swung around to see another officer approach him. "I wish you good morning," the man offered.

"Good morning, Pieter," Joseph replied dryly. He pulled his dusty coat sleeve up and glanced at his watch. It was still well before shift change. The other man, Pieter de Roos, was not supposed to relieve him for almost another hour. "A bit early aren't you?"

"Am I?" De Roos shrugged. "I thought I'd come out and keep you some company. Must be terribly boring out here this morning." Joseph simply nodded. "It'll give us some time to talk."

Joseph only slightly glanced at the other. He and Pieter had known each other for some years now but had never been on friendly terms. He could hardly recall any time when the other man simply wanted to speak with him. Pieter was known in the police department as a fanatical Marxist and unionist, while Joseph's politics tended to be much more conservative. De Roos's reputation among other officers in the department was that of a hardcore rabble-rouser, someone best avoided by others.

"Oh?" Joseph said with halfhearted interest. "About what?"

"Oh, just the current state of things," Pieter replied. "Wanted to check up on you. See how you're dealing with the changes." With the last word his voice changed. "The last few weeks have not been easy."

Joseph raised his eyebrows and shrugged. He really did not wish to speak with this man right now.

"What should I say? Things are the way they are. Not much we can do about it right now."

De Roos looked at him and gave the slightest nod. "Right now?"

"Yes. Right now." Joseph was trying to keep his impatience down to a minimum. It wouldn't do to have the locals see two police officers arguing with each other in the broad of day. He exhaled noisily enough for the other man to hear. "If you're trying to recruit me into one of your ridiculous communist—"

"No!" Pieter cut him off. The two looked at each other, and Pieter gave Joseph a friendly grin. "Nothing to do with communism. Look, I didn't come out here to start an argument with you."

"Then what did you come out here for? You knew that you weren't to relieve me for another hour. I doubt Captain Bauchau sent you out here early."

"Well, you're right about that. The captain didn't send me out here early."

Joseph turned his attention around the ruined town. The structures just blocks away were hollowed wrecks. Old buildings, churches, and homes that had stood for generations were now little more than piles of bricks and stone. The streets were littered with wreckage that city workers and civilian volunteers were still trying to clear away.

"Joseph, listen. I just wanted to see how you're dealing with all of this. I didn't want to start an argument with you."

"There's no argument," he retorted. "I can't imagine what you and I have in common that you'd want to talk with me about."

Pieter gave him a momentary look of disbelief before averting his own eyes. Down the road, in the distance, he could make out a single German tank sitting just off of the main road.

"You're wrong," he replied. "We do have something in common. Maybe more than you realize." He stepped closer to Joseph, clasped his hands behind his back, and casually looked around as if two old comrades were chatting away. Another car came up, and Joseph waved it past. "I've been speaking with some of the other officers. As well as some other people around."

Joseph gave Pieter a tired glance. "And?"

Pieter shrugged. "Just speaking. There's a lot of animosity right now. Did you hear about what happened in Amsterdam last week with the roundups?" He shook his head drearily. "I heard some things from some people I know. About the Gestapo deporting people, our people, out of the country."

Joseph jerked his head away. "Stupid rumors. They said the same thing in Nineteen-fourteen."

"No. These aren't just rumors," Pieter told him. "I've got contacts with people up there. Railroads have been commandeered by the Nazis. It's reliable I assure you."

"Yeah. From the mouths of your communist friends? Honestly, I'm surprised that they haven't all been rounded up by the Gestapo themselves. I wish the Nazis would round you people up." He said the words, then felt a surge of guilt for it. He didn't want anyone to be carted off by the Germans. He waved his hand in semi-apology for the remark.

"Just hear me out," Pieter replied without any animosity in his voice. "The Germans are rounding up communists. But they're also singling out a lot of others; democrats, monarchists, cabinet officials, all sorts. Anyone they suspect is loyal to the King."

"The King is dead," Joseph replied.

"There's a new one. He's in London. Look, all I wanted to do was just speak with you. I know you don't have a wife and kids, and you don't subscribe to some of the other politics. But good Lord, this is our country. These Nazis are the absolute worst."

Joseph didn't look at him, but he did listen. Frankly, he was shocked to hear this from the man. He wasn't friends with De Roos by any means, and right now the atmosphere in the country was as tense as it could get. Just talking a certain way could potentially land one in serious trouble. He didn't want to say it, but he'd heard the same rumors about deportations too. He'd expected some sort of period when political leaders and potential opposition would be rounded up for questioning. But he'd heard from people that the German occupiers weren't just taking political figures away. Entire families were being snatched up.

"I don't want to hear this nonsense," Joseph told him. "This isn't going to end any time soon."

"Listen, just hear us out," Pieter said and instantly drew a scrutinizing look.

"Us?"

"Some local people. Your friend Jules is one of them." Joseph looked hard into Pieter's eyes, trying to determine if the other man was trying to draw him into something or not. He and Jules had done in two German soldiers during the initial invasion, then dropped their bodies in a canal. They'd both vowed never to speak of it. Had Jules said something?

"I don't want to be associated with your meetings," he told Pieter.

"Just hear us out. One time." He had a seriousness in him. "Tomorrow night. It's just a few of us. Think about it. Let me know tomorrow sometime. I'll be around."

Joseph looked at him, then slowly, reluctantly nodded but said nothing. Pieter smiled back.

"Good. Just talk to me tomorrow and I'll let you know more. In the meantime, I'll take over for you here." He gave Joseph a tiny salute and took over in the middle of the roadway.

* * *

The stairs to the cellar squeaked as Joseph descended into the dimly lit basement. The hushed tones he'd heard before suddenly quieted as his footsteps were detected. A thin wooden door was half-open, and he pushed it all the way, revealing himself to the small group of people gathered. He looked at them cautiously and they at him suspiciously.

There was only a single small lightbulb hanging from a wire from the low ceiling. There must have been two dozen people, most of whom Joseph did not recognize, but two faces, in particular, did stand out to him. His friend Jules was there, the one who'd helped him murder two German soldiers and then dispose of the bodies, and Pieter de Roos. A smile flickered across Jules's face, and he nodded a greeting to his friend.

Pieter stepped out from the middle of the room where he'd been talking with others and gave Joseph a grateful look.

"Welcome, Joseph," he greeted. Joseph put his hands in the pockets of his overcoat and replied with a wry grin. "I was hoping you'd come."

"I told you I'd be here. I'm not signing up for anything, but I'll listen to what you have to say."

Pieter nodded gently. "Fair enough. Let's get this started then. Some of you know each other, but most do not. I thought that we should meet to discuss our situation. I made sure to only invite those who I was absolutely sure could be trusted. No one here has any hardcore political affiliations. When I thought about who might be willing to take action against our occupiers, I thought it best to keep the circle as small as possible, and not to bring on a bunch of crazy extremists."

"What action are you talking about?" a woman asked.

"I think that would be obvious," the man standing behind her answered sardonically. "Look at what has happened out there!"

"Shh," another voice cried out. "Keep your voices down."

"Please. Let's not get out of control," De Roos said holding his hands up for calm. "Things are tense as they are. Let's not add to the tension. Jan is correct. Look at what's happened to us, and to our country. Most of you here know me. You might not care for my politics, but that's beside the point today. Many of you know that I'm not someone who can sit idly by and do nothing while our nation and our people are suffering through an occupation. There's a foreign army out there right now, holding us at gunpoint. Occupations must, must be resisted. It's our duty to see the city occupants through to safety."

"How?" the woman who'd spoken before asked.

"Yes," another woman spoke up. "The Germans are already cracking down on political dissidents. People from the previous government are vanishing in the night. They have tanks and machine guns and who knows what else. What can we do against that?"

Some people rumbled, offering up a reluctant agreement. Joseph watched the interaction play out. People quietly asked questions of others. Some suggested taking direct action; others who thought it was too risky hesitated. Most remained silent.

"One thing is for sure, we cannot sit still," Jules told them. "These Nazis are not invincible. I say we hit them. We get some guns and—"

"Get some guns?" a man cut in. "Are you mad? And do what? Twenty of us against the German Army! We'd just be target practice for the Huns. I agree that we should do *something*, but let's be realistic here. If the entire Allied armies couldn't stop the Nazis before, what chance do you think we'd have?"

"I don't believe we should confront the Germans with guns, Jules," De Roos told him. "I don't know what the answer is right now, but I don't think we'd win in a street-to-street fight with those armored vehicles out there now. Jules has one idea, but there are others we can discuss."

The group erupted in a cacophony of discord. Several of them began talking over one another, some making accusatory remarks to others of being far too radical, while a few present, like Jules, accused those same people of being far too conservative. It began as a quiet disagreement, but as some began speaking over others, voices grew louder.

"This is not a time for caution," Jules said to the person who'd interrupted him, drawing an ire look from the other man.

"No? I'm sure your idea of charging right in with rifles blaring is the way to go. Right up until those Nazi machine guns wipe us out! Use your head, you fool!"

The mountainous Jules took one step toward the smaller man when Pieter put his hand on the large man's chest to stop him. The other had a threatened look on his face, and backed away a step, in response.

Joseph stood in the back of the crowd, watching in silent disgust. He'd come here tonight with the anticipation of listening and hearing what people had to say. He knew full well that there would be disagreement, but he thought—hoped really—that the people would come to the understanding that they were each in the same situation. But he watched as the gathering broke into small groups, their voices becoming louder as frustrations grew.

The discussion went back and forth for another minute with confused chatter. For a moment it looked as if De Roos was going to lose control of things when someone suggested that the Belgian government had capitulated and that they should simply accept the occupation as a reality.

"If the government in Brussels has—," a man named Michel began, but another voice cut him off.

"Our government is not in Brussels," Joseph said, then found himself completely shocked that the words had come out of his own mouth. He stood silent for half a second as the others in the cellar gazed at him. He gulped as he looked back at the faces staring at him. He had not intended to speak. "The Belgian government is in London," he said quietly. "The government in Brussels is a puppet regime, set up by Berlin."

"Yes," Jules agreed. "Collaborators."

Pieter shot a glance at Joseph, then looked around at the faces of the others. "Exactly. There's little difference between German Nazis and Belgian Nazis. This is a military occupation, and it must be resisted. We're not looking for a fight with our own people. However, with every foreign occupation, there brings with it collaboration. We have to accept that as a fact. We also need to be careful about who we associate with." His eyes scanned the room almost as an afterthought. "We can't risk exposing ourselves."

"In order to do what?" Michel asked. "Do you really think we'll liberate the country? Bring the King back from exile, and drive the invader out?" He shook his head in disbelief.

"No!" Jan snapped. "But we make them pay. Every day we make them pay."

"Every day more and more Germans are arriving," Michel shot back. "I see them go by. Every day brings more airplanes, more tanks, more of everything. The Nazis seem to be everywhere nowadays. Look at what they have behind them. Armored cars, machine guns. What can we do about that?"

"I agree," a woman who Joseph recognized said. Her name was Genivee, a clerk for the city. "I want to do something. For my children. For my husband." Her eyes teared up. "I don't even know if he's alive or not. But what can we here do?" She shook her head vigorously.

Again the discussion broke down into a scene of disarray. People began to make ridiculous suggestions of open confrontation. Some were not willing to commit to anything whatsoever. One man even suggested just sitting out the fight in the hopes that the Germans would simply leave one day. Pieter tried to intervene in the squabble, but the raucousness seemed to grow out of his control.

"The Germans are not simply going to leave," Joseph blurted out, and again the room went quiet. "Not anytime soon anyway, and not of their own accord." He let the words hang out there for a few moments. "Pieter is right when he says there must be resistance. Resistance comes in many ways." He thought briefly of the small town he'd hidden near during the German invasion. He thought of the people there, and the sound of machine guns firing, mowing half the people there down like blades of grass. He thought of the piles of bodies, and the smell that followed.

"What does that mean?" Genivee asked him.

"It means there is active resistance and passive resistance. Everyone has a role to play. You work as a city clerk don't you?" The woman nodded. "So the Germans need things done. Roads need to be rebuilt, bridges. They've taken over the old school for a barracks. They need things like running water and supplies. They'll undoubtedly use civilian labor for projects. That can be useful. When they requisition something, we take note of it. Occupiers don't take things that are of no value to them. We don't have to meet the enemy head-on, but we can lull them. Help them put up their telephone lines, then listen in on their conversations. The more we know, the more information we gather, the better positioned we'll be."

A quiet fell over the room. For a moment, the only sound came from the flickering of the light bulb dangling from the low ceiling. Even the air seemed to cease moving.

"That's, uh, a very good idea, Joseph," Pieter commented. His facial expression was that of sheer amazement. "I'm a bit surprised to hear you come up with it. I didn't know you were so well educated on revolutionary tactics." He grinned broadly at Joseph.

"I'm not," he replied, a moment later. "This isn't the first military occupation this country's seen. Does anyone think that our parents sat back and did nothing when the Kaiser's armies came marching in?"

"Family secrets, Joseph?" Jules asked, and Joseph shrugged.

"I know this," Joseph began. "If you want to begin to resist, then it's going to take a lot more than sitting around in dark cellars, arguing with one another. There're a thousand different actions that one can take. They don't all revolve around taking up arms." He looked squarely at Jules. "And I know you may want to, my friend. But it's simply not going to work. The Germans would gun us down in droves. And then they would retaliate."

"So, what are you saying?" Jules asked him.

Joseph chewed on his lip for just a moment as he thought about it. "We're not alone in this fight. There's still a war going on out there. The whole goddamn continent is under the thumb. There have to be others out there like us. In France, in Poland, in Czechoslovakia. All of Europe is a powder keg right now."

Pieter smiled. "Yes. Exactly. It's just waiting for the right spark."

Joseph nodded, and he noticed for the first time just how silent the cellar had become. "So we light the fuse, and set the whole fucking thing on fire."

CHAPTER TEN

Major Adolf Galland bit his lower lip as he maneuvered his Bf 109 just outside the gun range of the Hawker Hurricane that had been on his tail. The more maneuverable British fighters were formidable, and the RAF pilots were well-trained. He'd briefly underestimated their skill in aerial combat. He'd blown so many Allied pilots out of the air in France that he'd come to hold his enemy in low regard. But today was different. The Tommies and their allies were fighting with much more tenaciousness than he'd become used to seeing from them. Two small groups had come in from separate directions and caught him off guard. Now they were making a good showing, having gotten hits in on three of his planes, forcing one to retire back across the English Channel. Yes, he'd underestimated them, but he never made the same mistake twice.

He looked in his rearview mirror as the Hurricane became smaller in the reflection until finally, the other pilot peeled off from his pursuit. Galland banked his plane around in a wide arc, away from the Hurricane's path. Fifteen thousand feet below, the Dorset countryside looked like something out of a painting, with its squared-off hedgerows. In the skies around him, his fighters were fully engaged. Twelve Messerschmitts against eight Hurricanes. Well, seven now. They'd downed one enemy fighter, and he had personally gotten a tail end shot in on a second before picking up his own tail in the process.

A dozen flights of Messerschmitt and Focke-Wulf fighters had lifted up this morning from all across Normandy and the Pas-de-Calais. The English Channel was practically devoid of any ships that morning, except for some Royal Navy patrol vessels, and the odd fishing boat. The German fighter groups crossed the Channel, twelve thousand feet up. Nothing more than minor dots in the sky to the casual observer. Each group approaching the English coast on a different vector, each had been told to expect light to moderate resistance.

The Luftwaffe pilots knew that the Royal Navy ships would have spotted them and that the famed British radar stations had no doubt picked them up as soon as they reached cruising altitude, but there was no helping that. It was not as though the RAF weren't expecting the Germans to come eventually anyhow.

Galland turned toward the fight in the skies. German and British fighters whipped through the clouds in a game of cat and mouse. He searched around him and picked a new target. It was fighter on fighter, and Galland grinned at the thought of how well his pilots were performing. Not that he'd ever doubted their readiness or skill. Certainly not. They'd blown the Polish Air Force to bits, subdued the Dutch and Belgians as if they were nothing at all, and crushed the French at every encounter. Today, they'd prove themselves more than a match for the cocky British, and add another victory to their already prestigious record.

He lined his sights up on a single Hurricane. Its pilot steered the craft into a tight turn that only a Hurricane seemed capable of pulling off. The enemy plane's deep-brown silhouette darkened his canopy sights as he closed with it. He waited until he'd gotten well within gun range, then squeezed the trigger. A stream of bullet rounds filled the sky just ahead of the Hurricane, its pilot trying desperately to pull his plane away before it was too late. But his efforts were in vain.

The rounds raked the side of its fuselage, and black-and-white smoke trailed him as the plane spun in.

Galland watched as it turned over, and dove straight in toward the earth. The pilot fell out of the cockpit, his parachute opening up after a second or two. The German breathed a small sigh as he watched the plane fall away from the descending pilot. It was a small courtesy allowed between aerial combatants.

"Scratch one!" he said to himself. *Twelve on six.*

He scanned the sky again, like a hunter looking for new prey. Off to his right two Hurricanes chased after a single 109. He turned in toward them. These Englishmen were brave, but he could see they were inexperienced. He shook his head at it. They flew in straight lines for far too long, and he'd taken note of their failure to use the Hurricane's superior agility to their full advantage. Too many of them were trying to outrun the German planes. And it would be their undoing.

He nudged on the throttle, accelerating forward. In his peripheral, he caught a glimpse of two more of the gray-black 109s pull into formation on his wings. The three fighters went chasing after the two Hurricanes, who were weaving in and out in a chase of their own.

* * *

Flight Leader Andrews turned his fighter sharply, trying to keep the German he was chasing in his sights. He fired off a single volley, missing the 109 by a couple of yards. MacDonald, his wingman, kept with him as the two tried to get one good shot in on the bastard. The 109 was flying evasively, as he should be with two enemy fighters on his six o'clock.

The German pilot banked left, then right, then left again as it tried to shake off the two Hurricanes in pursuit. Any minute the 109's superior speed would take him out of range. Andrews tried to keep one second ahead of him, anticipate his movements, firing short bursts just ahead of the German. The faster Messerschmitts could escape gun range quickly, but the Hurricane could bank tighter, and get its guns just ahead of the enemy planes.

Number 213 Squadron had scrambled almost as soon as the first of them had been detected leaving French airspace. The Germans were already at peak cruising altitude by the time they'd reached the Channel. That had left the RAF desperate to get its planes sky bound to intercept. Despite their radar accuracy, there were simply too many gaps in the British defenses.

Andrews spotted the first of the westernmost group just as they'd crossed the coastline. There had been twelve Messerschmitts in all, and they'd charged straight in on the attack.

Bold, he'd thought when he saw them. *Very, very bold. Not even trying to be sneaky.* Number 213 had met the Messerschmitts head-on, and broken their formation. But the faster German planes, and the one-and-a-half to one odds they boasted, were proving to be too much for him and his pilots to overcome. He'd already lost two of his planes.

Andrews zeroed his sights on the German, squeezed the trigger, and fired a bright line of rounds from his twenty-millimeter machine guns. He caught a brief glimpse of metal flying off the enemy wing tip, then the German put his nose down, sending his plane into a steep dive. Andrews and his wingman followed, picking up speed in the pursuit.

His eyes were dead set on the 109 ahead. He hadn't even registered the three Messerschmitts in his rearview mirror. He squeezed the trigger again. His rounds cut into the 109's fuselage, shredding it to pieces. A small, bright explosion in the air a moment later and the German was gone from sight.

"Sir!" his wingman's voice crackled over his headset. By the time it registered with him, the German on their tail had already fired his shot.

His plane bucked violently, and shrapnel ricocheted around like small marbles in a tin can. His oil pressure gauge went to zero instantly, and he felt a sharp pain in his left shoulder, followed by a spray of blood across the controls. His instinct was to grab at the pain with his right hand, but he fought against it and kept his hand on the controls.

His propeller shut off, and the plane effectively died in midair. He watched frantically as his wingman peeled away from him. He rolled his craft over on its inertia, unbuckled himself, and simply fell out of the cockpit. Three 109s flew by just as he cleared his plane. For several seconds he was in free fall before his chute opened.

* * *

"Scratch two!" Galland called triumphantly into his mike. The Tommy's plane spun in and crashed into the ground half a minute later. The second British pilot pulled out of the fight and retreated. The major did a quick check around him. Eleven of his boys were still up, and he could only spot five Hurricanes. He grinned under his face mask, then squeezed his throat mike. "This is Group Leader, round up and head home."

He pulled his mask off, gave a victory salute to his two wingmen, then brought his plane around and headed south, across the Channel.

* * *

"Disaster." It was the only word that Churchill could come up with. The nub of his burned-out cigar moved from one side of his mouth to the other, and he chewed on it furiously. "A bloody disaster. Twenty-three fighter aircraft lost to the enemy's seventeen."

"And," Air Marshall Dowding began, "it's only the first day. We can expect daily sorties from the Luftwaffe. They're sending their fighters in to engage with ours. It gives them an opportunity to test our strength, and with losses like this they can wear us down. Less resistance when the bombers start coming."

"And they will come, Prime Minister," Cyril Newall added. Dowding nodded in wholehearted agreement.

Dowding was head of RAF Fighter Command, and the man responsible for meeting the Luftwaffe threat. The three-page report on today's initial engagements had painted a dismal portrait of his command thus far. Seven different engagements along England's southern coast had been costly for the service that was already struggling to catch up to Germany in terms of aircraft and pilot strength. Today's battle showed that they were still lagging. Twenty-three fighters lost and nine pilots were killed in action.

"We can't sustain losses like this day after day," Winston said. He took the chewed-up end of his cigar and tossed it in the small tin bowl on the desk in his private office. "Production estimates for new fighters is less than three hundred in the next thirty days. And the pilot situation?"

Dowding bit his lower lip and gave a single shake of his head. "Precarious would be putting it mildly, Prime Minister. Still coming up short in trained fighter crews. Some bomber pilots have volunteered for training, and we're putting men through the flight schools as quickly as possible. Even with other Commonwealth pilots in the country, we're spread thin in every squadron. On top of that, the Germans have only come in small numbers thus far. I fully expect that before the week is out, they'll be flying three or four sorties a day, with greater numbers."

"On the flip side, Prime Minister, of the German planes downed, we captured eight of their pilots. Two more are considered on the loose," Newall stated. Churchill barely grunted at the information.

"Gentlemen, I have to brief King George this evening on the situation. He's going to ask me what's being done and I'd very much like to have a realistic answer for him when he does." Winston patted down his coat in search of another smoke. Both Newall and Dowding nodded in understanding.

"I'll have something put together for you by then, sir," Dowding said. "VM Park and I have been bouncing around some ideas."

"Please," Churchill replied. He struck a match, lit the end of his new stogie, and the cigar began to flame to life as he drew on it. His private office was spacious enough, but the aroma of his famous cigar smoking could be overwhelming to some. Two open windows let fresh air in; however, the carpet was so full of smokey odor that one could hardly miss it. Churchill's eyes then turned to Admiral Cunningham. "Admiral, please tell me you've got some good news for me. It would be a welcome change."

Cunningham held up a folder. "After-action report, sir. The Casablanca operation." He placed it in front of Churchill, who promptly began looking through it.

Across from him, Anthony Eden watched Churchill eagerly go through the paragraphs, reading aloud the high points, and smiling at the attached photographs. The prime minister had OK'd the actions at Casablanca and Rabat, in French Morocco, as precautionary. Though still technically neutral, the new French regime under Laval had signaled its intention to align with Hitler. And the French fleet was still a powerful tool. Should that country become hostile its fleet could pose a serious threat to the Royal Navy.

"Casualties?" Churchill asked Cunningham.

"Surprisingly light, sir. Three planes shot down. Some retaliatory shots were fired from shore batteries. One of our destroyers took minor damage. There was some loss of life. It's on the last page, sir."

Black-and-white photos of the French naval squadrons at Casablanca and Rabat on fire drew a sigh of relief from Winston. He'd been given no choice. A Franco-Italian armada operating in the Mediterranean Sea would have been costly. Potentially cutting them off from the Suez Canal. Even a single French battleship operating against Britain's shipping lanes could have been highly deadly. Now that threat had been neutralized for the time being. It was a small glimmer of hope in an otherwise dark situation.

"We also took three ships in port at Alexandria," Cunningham informed him. "They'd been sitting there since the armistice. Our boys stormed the ships early this morning. There were skeleton crews aboard, and very little resistance. Admiral Harwood reported two destroyers and the cruiser *Montcalm* were seized." The news drew the faintest hint of a grin from Churchill, whose cigar was now piping smoke.

"That is good news," Winston agreed. "Do you have any idea of the damage inflicted?"

"Still sorting that out, sir. Between aerial reconnaissance and intercepted radio transmissions, we believe that the French battleships all took hits, with at least one of them sustaining considerable damage. Our torpedo bomber strikes sunk one destroyer berthed at Rabat, and the cruiser *Dupleix* at Casablanca."

Winston could imagine how the news was being handled in Vichy. Or for that matter, Berlin. The French population was still seething from their defeat by the German Army, and tensions across the Channel were high. Now, after this, their proud navy had just taken a pounding from what had recently been an allied power. But it couldn't have been helped. Even the slimmest possibility of Germany using the French Navy as a weapon against them was something that the government could not gamble on.

"Has there been any word through diplomatic channels?" Winston asked Eden, who shook his head.

"Nothing at all. In fact, so far as I know, there hasn't even been any increased communication between their new government and their overseas embassies. But I don't believe things will remain quiet for long. There will be blow-back."

"Well, we'll deal with that when it comes," Winston replied. In truth relations with the French had been strained under Pétain. Diplomacy with Vichy following April's armistice had been soured to begin with. The now-former head of state had not been happy when London had allowed a delegation of former officials and military officers to maintain an unofficial embassy there. That alone strained the relationship between the two former allies enough, but then General Giraud's broadcast calling for a united resistance against German occupation had been considered a slap in the face by Pétain. After this morning's attack on their fleet in Africa, it was going to get messier.

"Incorporate any captured French vessel into our forces," Winston said. His office had already been getting a steady stream of phone calls from the general in exile, and those rallying around him, who called the current regime in France illegitimate. Churchill had carefully avoided allying with those elements, even outright refusing to recognize them as the legitimate successor to the French Republic. After this morning's operation, however, he'd have to carefully reconsider the situation. "Also, I want the Admiralty to have plans prepared to seize French bases should the need arise."

Admiral Cunningham nodded in return. "I'm already having them drawn up, Prime Minister."

A swirl of smoke ascended around Churchill's head. "Things are bad enough in France, but this will, no doubt, be seen as an act of aggression by this new regime." His face abruptly became troubled. "We have to prepare for the worst possibility." He took a long draw from his cigar, looked at the clock on his desk, and realized the time. "Oh. It seems I've lost track of the time. I have a telephone call scheduled with the American president that begins shortly. Was there anything else?" He looked around.

"Um," General Dill sounded off. "There was North Africa, sir." His voice sounded grave, and Churchill grimaced at him.

"Yes. North Africa." Churchill rubbed his jaw. "The situation?"

Dill looked down at some notes held in his hand. "The Italians have an entire army threatening our forces in Egypt, and intelligence suggests at least four more divisions are being prepared to ship out from ports in Italy. With those kinds of reinforcements, our position may become untenable."

Winston had seen the newest reports. Every day the situation in North Africa seemed to bring more and more bad news. As if things at home were not already bad enough, the thought of a major enemy campaign against the British in Egypt hung over them.

"We do still have the options I presented to you before, sir," Dill stated, and Churchill instantly sighed.

"I'll bring it up with the King this afternoon," Winston replied. He didn't envy the thought of bringing forces from the Far East, thereby weakening an already tenuous position. "Now, if you'll excuse me."

He pushed himself up from behind his desk and looked to Tommy Thompson, waiting near the door. The officers and officials began to excuse themselves from the office. Foreign Secretary Eden remained behind as the door shut behind General Dill.

"Getting ever more desperate," Winston commented quietly. Eden nodded a grim agreement.

"The president will be on shortly, sir," Thompson informed them. He double-clicked on his telephone line and listened as the operator on the other end gave him an update.

"The other option?" Eden quietly inquired about Dill's suggestion.

Winston puffed away. "Singapore," he replied just as quietly. Eden's eyebrows raised in response.

"The president, sir," Thompson said aloud, breaking the eye contact between the two men.

"Mr. President," Winston said, picking up the receiver.

"Prime Minister," Roosevelt's voice came through over the crackling telephone line. "It's good to hear from you. Are you well over there?"

"As well as can be expected during such times. And you?"

There was a short pause at the other end. "Personally, very well. However, I pray every day for you. I've been informed by my people that you're facing quite a situation over there."

"Hmm. That's an optimistic way of putting things, Mr. President. I just ended a meeting with my people, and the picture over here is ... well, it's not good. We will, very soon, find ourselves accosted on all fronts." He paused dramatically. "I will honestly tell you that I genuinely fear for our country's survival. Our situation at sea is bad enough, and now we're being engaged in the air."

More static interrupted the line. "... been informed that the Germans have sunk ships just off the coast of North America. I regret to say that one of our own commercial vessels was torpedoed just last night off the New Brunswick coast. We've already lodged a protest with the German government."

Winston inwardly discarded any thought that it would be met with anything but laughter by those people in Berlin.

"Mr. President, I must inform you of action that we took just this morning. The recent events in France have forced us to take drastic measures." He and Eden swapped brief looks. "I ordered the Royal Navy to take offensive action against the French squadrons in port in Morocco. Several ships were heavily damaged. We also seized additional vessels in the Port of Alexandria."

There was a long silence on the other end of the line. Then, "I see," Roosevelt replied. "I'm not sure if that will make things better for your position, or worse, Winston."

"I understand completely, my friend," Winston replied. "Desperate times, I'm afraid. It was the French situation that I wished to confer with you about. We're terribly worried about the possibility of their navy becoming a weapon used against our shipping lanes. Their naval bases pose a considerable threat to *both* of our nations. Should the islands in the West Indies be used by the enemy, they could launch operations against our territories there"—he paused again—"as well as American territory." He desperately wanted those last few words to sink into his American counterpart.

"Yes," Roosevelt replied softly. "My naval planners have said as much. In fact, Admiral Stark over here has suggested that we take some form of action to prevent such a thing from taking place." Winston's brows rose at the sound of it. Any possibility of the United States taking some form of action would be most welcome news indeed. "However, the fact remains that any action would require congressional approval. While many in our Congress would vote for such a measure, I don't believe that it would find overwhelming support. And it may cost us dearly with the American public. There's also the other matter: that our relations with the French would be in peril. We do recognize the sovereignty of the French government. Despite recent events."

Winston balled his fist and lightly pounded his desk. He'd hoped against hope but knew that Roosevelt's hands could be tied against such a move.

"I see," was all he could eke out.

"However," the American president's voice crackled back. "I've been conferring with some of my people over here ... concerns of their own. As well as some solutions of our own. We're still working out some details over here, Winston, but the consensus is that we can declare some of our older naval assets obsolete. Thus freeing them up to be sold."

"Sold?" Winston replied, pouting at the suggestion. A good idea should the British government not be teetering already on the edge of the financial abyss.

"We're working out some details here in Washington, but we have an idea on how to make this work for both of our nations."

Churchill listened intently as the American president spelled out the details. His expression perked up as Roosevelt laid out the plan. Across from him, Eden grinned widely as he listened in on the phone call.

CHAPTER ELEVEN

Vice Air Marshal Keith Park pumped his feet up and down as he stood looking from the balcony of the operations room at the situation that was playing out below. The table below was so large that it had to be brought into the operations room in pieces. The map of England and the French coast had been enlarged to the point where nearly every single town and village between the English Channel and Derbyshire were marked. Every RAF airstrip, every Naval and Army base, tagged in green, red, and gold.

Along the far wall, a string of telephone stations had been set up, with RAF noncommissioned officers taking calls, scribbling out notes hastily on small pads of paper, then handing them off to the group of female plotters moving pieces around the board. The constant flow of communications between forward radar stations and aerial observation posts, and these command-and-control hubs always seemed to impress the air marshal. It was remarkable to him just how coolly and professionally all the information passed from one command to the next in such a constant stream. The vast network that had been put together for just such a purpose was truly impressive. Should any one radar station, communications center, or aerial observation post be destroyed by the enemy, there were several redundancies that kept the information flowing. That cool professionalism was something that was very, very British. Park appreciated that.

The native New Zealander had been in the RAF for almost twenty-five years now, and he understood, probably better than anyone, the inner workings of the service. Britain had learned many lessons from the Great War. Some had been forgotten, but one that seemed to stick was the crucial need for such a steady flow of information going back and forth between commanders and their subordinate units in the field. Far too many disasters could have been averted in his early days if only the British military system had maintained such a communications network. Gone were the old days of sending runners and couriers to forward units.

"Sir," a soft voice said to him. A young man entered through a side door holding a cup of steaming hot tea in his hand.

Park smiled and nodded. "Thank you," he said, taking the cup and saucer. A thin slice of lemon bobbed up and down in the cup. He took a sip and watched the situation below. Light bulbs on the opposite side of the huge room were lit up in yellow, indicating that a sector was currently calm, but units were on standby. A red light would indicate enemy activity. If a red light was on, it meant that enemy aircraft were detected heading toward a target in England. If that was the case, then Fighter Command, and more specifically his command, Number 11 Group, would coordinate the defense.

So far today, the boards were clear, and the bulbs remained at a cautionary yellow. But the day was still young. The last week had consisted of wave after wave of German fighters coming across the Channel. Two or three sorties a day were coming at their defenses, engaging the RAF squadrons, then fleeing back to their bases in France. That tactic was becoming routine. And also costly. The strain being put on Britain's pilots as they scrambled to meet the attackers head-on was starting to show in their performance. It was difficult for squadrons, which were already undermanned, to go up three times a day to engage with attackers twice their strength. Then to do it the next day, and the day after that. His pilots were already becoming tired.

He took a sip of the steaming tea. He preferred Darjeeling over Earl Grey. Down below, a corporal hung up his phone, then flipped a switch. A single yellow bulb shut off, to be instantly replaced by a bright red one. Messages were passed along, and the board plotters began moving the markers across the giant map.

There was a dull double buzz of a telephone.

"Park here," he answered. "Very well. Scramble Forty-one Squadron." He mentally checked the box. He had to know which of his squadrons was airborne at any time. Should there be bombers in any given attack, his airfields would most likely become their first targets. "Inform Ten Group of the situation, and ask them to have their wings on standby."

He hung up the phone and looked at the plot board. Two groups were moving north from Caen, straight toward the Solent, in southern England. A corporal writing on the chalkboard slowly wrote out the projected enemy's speed and their estimated strength. Park watched the man take in the information, before writing out the details.

"Damn," he muttered as the corporal put the numbers on the chalkboard.

Thirty-plus fighters escorted a bombing group of over a hundred in the first group. The second was on a parallel course with similar strength and was heading directly for Portsmouth. Two bombing groups on a route for Hampshire and the Isle of Wight would be only the beginning of what promised to be a very busy day.

Park put down his tea, picked up the telephone receiver, and gave it a double tap. On the other end, the operator answered. "Have Numbers Three and Seventeen Squadrons stand by. And put me through to the prime minister, immediately." He tapped his foot as the operator put him on hold. A minute later, a couple of cross-connections and another voice picked up the other end.

"Churchill," the voice answered.

"It's Park, sir. We have confirmation of large enemy bombing formations leaving French air space." He paced back and forth but kept his eyes on the board. As he spoke, another red bulb flashed on, and the small army of plotters pushed more pieces out. In a handful of seconds, he absorbed the information. A wall of enemy aircraft was quickly emerging.

"Strength?" Churchill asked. Park could hear him exhaling stressfully on the other end.

"Approximately five hundred plus aircraft," Park replied. Markers were pushed out from France toward the English coast in six large formations. "I think this is the beginning of the big push, Prime Minister."

"I understand. Do we know their intended targets?"

"We can expect that airfields will be their primary targets. I'm scrambling our own fighters in response, and I've asked Ten Group to cover our fields. However"—he let out a long sigh of his own—"it might behoove you, sir, to move to a safer location."

On the other end, Churchill remained silent for several seconds. Both understood just what Park was suggesting. Westminster could well become a target before the day's end.

"I'll remove myself when it becomes absolutely necessary," the prime minister told him. "Do your best, Park. We're all praying for you."

"Yes, sir," was all Park could manage before the prime minister ended the call. He slowly put down the receiver and continued to watch as more and more enemy formations began to appear on the plot board.

* * *

"Wheels up!" the communications officer shouted from the open window of the radio hut. "Wheels up! Wheels up!"

From above a young enlisted man stomped up the flight of wooden stairs as fast as his feet could take him to the top of the stout shack. He grabbed the alarm and began to crank the lever. A repeating air siren sounded, and the entire field jumped into action.

Squadron Leader Sharp grabbed his headgear from the hook of the outside wall of the pilot's house and jogged toward his plane. He barked out orders to his pilots as he went. Half of them had been out on the airfield when the alarm sounded, and the other half napping in barracks.

"Reynolds!" he hollered, pointing the man to his plane. "Davries! Courtland! Move! Move!"

The pilots of 239 Squadron rushed to their planes, putting their headgear on as they climbed into their cockpits. He did a mental count as he jogged toward his own Hurricane. Most of his boys were accounted for. A couple of them were running late, and he'd straighten them out later. He'd drilled his men mercilessly when it came to a fast scramble. It was one thing to take your time when going up on a standard patrol, but as soon as that siren sounded you'd best be in your plane within sixty seconds. Most of his squadron pilots were either fresh from flight schools or had minimal experience, and it had taken a while to train them up to standard when he'd been given the command. He wished now that he'd had another two weeks to get the men ready. Unfortunately, Hermann Göring had other ideas.

"Sharp!" a booming voice bellowed over the sound of airplane propellers starting up. Sharp turned quickly to see Group Captain Bushwell walking toward him. COs didn't run by nature, but his stride was wide enough that he moved quickly toward Sharp. "You're covering for Six-oh-nine. That squadron's up now, but they need their field covered in case Jerry tries to hit it. You have the command."

Sharp gave him an abrupt acknowledgment, then sprinted for his Hurricane. He understood what Bushwell was telling him. This would be his first combat action since Poland, and he'd be the one calling the shots. As he stepped up onto the ladder rung, he knew that he'd be responsible for any losses incurred. That, by itself, was a sobering thought.

The squadron took off in pairs, with Sharp inching into the lead of the formation. The runway fell away quickly as the flight of Hurricanes ascended and headed off southwest. It was right around midday now, and he swore to himself. The sun was at its height, and flying into it was like flying blind. German pilots were notorious for hiding themselves in the brightness, and they typically seemed to have the advantage of the sun at their backs.

There was some background chatter going on between RAF squadrons and their ground components. Sharp listened in, trying to paint a picture of the situation. As he listened in on the open channel, it was painfully obvious that the Luftwaffe had launched a massive airstrike. That by itself was not surprising. The Germans had the superior numbers advantage. They'd done the same thing in Poland. Huge fleets of bombers had launched against multiple targets simultaneously, overwhelming the defenders. In Poland, however, they'd had to deal with a lightning-fast German armored advance as well. That had made keeping the airfields operational an impossibility.

The flight southwest from Chilbolton was barely half an hour. It was just enough time for him to understand the strategic situation. Portsmouth was being hit, and bombs were falling on ships around the Isle of Wight. Further east, there would no doubt be more raids along the coast. Radar stations and RAF airfields were priority targets for the Germans. But he'd learned quickly in the war that the Luftwaffe didn't discriminate when and where it came to dropping their payloads. As Warsaw could attest to.

"Bandits!" a voice called over the mike. Sharp instantly sat up, craning his head left and right. "Bandits!"

He grabbed the mike. "Where, dammit?!" he snapped angrily. "What bearing?" He'd rip the pilot for his lack of proper communication, if and when they landed.

"Ten o'clock high!" a second voice answered moments later.

Sharp scanned the sky. The bright glare of the sun made it impossible to see anything.

"Climb! Climb!" he shouted. Just as he shifted the nose of his plane he could see them. Just shadows at first, then those shadows got larger. "Damn." There were four of them emerging from the sun, coming down on them fast. Sharp strapped his facemask and adjusted his goggles. "Break! Break!" he screamed into the mike.

He rolled his plane just as the first enemy rounds began to shoot past his undercarriage. The first German plane whipped by him, missing him by just a few yards. He looked over his left shoulder as the Messerschmitt buzzed him. A little further out from them, a second pair came streaming in. They dove through the formation, forcing them to break up.

Sharp leveled his nose out and calmly scanned the horizon. He was satisfied that there were only these four, and for the first time since the war had begun, he felt a small surge of relief. He'd never fought the Germans with a numerical advantage.

"Foxes Three, Seven, go high and get a bird's-eye view. The rest of you, engage. Engage!" There was some cross chatter between planes, and it got panicked enough that Sharp had to issue a profanity-laden order to stay calm and off the mike.

He craned his head over his shoulder and locked onto the German. The 109 pilot was bringing his fighter around in a turn so tight that Sharp gave him a momentary note of respect for the maneuver. He'd seen action in Poland, and he knew just what a good pilot was capable of behind the stick of one of those Messerschmitts. This one was as good as any pilot he'd seen. For a second Sharp wondered whether they'd crossed paths together there. The German picked up speed and bore straight in on a Hurricane.

"Fox Two, you've got a tail," Sharp said. The 109 closed in on Fox Two, weaving with the RAF pilot, trying to line up his shot.

Sharp, already on his turn to assist, lined up his sights between the two fights, then squeezed at the exact moment the German let loose a torrent of machine gun rounds. Tracers filled the sky. As the first of Sharp's round passed between Fox Two and the pursuing 109, the German peeled out without landing a single hit.

"Stay with your wingman!" Sharp ordered. "And for God's sake, don't fly straight for more than a few seconds." He shook his head in aggravation. He'd tried repeatedly to drill basic combat maneuvers during training. Most of his boys barely had the minimum number of flight hours as it was, never mind the fact that this was their first combat engagement.

The faster 109s moved in and out of range, firing off short salvos before peeling away. It was ten against four, but as the engagement went on, Sharp realized that the Luftwaffe pilots didn't seem that interested in pressing the attack. One would engage while another pulled away. Likewise, his own pilots were giving chase clumsily.

"Dammit!" he cursed. He knew the game the Germans were playing at. "Stay in your formation! Fox Five, fall on my wing, now!"

The 109s were drawing his pilots off into small groups, where they could be picked off. It was a veteran move when you were outnumbered. The German pilots drove their planes like champion horse riders. When one or two Hurricanes got isolated, they'd barrel in, guns firing, hoping to score a hit.

Sharp, with his wingman falling in, accelerated toward two enemy fighters circling two of his own.

"I've picked one up!" a voice screamed over his headset.

Sharp saw one of the Germans settle in behind a Hurricane. He gritted his teeth as he watched the 109 saturate the air around the

Hurricane with gunfire. The Hurricane danced left and right, but the faster Messerschmitt closed in, and its guns found his target. A puff of smoke, then a tail of thick white trailed behind the Hurricane. Sharp was too far out of range to do anything. He watched as the German machine guns chewed into the Hurricane's tail and ripped into the fuselage. The Hurricane rolled over and dropped like a rock from the sky.

Just as suddenly as that, the German fighters turned south and ran. Sharp watched them go, knowing it was useless chasing them. Most likely they were at the end of their fuel and were rushing for the safety of the English Channel. He kicked himself as he watched the burning plane in the sky tumbling down to the earth.

For a long minute, he remained silent.

"Fall back into formation," he ordered, his voice strained and exasperated.

"Fox Seven to Fox Leader."

Sharp grabbed his mike. "Go ahead."

"We've got an enemy formation moving southwest, sir," the other reported. "Bombers."

Sharp nodded. They were flying over Dorset. RAF Warmwell was nearby. In Poland, the Luftwaffe had made the Polish airfields their primary target. Number 609 Squadron was off to meet the German bombers hitting Portsmouth. That left their fields vulnerable.

He sighed as he saw the explosion ten thousand feet below. He saw no parachute open up. "All craft, on me."

He dropped the mike angrily.

"It was Fox Nine, sir," a voice told him somberly over his headset. He shot a look across the air at his wingman.

Galloway, he thought, and mentally crossed the name out in his mind.

That would pit nine against whatever was heading toward Warmwell. With first blood to the Luftwaffe, Sharp put the situation together in his mind. He wasn't just some pilot anymore, and he knew he couldn't just run off to every engagement. Squadron leaders coordinated attacks; they didn't just wade into every situation. He fought his instincts to do just that. Bushwell had warned him of this just before takeoff.

On the distant horizon, the small dots became larger. Enemy bombers began to take shape. Once again they were flying with the advantage of the glaring sun behind them, moving level across the English shoreline. The group was spread out across several miles, with, what appeared to be, lighter Dornier Do 17s in the lead.

"I've got them," Sharp said. "Heads up. They'll have fighter escorts with them."

The center formation was arrayed in a finger-four, with two wings on Sharp's left and another on his right. To the left and right, the planes were in two separate Vic formations. A Flight had three planes; C Flight had two, without Galloway. The bombers were arranged in multiple three-wide formations of their own. It was meant to bomb their intended targets like a paver pours a roadway, with long stretches of terrain impacted.

Sharp saw their targets dead ahead and could see a handful of smaller fighters peeling away. There were no less than forty bombers and perhaps half a dozen escorts. He did a quick evaluation. His primordial pilot's instinct was to charge in with the group attacking the bombers and blow them into pieces. But he remembered Bushwell's words. His squadron was understrength and had never engaged in combat before today. Anyone he sent to deal with those fighters would most likely be dead.

"B Flight with me," he called into the mike. "We'll engage with the fighters. The rest of you, go around the flanks. Hit the bombers. One pass, then run like hell."

The Germans came straight down the middle, Sharp's formation moved to meet them head-on, and the two groups exchanged gunfire as they whizzed by each other in midair. A couple of rounds pierced his left wing, and splinters and shards flew off. The flanking formations shot in toward the bombers.

A Flight broke into pairs to engage with the German fighters. Sharp tucked his nose in tightly and tried to keep the 109 in his forward view. The Messerschmitt was moving fast, but his Hurricane could bank harder. With his wingman right behind him, he brought his fighter around in a 120-degree arc, lined his sights up ahead of the fleeing German, squeezed the trigger, and unleashed a barrage of rounds that caught the enemy plane squarely in the fuselage. He didn't hold back either. As the first rounds impacted the 109, the enemy plane shifted in midair, and he opened up with everything he had. The German exploded in an instantaneous fireball. He allowed himself half a grin for the quick victory. A reprisal for Fox Nine. He felt no guilt for the kill.

A second 109 pulled into view off to the left. Sharp saw the plane out of the corner of his eye. It was trying to make a run for it.

"Get on him, Fox Five!" he said into his mike. His wingman didn't waste a single second, peeling off Sharp's wing and chasing after him. "I've got your wing."

Sharp fell in behind Fox Five just as the other turned and sped toward the German. The Messerschmitt flew straight off, not even bothering to maneuver. With Sharp just yards behind him, Fox Five opened up on the enemy plane. At first, the rookie pilot's fire was erratic and uncoordinated.

"Get ahead—," Sharp began, then cut himself off after the Hurricane's rounds found its intended target. The rounds clipped the German and gray smoke erupted behind him.

"I got him, sir!" Fox Five said enthusiastically over the speaker. Sharp could hear the lad's pride. But there was no time for it.

"Davries, let him go," Sharp told him. The German's tail was piping gray smoke, and the pilot was pulling out. Sharp knew he wouldn't make it across the Channel at the rate he was burning off fuel. "Fall in on me."

He wanted to let Davries take the lead, but the rookie was still a rookie, despite what would, no doubt, be called a probable kill. Sharp and Davries turned east, into the wind. The German fighters were dueling with B Flight's Hurricanes, but for the most part, his pilots were holding their own quite well. His orders about not flying straight for long were being taken seriously.

"Stay with me." Sharp nudged ahead of Davries. The two headed straight in for the bombers. A part of him wanted to break for the enemy fighters, and for a moment he was sorely tempted to do just that. But the German fighters, he knew, were just lures. Feints to take his strength away from the bombers. He just hoped that Cross and Hughlett could hold their own for the next few minutes.

The part of 239 that he'd sent in against the bombers had already hit the German formation. He could see the Hurricanes interweaving in between the bombers, lining up shots, firing, then pulling away, and for a brief moment he felt a surge of relief. Despite little training, his boys were doing just what he'd instructed them to and didn't give the Germans a stable target to shoot at.

"I got one!" Reynold's voice crackled.

A single Heinkel lit up, then turned over in the air before spiraling down. At least three other bombers had been knocked out of the sky, and another was smoking lightly but still moving on.

"Go for the Heinkels!" Sharp ordered seconds before opening up on one himself. He barreled into the side of the wedge, unleashing his guns on one of the 111s, the bomber's side gunner sending a spray of bullets in return. Sharp whipped by him. He didn't want to swing back for a second pass, he just found himself another target. A second 111 was two hundred yards ahead. Again he sent a barrage of rounds into its center compartment. Shards of metal plating exploded outward.

"I'm hit!" Sharp searched the sky but couldn't see which of his planes had made the call.

"Peel out!" he hollered into the mike. "Head for home. Bail out if you must!"

To his right, he caught a glimpse of the lead bombers opening their bomb doors. A wing of Dorniers led the approach.

Damn, he thought to himself. They must've been closing in on their target.

One of the Dorniers exploded, and a single Hurricane came flying out of the fireball, its propellers churning up the fire and smoke.

He brought his plane back around for a second run on the formation. But it was already too late. The German fighters had broken off and were now headed back toward them, and the lead bombers were already dropping the first payloads on the fields below. He could see them streaming downward.

"One more pass," he told himself. Most of the rest of his squadron had already broken off, just as he'd instructed them. Now it was him, Fox's Seven and Ten. He circled back around, Davries right with him. Machine guns on the bombers opened fire at their approach. Together the three Hurricanes shot down another Heinkel and damaged a second before the Messerschmitts closed in.

"Break off!"

They disengaged just as the enemy fighters came into range. Sharp fired off a salvo at them, just enough to make the closest of them think twice before pursuing. The Hurricanes broke out and made off just as the heavier bombers began unloading their payload. They screamed as they plunged through the air.

Sharp and the remainder of 239 Squadron watched in scornful silence as the bombs impacted the fields far below. Even at twenty-thousand-feet altitude, the bomb explosions could be seen with horrifying results. Gray-white plumes rose from the center of the bombsite, followed by waves rippling outward. Dozens of bombs found their targets, and the results were devastating. Fires and secondary explosions could be seen, and Sharp knew what that meant. Ammunition depots and fuel supplies were going up on the ground.

With a profound sense of failure, he clicked his mike.

"This is Fox Leader," he said, his voice full of grief. "Fall in on me. Mission failure." He yanked the control stick over and headed back home.

CHAPTER TWELVE

"Speer!" Hitler greeted the man happily. The Führer launched up from his chair and extended his hand warmly. "My dear, Speer. It's good to see you."

Reich Minister of Production Albert Speer smiled back as he embraced Hitler's hand. The Führer placed his hand affectionately on his shoulder and squeezed. Speer looked around the grand ballroom with amazement. He had not seen such an event since before the war started. The enormous hall at the Reich Chancellery hadn't been used for quite some time. Hitler's time these days was mostly taken up by more pressing military matters that the softer side of the German chancellor was rarely shown in public anymore.

Looking around, Speer was quite impressed with the people who were attending tonight's event. Naturally, half the attendees were military officers, all dressed in their finest uniforms, sipping on glasses of wine and cavorting with the upper crust of German society. Speer recognized most of them, as he worked with Wehrmacht officials on a daily basis. There were also many civilian officials from all different branches of government and private sector. And, of course, the ever-present Nazi Party members who frequently showed up to such events. The brown-shirted upper-party leaders could always be counted on to be at functions such as this. Martin Bormann and Rudolf Hess, both dressed in their Nazi Party overcoats and jet-black trousers, steadily made their way through the enormous room, shaking hands and passing out party pins for those who weren't wearing one.

The center of the ballroom was usually to be used as a dance floor for certain events, but tonight was being used as a standing area for the many foreign delegates and government officials to mingle. Speer recognized some of the foreigners. The Japanese delegation, for instance, he'd been introduced to last summer during the Tripartite Pact signing. Also present this evening was a diplomatic mission from Bulgaria. Their resident ambassador, along with his wife and aides, as well as several top military officers, were also here, mingling in the great hall that was practically standing-room only.

Beyond the dance floor was an arrangement of tables where many of the Germans were sitting, sipping away on drinks. Speer locked eyes with Field Marshall Keitel, who raised his wine glass from across the room. Grand Admiral Raeder was present, as was Karl Dönitz, one of his subordinates. Dönitz was the man most responsible for Germany's U-boat war. His disagreements with the Kriegsmarine commander were legendary, but his results spoke for themselves. His fleet of submarines was even now sinking more Allied ships than any of the great surface vessels in the Navy. His tactics at sea were reportedly bringing Allied merchant shipping to its knees.

"Thank you for the invitation this evening, Mein Führer," Speer replied.

"Pah," Hitler replied, "You're as much the reason for this as anyone. You've done more for Germany than just about anyone has."

"Thank you," Speer replied self-consciously. He tried to put as much humility into his voice as he could. His persona was anything but humble. The architect turned minister of war production was known high and low as a man who did not engage in modesty. His reputation in Germany, and abroad, as an industrial genius was as much self-promoted as it was outwardly apparent. He loathed the "old guard" of industry and took every opportunity to modernize the country's infrastructure as he could. The man had come up through party ranks by way of promoting those above him, but secretly, he disdained many of them. His predecessor, Fritz Todt, for instance, he'd felt had been far too conservative in his approach to the control that man had exerted over the Reich's economy. His death in August of 1939 had elevated Speer to the post that he currently occupied. And with the Führer, having not recovered from his injuries until the middle of the following year, Speer had unfettered control over the nation's industrial production. By the time Hitler had regained command of things again, Speer had cemented his position as master of the German economy. The swift victory in Poland, and his convincing Hitler to turn the economy into a wartime one, had sent lightning bolts throughout the industrial sector. Now, factories that had once produced home goods were churning out weapons of war.

"Tonight is as much your victory celebration as it is my own," Hitler went on. He half-turned and showcased Speer to others in the room. "Our own industrial genius," he proclaimed. Others around Hitler smiled at him, lifted their wine glasses in a toast, and gave him praise. Hitler laughed joyfully. "And our work will continue," he said as he turned back to Speer. "We've only just begun to see our potential, my friend."

"I agree with you, Mein Führer. In fact, I've been looking over our numbers for the next six months of production. I believe that we're on the cusp of an industrial breakthrough." He paused, then said, "Provided the raw resources keep flowing."

Hitler laughed again. "There you go again, Albert. Always planning, always coming up with new ideas. I wish that I had a hundred more like you. My God, we could put men on the moon before the end of the decade. Haha." Others joined in the laughter. "Every day brings new trainloads of resources in from Russia. Resources that keep your factories pumping out the very things that we need. And we're going to need each one of those factories working in order to bring us the security that I promised the nation."

"And we will respond as we always have, Mein Führer," Speer replied, and Hitler proudly patted the man's face.

"Come, I want you to meet some of our special guests." Hitler pulled him into the crowd.

Most of the people around Hitler, Speer was already familiar with. Some Wehrmacht officers were standing around with a group of officers in a foreign uniform, as well as a score of civilian officials congregating in the very center of the hall. A solidly built man in uniform was standing in the middle of the gathering. He was holding a glass of wine and entertaining the group around him. Seeing Hitler's approach, the group parted. The man in the center gave Hitler and Speer a gracious look.

"Conductor Antonescu, I am delighted to present my minister for war production, Albert Speer." Hitler smiled as he introduced Speer.

Speer snapped his heels together smartly, bowed his head slightly, and the two men shook hands. The Romanian stood as still as a statue. His uniform was perfectly tailored, and his frame pronounced the fact that he'd probably been a soldier his entire life. The man's reputation, both in his home country and Germany, was nearly legendary. He'd been imprisoned by the former regime as a revolutionary. But his popularity among the military elites in Romania had made it impossible to keep him there. With social unrest in Bucharest and military support behind him, he'd overthrown the former monarch in a late-night coup and become the head of state. He'd immediately allied his country with the Axis powers.

"Ah. I was hoping that we would get the opportunity to meet," Antonescu said. "Your name is spoken of with much enthusiasm. I would congratulate you on your achievements in Germany."

"Thank you very much, Conductor," Speer replied. "It's a great pleasure to meet you. Your reputation speaks volumes itself." Antonescu didn't even balk at the compliment. His demeanor was dispassionate.

"Herr Speer's talent for central planning is quite remarkable," Hitler stated. "His organization has streamlined our military production by leaps and bounds. As well as completing a number of national projects. Our autobahns have become a source of great pride for us. And soon he'll be connecting them throughout the Greater Reich. From Warsaw to Prague to Rostock."

"Yes," Antonescu agreed. "Quite an achievement."

"And, of course, we still have much more to do," Hitler went on, pumping his arms around. "What we can do for Romania can transform your country as well."

Speer nodded in agreement. A waiter came by, offering a beverage. He took a glass of white wine.

"I'm very curious, Herr Speer, about what you can do for Romania. Your Führer speaks very highly of you. And Minister Ribbentrop sings your praises at every opportunity. One of the benefits of our great alliance is the ability to learn from one another. I make no secrets that Romania could learn a great deal from the German model."

"Yes. Now that we've formalized an alliance, one of our main goals is to support our friends in any way that we can," Hitler added. They both turned their gaze to Speer. "Speer here, I'm sure, has all the information that he needs to begin."

"What truly interests me, and my country most, are your armored vehicles," Antonescu replied. "Truth be told, we're years away from a truly modern industry like the one Germany has. But what we could use right now, what we need now, are tanks. Those Panzer Threes for instance. From what General Jodl has told me, you've already begun replacing them with the heavier Fours in mass numbers. Romania would be very grateful to receive some of your surplus panzers."

Speer nodded, looked Antonescu in the eyes firmly, and grinned politely. "The Führer and I have spoken on this very subject before. Of course, we're very happy to supply our friends and allies with whatever they require. The defense of Romania is very important to us. I understand that German Army advisors have been training your military forces for some time. It really wouldn't take much, I'm sure, to train some of your soldiers on our heavy tanks." He shot a quick look at Hitler. "I can have some details worked up for our next meeting."

Hitler smiled boyishly. "We'd happily discuss the sale of panzers with you. You know, Antonescu, I've always felt that our two countries have much to trade with one another. Right now the time is right to strike a bargain that will redefine the sphere of influence in Eastern Europe."

Antonescu's eyes narrowed in intrigue. "I agree," he replied tepidly. "You're already getting our most valuable commodity, Herr Hitler. The oil from our Ploiesti refineries is Romania's lifeblood."

"Yes. And right now Germany is your primary export partner," Hitler replied. "For which we are enormously grateful. But it was not of oil that I was referring."

The Romanian sipped slowly on his wine, studying Hitler with his eyes. He knew the German Führer was not a man who minced his words. "Bessarabia?"

Hitler nodded. "It's still Romanian territory so far as Berlin is concerned."

"Occupied by the Red Army," the Romanian replied. "We were forced to abandon it."

"Yes. By the former regime. A weakness on their part. But yours is the new regime. You have the backing of your military, the support of the people. Every day you grow stronger. Together, we can right past wrongs." Antonescu was just about to speak up when Hitler preempted him. "In time. In time."

"A year from now, for instance," Speer added. "A year from now, with our assistance, Romania will be on much better footing."

"A year from now," the Romanian replied in a displeased voice. He sipped down the last of his wine. "That's a long time to wait. My people demand action now. We allied ourselves with the German Reich, partially, in order to secure the borders of our homeland. We were forced to concede a great deal of territory in the east."

"Yes. A terrible crime was inflicted on your people, to be sure," Hitler said to him. "But remember, you've gained territory the Hungarians ceded to you."

"Back to us," Antonescu corrected him in a friendly tone. "That land was ours to begin with."

Hitler, not wanting to get into a push-and-pull with the other man, simply nodded. His notorious temper was just under his skin, and everyone, especially Speer, knew that it could come out at a moment's notice.

"And we'll march together to right those past wrongs. You and we are the closest of allies. But we're not alone. Even the strongest nations need friends."

A waiter came, and Antonescu put his empty glass on the man's tray and took another full glass.

"It's rumored, Herr Hitler," Antonescu began as soon as the waiter had left, "that you've been secretly arming the Finns with artillery. Heavy guns, anti-tank weaponry. Things that made a difference in their war with the Soviets. All we ask is the same consideration that you gave to them."

For a moment Hitler's eyes went dark, and he did not answer. The rumors were, of course, true. But that didn't mean the German Führer was going to admit it publicly. One thing about the man that Speer knew well was that he did not like feeling like he was on the defensive. He remained deathly quiet, and it briefly seemed to Speer that he was simply lost for words at that moment.

"We did supply them with the heavy weapons they needed," Speer finally said aloud. Both men looked at him. "Pardon me, Mein Führer. I don't want to speak out of line, but the conductor is already aware of what we were going to inform him of anyhow. Obviously, we had to keep such a thing quiet, Conductor. If Stalin knew that the guns that had secured Finnish victory in the north were supplied by us, It would have most certainly meant another war in the east. Something that we are not looking for right now."

The Romanian's eyes widened in reply to Speer's directness. He'd half expected to be told that Germany had nothing to do with supplying the Finns with arms.

"But look at what those guns helped achieve," Hitler told him. "Victory for Finland. An entire Soviet field army was destroyed. Now Finland has secured its borders with the Bolsheviks when many said that it could not be achieved."

"And now word is that Stalin is once again purging his forces," Speer added.

Antonescu nodded. "Yes. We've heard this too. Many Ukrainians have crossed our border recently, bringing news of mass executions with them. We did not believe it at first. The Ukrainians are no friends of the Russians certainly, but we didn't take their words as truthful. However, our intelligence agency has also gathered reports. Hangings in Red Square, mass firing squads, deportations to Siberia." Surprisingly, he chuckled, then downed part of his new glass of wine. "It's like '37 all over again."

"Exactly," Speer replied. "Imagine what we can do over the next twelve months. While the fool in the Kremlin withers away his strength and terrorizes his countrymen, we'll be equipping our forces with modernized weaponry." He looked at Hitler, who nodded at him ever so slightly. "Give us time, Conductor, and we will help arm your armies with the tools that it needs."

"Victory in the east is within our grasp, Antonescu," Hitler told him, putting a friendly hand on his shoulder. "Ribbentrop will be returning to Bucharest in the near future. He'll bring with him many of our best military advisors. Rest assured, we will soon begin doing for you what we did for Finland."

"Panzers?" Antonescu asked hopefully.

"In great numbers," Hitler replied, smiling at him. "In the meantime, I would highly suggest you use your influence with your neighbors. As I said, we need all the friends that we can get."

"It was a pleasure to meet you, Reich Minister," Antonescu said to Speer. Both men shook hands again. "I look forward to working together in the future."

"As do I," Speer said. He and Hitler stood smiling as the Romanian dictator went about the room, eventually making his way over to his own foreign service staff who were gathered around a large table with several other diplomats. "You realize, Mein Führer, that we don't have the new panzers that he wants in the quantities we need, much less in what his own country would need?"

Hitler looked at him, and gave him a pouty smile. "That was a well-played part, Albert. Don't worry about that right now. Ribbentrop won't be in Bucharest for another month. Plenty of time to get anything we can put it on trains, and send it to him. Panzer Twos if necessary."

"Perhaps some of our newer field artillery or antiaircraft —"

"Never mind all of that," Hitler cut him off. "The Army can deal with the Romanian requests and pass them along to you. But right now I wish to hear about other matters. Preparations for the western offensive for instance."

Speer shrugged innocently. "The Luftwaffe will have more than enough aircraft to satiate their needs for the time being. I was going to talk with you about this in the coming days, but because we are here now, perhaps I should bring it up. I've been reviewing our production plans for the next year." He hesitated, and thought about how to word things that would not upset Hitler. "Mein Führer, given the resources that we've spent on aircraft production in the last year, I have serious concerns about adequately supporting other operational goals. I have penned a report that states my concerns. But, quite simply, I highly recommend that we dial down future aircraft production in order to meet other needs."

Hitler's forehead creased. "We're going to need as many aircraft as possible in the future. You know well the commitments we've made."

"I understand. However, right now we have more aircraft than we have crews for. The Army still hasn't received all of the armor that we promised. We've supplied them with as many of them as we possibly can, given the materials we have. But the Panzer Fours will not meet the production goals we set for them at the beginning of the year unless we divert additional resources. And now, we have the next generation preparing to come online. Furthermore, the Navy is again requesting that we finish up with many of the projects that we began some time ago. Admiral Raeder—"

"Admiral Raeder would have us stripping ourselves bare to build his dream of some grand fleet," Hitler hissed sharply.

"I understand, Mein Führer. However, I would recall the fact that we drew down, quite measurably, the original Plan Z. Most of the resources for the Kriegsmarine are now solely devoted to U-boat construction. We'll be short of our manufacturing targets if we don't shift those resources. That means, as I said, slowing down aircraft production and redirecting it toward other ends. Until the Reichswerke expansion is complete, we need to pace ourselves accordingly. However, the good news is that by the beginning of next year, we'll see a significant increase coming out of our factories in Poland and the occupied territories."

Hitler gazed around the room at the two hundred-plus people filling the great ballroom. He did not wish to show any sign of displeasure this evening.

"I thought we had enough resources to keep our industries booming," Hitler said with a quiet agitation in his voice. "Now you say we need to slow things down?"

"Not slow things down, Mein Führer, simply redirect our resources. We began a wide buildup of our air fleets because that was what we needed at the time. We had to make a decision whether to focus on aircraft or armored production, and my recommendations at the time were based on our goals at the time. We've expanded our factories greatly in the last two years. We're putting out almost twice the amount we were a year and a half ago under my predecessor." He looked around to make sure no unwanted ears were within range. He lowered his voice so that only Hitler could hear him. "Our future plans must now dictate our production goals. I highly, highly stress that we shift our assembly lines to armor production." He shrugged lightly. "Herr Göring has more than enough planes to accomplish what he needs. The Army will need all the support that we can give them. And, as for the Kriegsmarine, every U-boat that leaves one of the pens sinks twenty times its weight in Allied shipping. It would not be prudent to stop their construction." Hitler gave a grudging nod of agreement. "Those new panzers, along with our new high-velocity guns, will be what wins battles."

"You sound just like Keitel," Hitler replied. "I'll consider your recommendation. But tonight I insist we celebrate." He waved his hand around the crowded room. His lips curled under his short mustache, and it seemed to Speer that the Führer had all but forgotten about the disfigurement on his face. The scar that he'd incurred during his accident had never healed well, and at first, he had been most self-conscious about it. But, as far as the German people were concerned, it had become something of a badge of honor. A wound inflicted by Communist sympathizers. "We have new alliances to celebrate."

"New alliances?" Speer asked, and Hitler threw his eyes over at Antonescu, who was now mingling with other foreign delegations.

"Our friends over there."

"The Romanians?"

"I speak of the Bulgarians," Hitler corrected him. "Antonescu is just the beginning of expanding our reach into that region. The Bulgarians are already eager to sign the alliance, and they'll make important allies. Now, I will leave you, Albert. Our guests will demand my presence." Hitler patted him lightly on the arm before crossing the room toward a gathering of Wehrmacht and foreign military officials.

Speer took the first sip of his drink, and his eyes casually gazed around the room. In truth, he didn't care that much for gatherings such as this. Party functions aside, he felt wholly uncomfortable attending events like this, which were completely for show for foreign delegates, to show off the lighter side of National Socialism. He had wanted to shrug it off, but the order had gone out to all higher party members about attending. Speer, as the face of German industrialization, had no choice in the matter. Though right now he wished he was anywhere else but here.

"Good evening, Herr Speer," a voice said from behind. He turned to see a military officer approach him. He studied the man for a moment but did not recognize the face.

"Good evening, General . . . ?"

"Oster," the other man informed him. "Abwehr."

"Oh, yes," Speer said, giving recognition to the name. "So military intelligence was invited to tonight's event."

Oster gave a friendly smile and a half nod. "Yes. Well, we must have a face here. You know how things go. The Führer is always anxious to show off those behind our recent military successes. Besides, some of the visiting officials are military intelligence from their own countries. Seems fitting that we should be represented."

Speer nodded. "Especially since the Gestapo have no representation here this evening."

"Oh, I don't know about that. Reichsminister Frick is over there, Müller is having drinks with the Hungarian ambassador, and, of course, Reichsführer Himmler is around here somewhere. I'm sure there are one or two agents as well. Probably disguised as event staff."

Speer shot him a look of shock, then turned to look at some of the waiters making their way through the room. He felt a bit surprised that Oster would speak so casually to someone he didn't know. But he also didn't doubt that state security would indeed have observers in the room.

"No wine for you, General?" Speer asked, observing his empty hands.

"If you insist, Reichsminister," Oster replied and held up two fingers at the nearest waiter. The white-coated man walked over, Oster took a glass off the tray, and the man disappeared back into the crowd. "I wished to introduce myself to you personally. This felt like an opportune time. It's not very often that men like us get to step out of the office. Well, for myself anyway. I guess your travels take you all over the Reich."

"As deputy director of the Abwehr, I would think the same was true of yourself, General Oster. I understand that your boss never seems to leave the basement."

Oster laughed and sipped his wine. "He's not as … how shall I say this? Socially inclined as others are."

"Whereas your reputation speaks volumes," Speer replied lightheartedly.

Oster shrugged innocently. "I may have been a bit of a socialite. During my younger days, of course. These days I mostly run around, ensuring that our operations are running smoothly."

There was a friendly overtone, Speer observed, emanating from the man. He seemed habitually casual for a man who was both a general in the Army and the deputy of its intelligence branch. Especially toward someone to whom he had just introduced himself. Given the constant jockeying for power and authority that seemed to surround high-up officials in Berlin, Speer was cautious.

"I must congratulate you, Reichsminister," Oster went on after a few moments. "You've become the man of the hour. Not just in Berlin but in capitals around Europe. I hear your name spoken of from Paris to Budapest. The man responsible for supplying our forces with the tools necessary for victory. In fact, I wanted to personally thank you. I have friends who commanded units in France and Belgium, who might not be alive today if the Wehrmacht hadn't been so well equipped. Some of my old friends have a very bad habit of getting far too close to the fighting."

"Well," Speer began, "we all do our part, General. Military intelligence played just as important a role in our victory. May I ask you a question?" Oster nodded. "The Führer seems unusually conciliatory toward the new French government. Considering that it has not publicly taken a commitment concerning the war since its takeover, I find his attitude toward Prime Minister Laval to be strangely puzzling. I thought, as second in charge of the Abwehr, you may have had some insight."

Oster considered himself briefly. The eyes fluttered, and for a moment Speer thought he saw a flicker of uncertainty in the other man's expression. But it was only momentary and followed immediately by a friendly smile.

"I'm afraid that I don't," Oster answered. "I'm only in the intelligence gathering business I'm afraid, Reichsminister. I leave the politics to those better suited toward it."

"Understandable. If you're not accustomed to how that game is played, it's probably best to stay out of such things. I try to do the same thing out of convenience."

"Yes. But your position makes it a bit more difficult," Oster replied. He indicated to the people around the room. "As a minister of state, you're expected to be involved in the politics of it all. I would think that you would have more insight into the Reich's position than I ever would."

He inwardly sighed. "I just thought that you might have an answer to the question. The Führer has said nothing on the subject of the French. Given recent events there, I simply thought you would have some insight. Apparently, I was wrong."

"The coup in France was not a military matter. The SS seems to have orchestrated it. Why do you ask?"

"Mere curiosity," he told Oster. "Just two months ago we defeated our old adversary in a stunning victory. We imposed a series of, what some call, crushing terms on them. Now, there's talk of conciliatory gestures being made. I just wished to be prepared for anything. As minister of war production, I don't think it's outrageous to want to know what to prepare for."

"Of course. If I had any insight, or if I get some, I'll be more than happy to share it with you. As it is I think you'll have more than enough to prepare for. I understand that our allies have been making requests for heavier weapons." He gave a casual nod toward the foreign delegations on the other side of the room. The members of the Hungarian and Romanian embassies were mixing in a surprisingly friendly manner. Hitler had moved on. Both he and Keitel were standing with the Bulgarian prime minister who had made the trip to Berlin to finalize his own nation's treaty signing.

"That's an Army matter," Speer shrugged.

"Of course," Oster replied. "Well, I don't wish to take up any more of your time, Reichsminister. I'm sure you're a busy man, and there's more than one person here who'd like to speak with you. I simply wanted to introduce myself." He smiled again, and Speer found himself giving him a friendly grin in reply.

"My pleasure, General, my pleasure. I hope to see you again."

"As it happens, I'll be at the Armaments Ministry next week. Perhaps we'll see each other then."

"Oh?" Speer said. "I wasn't aware of anyone from the Abwehr visiting the ministry. What's taking you there?"

"Normal counterintelligence duties," Oster replied.

"That requires the presence of the deputy chief of intelligence?" he asked with a confused look.

"We're implementing some changes to our security procedures. Nothing to be alarmed about. But war production is a sensitive area that requires us to run countersurveillance from time to time."

"Isn't that the purview of the SS?"

"They have their responsibilities; we have ours. As I said, it's nothing to be alarmed about." With that, the general bowed his head slightly, then walked off into the crowd of partygoers. He watched Oster for a moment until the man disappeared from his sight. Something in the back of his mind caused him to be slightly bothered by the encounter. The Abwehr deputy chief had been friendly enough, but he was an intelligence officer. They tended to have ulterior motives behind things. He shrugged the feeling off. It was probably nothing.

CHAPTER THIRTEEN

Harkins reduced his altitude, bringing his plane down to twelve thousand feet, then leveled out. His wingman pulled in beside him. The other pilot was Jimmy Ringo, a second lieutenant out of some God-only-knows-where kind of place down in Texas. The younger pilot was full of himself for sure. He made Harkins look like a responsible adult, rather than the cocky flyboy that most people took him for. Ringo was that narcissistic type who thought that they were the center of the universe and showed it off at every opportunity. At times flying with the kid made Johnny feel like he was watching a sort of rodeo, with the other pilot throwing his fighter into some pretty fancy, and at times dangerous, high-speed maneuvers.

Johnny looked at the view from twelve thousand feet. Long Island stretched out for miles and miles. Behind them even the faintest hint of New York's outline had faded away in the rearview, and to either side of them was the wide-open ocean. He shut his eyes for a second and let the warm summer air wash over the open cockpit. He'd only flown out of Mitchel Field once before, and it had been in wintertime. His Pennsylvania upbringing aside, he'd been spoiled by being posted to so many warm locations that flying out of an airfield in the middle of the night in January had been brutal. When orders had come in that he was being placed on a special assignment, he'd been relieved to find out that it wouldn't be in the middle of winter. Long Island in the summertime was beautiful.

"Hey, Harkins," Ringo's voice blared over the headset. "How 'bout we skim the treetops?" His voice was overly excited, and Johnny could hear an almost boy-like tease in his voice.

"I don't think so," Harkins told him. "Just stay on my—" He broke off his words as the other pilot sent his plane into a steep nosedive. "Jesus Christ!"

Ringo put his North American T-6 into a vertical drop. Johnny put his head over the side of his plane as he watched the other pilots' antics. Ringo was laughing over the headset and Harkins shook his head at the other pilot.

Stupid damn kid.

Ringo's T-6 picked up speed as he dove down. At twelve thousand feet he'd only have a matter of seconds. Johnny's heart began to beat quickly now, and he nosed his plane downward just enough to keep Ringo in his forward sights. On the ground below there was nothing but empty land and farms for as far as he could see. He was silently thankful for that. Should the worst happen at least nobody on the ground would be hurt. Hopefully.

"Stop screwing around," Harkins told him, but his words were drowned out by the other pilots' howling. Ringo was stupid enough to have one hand on the mike, leaving him only halfway in control of the two-seat plane. Down, down he dove, picking up speed as he went. Harkins inwardly swore as he watched the plane go. "Pull up now!"

But the other plane kept diving. He hit six thousand feet, then five thousand, but he stayed in the nosedive. Four thousand, then three, then two thousand feet. At one thousand feet the landscape became so clear that each tree or shrub was as visible as if he were only feet away. Finally, in a single move, Ringo brought his throttle to the bare minimum and then pulled back on the stick. His plane skimmed just feet above the Long Island treetops. Johnny watched as the other man brought his nose back up and pulled away from the ground. His laugh made an eerie sound over the headset and all Harkins could do was mentally shake his head at the other pilot's sheer stupidity.

"How 'bout that, Johnny boy!" Ringo's voice was so full of brash arrogance that Johnny found the young cowboy's actions offensive.

"Stupid! That's what that was!" Johnny lost it, and let the other man know it. "Sheer fucking stupidity!"

"Hey, listen—" His voice was cut off by a sharp static-filled shriek on the line.

"G Flight, this is control," a voice hummed over the headset. "Uh," the young voice on the other end stammered. "We've got orders to have you return to—" The operator's voice ended abruptly only to be replaced a moment later by another, more booming voice.

"G Flight!" The voice was unmistakable. It was Doolittle. "Both of you get your dumb asses back here now!" The colonel's voice was as loud and harsh as the earpiece could make it sound.

Johnny let out a long breath and shook his head in disappointment. He didn't know who Doolittle was going to tear into worse, him or Ringo.

"Copy that," Harkins replied.

The two fliers brought their aircraft back around, toward the Army Air Force field they'd lifted up from. Johnny set his plane down first, followed half a minute later by Ringo. The cocky Texan looked around at the faces of the ground crew as he shut his engine off. Johnny watched him for a moment, sneering at the dumb kid's arrogant behavior. He took his headgear off and left it in the cockpit before climbing down the side of the plane. Ground mechanics gave them both sideways looks as the two pilots walked away from their planes. A sergeant was standing in the grass beyond the airstrip, near the line of hangars. He was Sergeant Pappas, the ground crew chief. The cautionary look on his face told Harkins everything that he needed to know about what was coming.

"Sir," Pappas greeted him.

"Sergeant," Harkins replied in a quiet tone of voice. "What's the word?"

Pappas scowled, gave an appalled look at the approaching Ringo, then pointed to the CO's office with his thumb. He didn't say anything else. He didn't have to. Harkins could read it on his face. He and Ringo walked past the hangars, toward the office. Another sergeant approached them.

"Sir, Colonel Doolittle wants to see the both of you," the sergeant said but Harkins strode right past the man, not even bothering to say a word.

"Come," a voice answered after Harkins knocked lightly on the door. He and Ringo walked right into Doolittle's office. The colonel was standing in front of a large chalkboard that had all of the pilots' names on it. Another officer, a captain, was standing with him holding onto a stack of papers. Doolittle gave them both a sour look as the two came to attention in the center of the room. The colonel tossed the piece of chalk he'd been holding and gave the captain a sharp nod. The captain tucked the papers under his arm, put his cover on, and left the room.

For a half minute Colonel Doolittle just stood facing them. His hands were resting on his hips, his foot tapping relentlessly on the hollow wooden floor.

"You two knuckleheads really fucked up," he scolded them. He stared at Harkins intently, to the point where Johnny couldn't look him in the eye. "What the hell do you think you were doing up there?"

"It was my fault, sir," Johnny replied after a few empty seconds.

"No, sir, it was—"

"Shut up!" Doolittle screamed as Ringo started to interject. Doolittle took two forceful steps forward, looked at Harkins then at Ringo.

He got right up in Ringo's face. "Where the hell do you think you are? Huh? This ain't San Antonio! You were both on a training flight. What part of training flights include crazy antics like the one you pulled up there!"

Ringo looked like he was going to reply, but Doolittle's gaze told him to stay quiet. Harkins stood there like a statue, disappointment in himself coursing through his veins. Finally, Doolittle stepped back, and leaned himself against the edge of his desk. He looked right at Harkins and shook his head.

"You two came to me by way of recommendations of your commanding officers. You're both supposed to be professionals. Emphasis on supposed to be." He threw a single nod at Harkins. "Speak."

Johnny let out the breath he'd been holding in.

"We fucked up, sir," he said sorrowfully.

"You're damn right you did." He turned his gaze to Ringo. "So what the hell's your excuse?"

Ringo gulped visibly. "I have none, sir. The exercises were over—" he tilted his head awkwardly—"I just thought . . . we'd let loose a bit."

Colonel Doolittle crossed his arms and gave Ringo a look of disbelief.

"Let loose," the words came out scornfully. "Listen to me, son. You don't get to let loose with a thirty-thousand-dollar aircraft. Do you understand me!"

"Yes, sir," Ringo replied. "I'm sorry, sir—"

"You're at attention, Lieutenant!" Doolittle stepped back toward Ringo, stared him right in the eye, and for a minute it seemed to Johnny that he was going to belt the kid. A part of him wanted to see that happen after today's embarrassment. "What would have happened if you'd crashed? Did you think about that?"

"No, sir," Ringo answered.

"No, sir," Doolittle repeated back. "If you think antics like that are going to impress anyone, Lieutenant, then you are sadly mistaken.

And I won't have someone under my command who doesn't give a wit about either his plane or his squadron." He turned around letting his back face the kid. "Ringo, you've got ten minutes to go pack your shit up and get the hell off my airfield. I'm sending you back to Texas. A reprimand will be entered into your file. Dismissed."

The kid stood there, unable or unwilling to move. Johnny watched him out of his peripheral vision. The look on the other's face was that of pure shock. He had the look of some teenage kid who'd finally learned that he couldn't just do whatever the hell he wanted without facing the repercussions. But Johnny didn't feel sorry for him. He screwed up and he may have sunk Johnny right along with him.

Finally, the kid turned and walked out of the office. The wooden door slapped shut with a thud after he left.

"I expected better from you," Doolittle said after the two had been left alone. He turned back to face Johnny. "At ease."

He widened his stance and relaxed visibly. Colonel Doolittle stepped back behind his desk, but his eyes were still full of anger. Johnny gave him a half-apologetic look, but he could see that Doolittle wasn't going to buy it.

"So he's gone," the colonel said. "His little show-up there will get him a reprimand. Possibly even cost him his wings. So far as I'm concerned he deserves whatever punishment the Army doles out to him. Either way, he's outta here. So what's your excuse?"

"Sir, I ...," he stammered. "I wasn't aware of Lieutenant Ringo's idea until he was already doing it. I ... I, just—"

"You're a first lieutenant, Harkins. He's a second louey. You were senior up there! Jesus, man. You think I don't know what happened. Christ almighty, I was in the tower listening in when he decided to do his rodeo trick. I know who did what. What I'm talking about is why you didn't stop him."

Johnny looked at him confusedly. "Sir?"

The colonel rolled his eyes at him. "Did you not just hear what I said? You were the senior officer up there. That puts you in charge of the flight. Not once did I ever hear you give that moron a direct order to fall back in. Not once! If you had, at least you could've hung your hat on that. But you didn't once execute your authority to get your wingman back in line." He held up his finger between the two. His stare was piercing but it lightened after a few seconds. "You came well recommended, Harkins. Your CO told me that you're a bit of a hotshot at times, but that you're a damn good pilot. Well, that might be alright if you're flying on someone else's wing, but when you're in charge the picture changes. Do you understand what I'm telling you?"

"Yes, sir. I do," Johnny replied, and meant it.

"First and foremost, Harkins, you're an officer. Start acting like it. Your record is good, you've got good chops for flying. Six months from now you'll probably be a captain. Start giving orders, Harkins." He ended with a curt nod.

Johnny felt a surge of relief swell up in him. He knew he was going to get it, but he thought he'd be busted out like Ringo just was. But Doolittle was right, and he accepted it.

"Now," Doolittle started, his voice much more casual. "I want you to get some rest. Spend some time with that girl of yours. I expect you to be shipping out again any day now. I'll write you a week's pass, but don't be surprised if you get a call to report sooner than that." He nodded. "Dismissed."

The two men swapped salutes, and Johnny was off. It was a one-hour drive from the field all the way back to Williamsburg in Brooklyn. But Johnny made a couple of stops on the way. It was just now four o'clock when he pulled up to Gwen's apartment building. Some kids were playing out in the street, running through an open fire hydrant. He laughed as he saw them running around. Two other ladies, friends of Gwen, were sitting outside when he got out of his car. One winked at him as he walked by in his Army uniform. He walked around the hallway corner toward her apartment when he practically ran into Gwen's neighbor, Mrs. Simmerson coming around the corner at the same time.

"Hello," Johnny greeted her warily.

"Oh. It's you," the elderly woman replied in a negative tone, giving him a stern look. "I don't approve of you." She stuck her finger in his face and waved it about. Johnny tried to sidestep the old lady. "I hope you're not a Catholic."

"I'm not," he told her before continuing on. He came to Gwen's door and knocked. A moment later it opened and there she was. Gwen was standing with wet hair, and a towel around her. Her lips curled up in that gorgeous smile that he loved. Her green eyes squinted playfully at him as she stood there in the doorway.

"What are you doing?" she asked him. "You don't have to knock, baby."

"Your rather judgmental neighbor warned me on my way here," he told her, drawing an instant giggle. "Besides, I wanted to surprise you." He pulled out the flowers that he'd held behind his back. They were pink roses.

"Well. I'm surprised," she said, taking the flowers. He stepped into her apartment, leaned in, put his hand behind the small of her back, and kissed her. He kicked the door closed gently with the back of his foot. She giggled, then pushed him away playfully. "They're beautiful."

"So are you," he told her and began to unbutton his tunic. Then something caught him. "So you didn't know it was me at your door?"

"Nope," she replied. She walked into the kitchen and pulled a glass vase from the cabinet, filling it with water.

"Really? So you answer the door wearing nothing but a towel for everyone?" he asked. She laughed from the kitchen.

"I thought you were Ginger." She came striding out of the kitchen, threw her arms around him and they kissed again. "But this is better. You're home early."

"Yeah. The bigwig gave me the next few days off." She smiled again. "I thought we'd go out tonight. Maybe go over the bridge." Gwen's eyes widened at the suggestion.

"Manhattan?" she asked, and he nodded back. "Well, how can any girl say no to such a handsome man offering to take her out? Gatsby's?"

"That sounds good. I see you've already taken a shower. Let me do the same and get into something more comfortable, and we'll go."

Johnny took his uniform off and started the shower. Gwen got dressed and put out some clothes for him. When he got out of the shower he found her sitting in front of her mirror brushing her hair. He watched her for a moment, relishing the experience. She always seemed so innocent when she thought he wasn't looking. So natural. He loved that about her. She turned her head and smiled at him.

"I poured you a little drink," she told him. There was a glass of whiskey sitting on the edge of the night table next to the bed. He kissed the top of her head as he grabbed the drink, then started getting himself dressed. "Good day today?"

He chuckled a little. "It was an interesting one, that's for sure. What about you?"

"Slow. I swear if Bobby didn't come in just about every day, I wouldn't have had any customers today. I think he comes in to see Sue."

"Bobby who?" he asked as he finished tying his shoe.

"I've told you about him. Bobby. He works as a welder. Don't you listen to the things I say?" She was toying with him.

"Of course I do, baby." He buttoned up his shirt and took a swig of his whiskey. "Every word of it."

She looked at him and squinted. "So. You wanna talk about it?"

He gave her a confused look. "Talk about what?"

"Don't do that. I asked you about your day, and you pretty much shrugged it off. You came home early, and you've got the next few days off." She turned in her chair, threw her arm over the top of the back, and stared at him. "So?"

He looked into her eyes and snickered. Her eyes widened as if she were expecting an answer. She knew him better than anyone. He gulped down the rest of his drink in one shot, then reluctantly nodded.

"OK, OK." He held up his hands in surrender. "I think it's going to happen soon."

"You're shipping out?"

"I think so." Her eyes instantly fluttered. "He hasn't said when, but he basically hinted that it was going to happen soon."

"God," she whispered. She turned her head away from him and wiped her left eye. "Well ... we knew it was going to happen." She sniffled. He stepped in behind her and put his hands on her shoulders; she ran her hands along his. "Do you even know where yet?"

"No," he said, shaking his head. "They typically don't tell you until the last minute. But ..."

"It's China, isn't it?"

"Probably."

She nodded her head subtly. Some tears ran down her cheeks, Johnny smiled at her in the mirror's reflection. He was glad she didn't wear makeup, as it would have ruined her natural beauty. She didn't need it and he was glad for it.

"Maybe we should just stay in tonight," he suggested. Almost instantly she put on a genuine smile and looked at his reflection.

"Nope," she stated. "We're going out tonight. If we've got limited days together now, then I want to make the most of each one with you." She stood up to face him. He wrapped his hands around her waist. "Tomorrow I'll call Carl to let him know I'll be gone from work for the next few days."

"Baby," he whispered back. "You don't have to—"

"Shh," she cut him off, putting a single finger on his lips. "You don't get a say," she whispered back to him. He leaned into her, and they kissed.

CHAPTER FOURTEEN

Admiral Yamamoto stood in the center of the office, staring down at the chief of the Imperial Japanese Navy. The other man, Admiral Nagano, sat still behind his dark oak desk, his left elbow propped up on the arm of his chair, and his chin resting on his balled fist. His eyes were thoughtful, and his breathing almost rhythmic. Yamamoto waited, patiently, and quietly as his superior officer pondered on what he had just been told. Finally, he brought his gaze back up to Yamamoto, then slowly shook his head.

With a great sense of disappointment, Yamamoto exhaled heavily through his nose. In all of his years of service, he had mastered the art of suppressing any outward sign of emotion, never allowing his enthusiasm, or disappointment, to bubble to the surface. When in the presence of the officers who served under his command, it would have taken no effort whatsoever to do. But today, with only him and his old friend and commanding officer in the room together, he could not help but release the tiniest hint of disappointment.

"The emperor has made his decision," Nagano told him. His voice was laced with both sternness and something else. *Was it sympathy?* Yamamoto wondered as he studied Nagano's face. "I'm sorry, Yamamoto."

The commander of Japan's Combined Fleet averted his eyes, looking out toward the light beaming through the expansive glass window that overlooked Tokyo's government sector. He let out a long, audible sigh. It was the only outward semblance of emotion that he would allow himself. But inside he was seething.

"Once the Emperor has spoken, it is our duty to see it through," Nagano told him. Yamamoto nodded in agreement. He didn't need to be told by anyone about what his duties and obligations were. But he understood Nagano's sentiment, and that his superior could do nothing.

"So, once again the Army will get its way," Yamamoto said in a sorrowful voice. "Have they learned nothing?" he asked, but it was rhetorical.

Nagano pushed himself up from his seat, and slowly began to pace back and forth around the side of his desk. He clasped his hands behind his back and looked self-consciously down at his feet, grumbling an agreement in reply. Both of them knew that he had pushed hard for a different strategy. He'd steadfastly argued to the cabinet, and to the Emperor himself, about the many concerns that he had about another war with Russia. But in the end, his argument seemed to fall on deaf ears.

"I believe this to be madness," Yamamoto said to him. His tone was hushed, even though they were the only two in the room. "I firmly believe that we'll be met with disaster if we are set on going down this road."

Nagano had already begun to pour two cups of tea. He pushed one cup toward Yamamoto and held up his own. Yamamoto took his tea, bowed his head in respect, then let his lips touch the rim of the cup.

"We both know war is nothing but madness," Nagano replied. "Be it with Russia, or with China."

"Or the United States," Yamamoto added. "I tell you now, old friend, in confidence, that I am beginning to feel"—he searched for the right words—"a great uncertainty swelling up within me. As if we are being swept about by a great storm." He sipped on the hot tea.

"Such is the way of things in these days. What do the Chinese say? May you live in interesting times? Well, we are living in those times now." He turned back around, and lifted his teacup to the giant portrait hanging behind the desk. Emperor Hirohito was dressed in his finest military uniform, seated on an elaborately decorated stool, a half-unsheathed samurai blade in his lap.

Yamamoto shared in the moment. He knew the saying well and knew it was as much a warning as it was a hopeful blessing. He also knew that his superior had gone well beyond his position in arguing for a strategy other than the one that the government had settled on. In the long animosity between the Imperial Navy and the Army, and their opposing strategies, the Army had won out. Now Japan was seemingly going down a road that would take it into yet another land war in Asia.

Although there was no proof of it, rumors swirling about suggested that their distant German allies had offered up some sort of incentive for Japan. Nobody in the Navy seemed to know exactly what that incentive was, but it seemed to be enough to persuade Hirohito to side with the Imperial Army.

Yamamoto and other top Imperial Navy planners saw nothing but folly in this move. Japan had a number of border confrontations with the Soviets years earlier. They had been costly and ended in failure. The massive invasion the Army was proposing now would require vast numbers of troops, tanks, artillery guns, and naval support. That did not even include the huge supply and logistical support they'd require. Should they manage to assemble all those things, such a campaign would be difficult enough due to the vastness of the territory involved. Then added to that was the fact that those troops would have to be drawn from other parts of the empire, potentially weakening their positions elsewhere.

"I would have it known now before we begin this operation, that I again strenuously argue for a preemptive invasion of several Pacific Island groups," Yamamoto said. Nagano turned back to him, finished off his small cup of tea, then gave a curt nod.

"Your arguments are known, and your opposition has already been noted," Nagano replied. But his words ended there, and his tone gave an air of finality on the matter. "Go now, my friend. You have been given your orders. I expect you to carry them out accordingly."

The two stood there for a few silent moments. Finally, Yamamoto up-ended the last of his drink. He put the cup down on the edge of the desk and bowed to the other man. They saluted one another, and Yamamoto turned and strode out of the office without another word. All that needed to be said had been and there was nothing further that either man could do. He knew Nagano was as hamstrung as he was, and that he was following orders that he had vehemently disagreed with. But as Nagano had expressed, the Emperor had spoken.

The main hallway of the Imperial General Headquarters was as modest as it was empty. Only a few staff officers walked through the main corridor. One of those officers was Admiral Tamon Yamaguchi. He sat patiently on a simple wooden bench, his hat in his lap. His attention turned toward the door that led through a series of small offices, and ultimately to the chief of the Imperial Navy. The door swung open, and Admiral Yamamoto exited, his hat tucked under his left arm. Yamaguchi stood up at Yamamoto's approach.

"How did things go?" Yamaguchi inquired, and Yamamoto grunted.

"About as we both knew it would," he replied. The two men started toward the main door. "It seems that the Emperor's mind has been made up, and the final decision is no longer open for debate. There is no dissuading him from this decision."

A sailor held the door open for the two admirals as they left the building. A car was waiting for them at the bottom of the steps. They slowly walked down from the main entrance.

"I don't understand their position," Yamaguchi commented. "Seems like a fool's choice."

The driver jumped out of the front seat and opened the door for the two men. Yamamoto stepped in, tossing his hat beside himself on the back seat. Yamaguchi followed, and a moment later the car started off. The streets outside of the complex were generally packed with people walking on either side of the street. Today was no different.

"They're convinced they'll be victorious," Yamamoto replied, shaking his head sadly. "They've given up on common sense, Yamaguchi. Four years in China now without a victory. You'd think that they'd have learned." He lowered his voice and added, "Too many damn wars."

"We knew that this was always a possibility," Yamaguchi told him. Yamamoto always appreciated the other man's opinion and the manner in which he gave it. Without remorse. "They've been pushing the Emperor just as we've been pushing for a southern strategy. Shame. All those islands in the Pacific, ripe for attack, rich with resources. I do not wish for war, but if we are to fight one, give us one we can win."

"I'm not sure if we could win that war, Yamaguchi." Yamamoto's voice had enough remorse for both of them. "For a while perhaps, but not long."

"We wouldn't have to attack the Americans directly," Yamaguchi told him. "If we take control of the Dutch colonies. Maybe some of the British possessions. The Americans won't stand in the way of that. They're not interested in fighting for some other country's colonial possession."

Yamamoto sighed at the remark. He rubbed a gloved hand on his chin in thought as the car drove through the streets. Outside, merchants and peddlers were trying to sell their goods, women walked with their umbrellas open above them, and children played on the sidewalks. A part of him wanted to tell Yamaguchi that it didn't matter, and that, in time, they'd be at war with the United States anyhow. But he knew the other admiral already understood that fact. The American government was not going to sit by and allow the Japanese free rein any longer. And any move by Japan into the southern and central Pacific would not be tolerated. Now, on top of the possibility of a war with America, they were certainly on the path to war with the Russians. Those two things combined with the unresolved war with China, meant the empire would be fighting on all fronts. He closed his eyes for a moment and said a silent prayer.

"Do you know when they are planning this operation?" Yamaguchi asked.

"No." Yamamoto shook his head. "But it won't be this year, I'm sure. They won't have the time. It'll have to be next year, '42, at the earliest. By then some of the generals think the situation in China will have improved. But ... who knows. They're being driven by fear. Two years, Yamaguchi. That's how many years of oil we have left. And when it runs out, everything stops." He could hear Yamaguchi sneer at the words.

"The East Indies have plenty of oil. All the oil wells we'd need. And we would shed a lot less blood taking them than we will going north."

"It doesn't matter anymore," Yamamoto told him in a grim voice. "We're now on a course that will take us down that road. The Emperor's mind is made up. As Nagano told me, all we can do now is our duty. I know that I don't need to remind you of that." He looked his friend squarely in the eye. "You've never disappointed me, Yamaguchi. I know you will do yours." He put his hand on Yamaguchi's in a friendly gesture.

"So what do we do now?" Yamaguchi asked him.

"You get your ships in for their expected refits. After that . . ." Yamamoto waved his hand around. "We wait, and we pray."

CHAPTER FIFTEEN

His Excellency Francisco Franco, Generalissimo of Spain, went through the pages of the final action plan, line by line. He closely skimmed through the most important details of each page of the report, giving off only subtle grunts here and there as he read. The group of civilian and military advisors gathered around him stood quietly by, patiently waiting for the Spanish dictator to give his final up or down. The pendulum on the ancient clock in the corner of the elaborate office swung back and forth as the seconds ticked by. For a while, it was the only sound in the room.

They'd been over the details of the operation no less than a dozen times in the past few days. These refined articles were nothing more than a formality at this point. Franco knew the details of it just as well as anyone else in the room. But he didn't mind taking his time to review the written details. It was almost as if by reading through them that he was somehow being absolved of any responsibility should things not go according to plan.

Minutes quietly ticked by, and it seemed to the others present that Franco was simply glancing blindly at the plans that the Army commanders had drawn up. His tongue protruded from his lower lip, and his mouth moved silently with the words on the paper. Finally, after what had seemed like an exceedingly long time the man closed the file and ran his hands over his bald head.

He gave only the smallest of nods before looking back up at the men surrounding him. This was a top-level operation. Its secrecy was paramount, and only the most senior civilian and military leadership, as well as a handful of field commanders, were even aware of it. That by itself would not be well looked upon by others in the government who had supported him in the past, but that couldn't be helped. This was concerning the very future of Spain, and only those directly involved could be trusted with this information. Some might not like the direction that Spain was about to take, but they'd return to the fold once it became obvious Franco was leading them in a better direction. Besides, he was the generalissimo of Spain, the highest authority in the nation. No one would challenge his decision.

"The odds of success?" Franco asked.

The man standing in the center of the group shrugged slightly. General Carlos Asensio Cabanillas was Chief of Staff of the Army. A tall, slender man with an immaculately trimmed mustache, and a favorite of Franco's. Asensio Cabanillas pondered the question for a strategic moment. He'd been down this road with Franco before and had tired of the repeated indecision. But he knew the dictator well enough and knew how to dress his answers theatrically. Franco was no fool, he could see when others were lying to him. Words had to be crafted carefully.

"Almost certain," he answered, only because that was the only answer Franco seemed to accept. The plans had been submitted, revised, and resubmitted a dozen times before now. The papers presented today were virtually identical to the originals. Only subtle language differences had been made, and only to satisfy the whim of the Spanish dictator. "Six brigades, a score of naval ships, and ninety-four aircraft. Not a token force by any means. The guise of training maneuvers should not draw any unnecessary attention. Those kinds of things are not uncommon. And with the vast majority of our armed forces maintaining their positions in the north, we have high expectations that the British will not expect a thing until it's too late. Furthermore, our observation posts report few of their warships are anchored in Gibraltar these days. Confirming intelligence that they are spread thinly in the Mediterranean. We've also been given assurances, through the foreign ministry, that the Italians have guaranteed us naval support. A flotilla will be pre-positioned on the night prior to the attack. Once we commence, they'll sweep in from the east."

"And the other commanders?"

The general sighed and shrugged his shoulders. Only Spain's highest political and military leadership and a handful of field commanders knew of the coming operation. The reasons behind this secrecy were twofold. First, the fewer people who knew of the coming attack, the less chance there was of Allied intelligence operatives becoming aware of it. Second, Franco knew well that not all of his regional commanders would approve of the move. Many of his generals had argued for strict neutrality, a policy that Franco had previously favored as well. Others were more sympathetic to the British cause and saw Hitler as a potential threat to Spain.

"After our victory, they'll fall in line," the general told him. "Once it's shown that the British are vulnerable and that we can achieve success, they'll abandon this insane notion of non-belligerence."

"Hmm." Franco looked back down at the plan before him. He made the smallest movement of his hand, and tapped the files, and Asensio Cabanillas was half afraid that he'd open the paperwork back up and read through the extensive plan as he'd done two dozen times before now. But the dictator paused.

It had been a bold plan. Much bolder than he had originally thought the country could manage at the time. But with the fall of the French Republic and the retreat of the British Army from the continent, it seemed that their fortunes had changed, and Spain's future was looking a bit brighter. That, along with Hitler's promise to forgive much of Spain's monetary debt to Germany, and the possibility of territorial concessions by France, had enticed him just enough. With the real likelihood that Gibraltar might be rejoined to Spain after two centuries of British possession, this could mark a significant, historical turning point for his country.

His troops would be positioned and poised to cross the border into the British enclave while at the same time conducting an amphibious pincer movement. With a surprise attack by the Air Force and the support of the Cadiz-based naval squadron, the operation should stand a very good chance of rapid success. At least, that's what Franco was hoping desperately for. And it's what Foreign Minister Suñer had consistently assured him of.

The hardcore Germanophile Suñer had been a convincing voice for his brother-in-law, Franco, to see that the time was ripe. Despite Spain's hardship since the days of the civil war, now was as good a time for the country to reshape itself since the decline of its overseas empire over the last hundred years. Despite his own personal leanings toward the likes of Fascism and National Socialism, he had absolutely no plans to just throw in blindly with Hitler and Mussolini. He'd accepted both their support during the days of the war with the republicans, and the Germans and Italians who'd flocked to him had performed miracles and helped to give his nationalists the victory. But Franco had zero intentions of just turning his country into some vassal of Germany, or worse yet, be absorbed into some greater Reich like Austria and Czechoslovakia. No, Spain would set her own course. It all began in Gibraltar.

"I see," Franco replied. "I want to know that the British will not see this coming. I want to know that their defenses will not hold. Can you guarantee me this?"

General Asensio Cabanillas pouted his lip and nodded. He turned his head to the other officers assembled, who themselves nodded an affirmative, then looked back to Franco.

"Of course," he answered casually. "All of our intelligence sources say that Gibraltar is only lightly defended right now. So the civilian casualties should be minimal. Most of them were evacuated after Poland. A swift, decisive operation should give us the victory. After that, British prestige will suffer, and they'll have no base of operations from which to counterstrike."

"The strategic initiative will be ours," Minister Suñer added. "Besides, Herr Ribbentrop and I have developed a good relationship recently. He's assured me that shortly the British will be forced to sue for peace with Berlin." He shrugged again. "Take from that what you will. But I suspect that the Germans are planning some sort of offensive against them. Possibly an invasion of their island. Under those conditions, London would be hard-pressed to mount a rescue expedition. Their empire is dying, and everyone knows it. Germany is the future. We'd be wise to align ourselves accordingly. Either way, once the territory is back in our hands, and we've removed any British threat near our shores, Germany will provide us with any military aid we may require."

Franco looked up at his brother-in-law and studied his face. He'd trusted him up until this point, and given him extraordinary power to craft Spain's foreign policy. Though personally he may harbor some inner doubts, he saw no reason not to trust the man. After all, what could the British possibly do after the fact? It's not as though the Americans were clamoring to come to their rescue.

Franco flipped through the pages until he got to the final paper. He unscrewed his pen, and with only the slightest bit of trepidation, he penned his signature to the bottom of the page, then put his personal seal next to it. He knew full well that this was as good as a declaration of war. But with its ultimate success, Spain would begin the long road of reversing its past failures.

He flipped closed the pamphlet of folded papers and held them up for the general, then held them back just as the other man reached for them.

"I want your best man in command," he told him firmly. "I will not suffer defeat, Carlos! Do I make myself clear?"

"Yes, Generalissimo. I'll make sure of it. He'll come back victorious, or I'll personally order his execution," he managed with the slightest grin.

CHAPTER SIXTEEN

General Udet stood quietly in the very center of his headquarters briefing room as the procession of staff planners updated him on the strategic situation. Everywhere around the room there were maps and charts, enlarged photographs of enemy airfields, ports, and industrial centers. There were boards with unit casualty reports chalked on them, probable kill statistics, and logistical and readiness status updates. From this room, he could get nearly real-time updates on every unit under his command.

General Vleck, the chief of operations, was updating him on the outcome of the most recent bombing attacks on British soil. As if the map and the chart of casualties, and known inflicted losses hanging on the wall, didn't speak volumes by themselves. But he gave his staff the consideration that they deserved. He listened to each and every word, but his eyes carefully studied the influx of information that was displayed around the headquarters situation room.

The fact was that they were winning. That the *Luftwaffe* was inflicting heavy losses on the RAF. Every day brought in more reports of successful raids on the British homeland. The fact was that his supplies were in good shape, that his logistical support was performing admirably, and that his reserves were intact. He'd had to admit that Göring had done just what he'd said that he was going to do; supply Udet with everything that he needed to get the job done. And despite some serious losses taken, he still outnumbered the RAF by a substantial margin.

That is if you took Luftwaffe Command's word for it.

They'd sent wave after wave over England. Groups of fighters wore down the British pilots, and the bombers had so far done an outstanding job of hitting their targets. But not without loss, and certainly not with achieving the air supremacy that so many in the Luftwaffe High Command had hoped for at this point. In the weeks since the attacks began, his command in particular had taken more losses than they'd anticipated. Or, at least, what Luftwaffe Command had anticipated.

Udet nodded emphatically as General Vleck went on with the operational part of the briefing. The bombing groups had continually hammered RAF airfields in the south and had forced some closures, which was giving the Luftwaffe a small advantage.

"I understand all of this," he told Vleck. He turned his head and watched as the massive plot board moved in a reflection of what exactly was happening right now above that country. "But is the strategy working?" He asked pointing to the board. Vleck turned his head and saw what the general was pointing out.

"Well, General, as you can see we've forced them to move some of their airfields farther north. I would have to say, as of right now, that yes, the strategy appears to be working."

Udet bit his lower lip. Three bombing groups had made the English coast, with one more crossing over the Channel toward Kent. There'd be two more groups crossing the North Sea from Norway that would hit targets in northern England and Scotland. Then there would be four more sorties out of Germany and the Netherlands. But despite all the strength they kept hitting the enemy with, the RAF kept putting up a stiff defense. There was a part of Udet that gave the enemy respect for the fight that they were putting up. The RAF had been outnumbered at every encounter, but still, they came on in defense of their homeland. Berlin had assured all of its subordinate commands that the RAF was close to breaking, that their numbers were dwindling. But General Udet had a difference of opinion.

He'd warned his superiors. He'd even warned Göring before the operation had commenced, about what he'd felt was faulty operational intelligence. That was one reason why he'd secretly ordered his own reconnaissance flights. So that he could get direct, reliable information on enemy strength. He'd never been convinced that the RAF was as weak as Luftwaffe intelligence had made it out to be.

"That would be easier for me to swallow, Vleck, except for that." He indicated the list of casualties spelled out on the board. Bombing groups had been reduced by as much as thirty percent in some cases. "How is it we're inflicting these crippling damages on the enemy, but still they're able to sortie against us? I was up late last night reading through after action reports filed by our own pilots. Intelligence reports aside, they paint a picture of an enemy that doesn't seem to be on the cusp of collapse."

Vleck winced slightly. It wasn't meant as a rebuke of the general's ability of course. He'd simply been stating a fact.

"Well, General, I can only assume that they're repairing their damaged planes and fields faster than we knock them out," Vleck replied. Udet knew Vleck well and knew that his tone of voice made it obvious the general didn't believe in that last statement.

Udet sighed. "I believe that it's more likely that the RAF has greater strength than what those reports we get regularly say they do." He shook his head in dismay. "I believed that a month ago, and I believe that still. If OKL was correct, we would have gained air superiority by now. We have not." He looked at his chief intelligence officer. "What do you have to say, Colonel?"

His head of intelligence for Air Fleet *3* was a straight-shooting type of officer. He'd consistently backed Udet's statement that Luftwaffe

Command had routinely underestimated enemy fighter strength, either deliberately or due to faulty intelligence gathering. Though Udet would never admit it to others, the man had quietly confessed to him that the blame was most likely on Schmid, Göring's chief intelligence officer.

"I agree with you, General," Colonel Voight replied. "I've personally been through scores of reports from our own group leaders and squadron commanders. They are vastly different from what Berlin has said about our opposition. I don't wish to contradict anyone, however, if Berlin's reports were true, we'd be seeing a substantial decline in the number of enemy fighters that we're engaging. But we aren't."

"That could just mean that they're turning their fighters around quicker than we anticipated," Vleck countered. The two men were usually on the same page, but it seemed to Udet that Vleck was simply touting the party line. He didn't blame him. Vleck's job, as operations chief, was to keep the pressure up on the enemy, and he was accomplishing just that.

"That could be," Voight began to reply. "If that's true, it would also mean that we underestimated their logistical capacity. If the British can turn a damaged plane around, and get it back into the fight so quickly, then either way we're not assuming those things that we should otherwise be assuming."

Vleck briefly appeared as if he wanted to say something, but fell silent instead. Udet rasped his knuckles against the tabletop. Both generals knew that Colonel Voight was correct. For a minute he felt like kicking himself or perhaps kicking some of those above him. Military decisions were being made without proper consideration. As military officers and strategic planners, they should have been assuming things like higher enemy numbers, stiffer resistance, and better-quality pilots. But Command seemed to be telling itself just what it wanted to hear. Another commander may have remained silent, and simply followed his instructions to the letter, regardless of what the facts were telling him.

"No," he whispered. "We knew from the beginning that the RAF had greater numbers than what were reported to us." He balled up a fist and gently pounded the edge of the table he was standing over. He wanted to say aloud that Berlin had spoon-fed them exactly what they wanted to, rather than give them the information that they needed to know, and that Schmid was nothing more than an incompetent fool. But, for the sake of those working around the room, he didn't. No use spreading uncertainty among the men, or speaking ill of another fellow officer. "As of right now, we are to assume enemy strength is higher than what we've been told. I want revised estimates. Assume a twenty percent increase in strength."

"We'll have to reconsider our own sortie strength as well, General," Vleck told him. "Launch larger bombing groups."

"I understand that. But we cannot take for granted anything any longer. Our supply situation is very good right now. We have the resources to make the change. We'll coordinate larger attacks against enemy targets. Airfields and supplies will be priority targets. No more of this nonsense of hitting industrial centers. We'll concentrate on fewer targets. One by one we'll wipe them off the map."

"What about the other commands?" Vleck asked him. "Our orders from OKL –"

"Are vague, and indecisive, Karl," Udet stopped him before he could go down that road. "There are no conclusions to be drawn about our cooperation with the others. Kesselring and Stumpff are free to interpret their orders, and I am free to interpret mine. Beginning now we're going to approach things from a bottom-up perspective. Understood?" Both men nodded.

"My only fear is that Berlin may not like this change, sir," Voight stated. "Not without clearing things with them. I've been told that

Göring is preparing to visit the frontline commands. He may not appreciate being kept out of the loop."

The remark drew an instant shrug from Udet. He'd spent years working in Berlin, wasting away behind some desk. Now he'd been given command in France. Not someone else, but him. Udet was a fighter pilot by nature, and he intended to use those skills. Not fall into silence like so many other generals might have done. Fear had kept too many of his friends and fellow field commanders silent about many things. It seemed to be a contagion these days in Berlin. Paris too for that matter. Which was why he'd relocated his headquarters to Rouen. Out of the reach of prying eyes and ears.

"Leave Reichsmarschall Göring to me. Until the day that I'm relieved of my command, I will accept any and all responsibility. Colonel, update your intelligence information to give more weight to our surveillance sources. Photographs, reports from squadron leaders and wing commanders, that sort of thing. Of course double-check with OKL reports to see how our information matches up with theirs. We'll assign targets based upon your intelligence. We have the strength of numbers, and the quality of our pilots is second to none. I have some thoughts about how we can capitalize on some things that we've failed to do. Let's plan an informal briefing at dinner tonight. We can go over any recommendations that anyone has. Tomorrow we'll brief the entire senior staff. But I'll let you know that as of now, I have no intentions of playing this game by someone else's rules any longer."

* * *

The train whistle sounded as the locomotive broke to a stop at the station. Himmler did not even wait for the train to come to a complete stop before stepping off onto the platform. His staff came filing out of the passenger car behind him. Underneath the roofed platform, safe from the torrential downpour, was a large reception consisting of German and French officials.

Two men were standing apart from the others. One wore the uniform of an SS officer. He was young, his facial features were sharp, and he had that dark, brooding look in his eyes that the SS chief liked to see in his young underlings. Klaus Barbie was one of Himmler's more enthusiastic protégés. The young man was a devout Nazi, and his professional record with the SS reflected that. He did everything by the book according to party ideology, and he was known to be quite an efficient officer, despite his young age.

The second man was dressed in what looked like a cheaply made suit. His hair was pitch black, his mustache was unkempt, and Himmler thought that the man looked more like a Greek or Italian than a Frenchman. But underneath the shabby exterior, the man was as hard and cruel as anyone that wore the uniform of the SS. He was also politically sharp. Qualities that made Pierre Laval the perfect successor to the old French marshal, and a solid ally in unoccupied France.

"Heil Hitler!" Barbie saluted, and Himmler returned the greeting and then shook the man's hand.

Himmler gave the Nazi salute to Laval as well before shaking his hand also.

"Welcome to Unoccupied France, Reichsmarschall," Laval welcomed him. The man's grip was firm, and he met Himmler's gaze straight on. Himmler could smell the cheap French cologne on him.

"Thank you," he replied, and the group began walking down the length of the station.

Standing behind Laval and Barbie was a double line of honor guards. For a moment Himmler thought that they were an SS unit, but then he realized that they wore the jet-black uniforms of the newly formed French Service d'ordre legionnaire, or SOL. They were mostly younger men. Instead of helmets, they wore black berets. They reminded him of his own guard units or the Brownshirts that had been instrumental in putting the Nazi Party in power. He gave them a salute as they walked by. An officer saluted him back with a snap of his sword, and a young drummer beat his drum as he gave them an honoring inspection.

When the short greeting ceremony was over, the group assembled inside the train station building. It was vacant, except for several Frenchmen who were serving on Laval's staff. There was a table with a white cloth draped over it, and coffee cups set up in the center.

"It's far too rainy to stay outside," Laval said. His manner was friendly enough, but he also had an air of impatience. His hands moved about at his sides, and he seemed to fidget a lot as all of the proper introductions were being made between the French and German staff members. "Reichsmarschall, this is our new Interior Minister, Jacques Doriot. And, I believe you know Admiral Darlan."

"Yes. We met at the surrender ceremony at Compiègne," Himmler stated. He grinned slightly. It didn't hurt to remind his hosts of who had beaten them in the field. Darlan lowered his head respectfully, but he did not indicate whether he'd been insulted by the reminder. "So, your new government has really fallen into place," he told Laval. "I approve of the manner in which you seized the moment. Reminded me of our victory in '33."

"Yes. Well, it wasn't quite that way. But the people needed leadership. Real leadership. I'm afraid that the previous government wasn't doing that. They were moving in a direction not compatible with the views of the majority of the nation. But, we've since corrected that. I've been anxiously waiting for this opportunity for us to meet. Our correspondence and telephone conversations really made me feel as if we had a strong ally in Berlin. I will admit to you, that I don't think we would have moved on Pétain when we did, had we not had your support." Laval cackled a little. "Also, it didn't hurt to have some help from your people." He looked at Barbie and nodded in appreciation.

"Well, we saw the opportunity, and we seized it as well." Himmler grinned, crossed his arms, and let his body relax. "I see a real friend in you, Prime Minister. Germany needs friends. Friends that offer us secure borders."

"Thank you," Laval replied to his compliment.

"So long as you govern yourselves appropriately, and in the best interests of the German Reich, you'll receive all the support that you need from us," Himmler told him. He took an offered cup of coffee, looking Laval in the eye as he sipped on it. The Frenchman seemed to be taken aback at the language but quickly found his diplomatic voice.

"Of course. Of course." He waved his hand. "I believe that France and Germany should walk hand in hand. We're natural allies I think. Together we can do good things."

"So, you don't have any regrets then?" Himmler probed him. "Ousting the former regime?"

"None whatsoever."

"And the British?" Himmler kept probing. The viper was a master of observation. Even the slightest facial twitch or movement of the hand would catch his attention. "You have no worries about tearing up any agreements you may have with them?"

"The British?" Laval sighed. "Worthless people. We are not at war with them, and what do they do? Attack our naval bases in North Africa. Did you know that over two thousand of our brave sailors lost their lives in that attack? No. We don't owe the British anything."

Himmler continued to sip his hot coffee, looking around at the Vichy delegation, studying each one of them. Except for Admiral Darlan, who stood as still as a marble statue, the rest all nodded in agreement with the Prime Minister. He gave them all a friendly look.

"I'm glad to hear you say that, Prime Minister. Very glad. The Führer wishes nothing but good relations between Berlin and Vichy."

"Good," Laval replied to him. "It's on good relations that I wish to speak." Himmler gave him his attention. "It's important that we begin our new relationship with a symbol of, shall we say, mutual trust. On that note, I'd like to discuss the prisoners that are being held in Germany. You're holding over three million of our soldiers. We'd like to open a dialogue concerning their repatriation."

Himmler nodded. He put down the coffee cup and rubbed his chin. He'd prepared himself fully for this subject and found himself strangely appreciative that Laval could get straight to the point of things. He didn't care to waste time as so many others did when it came to politics. Even Hitler was guilty of filibustering sometimes.

"The prisoners that we captured during the collapse of the old republic are well cared for. I certainly can understand your position on their returning to France." He allowed for a few seconds of silence, then placed his hands behind his back as he typically did. "I'll broach this subject with Hitler, and give you all the support that I can. The Wehrmacht are the ones holding all of the captured prisoners, and their release is out of my authority. However, should Vichy show a gesture of cooperation to us, it would certainly go a long way with the Führer. He's a reasonable man."

Laval grimaced a little, then pulled together a grin and nod. "I understand his position, and yours. However, consider that this is a newly formed government. The instability of the Pétain regime was partially based on his inability to resolve certain matters that are sensitive to us here in France. Should we begin by curing this matter to some extent, then I believe that would be looked upon highly by the French people. Perhaps even alleviate some animosity."

"Hmm." Himmler thought about it for a moment. He was no politician, and ultimately Hitler would have final say on the matter anyhow. But he realized that Laval was giving him an offering to some degree. "I do see your point. Maybe we have the opportunity to make a simultaneous exchange." He put his hands up instantly. "Understand again, that I have no authority to make such a deal. But, theoretically, should France make a gesture to us, then it's possible that Hitler could order the release of some, not all, but some of your prisoners that we're holding. That could go a long way to solidifying your position."

He'd thrown out the bait. Now it was time to see if the Frenchman was truly an ally in fact or name only. Germany, and Himmler personally, had gone out on a limb in supporting the coup against Pétain. Even though from a distance it appeared to be an internal French matter, the truth is the SS had invested people and resources, and now had to justify it. More than that though, Himmler himself needed to ingratiate himself to Hitler. To reinforce to him just how capable he and his organization truly were, and that his power didn't stop simply at state security.

"We are still recovering from the collapse of the republic," Laval told him. "But we here," – he gestured to the men around him –, "are interested in whatever helps us get the country back on its feet. To this end, we'll be reliant on whatever assistance we can receive. And, of course, we shall reciprocate."

Himmler stretched out his arm and gestured to one of his aides. The man took out of his briefcase some papers and gave them to Himmler, who promptly held them out for Laval. The Frenchman took them. His people stepped closer to him, reading the documents from over his shoulder. He flipped through the pages until he was done.

"You cannot be serious?" he asked Himmler, his voice skeptical.

"Very serious," Himmler responded, his voice was commanding. "I'm having my people in Berlin put together some details now. But, I can tell you right here, right now, that should you accept my proposal, you'll not only receive whatever assistance we can offer but I will personally vouch for you with Hitler. If you read through those carefully, I think that you'll see that what we're proposing is of considerable value to you."

Laval looked at Doriot, then Darlan. The admiral grunted softly but said nothing. Doriot whispered something briefly into his ear, causing Laval to give the smallest of nods.

"Doesn't your Army High Command have to give its approval for this?" Laval asked.

"There are ways around that," Himmler replied. "We have an agreement?"

Laval bit his lower lip, and thought about it. He looked briefly at Darlan, who replied with a silent nod of his own.

"I will call for a meeting with my cabinet ministers this evening," Laval told him. "I'd like to carefully review this. However..." he gave himself a moment. "If you can do what you are proposing, Herr Reichsmarschall, then I think we can accept your offer. But I still need to pass it through the parliament. Otherwise, it would not be considered legally acceptable."

"Of course, Prime Minister, of course."

CHAPTER SEVENTEEN

It was dark outside of the White House. City streetlights started to flicker on as the last rays of daylight slowly dimmed. Roosevelt sat behind the Resolute Desk, looking out of the window. For a few moments, he watched as the city lit up, and just for one brief moment, he wished that he'd had the use of his legs once again. It was a beautiful summer evening outside, and he could imagine strolling down the city street with Eleanor on his arm, enjoying the nightlife as they had years earlier in New York.

His personal secretary, Margaret LeHand, came by with a teapot. She stooped over a little and began to fill his cup back up. He turned his attention from the window, looked up at her, and grinned.

"Thank you," he whispered to her.

"My pleasure," she said and smiled back.

The moment's diversion was over, and he brought his attention back to the men sitting in the center of the Oval Office. Miss LeHand went around the room refilling each man's cup of tea, then left, closing the door quietly behind her.

There were three men in the Oval Office with him. Averell Harriman had just been appointed the new Ambassador to the United Kingdom, replacing Joe Kennedy. Kennedy's personal correspondence, condemning both the British government and Franklin Roosevelt himself, had just become much less private. The Boston Globe had gotten their hands on some of Kennedy's letters in which he'd brutally hammered the administration for its support of Great Britain and called the situation over there a hopeless cause. Frank Knox was present as well. The Secretary of the Navy had become an almost permanent resident at the White House these days. More than just about anyone, the man was working around the clock, working both houses of Congress to get more support for the service he led. The last man was the newest addition to Roosevelt's Cabinet. Carl Vinson, until recently a congressman from Georgia, had just been confirmed as the new Secretary of War, replacing Woodring. Vinson had wasted no time in getting right to work, undoing any number of his predecessor's policies. The generals under his charge were already more hopeful than they'd been under the isolationist Woodring.

"Where were we?" Roosevelt asked.

"The Philippines, sir," Vinson answered.

"Oh, yes." Roosevelt grabbed his briefing book and flipped through the pages. "General MacArthur." The name came out in a tiresome tone. The US military governor in the Philippine Islands was quite a famous character. His flamboyant style had made a name for the general, and he was clamoring every day for more and more support. More guns, bigger guns, more ships, more aircraft, ammunition, radios, medical equipment, the list went on. "What is he asking for now?"

"What isn't he asking for," Secretary Knox joked in a hushed voice. Roosevelt chuckled himself.

"He's scheduled a series of wargames," Vinson told him. "Previous exercises have shown, what he terms, 'a serious deficiency in preparedness'. Bottom line, Mister President, is that MacArthur has serious doubts concerning the ability to hold the islands in case of invasion."

"Did he say it like that?" Roosevelt inquired.

"Well… no, sir. He said it in his usual, MacArthur style," Vinson replied. "He's been making repeated requests to the Chief of Staff for additional heavy weaponry. Everything from scout planes to coastal artillery. I've spoken with General Marshall concerning this. He agrees that we need to supply the Filipinos and MacArthur with more than what they've currently got. The problem is supply. The Army isn't exactly sitting on an excess of heavy coastal guns. We're working out a solution even now. But, truth be told, even if we began construction on additional defenses, it would be years before we saw the final results. In the meantime, I'm having my people put together a plan to reinforce the islands. Perhaps, cycle some of our reserve or national guard units in and out on training missions."

"Frank." Roosevelt looked over at Knox. "What's the Navy's situation?"

"Sir, the Asiatic Fleet is in even worse shape than the Army is. We've updated a lot of our shore facilities and defenses in the area. However, the ships we've got stationed out there are mostly older ones. We've been updating and refitting them as fast as possible, but I have serious doubts about their ability to deter. Admiral Stark has even more reservations than I do about posting some of our newer ships out that way. There are no facilities in the Philippines or Guam to be able to properly service our bigger ships. Besides that, Admiral Stark firmly believes that we should hold our larger ships back, out of the reach of a first strike. It's a view that I happen to share."

President Roosevelt had agreed with Admiral Stark and signed off on the strategic recommendations that the man had made. But the Philippine Islands were about as far away as the moon was, so far as your average American was concerned. Even members of Congress were hesitant to supply the territory with that much weaponry. A far-off US possession that drew closer and closer every day to the front line of a growing conflict in Asia. If it fell tomorrow to an invader, he doubted very much that most Americans would give a damn.

"Well, we're gonna have to do something," Secretary Vinson stated, taking a sip from his cup. "I've reviewed the new plans from the War Department, and I have to say, that as much as I believe in strengthening the US mainland, our outlying territories are as much a part of our defense as Hawaii or Alaska are. Secretary Knox here and I have been working together since my confirmation. We've got a slew of potential actions that we can take jointly that should bolster those territories. I found out yesterday that there's a stockpile of anti-aircraft guns sitting in an armory outside of Des Moines." He chuckled ironically. "I don't see any German or Japanese planes flying over Iowa anytime soon. They'd make a difference out in the Pacific though."

"Or to the British," Averell Harriman added.

"I'd much rather see them sitting in Manila," Knox replied. "No offense to the British, but we can't strip down everything we've got and send it to them, even if we wanted to."

"The point is, Mister President," Vinson continued. "that we can get some things out to people like MacArthur, but it's not going to be much and it's not going to be the new stuff. Until production is in full swing, we're making do with the bottom of the barrel. Which brings me to my next point, sir. Military production. I know that we've expanded manufacturing in order to meet our needs, but I'm concerned that it's not as streamlined as it could be. General Marshall and I have been going over new figures for weapons and equipment coming out of factories, and quite frankly, I think we could be doing better. Much better. I'm an old legislator, Mister President, and part of me still thinks like one. I'm going to formally propose to you that we form a board. Much like the War Industries Board we had for the First World War. Its mandate would be to oversee all matters concerning military production and to make sure both branches of service are getting just what we need. It should have the authority to supervise all aspects of production and purchases. If you give me the go-ahead,

Mister President, I think it can be put together rather seamlessly. I've got some good ideas about who'd support it in Congress too."

"I think that's a fine idea," Roosevelt replied. "Send me the proposal. I'll confer with Speaker Rayburn on it. Seems to me like there shouldn't be any problems ginning up support for it, but if you have anyone in mind in the House, feel free to mention it."

He jotted it down on a note. Secretary Vinson was already proving to be an immense improvement over Harry Woodring. This was his first full week on the job, and he'd already gotten along better with the Chief of Staff than the other man had in his entire time as Secretary of War. Vinson's approach had been much more open-minded and considerate. He wasn't afraid to hear the opinions of the uniformed service members and didn't claim to know everything about everything. He'd been a reliable ally in the House of Representatives and had championed many of FDR's policies, including the Two-Ocean Navy Act, making him very popular with the Navy Department. When Harry Woodring had been forced to resign from the post, Vinson's name had been on Roosevelt's short-list. Now, seeing him at work, the President was glad to have the man filling such an important position, particularly now, in the face of threats from abroad.

"What about those destroyers we sent to the British?" Roosevelt asked.

"They were all handed off to the Canadians, sir. I understand most have made their way to Britain by now. Though in reality, it's going to take the Brits some time to repair and refit them. They weren't properly cared after when they were sitting in mothball. Some of them are going to require extensive work to get them up to snuff."

"It was better than nothing at all," Roosevelt replied. "We can't give them fully armed ships, I'm afraid. Unless someone else has a better idea, then I'm not sure what else we can do."

"If I may, Mister President." It was Averell Harriman. Roosevelt gave him a nod. "I've been doing some thinking on the subject. Since

I'm the one who'll be in London, working with the British, I thought it a good idea that I have a good working relationship with them. In my mind, that means bringing new ideas to the table. I've been considering the use of national security as a legal pretext for taking direct action. Well, maybe direct isn't the right word."

"I understand," Roosevelt told him. "Please, continue."

"If we rationalize that aiding certain parties can better secure our borders, and ensure our sovereignty at the same time, then we can further rationalize that a steady stream of support by us to, say Britain, could make sure that the conflict remains as far away from our shores as possible. Thus, keeping our own citizens safely out of harm's way, and at the same time give our overseas allies the materiel that they need."

"Isn't that what we just did?" Knox asked him. "They gave us bases, we gave them destroyers."

"My point exactly," Harriman nodded. "We provided them with warships, in exchange they gave us bases in which to defend ourselves with. But, forgive me Frank, the ships we gave them were old, obsolete, and stripped bare. You said yourself, it could take the British months to get those ships up to par. Under the legal pretext that their defense was by de facto our own defense, we got around the Neutrality Act. Better to send a few empty warships than our ships right?" Roosevelt nodded. "So then, if we follow that theory to the logical next step, is it not better to send a hundred bombers, or a hundred tanks, if doing so ensures our security."

"That's a nice sentiment, Averell, but I think it flies in the face of the law," Knox said. "I don't think it's going to fly."

"Why not?" Roosevelt asked him, genuinely interested in hearing the answer.

"I'm as much in favor of supplying Britain with the things they need to defend themselves as you are, sir. I agree with everything that Averell just said. But the Congress –"

"– Congress shouldn't have anything to do with it," Roosevelt pre-empted. "I don't mean that they can't rebuke me, and my actions. But I think Averell is going down the right road. By aiding in the security of the eastern hemisphere, we're by default securing the western hemisphere. We're not talking about propping up semi-dictatorships here, these are democratic countries, whose own sovereignty has not only been violated but in some cases crushed." Knox threw up his hands in concession. Roosevelt gave him a soft look. "Go on Averell. I want to hear more."

"Well, sir. It just so happens that I was reading about Lincoln a few nights ago. What struck me, as I was reading, was his use of General Orders. Particularly Proclamation Ninety-five."

"The Emancipation Proclamation?" Vinson asked.

"Lincoln's declaration that slaves were being used to further the Confederate war effort to subvert the United States." Averell paused, and tapped his fingers up to his lips as he reasoned his thought into words. "Lincoln reasoned that to keep the rebellion from spreading, he needed to deprive it of anything and everything that kept it going. The Southern economy was based on slavery. Freeing those slaves would cause their economy to collapse, thus ending the war sooner, thus saving American lives."

Secretary Knox let out a tiny sigh. "It's a good theory. Though, it could also be interpreted as a slippery slope." He shrugged at the idea. "I can certainly see the isolationist wing of the party raising some hell over it. They'll publicly attack it on legal grounds."

Roosevelt sank back into his wheelchair. He was an old New York lawyer himself, and he was no stranger to making a good legal argument. He was also no stranger to pushing the limits of some of those arguments, or some of the executive orders he'd issued since taking office. His political opposition had consistently accused his administration of breaking the law. Though the courts said otherwise.

Frank Knox could see that Roosevelt was attempting to justify this in his mind. "In cases of such moral dilemmas, I sometimes ask myself what T.R. would do in such a case," he said, good-naturedly.

Roosevelt came out of his little reverie for just a moment and smiled at the mention of his cousin. "Oh, I think I know exactly what Theodore would do. He'd grab his old Winchester, put his boots on, and head out the door. Teddy didn't care much for bullies." And in that light, the pieces in his head began to come together.

Where there's a will, there's a way.

"Hmm." It was Secretary Vinson. He leaned forward. "I agree with Averell," he said. "It's one thing to send American soldiers into combat without Congressional approval, it's quite another to provide aid and assistance to a nation whose survival is in the best interests of the United States of America. Since the survival of the British Empire and its dominions would lead to a more stable world, and one more aligned with democracy, then its continued existence is in our national interests." He held his hands up, his palms out. "Far be it for this old legislator to tell the executive branch how to surpass Congress – legally –" he grinned. "But I think there's more than one leg to stand on here. I think we're on solid ground with this."

Roosevelt smiled at him. "Seems like you've been giving this some thought, Carl?"

"Maybe, Mister President, maybe," he replied with a chuckle. "But I'm not exaggerating when I say that as President of the United States, the Constitution does give you broad authority to use whatever means are at your disposal in order to keep the country safe."

"Both Germany and Japan represent a clear and present danger to that security," Knox added to that. "I agree, Mister President."

The room became so suddenly silent that one could hear the evening wind blowing the shrubs outside the window. The President became thoughtfully relaxed, giving credence to the words here today.

"Clear and present danger," he mumbled just loud enough for them to hear him. "I wonder how many other future Presidents might use those exact words to justify action."

"Extraordinary times, Mister President," Knox said reassuringly.

"Extraordinary indeed. Alright, Averell. Let's see where this train takes us. Tomorrow I'll run this through Justice. I agree that we're on solid legal ground here, but it wouldn't hurt to have their stamp of approval on it. You'll be off to England in a couple of days, but it wouldn't hurt to put all your notes and memos together on this subject. I think you'll be a good addition to Churchill's circle. He hates Joe Kennedy, but I feel that he'll like you. And he'll value your opinions, so don't be afraid to share them with him. We here'll put this thing together in the meantime. Seems like the Speaker and I will have much to discuss, so I guess I should invite him to dinner tomorrow. Carl, I'd like you to reach out to some of your old colleagues in Congress, particularly the more conservative ones. It wouldn't hurt to have some support from them as well." Vinson nodded. "Alright then, gentlemen. Let's get to work."

President Roosevelt wheeled himself out from behind his desk. Harriman, Vinson, and Knox rose up and gathered their belongings together. Roosevelt wished Vinson and Knox a good evening. Then he clasped hands with Averell Harriman.

"Averell, if we don't speak before you leave, then I want to wish you good luck."

"Thank you, Mister President."

"I think you're the right man for the job." He patted him on the back of the hand lightly. "When you see Winston, tell him for me, that all of my thoughts and prayers are with him. Tell him that one way or another we won't let England go. Tell him that."

CHAPTER EIGHTEEN

The pilot's club was solemnly quiet when Sharp entered through the flapping double doors. There were only a handful of pilots in there having a drink, reading a book, or smoking a pipe. Whatever it was that got them through the hell that they'd been put through. Some soft music was playing in the backroom behind the bar.

Christopher ran his hand through his hair and leaned up against the end of the makeshift bar. The bartender, an enlisted man who clerked for some air commodore or some such thing, made his way down to him, apron around his waist and towel draped over his shoulder.

"Evening, sir. Drink for you?"

Sharp rubbed his sore cheekbones then replied, "Brown ale, please."

"Coming right up, sir," the man answered and walked back toward the taps.

Sharp took a brief look around the room. There couldn't have been more than a dozen people here. Normally, after a long day, half the pilots on base would have been gathered here for some well-deserved downtime. But they'd taken such a pasting this afternoon that he wasn't surprised that so few pilots were here this evening. But, everyone was entitled to a free drink after every fight. The bartender returned a moment later with the frothy ale.

"Thank you," Sharp told him and dropped a wooden coin on the bar along with a couple of pence for the man.

"Thank you, sir."

Two of the other pilots at the end of the bar nodded a greeting to Sharp that he returned.

"Sir," a voice called over from the lounge part of the makeshift club. Between two wooden pillars was an area set up as a sitting area with leather chairs and a couch. Pilots often looking for a quiet area to just sit and enjoy a few restful minutes would often go there rather than sit up at the bar or at one of the small tables dotted throughout.

Sharp picked up his drink and made his way over. Lieutenant Davries, one of his, was sitting in one of the luxurious cushioned chairs, sipping on an ale of his own. He started to stand up at Sharp's approach, but Christopher quickly waved him back down.

Today had been an ordeal and Sharp wasn't much in the mood for protocol. 239 Squadron had gone up today to meet a flock of German bombers heading toward the Bristol Channel. Forty or fifty bombers escorted by a wing of the newer Focke-Wulf that had just been introduced. Reports on the new German aircraft had been mostly accurate enough, if not a bit conservative. The truth was the new fighter was incredibly versatile. Ten of them had been present during today's encounter, against six of Sharp's Hurricanes. And it had not gone well for the RAF. Despite a valiant effort, and an assist from 87 Squadron, they'd only managed to shoot down half a dozen enemy bombers and a single fighter, compared to three of his planes shot down with one pilot KIA. The Luftwaffe bombers managed to push through and hit the dockyard at Bristol. Not a good day.

"Evening, sir," Davries greeted him. Sharp nodded quickly to him then looked over at the man sitting in the chair next to him. The other man was dressed in a drab green service coat and lighter color trousers. Some service ribbons were pinned to his chest, as opposed to sewn in like RAF officers and silver bars sat atop his shoulders.

He had a gracious smile on his face and gave a friendly nod to Sharp as he took a seat across from the two men.

"Davries." Sharp nodded back to the stranger.

"Sir, allow me to introduce you to Lieutenant Harkins. Recently arrived from Plymouth." Sharp's forehead creased at the pronunciation of the other man's rank.

"Loo?" Sharp asked after taking a small sip of his ale. "Not leftenant?"

The other man smiled back and ran his fingers up and down the icy glass sitting on the table next to him.

"No, sir. Loo-tenant." He replied.

"American?"

"Yes, sir," Harkins replied.

Sharp sighed and gave the younger man an appraising look. He was a few years younger than Sharp and had the eyes of a man who had something he was trying to prove. His gaze fell to the silver wings on his uniform breast.

"Pilot, Lieutenant Harkins?" He inquired.

"Yes, sir. United States Army."

"Has America entered the war on our side?" Sharp inquired lightheartedly and took another drink.

"No, sir," Harkins laughed. "Just part of a cooperative commitment." He picked up his glass, filled with a dark-brown drink and iced cubes. "The Army sent a few of us over here to help train some of you RAF guys on our planes." He took a sip and winced as he swallowed. "So here I am. Fresh off the boat."

Sharp bit slightly on his lower lip. "Fresh off the boat and you managed to find the single pub on post?" His eyes drifted around the room then back to Harkins. He tried to give the other man a friendly grin, but the stress of today was just under his skin. Harkins pouted and shifted uncomfortably in his chair. "Apologies, Lieutenant. I didn't mean to suggest anything. It's just... today's been a tough one."

"I understand, sir," Harkins replied, and exchanged a quick look with Davries.

"The lieutenant is training some of our boys on those..." he lost the word, "What do you call them again?"

"Aircobras," Harkins answered.

"Yes. American built fighter planes. RAF purchased a lot of them. Bunch of Yanks come over to help train on them."

"Oh. I see," Sharp said. "Well, God knows we need all the fighters we can get our hands on. So, Lieutenant Harkins. Where does the US Army have you stationed?"

"I'm on detached assignment right now, out of Long Island. That's in New York. But my duty assignment is at Hickam Field in Honolulu?"

"Honolulu?" Sharp inquired and shook his head.

"Hawaii, sir," Davries told him. "Used to be called the Sandwich Islands." Sharp instantly nodded his understanding.

"So the Pacific then?" Sharp asked and Harkins nodded. "Interesting place to put an Army airfield isn't it? On an island surrounded by water."

Harkins chuckled. "Well, sir, isn't that what Britain is? An island surrounded by water?"

Sharp sat silent for a moment. He found the American to be a bit on the naïve side but decided that the intensity of the day was partly to blame for his demeanor. The younger American pilot surely wasn't to blame for the edge that everyone was feeling right now. He brushed it off.

"So, you've just arrived in England. What do you think of our country? Not exactly the best time for a visit is it?"

"Hmm. Well, Captain, I've only been here for a couple of days now. But from what I've seen so far, I have to say that I'm a lot more impressed now."

"Really? Impressed how?"

Harkins downed another sip and shrugged his shoulders. "Well, the only news we get over in the States is over the radio, or short newsreels in movie houses. Doesn't show a very good picture. But, having seen some things since I've been here already, I gotta say that it wasn't like I thought it would be. The people here have a determination. Coming from the States, it's not like anything I've ever really seen before. Considering what you Brits are going... Excuse me. What you folks are going through, it's incredible."

Sharp studied the American for a few seconds as he slowly downed more of his brown ale. Despite the younger man's lack of worldly experience, he found this Harkins fellow strangely entertaining.

"Yes," he replied to Harkins, the slightest grin touching his face. "Well, we Brits can do amazing things when we set ourselves to task." Harkins raised his glass in the air in salute and Sharp followed suit.

"Yeah. You're some tough nuts to crack," Harkins commented, Davries laughed. "What about you, sir? Seen action before now?"

Davries spoke up first. "The Squadron Leader is one of the few pilots around here who saw action in Poland. Three kills." He drank his own ale down generously.

"Really?" Harkins sounded impressed. He wiped his mouth with the back of his hand and leaned slightly forward in his chair. "What was that like if you don't mind my asking? We hear all the time that those Nazi pilots are pretty good."

Sharp looked back at him. He was an audacious kid for sure, and naïve as all hell. He studied him and thought for a moment whether or not he wanted to knock him on his young ass or not. Maybe it was just the stress and the alcohol. He exhaled and let it go.

"Plenty of my mates were shot down by those Nazi pilots," Sharp replied. "So I guess they must be pretty good. I'll tell you this, Lieutenant. Anyone who doesn't respect the pilots they fly against up there is in for a damn short life. Damn short. This is a messy business. Messy business indeed. Just ask your new friend here, he'll tell you." He looked at Davries. "You've been in now what, six months, Davries?" The other man nodded. "Five combat sorties under his belt. Two confirmed kills. But this nonsense has a way of knocking the bravado out of those seeking some sort of glory." His words came out snappishly.

Harkins sank back, and sat motionless, cradling his drink. Sharp had not intended to sound harsh but couldn't help himself. This week's death toll alone was enough to drive anyone to frayed nerves. Three of his pilots dead, three more hospitalized, and replacements were becoming scarce for Fighter Command. Then there was the civilian casualties, probably the worst part of it all. Every home destroyed, every bomb dropped on England was a failure on their part. It wasn't the American's fault, and he knew that. The kid was just so...

... Well. It didn't matter.

"What are you drinking, Lieutenant?" Sharp asked politely.

Harkins held up his nearly empty glass. "Scotch, sir."

Sharp waved over at the bartender then finished off the rest of his own drink.

"If I seem a little cross, I don't mean to be. We've just had it tough these last few days." The bartender approached. "The next round's on me."

"Of course." The bartender took the empty glasses and made his way back behind the bar.

Sharp let out a loud exhale, reached into his pocket and drew out his Pall Malls. He offered one to Harkins and Davries, who both accepted, then lit them up with his lighter. Harkins looked every bit the Yankee flyboy that he'd heard of. A young, brown-haired man with good, sharp features. He imagined that the man was popular with the ladies. But his fingers were raw looking, and his eyes were keen. Sharp figured that he spent a lot of time in a cockpit. Since he'd been given a special assignment to England to train RAF pilots on

American-built fighters, he assumed Harkins was better behind the controls of a plane than he might have initially thought.

"Here we are." The bartender arrived with a tray of drinks. He set one in front of each. Sharp dug into his pocket and put some coins on the tray.

"Let me ask you something, Lieutenant," Sharp said, raising his glass to his mouth. "What do Americans think of what's going on over here?" The question was asked casually.

Harkins took a small sip of his whiskey, then took a few seconds before answering. "Well, sir. I suppose most of us feel like we should be doing more to help out. We're not fond of those Nazi sons-of-bitches. Pardon the language, sir."

Sharp shrugged. "We're not too fond of the Nazi sons-of-bitches either, Lieutenant. But what I meant was... does your average Joe, as you say, have any real idea of what's going on? Outside of movie houses and short newsreels, I mean. Do you understand the gravity of the situation and the stakes at play?"

Harkins ran his finger up and down the icy glass. He gave Sharp an almost embarrassed look. Finally, he just shook his head.

"No, sir," he replied.

Sharp gave him an approving look that said he appreciated the direct honesty.

"I have to tell you, sir. Probably most of the guys back at Hickam don't either. Or anyone else in the service. Maybe the generals and admirals do, but not the rest of us. I don't know. It's not like we've suffered through these kinds of things." Sharp gave him an inquisitive look. "What I mean is: we haven't had to fight a war like this. Not for a while anyhow. Civilians being targeted, towns bombed, all that is just beyond what we can imagine. Maybe we're spoiled. I can certainly see how some might see things that way." He tipped his glass and took a sip, but he kept his eyes on Sharp.

Sharp let the words sink in. "Well... I've been put in my place."

"It's helpful to have two very large oceans on either side of your country," Davries added.

"Well, there's more to it than that," Harkins replied, swallowing another sip of the whiskey. "I'll be the first to admit that we, as Americans, can be quite –" he hated using the word, "– sheltered at times. I mean, we've got it made in a lot of ways. I'm from a pretty quiet corner of the country originally, but most of my time nowadays is spent in Honolulu or New York City. We've got everything right at the end of our fingertips, and there seems to be no end to what we can produce. So we'll never run out of anything." He took a long swallow. "Even during the Depression, with the long lines of guys waiting around for work, things were never so bad. FDR comes along, makes sure every family can feed itself, keep the heat on in winter. Even then we didn't have to worry about bombs falling on our heads. When I drove in today, we could see smoke in the distance. The Germans hit it this morning, I guess. Somebody's village got burned down to the ground..." He didn't go on, just shook his head.

'Well," Sharp began, "the unfortunate business of war. The part of it that the poets don't seem to get right. Well – Shakespeare perhaps. Everyone here heard the stories from our fathers or uncles, of 1914 and '15. The Somme, the trenches, the long weeks spent just trying to keep warm, and the Hun out. As horrible as that war was, this one is even worse. We see it every day in the eyes of the old veterans, our superiors who fought that war. No, this time we're in it for our very lives. There's a madness that's infected Europe." He drank generously after that.

Harkins didn't answer, only grimaced, and shared in a drink. His uncle had gone over to France with old General Pershing and the American Expeditionary Force. He'd only ever hinted at what he'd experienced during that war, but even as a kid Johnny could see that it had been a traumatic ordeal. Every American who grew up after those years learned that the war, the so-called War to End All Wars, had been a devastating event. Maybe it was that reason that Americans didn't want to get involved in another such conflict.

"So you came directly from the Sandwich – I mean, Hawaii, did you?" Sharp asked, and Harkins shook his head.

"No, sir. Long Island, New York."

"Of course. Still, a long flight from Hawaii to New York. I hope the Army gave you some leave time."

Harkins grinned and nodded. "Yes, sir. Got a week. Spent it in the city. Manhattan, that is."

Sharp's eyes widened. "Manhattan," he repeated back to him, in an almost envious voice. "Family there?"

"Uh... no, sir. But..." he trailed off, gave a short shrug.

"Lady friend?" Sharp guessed, drawing a smile from Harkins.

"Yes, sir. Someone."

Sharp grinned lightly. He was beginning to warm to this American. A bit of a cocky one, Harkins, but he could pick up on something else underneath the exterior. There was just something behind the other's eyes that reminded Sharp momentarily of a younger version of himself. He laughed at the thought.

"You, sir?" Harkins inquired.

"Me?" Sharp replied. He sighed in mild amusement that the younger man would ask. But, he supposed that all was fair. "Divorced," he replied. He held up his left hand. There was a hint of pale skin around his ring finger. "Marriage doesn't do when your husband is stationed on the other side of the world."

"Oh. Sorry, captain. I didn't mean to pry."

"It's group leader actually," Davries told Harkins. He glanced at Sharp, then back to Harkins. "Though, I suppose if this was the Army, he'd be a major."

"Captain is fine," Sharp replied. "Technically, I'd be a captain anyhow. My promotion still hasn't been signed off on." He took one last gulp of his ale and put the empty glass on the small table next to him.

"I'm afraid that I've had quite the day today. So... if you'll both excuse me." He pushed himself up from his chair. Harkins and Davries both stood up respectfully. "I've got a report to file. Tomorrow's another day."

"Good evening, sir," Davries said.

"Good evening," Sharp told him, then turned to Harkins, and extended a hand. "Pleasure meeting you, Lieutenant." The two shook hands. "Welcome to England."

CHAPTER NINETEEN

Jock Colville was already standing outside of Windsor Castle when the Prime Minister emerged. A footman held open the door as Churchill emerged, putting his distinctive bowler hat back on as he exited. He slowly walked the twenty paces to where Jock was standing, his walking stick moving with his feet, the gravel crunching under his shoes. It had been a long lunch meeting with the king. Longer than usual, and the expression on Colville's face seemed almost concerned.

"Did everything go alright, sir?" Colville asked him delicately. "You were in there longer than planned."

Churchill grumbled, reached into his breast pocket, pulled a Cuban out, then searched his other pockets for his lighter. Colville pulled his own out instead and flicked it. Winston bit the end off and spit it out then puffed the stogie to life. He motioned for the two to continue on to the car that was parked and waiting for them.

"Aside from his briefing, the king had several other concerns that he wished to discuss," Winston told him, looking up at the cloudy skies. "Things of a more personal nature."

"Oh. May I inquire, sir?"

Winston paced himself on the walk down the brick walkway. Large lunches tended to slow him down.

"He's worried, as any father would be," Winston replied lightly. "Concerned for the safety of his family. I tried to reassure him that they were as safe as any other in the country. Probably safer." He puffed on his cigar. "But he's considering removing himself."

"Removing himself?" Colville asked stunned. "To where, sir?"

"Canada, possibly." Winston coughed slightly. "He feels that having a monarch, even one in exile, would be better for the nation, and the Commonwealth, than no monarch at all."

Jock's eyes fluttered at the suggestion, and Winston heard him give off a tiny sigh. Jock was an excellent private secretary, as well as a devout monarchist. Churchill knew that the man would never discuss any of his private conversations with others. His professionalism and character wouldn't allow for it. If word spread that King George was considering leaving the country, it could well cause panic.

"Canada," Jock whispered. "He's the father of the nation – the empire!" He shook his head ever-so-slightly. "What would Britons think if he removed himself to Canada or Australia?"

The driver of Churchill's private Humber Pullman opened the rear door and stood waiting for the two men to get in.

"Well, he must do as he feels is fit for his own," Winston told him as the two reached the limo.

"I understand, but..." Jock paused for a moment. "No monarch in the country? It's never before happened. What would we be then?"

Churchill took the cigar out of his mouth and looked at him. "I suppose that would make us a republic," Winston replied jokingly, then stepped into the rear seat.

"A republic!" Colville could hear Winston chuckling at him, then stepped into the car beside him. "Flies in the face of everything British."

The door closed behind him and the driver, Reginald got back behind the wheel, pulling away from the palace. Winston pulled out the ashtray he'd had built into the car and knocked away the ash tip of his cigar, then rolled the window down just enough to let the smoke out. Beside him, Jock was holding a file. He held it open for the Prime Minister to look at.

"What's this?"

"Tommy Thompson's report. He came by an hour ago and left it with me."

"Important?"

Colville handed it to him to look at. "Mostly after-action reports from Fighter Command. Some general notes from the IGS. The American destroyers finally arrived, as well as North Africa." He cleared his throat. "There was some rather distressing news, however. It's on page eight."

Churchill exhaled smoke out through the cracked window. He flipped to that page, mouthing the words silently as he read. It hit him like a brick as soon as he saw what Jock was referring to. His heart seemed to come to a stop, and his whole body went numb.

"My God," he said in a tone so distraught that for a brief moment Jock thought that he was sobbing.

The report from the Royal Navy had come in within only the last few hours, and it had been confirmed. A ship carrying children from London had been torpedoed on the high seas, on the crossing to North America. A U-boat had caught them just a hundred miles off the Irish coast, sending the ship loaded with civilians fleeing the bombing, down with no survivors. Over two hundred children had been lost. The vessel had sunk so fast that the escorting Royal Navy ships had not been able to rescue anyone. Page nine of the report included a ship's manifest. Winston looked at it. His stomach turned inside-out when he saw the names and ages of the dead.

"Two years old," he mumbled. "My God." He could feel Jock's eyes on him. His eyes watered a little and he turned his head away, blocking Colville from seeing him wipe his eyes. It was the terrible business of war to lose people, but nothing made war worse than the killing of children. The fact that it had been a German U-boat firing a torpedo from a distance meant nothing to him. So far as he was concerned it was like shooting them in the open.

"I'm sorry, Prime Minister," Colville said in a comforting voice. Winston looked back at him and forced a small smile.

"I'll wish to meet with the parents of some of the deceased. Do we know if they've all been contacted yet?"

"Not yet, sir."

Winston gave him back the report. He sat quietly for a few minutes in the back seat, piping on his cigar. They'd tried to evacuate as many children as they could out of the cities. Sometimes even out of the country if possible. Ireland had refused to give shelter. Perhaps they'd be willing to reconsider that policy after this tragedy.

The drive from Windsor to Westminster took just under an hour, and Churchill and Colville had discussed a bevy of topics after he shook away the sad news. Londoners were out in droves today. The roadways were lined with makeshift shelters and sandbag walls. There were soldiers and policemen out on every corner it seemed, but he saw the faces of the ordinary citizenry as they drove by. They were smiling, greeting one another on the sidewalks, everything that they would normally do if there had not been a war on. It gave him some comfort to see it this way.

Tommy Thompson was waiting at the front door of Number 10 Downing when they pulled up. He opened the door for him and helped Churchill exit.

"Afternoon, sir," Thompson greeted him. "I hope your lunch with the King went well." Churchill nodded. "The Cabinet officials are waiting for you in your study. Air Chief Marshal Dowding is with them. Mrs. Churchill is entertaining them, and you've got tea with the Lord Privy Seal this afternoon. I've also set up the telephone call for you with the Foreign Minister at five-fifteen. Also, sir, General Giraud once again reached out. He was quite agitated that his previous calls have gone unanswered."

Winston scowled. He'd put the French general on the back burner for quite some time now. Since the surrender, he'd been very vocal about getting official recognition from the British government. His multiple radio addresses since then had repeatedly bashed the Vichy government as completely illegitimate and was trying desperately to rally support to his own cause. Very few had.

"I think you'll have to handle him sooner or later, sir," Jock Colville told him. The three men strolled into the residence. Colville took Churchill's hat, and Thompson escorted him into the study.

The wooden oak door opened, and Winston strode across the room. Clementine was sitting at the round wooden table, sipping on a cup of tea. The others stood up as the Prime Minister entered. Present were First Lord of the Admiralty, A.V. Alexander, Minister of Supply, Lord Beaverbrook, Air Chief Marshal Dowding, and Herbert Morrison, the Home Secretary. Winston bent over and pecked Clementine on the cheek.

"Good afternoon, gentlemen," he said warmly and shook hands with Lord Beaverbrook. "Either you're early, or I'm late. My money says the latter."

Clementine stood up and gave them a genuine smile. "I very much hope I was good company for you all. I'll leave you to your affairs now." Winston took her hand, kissed it gently, and she walked out of the room.

"Apologies for my tardiness. The King had some personal matters he wanted to discuss. Please." He sat at the round table and everyone else followed suit. Tommy Thompson, dressed in his naval uniform, sat down in a chair between one of the tall bookcases and the door. "I suppose you've all heard the dreadful news about the *SS Kingston*?" Heads nodded.

"Terrible tragedy," the First Lord commented.

"We can only pray that this will be an isolated incident," Winston said, but he knew it wouldn't be. "So, A.V., I understand those American ships arrived."

"Yes," he replied dispassionately. "Though I'm not sure I would say arrived intact. Not much more than hulls with engines. They've been completely gutted, top to bottom, and several of them barely limped into port, their hulls are so corroded. The really bad ones will be transferred to Belfast. Others, the ones we deem a bit more serviceable, will get the speedy treatment. We'll install some basic equipment, depth charges, and all that, then put them out on submarine patrol. God knows that's where we need them most."

There was unanimous agreement around the table. U-boats were sinking merchant vessels left and right, and there was a severe shortage of smaller ships to combat them. Shipyards were working around the clock to build more, but they weren't planning to see any significant number of new ships roll out until early next year. That put the country in a tight pinch.

"With *Glorious* out of the water for repairs, and *Repulse* reassigned to the Mediterranean Sea, we'll also have some gaps in the North Sea. Should a German heavy ship try to sneak away into the North Atlantic, we might not be able to do anything about it. I certainly cannot reassign another one of our other carriers for the time being. It would mean cutting down on other commitments."

Churchill understood perfectly. He'd green-lit an operation in the Mediterranean that was going to require the presence of several of the Royal Navy's carriers. But that was a classified matter, and not everyone present had been cleared to know it.

"And we still must keep a sizeable force in the Far East," Winston added, drawing an instant agreement from the First Lord.

"Yes. With the redeployment of troops from Singapore, we'll need to keep a deterrent out there. In fact, on that note, I'm planning on having a special reviewing officer dispatched shortly. He's with Operations. I want a full review of our naval assets in the Indian and Pacific Oceans. As well as a threat assessment from the Japanese. I don't want to get caught with our pants down out there, while we're dealing with matters here."

"Any officer in particular?" Winston inquired.

"Why yes. After speaking with Operations, they've recommended that Chadwick fellow." Churchill's eyes squinted as he tried to place the name. "He was the submarine commander who helped catch the *Admiral Graf Spee.* He's been assigned to the Naval Planning Office. From what I hear he's making quite the impression over there."

"Chadwick," Winston repeated after recognizing the man's name. "Isn't he just a lieutenant commander?"

"Yes."

"Well, I think that the commanders in Singapore might disapprove of someone so junior on the scale from conducting a review of their assets."

The First Lord blinked, then shrugged. "I suppose we could bump him up to full commander. I'll ask personnel to look into it. So long as he has time in rank, I guess I don't see the problem."

"Get him out there as soon as humanly possible," Winston ordered. "I'd like a bottom-up review. Anything else?" The First Lord shook his head no. "Lord Beaverbrook."

The Minister of Supply looked at the short list he'd brought with him. "Continuing to provision the Army, and get it back on its feet after Boulogne and Dunkirk. We've got enough new equipment to properly provision two infantry and two armored divisions, and make them deployable should the need arise. Within a fortnight, we'll have another four divisions provisioned. That'll bring the strength of the evacuated expeditionary force up to just about forty percent. Additionally, according to the General Staff, the entire First Canadian Corps and the Ninth Australians have arrived fully. We've also got somewhere in the vicinity of twenty-thousand Indian soldiers that have arrived in Portsmouth in the past week and a half. We need to expand our warehouse capacity in Wales and Scotland to support future units arriving. I think that by the beginning of September, we'll be putting out enough from our factories to have replaced most of the losses we incurred."

"The Air Force?"

Lord Beaverbrook waved his hand. "More than enough planes, just not enough pilots. We've got fighters sitting around fields that haven't even been flown yet. Although, our bomber losses in France, covering the evacuation, did cost us. We won't have a substantial number of replacements until. . ." he thought about it, ". . . the end of the year perhaps."

Winston coughed on his cigar smoke at the disappointing news. He'd had no choice but to deploy those bombers in order to stall the German advance on Boulogne, giving the expeditionary force the time it needed to evacuate from the continent. But it had cost them dearly, and now, with so few of the aircraft left, they had no offensive arm to use against German targets.

"And the other thing? What we discussed yesterday?" Churchill inquired.

"Ah, yes." Lord Beaverbrook hesitated for a moment, looking quickly around the table. "We've inventoried our supply of chemical weapons, and I've ordered their disbursement to safe locations around the country. As per your instructions, Prime Minister, they'll only be employed if given the order directly by you."

A soft murmur went around the small table.

"I'll tell all of you here and now, that should there become a necessity to employ our stockpile of mustard gas, I shall not, for one moment, hesitate to order it," Churchill told them, getting a series of reluctant nods. "It's a difficult decision, but the alternative would be to allow the German Army a foothold on our island. That, none of us here can allow."

"Hopefully, it won't come to it," Lord Beaverbrook said softly. "That's all I have, sir."

"I've asked Air Chief Dowding to be here today. I thought it important that we get a handle on the situation in the skies." Churchill motioned to Dowding.

"Well, as the Minister of Supply has said, we have plenty of aircraft, and new ones coming out of factories every day. However, I cannot, CANNOT, stress enough the need for additional, trained pilots. I'm sorry for sounding like such a broken record, but this is a problem that we've been confronting since the war began. Prime Minister Chamberlain did much to improve our aircraft production, which is good on one front, along with the losses we incurred in France, as was said before, we have more fighter planes than we have men to fly them. We've cut down on training hours just to fill cockpits, but sooner or later, we're going to need bodies. A lot of them." He opened up a leather-bound book and read some numbers. "We have six hundred twenty-two pilots from occupied nations, mostly Poles, Czechs, and Frenchmen. We've been keeping them in reserve for the most part, and not assigned them to front-line units. I plan to now countermand that policy." Again there was some small grumbling from others.

Lord Beaverbrook shifted uncomfortably in his seat. "Don't you worry about their lack of training? And, quite frankly, their lack of understanding of basic English?"

Dowding nodded. "I do. That's why I'm having them all put through training on our Hurricanes and Spitfires. Even a week's worth of flight time can give them the basics they need. And honestly, some of them flew in Poland. Nothing like our planes, but they're not wet behind the ears. Some have seen real combat. They'll also have to attend classes in basic English. We can assign some of the French-Canadian pilots to serve with the French, to act as interpreters.

In fact, we should be able to activate three additional squadrons almost immediately that way. We have the aircraft, and we're going to need them in the air. Things are only getting worse.

"Every intelligence report that I've read about Luftwaffe operations, seems to suggest they have huge numbers of reserves. In the past two weeks alone we've suffered higher losses, particularly in the south and southwest of England. The Luftwaffe commander, Udet, has shifted his tactics, and it's caused real gaps to begin to form. Waves of fighters engaging our pilots, succeeded by larger, more focused bombing groups, followed up by dive bomber strikes on critical infrastructure, have simply stretched us to our limit." He looked down at the words scribbled out in large print, then brought his attention back to them. "Gentlemen, if that keeps up, we could be looking at a full-scale collapse of the Royal Air Force in southern England in less than thirty days."

He emphasized the word collapse, then let his language sit out there. The ministers looked at each other and instantly a torrid of excited talk went up. It ended when Winston tapped the table with the palm of his hand.

"You must do whatever is necessary," Winston said to Dowding. "You have the fullest support of the Cabinet, and me. Your position makes you responsible for the aerial defense of the country, so I expect you to do just that, by any means necessary."

"Understood, sir," Dowding replied.

"I'm afraid we're going to have to wrap this up shortly," Winston said, gazing at the clock on the wall. His meeting with King George seemed to have set him back farther than he realized. "I have a radio address to prepare for, and the Lord Privy Seal will be arriving shortly." He looked at Herbert Morrison. "Herbie?"

The Home Secretary adjusted his glasses. "Won't take long, Prime Minister. I wish to report on the recruitment of volunteer firefighters. We've seen a notable increase in volunteers these past few days, but we are nowhere near where I'd like to see the number. Particularly in London. The damn Germans have so far steered clear of the city, but as Home Secretary, I can't risk not being prepared in case. Londoners have been remarkably well trained in the use of the underground for shelters, but should the city proper be hit with bombs, fires could rage out of control. I'll be appealing for additional volunteers.

"Furthermore, it's of the bombing civilians that I want to make my next point. It's the opinion of a great number of my staff that we should discontinue school services in Greater London." Winston's eyes widened at the suggestion. "Until further notice."

"Call off schooling?" Lord Beaverbrook sniffed at the statement. "Has it come to that?"

"I believe it has, Max," Morrison answered. "Consider what just happened to the *Kingston*. It won't be popular, I understand that. If it becomes too unpopular, and there's a backlash, then I'll accept responsibility and tender my resignation. But after careful consideration, I believe that this is the best option."

Winston smoked on his cigar for a minute, thinking on the subject, thinking of the boatload of children who'd died aboard the *Kingston*. Then he leaned forward and pointed two fingers at the Home Secretary.

"I'll give it serious consideration," he told Morrison. "You're right when you say it won't be popular, but I don't wish to have to see the bodies of deceased boys and girls on the front page of the newspapers either. I believe it's unavoidable as it is. Anything else?"

"One last thing. We've had a number of refugees come in from North Africa recently. Not many, but their arrival has caused a bit of a stir. I've had reports of some confrontations between them and our own citizens. I think it may suit us to not take certain people in at this time." He shut up abruptly. He was met by stares from those around him.

"What's the nature of these confrontations?" Winston asked.

"It revolves around their religion, sir. They're mostly Jewish or Muslim. Some of the people are, uh, a bit suspicious of their practices. My office has gotten several complaints from local officials."

"Good Lord," Beaverbrook muttered. His personal feelings toward Jews were quietly known.

Churchill looked over quickly at Tommy Thompson. His military aide sat quietly against the wall and subtly rolled his eyes at the comment. Winston had no desire whatsoever to broach the subject of religious refugees seeking shelter. He genuinely felt for any people who'd had to endure subjugation and repression. Many in his Cabinet, however, and in Parliament, had different views on the matter. He was amongst some of them now.

He cleared his throat. "I will not, at this time, prevent any minority, religious or otherwise, from reaching these shores. I believe, as I think most Britons do, that we have an obligation to take in the most oppressed, and repressed people trying to flee tyranny. I don't believe we should cater to the most... unchristian-like behavior. This country has always had a segment of its population adhering to foreign religious beliefs. Why should now be any different?" Nobody rose a voice in disagreement. "I'm sure, if there are some who don't wish to patronize foreign populations, then there are those who will. Let us turn our attention to more pressing matters."

Just then the clock in the corner began to chime. Tommy Thompson stood up and Winston gave a curt nod of dismissal to the group. Some small words were exchanged between them on the way out. Winston clasped Morrison's hand as the Home Secretary made his way out of the room, and he thanked Churchill for his time.

"Whew," he finally said as soon as the door had closed behind the last of them. Thompson was already putting the details of his next briefing in front of him. "You'd think we'd be beyond all of this by now." He snipped the end off of his chewed-up cigar. He looked at Thompson. "Are you a religious man, Tommy?"

"The service is my religion, sir," the other man answered, and it drew a laugh from Churchill.

"Good answer. A good religion it is too. Pour me a Scotch please." Thompson nodded and went toward the cabinet that housed the liquor. "Sometimes it feels to me like we're back in the fifteenth century. Oh well." Thompson topped the Scotch off with a little soda and put the glass down in front of the Prime Minister. "I suppose, I really should give the French general the courtesy of a phone call." He drank down some of the Johnnie Walker and looked at Thompson who stood nodding his head. "I believe we may need to reevaluate the French situation. Put him on my schedule as soon as possible. I'd like to take a few minutes before the Lord Privy Seal arrives to do a little praying of my own."

"For victory, sir?" Thompson asked him good-naturedly.

"For a little common sense in my fellow Englishman."

CHAPTER TWENTY

General Udet paced back and forth in his personal office, smoking on his third cigarette of the day, occasionally ceasing to sip on the dark cup of coffee that had turned lukewarm. Since coming to France he'd developed an appreciation for the local cigarettes here. Given the increasing prices of the German brands, it was no wonder. But prices aside, he did prefer the more aromatic Turkish tobacco over that of the blander, German tobacco, which mostly came out of Ukraine and Poland.

His office had previously belonged to the general manager of the lodge that was now his headquarters. The former manager had been allowed to remain on after the occupation but was now occupying a much less significant office on the kitchen level. Udet didn't much care about the size or grandeur of his office, given what he'd had in Berlin, but appearances were important in today's Wehrmacht. Both Göring and Hitler frowned upon their highest-ranking officers taking anything but the finest establishments as their field headquarters. Which was probably why so many in the Wehrmacht had set up their flags in some of the best hotels in Western Europe. But on occasion, Udet longed for the days of the old Imperial German Army, where results, not appearances mattered.

Around the office, his staff was at work. Telephones were ringing, couriers were coming and going. Every so often outside came the winding sounds of propellers, as airplanes were taking off. Everywhere around his headquarters, personnel were getting ready for the arrival of their anticipated guest. They'd only received notice of it just after dawn this morning, just as the first waves of bombers all across northern France were preparing for takeoff. Hermann Göring was once again on his way, and the unexpected visit had caught Udet completely off-guard for once. In addition to the Luftwaffe commander, Field Marshall Rundstedt was also on his way. Though for the life of him, General Udet could not understand why. He knew how Hermann Göring was, and knew that he could be unpredictable at times. But he didn't care for these unannounced visits, and could only assume that it had to do with his change in strategy.

Change in strategy? There was no strategy. He mentally shook his head at the thought. As strong as the Luftwaffe was, as much of an advantage over the enemy as they had, the High Command had routinely squandered that advantage by only vaguely defining the battle they now found themselves in. Various commands had been given the leeway to conduct operations as they saw fit, so long as it led to the destruction of the Royal Air Force. But there'd been no coordination between those commands. Stumpf in Norway, Kesselring in Belgium, and he in France had been allowed to prosecute battle plans as they saw fit. But the targets assigned to them had come directly from Berlin. Normally General Udet would not see a problem with having central authority during battle. Except that Berlin, more specifically, the Führer himself, seemed to be making all of the decisions. A task which the man was unsuited for. But Udet would keep that opinion to himself.

A lone sergeant entered through the open office door, coming to a halt halfway in, and snapped his heels together.

"General, Field Marshal Rundstedt's party just passed the outer gate," he reported.

General Udet sighed. "Very well," he replied, dismissing the sergeant. He looked at his Chief of Staff, Major General Ritter. Both men nodded at one another simultaneously. He upended the last of his lukewarm coffee, then extinguished his cigarette and waved away the rings of smoke in the air. "Well Paul, I suppose we should go meet our unexpected guest."

General Ritter tried to put on a smile, but the nerves in his face couldn't seem to manage. A wound he'd incurred on the Marne years earlier had physically scarred the general, but it hadn't slowed his mind any. He was one of the best staff officers that one could have asked for. Ritter picked up Udet's cap from his empty chair and handed it to him.

"Look at it this way, General," Ritter started to say. "At least we didn't have to drive to Paris. It's not every day that two higher-grade officers come to visit you at your HQ."

Udet exhaled sharply. "Yes. Well, that might be a good sign or not. Perhaps Göring means to sack me. I suppose we'll know soon enough. Make sure the kitchen has some food ready for the Reichsmarschall when he arrives. The man's mood sours quickly if he goes hungry." Ritter chuckled softly, out of the eyes of the other staff.

The day was sunny and bright when the entirety of the command staff stepped outside. A pair of 109s flew just a hundred feet over the building, then ascended skyward. The plane's propellers sent a high-pitched wave over the group. A pair of motorcyclists escorted the black automobile carrying the field marshal, followed by two other cars that would have brought his staff officers along. The guards outside of the lodge held their rifles up in salute.

Field Marshal Gerd von Rundstedt exited his car, followed immediately by a host of other Army officers. He put his cap on, gripped his baton, and ascended the steps.

"Welcome, Field Marshal," Udet greeted, walking to meet the man. They exchanged salutes. Rundstedt smiled and the two men shook hands. "Good to see you again old friend. Congratulations to you."

Rundstedt had just been made commander of all German Army forces west of Germany. It was a good decision on Hitler's part. One of few, so far as Udet was concerned. Rundstedt was not just an excellent, tested battle leader, but his reputation among the General Staff was that he was an even more able administrator. His new position would make him, possibly, the most powerful man in Europe outside of Germany.

"Good to see you. Thank you." Rundstedt began the introductions of his staff, most of whom Udet already knew. His staff was almost twice as large as Udet's was, and this was only a fraction of them.

"I apologize for the hastily thrown-together reception," Udet said to him. "We only just learned of this gathering. I had no foreknowledge."

Rundstedt waved the apology away. "No need to worry, Ernst," he said reassuringly. "I'm only here as a courtesy to the Reichsmarschall. I'm on my way to Tannenberg this afternoon. Göring requested my presence here before I left."

"Oh?" Udet's face went vacant. "I didn't know that you were leaving France. May I ask what about?"

"The Führer has asked for my presence there. I'm to give him a full briefing about Sea Lion." He shook his head. "General Manstein is already there, updating Hitler, but I guess the Führer feels that he needs my direct input on the matter. He's called for a formal briefing on the subject."

"Sea Lion?" It was the codename for the planned cross-channel invasion. "I see. Please, come in." They walked into the grand hallway, their respective staff falling in behind them. "Am I to assume that the Führer has seen fit to approve of the operation?"

"Assume?" The field marshal chuckled lightly. The inside joke being that it was not safe to assume anything when it came to Hitler. "If Manstein has gone through every detail of the plan to Hitler, and he's called for me specifically, then I suppose it's a fair bet that he's leaning toward approval. I know that most of the inner circle is pressing for it. Especially your boss."

Of course, Udet thought with a grin. *The successful invasion of Great Britain would be Hermann's crowning achievement.*

Men came to crisp attention as the group marched through the hallways until they came to Udet's office. Most of the staff had been removed prior to their arrival, and there were only a handful of officers that entered behind them. Field Marshal Rundstedt gazed around the room. Udet's private office looked more like the operations room of most headquarters than an actual functioning space fit for a man of his rank. Everywhere there were maps, status reports, and photographs of British airfields. Shelves full of books were hidden from sight by board after board. When he'd learned of today's visit, General Udet had briefly thought of taking them all down, but then thought twice about it. Upon Göring's arrival, he very much wished for the Reichsmarschall to see for himself just what his planners were telling him did not exist. A little dose of reality every now and again was good for Berlin.

"Please," Udet offered Rundstedt a chair in front of his desk, then took the one beside him.

Rundstedt put his cap and baton on the desk then combed his hair back. "Hitler likes to hear things directly from his most senior commanders," Rundstedt continued. "I guess it gives him a sort of a reprieve when it comes to his making a decision about something. I can't tell you how many times we at the War Ministry were meeting with him in the weeks before Poland. Look how easy that went."

"I'm still unsure why the Reichsmarschall didn't inform us of his visit earlier. Normally he's so studious in his scheduling." He looked at the field marshal, and Rundstedt squinted back at him, then relaxed visibly in understanding.

"I think you're misinterpreting him, Ernst," Rundstedt told him, in a calming tone. "If you're worried about being replaced, I wouldn't be." Udet saw an understanding in his eyes and let out a short, relieving exhale. "Right now, as I understand things, your command has been making more headway than others have been. I only get what I read in reports, but it looks to me like your pilots are making a real dent in the enemy. Between you and I," he leaned in closer so nobody else could hear, "the fat man isn't happy. Kesselring is a favorite of his. But numbers are numbers, and yours are better than his are."

General Udet didn't reply to the remark, but he did feel a bit less apprehensive about things. He'd had a personal relationship with Göring going back years, but he'd felt recently that their relationship wasn't what it used to be. The Reichsmarschall had been here weeks earlier, and Udet hadn't restrained himself when asked for his opinion on certain matters. Calling out Göring's head of intelligence the way that he had, didn't seem to sit well with the Luftwaffe chief. He'd provided Udet with all the aircraft that he'd asked for, but his personal phone calls to Berlin had also gone unreturned.

The two men sat for a while, trading friendly stories back and forth. Both had complimented the other on the seeming success of their commands. Rundstedt was still the hero of the hour for most Germans. The fall of France was continuing to be celebrated in the Fatherland. Though he claimed ignorance of the coup d'état that had so recently taken place in Vichy, he also praised it as a significant victory.

It was sometime just after noon that news of Göring's arrival came, and the entire procession again made their way outside, this time with a full honor guard. The red carpet had indeed been laid out for the man's arrival. Flags were unfurled, and a small band played up *Bomben auf England*, which was becoming quite popular back home.

As per usual, the Reichsmarschall's arrival was full of pomp. There were no less than two score escort vehicles that had arrived. The line of cars stretched around the circular drive, all the way back behind the tree line. Göring's car pulled up in front of the headquarters, and for several minutes had waited in the backseat. Udet and Rundstedt could see him conversing with another officer. It was not unlike Hermann to grandstand, and no doubt he was letting both men know that he was superior to both. Though Rundstedt did not fall under his direct command, both knew well that Göring was a man of image and pageantry. By letting the field marshal stand and wait, he was therefore sending a message about who was in charge.

Finally, an aide opened the door to let Reichsmarschall Göring out. Udet and Rundstedt met him at the bottom of the steps.

"Heil Hitler," Udet said, followed by Rundstedt. Both gave the Nazi Party salute, which Göring returned with a raise of his baton.

"Welcome back, Herr Reichsmarschall," Udet greeted warmly. He looked around Göring's shoulder to see Colonel Schmid was among those officers who'd accompanied him. "It's good to see you."

"General," he replied in an exhausted tone of voice. His face was paler than usual, and his eyes were bloodshot. He gave Udet a brief look, then marched up the steps without waiting. Even Field Marshal Rundstedt seemed surprised by the man's hastiness but fell in beside him.

The Reichsmarschall blew by the line of officers and enlisted men assembled to greet him, and did not so much as acknowledge the cart of snacks waiting in the main corridor. He knew Udet's headquarters and knew exactly which way he wanted to go.

"We're thrilled to see you again so soon," Udet again commented as they strode through the hallway.

"Yes, yes," Göring grumbled back, coughing into his gloved fist. "I'd like to see both of you. I'm not here on a publicity tour." They walked into Udet's office again. Göring stood in the middle of the room, waiting for the others to catch up with him. "I don't believe that we'll need all of you," he told them as more officers tried to enter. "Chiefs of staff only." His words were oddly curt. "Can we get some hot tea in here please?"

"Of course," Udet replied and nodded to a lieutenant standing near the door. He closed the door as he left. In the room were Göring, Rundstedt, Udet, and their respective Chiefs of Staff. The Reichsmarschall coughed again, then dropped into a cushioned chair at the end of a long table.

"It's been a long trip and I'm quite tired," Göring told them. "I apologize for the promptness of my visit. I had not planned on stopping here. But I thought it necessary." His eyes settled squarely on General Udet, and for a moment he thought that Göring was going to erupt in a tirade. "Gerd. I'm sorry to have had to ask you here, but I thought that before you left to meet with the führer, that you should get a bird's eye on the situation. That way you'll be better informed when you meet with the Führer. Ernst. I thought we should discuss some things."

The door flew back open, and a single enlisted man emerged carrying a tray with two pots of hot tea and some cups. He dropped the tray on the table near Göring, then left, closing the door behind him again. Hermann poured himself a steaming cup. Udet stood with his hands behind his back.

"Very well, Reichsmarschall." Udet and Rundstedt took seats across from him, their staff doing the same.

Göring dropped two cubes of sugar and stirred his tea around with a tiny spoon. "I spoke with Kesselring yesterday. He's given me strict assurances that the RAF is close to its breaking point." He took a sip, wincing as he swallowed the hot beverage. "He believes, as do I, that the British are getting close to the end of their rope. That they can no longer realistically contest the skies." He paused. His throat was evidently bothering him, and he took another sip. "I know that you've recently changed your tactics, Ernst. I've gotten reports that say you've scaled down bombing missions. May I ask why?"

Because the RAF is not close to breaking, he thought but instead shrugged innocently. He was tired of this ridiculous line of thinking that so many were attached to.

"Not scaled them down, per se," he replied. "If you've been reading our reports, you'll note that we've been hitting the enemy with all of our strength. As for our tactics," he hesitated briefly. He did not like to hold back. "Our tactics weren't working."

"Go on please."

"For weeks we'd been hitting our assigned targets, but seeing very little in the way of results. RAF pilots come up, engage a few of our bombers, break up their formations, then run. With some exceptions, they've adopted more of a Fabian strategy. Hitting our groups with smaller ones. But they could scramble two or three at a time, hitting us on the way in, and again on the way out. Bombers were barely scratching targets. I could go on."

"The numbers advantage is with you," Göring told him. "You told me six weeks ago that alone should guarantee victory."

Udet held in a laugh. "I said many things six weeks ago. For instance, I spoke of the existence of additional enemy fighter planes. Planes that we were told do not exist. Pardon me, but if we had assumed that to be true, we would have had victory by now." He stopped. He was surprised that Göring didn't seem interested in arguing the point. "I believed then, and I believe now, that the enemy has greater strength than what we were led to believe. I had to adjust our tactics to compensate."

"Please explain these tactics to me."

"Well. It's quite simple actually. Our fighters probe enemy airspace." He threw a glance and a nod over at the map behind his desk. Red arrows indicated recent Luftwaffe flight patterns. "Our own fighters are just as good as theirs are. Their only weakness is that they can only spend limited amounts of time over England before having to withdraw due to their fuel supply. But every time we engage them we wear down their pilots, making them less effective. We then launch our bomber groups, escorted by fighters. Again, our fighters can only last for so long, so while the bomber groups move against their targets, we launch a third wave. Again, our fighters move in, and engage the RAF while they themselves are on the attack. We're using their tactics against them. Any foe that's constantly fending off attacks is vulnerable.

"Instead of hitting a wide array of targets in England, we've narrowed it down to a handful. Airfields, and supply centers mostly. Pardon me, but there is little sense in bombing a factory in England while the airfields they use to attack our bombers are left untouched. No. I've ordered a reduction in daily sorties. But when we do hit them, it hurts. Our fourth and fifth waves are made up of Stuka dive bombers. As you can see, we've knocked out a number of their RDF detection and communications stations along the coast. Reichsmarschall, we are having an effect."

Göring drank his tea and gave him a hard stare. It was difficult to know if he was upset or if it was simply his health, but the man did not look well. Hermann gave the other group of officers sitting quietly an appraising look, then looked back at Udet.

"I promised Hitler that we would have British airspace cleared within weeks of beginning this campaign." Udet leaned back, silently nodding his head. Now he understood. Göring had done what he had always done: over-promised something he realized he couldn't keep. No doubt Hitler was pressing him, wondering where his victory in the sky was. And the Reichsmarschall was getting scared that he might look weak in front of him.

"I understand," Ernst said. "And I believe we can achieve success. In the last few days, we've seen a number of indicators that make me believe this. I could show you reports, but suffice it to say, our kill ratio has increased. Not drastically, but not marginally either. Enemy response time has been slower, our own time above targets longer, and we've successfully hit our intended targets at an increasing rate." He wanted to add the part where neither of the other two Luftwaffe fleets involved had achieved his rate of success, but he didn't wish to step on that land mine. For the first time since taking this command, Hermann Göring was listening to him. Udet had to believe that deep down inside, both he and Kesselring could see the truth of what he was saying.

"Well," Hermann began slowly. "Hitler seems to agree with you. He's been impressed with your results as of late." He bit his lower lip. "But don't believe for a minute that'll last. The führer is a man who demands victory of us." He tapped the side of his chair with a finger. "My visit here today was a surprise to you?" Udet nodded. "Ha. I'm sure some probably thought I was coming to sack you. I won't lie, Ernst. After our last meeting, I did consider it. But now..." he held up his hands. "It looks like you were the best choice after all. You know I originally planned to put Hugo Sperrle in charge out here. I'm not sure he would have been as bold as what you have been. I'm here to tell you personally, that I am, from this point on, placing you in charge of the main thrust. I'll have orders drawn up immediately to have some of our groups in Norway transferred to your command. Other reserves will be drawn from Germany and sent to you. That'll give you all of what you need to get it done."

Udet gave him a grateful nod. "Thank you, sir," was all he said.

"Don't thank me. Give me victory. Now, let's get down to a real debriefing. The Field Marshal will be on his way soon to convince Hitler of the credibility of the plan. Provided the Führer agrees to it, I very much intend to have Sea Lion launch before the end of summer." He stood up from his chair and everyone else followed suit. "Once we control the skies, we can finally knock Britain out of this war. Send that cigar-smoking degenerate to the hell where he belongs."

TAVIAN BRACK

CHAPTER TWENTY-ONE

It was a mostly cloudy night in the skies above the Ligurian Sea. Decent cover for the twelve Blackburn Skuas of 800 Squadron cruising at six thousand feet. The squadron had taken off just after nightfall, and had cloud-hopped its way the nearly three hundred nautical miles they'd come. The dark night skies and the cloud cover had concealed the flight's approach to the Italian coast.

Three air groups had taken off from two carriers, *Ark Royal* and *Illustrious,* and had taken three separate approaches to the Italian mainland. The flight out was a long and dull one, with little but empty sea under a half-moon. But now, looking out the front view from his cockpit, Lieutenant Commander Clifford Sinclair could just barely see the pinpricks of light that marked the coast of northern Italy.

For a long while during the flight, all he could think of was the possibility that his squadron, or the two others on the southern approaches, would be spotted and that the enemy would become alerted to their presence. Thus, the element of surprise would be lost, and the entire attack might well be shredded to pieces. And, of course, that could still happen. But Sinclair kept telling himself that if they had been detected, Italian fighter planes would have pounced on them long before reaching the coast. But so far there'd been absolutely no sign of another aircraft in the skies whatsoever.

"Thank God the Italians don't believe in radar," he said to his rear-seat gunner. The other man, Collinsworth, chuckled back worriedly. Sinclair could hear the nervousness in his laugh.

"Let's hope they don't believe in shooting back either," Collinsworth softly replied, drawing an instant burst of laughter from Sinclair. Those were the first words the man had said since they'd taken off almost three hours earlier. He'd only been with the fleet for a couple of months now, and this was his first combat flight.

800 Squadron had been the last of the attack to take off from their carrier. The other two squadrons were made up completely of the slower Fairey Albacores. The slower-moving biplanes had split off from one another and were moving in on the target by two separate approaches. 824 Squadron, would be coming straight north, up the Italian coastline. 829 Squadron, was heading in from the southwest. Both of those groups had been armed with the Mark Twelve torpedo. 800 Squadron, his group, were coming around from the northwest, each with a five-hundred-pound bomb pinned to their underbellies. All of these groups would then converge on their target from different angles, and release their deadly payloads in successive order.

The target: La Spezia. The naval base in the north of the country was one of only two that housed the majority of the ships in the Italian Navy. And if all went according to plan, would be lit up in the midnight darkness roughly fifteen minutes from now. The plan was to drop enough torpedoes in the water to hopefully cripple a capital ship or two, then drop his squadron's bombs on the shore facilities. It had been bold, and it had been daring, and when Admiral Tovey had told him about the plan, he thought it was crazy. Now, as the flight closed in on the coast of Italy, with hundreds of little lights getting larger and larger in his cockpit view, he recalled some words by Lord Nelson he'd read once. Something about the boldest measures are the safest.

With those words in mind, he nudged his throttle up and took the lead. The other planes of Swallow Flight came in behind his tail.

"Fourteen minutes, Collie," Sinclair said to Collinsworth. "Are you ready?" He was trying to be funny now, but it probably sounded cruel. There must have been something about those in the rear seat being scared out of their wits that gave some sort of perverse pleasure to pilots.

"I hope that whoever's in charge down there is napping," Collinsworth replied, then added, "Sir!"

The cloud cover was still good, with only some small breaks. A fishing boat passed by, followed by a trawler. Their lanterns bobbed up and down as they cut across the night sea. Off to the left, he could see the glow from the lights of Genoa. He reached down, pulling his map out, making sure that the coastline looked right, which it did. The town of Sestri Levante would be dead ahead. After they made landfall, they'd come hard right, straight south until they hit the naval base.

He'd had to admit that when he'd been told of the plan, he give it one chance in twenty of success. Not that Sinclair was a gambling man. But a nighttime attack, against a heavily defended target, deep inside enemy territory, with only thirty-six planes, might be considered madness by some. Now, as they approached, without so much as a single enemy plane sighted, or one round of anti-aircraft fire, it was beginning to look like the odds were taking a turn for the better. Then he began to think of the Light Brigade. Things had started well for them also.

"Seven minutes," he whispered to himself. The strike plan called for radio silence. That meant they were completely out of touch with one another and with the other strike groups. They were operating completely in the dark. If one group got lost or worse, then the other groups would press on without giving away their positions. The drawback being that attacks often went uncoordinated.

"Here we go!" Sinclair said. The flight passed right over the beachline, then banked right. Like some aerial circus, the twelve Blackburn

Skuas followed in column, one after the other with the sea off their right wing. Below them, homes, schoolhouses, cafes, and sleeping families.

He gave the plan one last go-through in his head, then mentally tossed it out. The plan was one thing on paper, but when that first torpedo hit came, and that first explosion on the ground went off, then the plan was as useless as a burnt piece of toast. Sinclair wished that he could draw upon years of experience, but like everyone else, this was his first taste of combat.

And none of them had to wait long. The lights of the Italian naval base were just up ahead, less than twenty miles away, at the bottom of a line of gently rolling hills. He could catch brief glimpses of vehicle lights moving around the perimeter. He found it odd that not a single spotlight was active, nor did there seem to be any air activity in the skies around them.

In the distance, five-thousand feet below, he could see the first planes of 829 Squadron flying off the ocean top like giant gulls. They were only shadows under the moonlight, but he could see them moving in lines of four. The base at La Spezia was now dead in his sights. He could see the building outlines, the old citadel that he'd seen the aerial photos of, the warehousing along the western shore, and the drydock in the distance. It appeared as though there was a ship sitting in the dock even now. As large as it looked at this range, it had to be either a battleship or a heavy cruiser.

The entire base was lit up like a Christmas tree. There were working lights all over the harbor. It was as if nobody down there thought there was any chance of an enemy attack, and took no precautions. He could see automobile lights on the civilian roads below, and he wished they'd get home and lock the door. It was going to get loud in the next couple of minutes.

Two small marker lights indicated the outer boom of the harbor. Outside of which there would be a collection of torpedo nets, chain linked together to prevent any enemy sub from firing into the harbor. But with a little hope and some skill, those Albacores were going to drop their torpedoes just beyond the boom, then run like the wind.

The first wave came in. Four Albacores came straight out of the southwest and reduced their altitude until they were just feet above the water. They skimmed the surface, and Sinclair couldn't believe that no alarm had been sounded yet. No enemy fire from the ground, no red lights, nothing to indicate any kind of awareness that something was going on.

He began dropping his altitude, and the squadron followed him, like a flock of birds following a leader. The picture in the moonlit distance became clearer. One of the Albacores, the one on the left of the line, pulled away from formation, followed two or three seconds later by the other three. Then there was a short period of time when nothing seemed to happen. Then the first explosion went off, followed almost instantly by two more. Inside the port, two ships could be seen lurching out of the water as the first torpedoes impacted.

The second and third waves set themselves up for their own runs. The second wave, passed over the boom by no more than fifty or sixty feet, dropping their loads into the harbor beyond. He could see the faint trails of the torpedoes as their propellers took over, skimming just below the waterline. Four of them streamed out in different directions. It was just now that the lights on the base began flashing, and bodies below could be seen running. Two of the torpedoes impacted uselessly into some wall or wharf, while the other two hit their intended marks.

What appeared to be a heavy cruiser, sitting in the center of the harbor motionless, shuddered as the two torpedoes got it at either end. Fireballs erupted in the air. A single AA gun on the opposite side of the base opened up blindly. Tracer rounds streamed out in multiple directions, but it seemed like panic fire. Seeing that there was no longer any reason for radio silence, he picked up the mike.

"This is Swallow Leader. Follow me in. You've got your target. If you can't get the prime, drop it on the base!"

Six Skuas broke away on their own track, and five followed behind him. Machine guns now flashed to life from half a dozen guns around the harbor, firing in the direction of the torpedo attack. The last wave of 829 Squadron was settling into their attack formation, four abreast. Sinclair looked around the horizon, expecting to see 824 somewhere in the distance, but couldn't see anything. The plan was to drop all the torpedoes one wave after the other. If 829 had gotten off course, they might soon become the victims of the Italian Air Force, responding to the attack taking place.

He pushed his stick forward, putting the nose of his plane into a dive.

"Oh Christ" He heard Collinsworth scream from behind.

One of the attacking Albacores fell out of formation, and the one on the right dropped his torpedo too soon. It must've gotten caught in the nets because no explosion came. The remaining two dropped theirs into the water just meters beyond the boom, sending the two projectiles straight into a pair of destroyers sitting at anchor.

The first spotlights came to life below, searching the sky around the base. The lights outside the hangars came on, as did the line of window lights in the arsenal below. By now every soldier and sailor down there would be scrambling to get to their posts, fully aware that there was an attack taking place.

His plane came down at a sixty-degree angle. He put the hull of the nearest heavy ship in his sights, and one hand on his bomb release. For his first combat mission, he found himself remarkably still. The ship filled up in his sights as his elevation dropped, and he could see metal doors swing open in the shadowy light below. Sailors came streaming onto the deck, running toward their action stations, seemingly oblivious to the flight coming down on top of them.

"Sorry lads," he muttered as he dropped his bomb and pulled out of the dive. A half second later a thunderous explosion followed in his wake. He looked behind him as he pulled up and away, to see the damage. A ball of fire was rising up from the center of the cruiser below. He gave out a self-congratulatory cry. Even Collinsworth shouted in glory. The young gunner fired off a volley at the forward deck as they flew away.

Sinclair pulled his plane over at fifteen hundred feet. He could see the shapes of 829 Squadron's planes as they made their escape. In the bay blow, another bomb fell on top of the warehouse closest to the arsenal. Jackson, who'd taken charge of the other six dive bombers, came down on ships at anchor. Jackson's plane lined up on the battleship on the far side of the harbor. He dropped his bomb and then pulled up. It seemed to Sinclair for a moment as if the bomb had missed until the center structure of the ship exploded outward. Another bomb fell, and a third, causing a ripple of smaller explosions to set off. The battleship caught fire and began smoking from a dozen different places.

"Woohoo!" One of his boys shouted over the mike. He couldn't help but smile. Three other vessels at anchor erupted in explosions, and a geyser of water shot up from a bomb that had missed its target. But the coup de grâce came when the dry dock got hit. The cruiser sitting out of the water in the center of it split in two. The explosion blew down and outward, kicking the supports out, and the wall of the dock collapsed in on itself. A wave of water rushed in, washing away the scaffolding around the heavy cruiser.

The last Skuas finished their runs and pulled away. He did a quick count and was relieved that nobody had been lost. Sinclair took his plane around the perimeter of the harbor for another view, to assess the damage and make sure all pilots got away. Some of his pilots traded machine gun fire with targets on the ground, before disappearing over the western shoreline.

The base was smoldering below, with fires raging both onshore and on the ships in the port. At least half a dozen ships, including a battleship, had been hit by bombs or torpedoes. Small secondary explosions went off around the dock, sending bursts of flame skyward. One of the destroyers that had been torpedoed was already beginning to sink. The fires around the warehousing spread, causing a half dozen smaller explosions to set off as flammable materials nearby caught fire.

"We have friendlies, sir," Collinsworth alerted him. "Four o'clock low."

Sinclair turned over to see the twelve torpedo planes of 824 Squadron coming in low. He grinned happily as the biplanes approached. It wouldn't be hard for them to find a target with all of that light.

"Better late than not at all," he replied.

Guns from one of the outlying destroyers opened up on Sinclair as he circled his plane around. Bright pyrotechnics seemed to fly all around him for a few moments like fireflies. But the shooting died out when the gunners lost sight of him in the darkness. He was tempted to take his craft down and buzz by them, then thought better of it. Best not to push your luck.

Towers around the perimeter of the base began firing in the direction of the incoming attackers. The rapid flashing of machine gun fire intensified as the torpedo planes drew close. Sinclair lined his sights up on the nearest tower and fired until there was nothing left of it, then moved on to the next one. He dove in steeply, riddling the next tower with his own guns. He flew his plane low enough to draw away some of the enemy fire from the slower biplanes, then pulled up and away, letting Collinsworth let loose parting shots from the rear, before cutting straight across the middle of the harbor.

824 dropped the first of their loads. A dizzyingly bright explosion took place where a second battleship was anchored. A torpedo struck

it, followed immediately by another, then an entire magazine seemed to erupt in a strange green-orange color. Other planes methodically began dropping their torpedoes in the water. Most of the fish hit their target. A couple didn't, but it didn't matter. The harbor and almost half the ships in it were casualties. One final pass and he could see the submerged cruiser that had been sitting in the wreckage that was the dry dock. Out-of-control flames, and a scattering of machine gun fire was the last thing he saw before turning back west. 824 Squadron's Albacore torpedo bombers right on his tail.

CHAPTER TWENTY-TWO

The concrete walls and hallways of the bunker known officially as Installation T, echoed the sounds of heels clicking together as the Führer entered the cramped meeting space. The bunker complex was small, compared to many of the others built specifically to act as personal headquarters for Hitler and inner circle members while they traveled around Germany. The installation was built deep in the heart of the Black Forest, in the southwest of the country, near the Franco-Swiss border. It had been buried deep into the mountains, oblivious to enemy aircraft. Trees grew up atop the roof of the bunkers for added camouflage, and only small dirt roads led into and out of the area. There were no windows in the room, but the thick concrete walls made it much cooler than the open wooden conference hut would have been in the middle of summer.

Hitler moved around the room, the cluster of officers parting to let the Führer take his place at the center of where the map table was placed. He was tired of attending these types of briefings. They often became rather too redundant. But he thrilled in the strategic planning of great campaigns and thrilled even more when those campaigns manifested some glorious victory. It was personal for him. Watching his armies snuff out Germany's many enemies one by one, planning offensives against the great cities of Europe, only to watch them fall. Warsaw, Prague, Amsterdam, Copenhagen, Paris. Then sitting at the negotiating table to dictate terms to those very enemies who had been foolish enough to try and resist the inevitable.

His eyes passed absently over the faces of the men in the room as if he didn't recognize any of them. His right arm hung at his side, and it seemed to some that he was pumping his hand in some uncontrollable way. His left hand was balled up under his rib, ad he gave off subtle grunts and nods as he took his rightful place.

Aside from military aides and staff, some of the top officers present were General Manstein, who was quickly becoming one of Germany's most talented operational planners, Field Marshals Rundstedt and Brauchitsch, Grand Admiral Raeder of the Kriegsmarine, and General Jeschonnek of the OKL, Luftwaffe Command. Albert Kesselring, commander of the Second Air Fleet, one of the principal units responsible for achieving the destruction of the Royal Air Force, had also shown. He was a favorite of Hitler and seeing him again was always a great pleasure.

Hitler leaned himself against the table, propping himself up with his hands. His gaze went around the room and fixed on General Jeschonnek. "Proceed," he spoke softly.

General Jeschonnek tapped the map, circling his fingers above the Franco-Belgian sector. "Mein Führer, since air operations began against England, seven weeks ago, we've neutralized a number of strategic targets. The Luftwaffe has decimated a large number of enemy aircraft, and we've pushed deeper into the industrial heart of the British Isles. Our airbases along the coast launch daily strikes, with the end goal of being to wear down enemy air defenses, and to wipe the RAF out. To date, we've killed a total number of –"

"I don't need the numbers," Hitler interjected. "Continue."

"Of course. With the recent redeployment of units from Norway, and with additional reserve units from Germany, Air Fleet Three, under General Udet, is now the premier field command conducting our operations. General Udet's strategy has been to concentrate heavily on a fewer number of targets, rather than the wider number of raids that we'd been conducting. My briefings with the general's staff has convinced me that this tactic seems to be the better alternative. British airfields have suffered, particularly in the southwest of their country, and some gaps are beginning to form." He circled his fingers along the English coast. "We know, both through civilian broadcasts and our own reconnaissance flights, that many towns and villages near known airfields have been evacuated following heavy bombing raids. By this, we deduce that those airfields have become untenable for the enemy, and their units withdrawn or destroyed. Enemy engagements, particularly in the south-central zone, have dropped significantly. Yesterday, one of our raids reported almost no enemy activity. That flight went on to hit its objective; an airfield near Tangmere."

"Recent attacks against their radar stations have also contributed to a slower response time by the RAF. General Udet's strategy of launching multiple waves during the attack phase, is blossoming." He moved markers around the map, taking pieces away as he spoke. "The British cannot defend against attacks in one place, as they are busy fending off attacks somewhere else. As we eliminate their early warning detection, we deprive them of a critical advantage. Once we remove enough of them off the board, then we assure ourselves air superiority in southern England. And that, Mein Führer, is when we launch our ground invasion."

Jeschonnek fell silent and placed his hands behind his back in a gesture that he was finished with his report. Hitler studied the map, tapped his hand on different points against it, then looked up at the general.

"So what is the delay?" His voice was soft.

General Jeschonnek gave a look of confusion. "Mein Führer?"

Hitler sighed. "Göring assured me weeks ago that this campaign would be over by now. That the British had lost most of their strength fighting in France and that they were on the verge of collapse. So why the delay? Why do they continue to fight?"

The general cleared his throat nervously. "Well, our timetable for victory has been quite consistent. Following our conquests of France, and the Low Countries, we needed time to consolidate our gains. To establish bases from which we could launch the attacks. That may have given the British some additional time to rest and recuperate and to prepare for our offensive. But, so far as their resistance goes, we've seen a substantial decline in the past few days. I would agree with the reichsmarschall's assessment that we are on the cusp of success in the air."

Hitler gazed into the man's eyes, and the general gulped nervously. Hitler's eyes were dark and those who knew him well, knew that when he was in a mood he could be quite intimidating. But the Führer said nothing. He just stood, tapping his fingers steadily on the tabletop. After a few moments of utter silence, he gave a small nod. Jeschonnek stepped aside, to be replaced by Admiral Raeder.

"What of the Navy?" Hitler didn't even bother glancing at the admiral. It seemed to those present that he was in a most melancholic mood this morning.

"The Kriegsmarine is prepared for the task of securing the English Channel, by blocking off segments here, here, and again here." He indicated points along the map. "We're still allocating most of our resources to sinking enemy shipping and harassing the Royal Navy at sea. However, I've allotted, what I believe, should be a sufficient number of naval assets to the invasion. The goal is to isolate pockets along the English coast, to bar the Royal Navy from engaging with the invasion force. We cannot reasonably block off the entire Channel, but we can, with Luftwaffe support, maintain areas for a considerable length of time. However, the longer the time period involved, the harder it will be for us to maintain that control. We cannot match the Allies in terms of strength of numbers. That is why I have developed the plan to begin with a narrow front, along the south of England. A wider front would be almost impossible for us to maintain. But a narrower one would be much easier to hold for any length of time. Time for the Army to disembark, and to gain a foothold on the island."

The lowest of rumblings went around the room, mostly from Army officers. Hitler's eyes rose up to glare at the admiral, and Raeder could see the dark, displeasure in his stare. His face was unmoveable, and the tapping had stopped. Both the Army and Air Force had argued strongly for a wider invasion front. Somewhere between one-hundred-fifty and two hundred miles was thought to be ideal. However, it was generally accepted that the Navy simply could not support such a wide area.

Hitler fought himself to remain silent, and Admiral Raeder continued when no objection was made.

"We've designated fifty U-boats for the operation. They'll act mostly as picket ships on the flanks. Some of them will tow mines into place, in four zones that we've designated as the most likely route the Royal Navy will use for a counterattack. Our surface fleet shall consist of the battleships *Gneisenau*, *Bismarck*, *Scharnhorst*, and *Schleswig-Holstein*. Around them, the cruisers *Admiral Sheer* and *Admiral Hipper*, and the *Prinz Eugen*, and fourteen destroyers shall form the bulk of the landing support. They'll be arrayed in three separate groups, which will enter the Channel, traverse the French coastline until they reach their assigned zones, then move north. Their objectives are – "

"Where is the rest of the fleet?" Hitler asked him, his voice turning suddenly harsh. "What of *Tirpitz*? What of *Seydlitz*? What of all those ships you convinced me to build?" His eyes widened as he spoke louder. Admiral Raeder blinked at him.

"Mein Führer, some of those ships must be used on other fronts," he replied in a cowed voice. "Some are even now being repaired and are not available. I assure you, we are committing the majority of our strength to Sea Lion."

The führer bit his lip agitatedly and ran his left hand through his slick hair, then let out a loud sigh of annoyance. His gaze fell back to the map, and he swept his hand over it in an encompassing gesture.

"Why not just attack them where they least expect it?" He snorted his reply. "The British fleet is sitting there!" He pointed at the collection of markers in the North Sea. "Neutralize that, and you should have supremacy. Then you can assist with the landings without interference. The British would not expect an attack on them. Am I the only one who sees this?"

The eyes of everyone in the bunker shifted uncomfortably around. Everyone, regardless of which branch of service they were in, knew that the Royal Navy outnumbered them four to one in tonnage. Germany simply did not have the strength at sea to openly confront their old adversary, and that had been clear since the beginning.

"If I may interject?" It was General Manstein. Hitler threw up his hand in validation. "The admiral's position is quite correct. Better to keep the fleet close to our shores, where it can be protected from an air attack. Consider this: if the fleet sortied into the North Sea to confront the Royal Navy, it would take days to assemble. By the time it reached the base at Scapa Flow, it would almost certainly be detected. The enemy could launch their bombers and sink it entirely. But..." he brought his attention from the North Sea back to the English Channel. "After a successful invasion of the island, after we've landed enough divisions to carry the operation through, the enemy will have no choice but to come at us. Churchill will have to commit his entire fleet to cutting off our invasion force. When they move south, our fleet, with assistance from the Luftwaffe, will be in a far better position to repel an attack like that. Our main objective should be put on suppressing resistance for the landings."

Hitler sighed again. He gave Manstein a thoughtful look, then he seemed to relax visibly. His minor tantrum over, he brought his gaze back to Admiral Raeder, then indicated for him to continue. The officers in the room breathed silent sighs of relief of their own.

"Once we've secured the landing grounds, we'll have to keep our ships on station until the supply and reinforcement situation allows for the Army to take to the offensive. As General Manstein has pointed out, Churchill will have no choice but to commit their Home Fleet once the landings occur. That's when we'll need to redeploy the fleet."

"And how long for their fleet to respond?" Hitler asked him.

"Two days. Three at the most." Hitler nodded. He went back to looking intently at the map as if running some grand strategy through his mind.

"And every minute, they'll have the Luftwaffe on them," Kesselring added. "We'll bomb them from beginning to end. If any of them even reach the English Channel, that's when Raeder's fleet will pick them off."

"And you agree with Kesselring?" Hitler asked Raeder. The grand admiral nodded softly.

"I feel, however, that it is my duty to tell you, Mein Führer, that I do not believe the destruction of the Royal Navy will be an easy task. Not at all. I agree with Field Marshal Kesselring, that his air forces will bomb them continuously until they reach the Dover Straits. However, I do not believe for one second that they will be easy prey. I do not like to underestimate my enemies, and the Royal Navy is… well… we can all remember Jutland in '16. We had twice as much firepower there as we do here, and we still couldn't match them."

"Ach." Hitler flipped his hand at the admiral. "You remind me too much of Beck. He was far too conservative in his thinking also."

Grand Admiral Raeder stood still at the deliberate insult. The Führer's almost instinctive dislike for the Navy aside, Raeder seemed to be ever more in his crosshairs these days. It was one thing for a commander to invoke the displeasure of Hitler, but it was generally agreed upon by other top leadership that the man's consistent attacks on the head of the Navy, only stoked fears of confidence in the lower ranks. But Raeder remained professional, and silent nonetheless.

"Let us get to the bones of it," Hitler demanded. His eyes were baggy, and he seemed to be growing quite agitated. "The invasion." His gaze fell on Field Marshal Brauchitsch.

The admiral stepped aside and let Brauchitsch take his place, Field Marshal Rundstedt standing right behind him.

"We've allocated twenty-nine divisions for the operation. A further fifteen will be held in reserve. Our ports in France are even now being readied to handle such numbers. We've gathered approximately three thousand seacraft at various harbors along the Channel coast, and we're still bringing more in. Small boats mostly, but there are some larger barges and ferries we're converting for armored vehicles and tanks. With the resources that the Kriegsmarine has, and in consultation with the General Staff, I've agreed that the landing grounds will be narrower, as opposed to a wider front. I would've wished for more maneuvering room, but aside from subduing enemy defenses, the Navy will have to provide protection for our landing craft. We've therefore adapted the original plan, which called for a one hundred-seventy mile landing front, to a seventy-five-mile front.

"Our first objectives in England must be to disrupt their communications and to prevent major reinforcements from reaching the landing grounds. To accomplish this, the day of the attack, we will drop specialized glider borne units behind the landing zones. They'll be equipped with special weapons and equipment. Anti-tank mines, mortars, PzB 38's. Anything that'll delay an enemy counterattack. They'll be reinforced by the Seventh Parachute Division, which will drop in this area. Between the woodlands and the hills, it should provide excellent places for ambushes. There are only a handful of roads passing from north to south. Those will be secured to prevent enemy armor use. The initial invasion force will depart, under cover of darkness, from Channel ports all across Normandy, all the way to Boulogne and Pas-de-Calais. They'll reach English soil sometime in the very early hours and begin their assault. The first wave will consist of the Twenty-second, Eighty-seventh, and Two-hundred-Nineteeth Infantry Divisions. All three will be equipped with modified Panzer Twos, to traverse the beaches. After they've secured their main objectives, the second wave will land, and push northward." He turned his head and gave a nod to Rundstedt.

"Thank you. I've been through the operational plan, and I've assigned the Ninth Army to act as our main ground force during the initial phase. Once General Vietinghoff has a secure footing in England, he'll move west, capturing Portsmouth, should it not already be in our hands. After that he'll strike north, linking up with the airborne units holding the line. The Sixteenth Army, out of Boulogne, shall reinforce, and hold Vietinghoff's right flank as he advances toward London. After we've secured Portsmouth, and hopefully Dover as well, we can transport our heavy armor across."

"Your timetable for this?" Hitler asked.

"Twenty-four hours for the initial assault," Rundstedt replied. "Forty-eight to seventy-two for the lead elements of the Ninth Army to cross. Provided objectives are met quickly, we should be able to mount an offensive against London in... perhaps a week." He chewed his lip as he answered, considering the movement of troops and supplies, then continued. "If the British are going to mount a counterattack, they'll have to do it within the first forty-eight hours. The bulk of their forces are south and west of London. It'll be vital that we hold this line, north of the beaches. Luckily, the majority of the enemy force is made up of their reorganized expeditionary force. They left most of their heavy weapons in France, so they shouldn't pose too much of a threat. They're also demoralized as a result of that evacuation."

"How many divisions will the British have waiting?"

Rundstedt shrugged. "Difficult to say. We know there's at least one division of Canadians that arrived after Boulogne. Possibly some of their other Commonwealth units as well. But the bulk will be those units that broke out of France."

"What are the British defenses like?" Hitler asked Rundstedt. "What will our brave troops face when they reach England?"

"We can assume that there are any number of units stationed along the English coast. Aerial photographs show the placement of large coastal guns, and pillboxes constructed just about everywhere. So we must assume that the landing units will encounter resistance from the moment they hit the beaches. But both the Navy and Luftwaffe will assist in knocking these installations out. Though we have no confirmation of it, it would be my strategy to have field artillery batteries placed behind the line of defenses. From there they can support the defenders from miles away. As our area of air superiority enlarges we should be able to get confirmation of this, and to eliminate those positions before landing."

"Hmm. And you're quite positive you'll be able to breach their defenses? To secure these ports?" Hitler asked. His voice sounded shaky.

"One can never be absolutely sure of anything in war, Mein Führer," Manstein answered instead of Rundstedt. "But the odds are as good as we're going to be able to make them. The more time that goes by, the more difficult it'll become for us to mount such a campaign with any reasonable chance of success."

Hitler began to tap his fingers against the table once again. "Yes. Success" he said silently. He groaned and grunted. "Once the Army has completely consolidated, then what?"

"As General Jeschonnek has already stated, we will have air supremacy," Rundstedt answered. "We'll be able to launch attacks on their ground units, using their fields as launch points. Even a few dozen Stuka dive bombers can carve a path the Army can follow. The

Ninth and Sixteenth Armies will be redesignated as Army Group Britannia. Once the British Army is destroyed, they should systematically capture city after city after that. Like France and Poland, organized resistance will be dealt with, and the rest will simply be mopping up civil unrest."

Silence fell across the room, and Hitler stooped across the map, rubbing his chin, absorbing the information he'd just taken in. The tips of his fingers moved pieces around like a chessboard. His frequent meddling with military strategies in previous campaigns was well known. The fact that all of those campaigns had been victorious only reinforced to the man that he thought he could do things better than the professionals. But today he didn't seem to carry with him the confidence that he'd had previously. The man who'd so assuredly projected victory in Poland, in Denmark, in Norway, in all the other countries, now looked uncertain. Whether it was of himself, or the plan, or if there was something else, no one could say.

"I offered him a way out," he said, not speaking to anyone in particular. His eyes shot up suddenly at Rundstedt who appeared confused by the comment. "Churchill, I mean. I offered the man a way to avoid all of this bloodshed." He held up his hand and waved it about. "And he pushed it away." He shook his head in sadness. "I dreamt of an alliance between us and the British. Their blood is Germanic, the same as ours. An alliance between us and them would have reshaped the world." He paused momentarily, then muttered, "But I didn't want this."

"Those people have made their decision, Mein Führer," Kesselring told him gently. More than anyone else present today, his was the only voice that Hitler would have heard out. Hitler eyed him for just a moment, and a flicker of a smile creased his lips.

"Jeschonnek!"

"Mein Führer?"

"How long can their strength hold out against ours?"

General Jeschonnek exhaled strongly. "A matter of days. Perhaps a fortnight."

"A fortnight. Then in a fortnight, I will expect to hear that we have secured the skies above England. Then..." he began to say, then stopped for an extended length of time, "...we will...take them. I didn't wish to have to invade their island, but now I see that nothing else will work. Nothing short will get through to them."

"Perhaps not," Kesselring replied. "If I might make a suggestion? General Udet has found a winning strategy. But consider this as well: should an invasion of their island take place, even a successful one, we would be the first to do so in almost a thousand years." He held up his forefinger. "But the will of the British people might very well be the deciding factor of whether there is a successful resistance or not."

"What do you mean?" Hitler looked at him puzzled.

"The British people are not like others. Not like Poles or Czechs. They're more oriented around this notion of freedom than other peoples are. Probably because they've known more of it than others have. Perhaps, it's their spirit that needs to be broken. If we can break their delusions of opposition, make them realize that it's futile to resist, then perhaps we can force them into submission before it becomes necessary to raze their nation to the ground." He made a gloved fist as he said that. "Before war comes to their shores, we demonstrate to the population the futility of their fight. Show them what we are capable of doing. To deter them from future acts of aggression."

"What do you suggest?" Hitler asked him. He was suddenly beginning to sound much more confident.

"So far we've avoided bombing large population centers. Concentrating more on reducing their air force. But, I believe that we have the strength to do both at the same time. I propose that we choose a target, and unleash an attack so devastating, that it forces their people to see the horrors of war firsthand."

Hitler grinned. "What target?"

"London," he answered bluntly. "We bomb London into submission. When Londoners see their city reduced, panic will spread throughout the British Isles. They'll see that we can destroy any of their major cities. Then, only then, will they come to the table with an offer of surrender."

Hitler seemed to consider this suggestion. He licked his lips as he thought about it.

"Mein Führer." It was General Jeschonnek. "With all reverence to Field Marshal Kesselring, I would highly advise that we stay with the plan General Udet has developed. Destroying enemy airfields and organization. A couple of weeks from now, we might well destroy them outright. It would be a greater achievement than reducing some city blocks to ruin."

"No," Hitler whispered back. He put his finger on London and tapped it gently. "Kesselring may be right. London is one of the greatest cities in all Europe. If we can destroy that..." He trailed off.

"I... uh..." General Jeschonnek stuttered. He gazed around, silently looking for support from his fellow officers. "It may also harden their resolve against an invasion."

"How?" Hitler asked him excitedly. "It will bring to mind images of Warsaw, Oslo, Amsterdam. No, no. I think Albert is on to something here. Churchill, the fat fool, will lose the support of the people when it becomes apparent that he cannot protect them from our bombs." His expression changed and he appeared much lighter on his feet after that. "And you can do this in strength, Kesselring?"

"If you give me the word, I can begin immediately. I have five hundred bombers sitting on my airfields, fueled and ready."

"Haha," Hitler giggled like a child. "I wish all of my generals were like you, Albert. You have my authority. Udet can do what he does, and you can have London. Bomb them, Albert. Send them back to the stone age." Kesselring snapped his heels together. Field Marshal

Brauchitsch stepped forward and looked as if he were about to say something, but Hitler cut him off with a hand. "The decision is final. But, should Kesselring not bring the British to the negotiating table, begging me for mercy, then we shall move forward with Sea Lion at the beginning of August. Six weeks. No more."

No one dared moved. Kesselring smiled and nodded his understanding.

"Now, I wish to go," Hitler said, shuffling his feet toward the doorway. "I feel a headache coming on."

CHAPTER TWENTY-THREE

It was nighttime when the bomber flight flew by overhead. There were no clouds in the sky that night, and the beginning of a new moon period meant no moonlight either. But even against the darkened night sky people could still catch the phantom-like shadows crawling across the heavens. Bells rang in the middle of the night, and villagers and townsfolk from all over southeastern England came out of their homes and watched in frightening horror as more and more bombers emerged from the south, flying in a straight line due north.

Everywhere in the city of London, the sound of air raid sirens wailed. In the streets, police officers with helmets on, directed civilians into the underground shelters, and fire trucks waited in pre-positioned areas, for the moment that they were needed. And every one of them knew that they would be needed on this night. The alarm had been sounding for close to half an hour now. Hundreds of thousands had removed themselves to shelters, and hundreds of thousands more were still running.

Below the streets, in tunnel stations and basements all over London, millions of residents waited in nervous silence for what was coming. Whole families huddled together in the darkness. Even under the city streets, deep in the long tunnels, the sounds of sirens, though muffled, could still be heard. Civilians waited and prayed. Here and there a mother could be heard whispering soothing words to her children, or a voice of a man reciting the Lord's Prayer. A baby cried and a puppy whimpered. The young and old alike gathered together in the darkness to wait out what was to come. And they didn't have to wait long.

When the first bomb exploded it sounded like a simple thud, as if someone had dropped a heavy book on a wooden floor. Then another one sounded, and then another, and then another. Soon after, a chorus of ground-shaking bombs exploded in rapid succession in the city above. Buildings, old and new were leveled. Churches were struck and homes were set ablaze. The lights of the underground stations flickered, then went out. Fifteen thousand feet above London, hundreds of Luftwaffe bombers flew overhead, dropping their deadly payloads onto the old city, and the millions of inhabitants below.

The outskirts of London's East End were struck first. It was a terror bombing. Its aim was simply to strike fear into the heart of the British populace, just as the Germans had done on the continent. Like Warsaw, Rotterdam, Brussels, and other major cities, civilian targets had not been deemed off-limits. Londoners gave this day a name, Black Tuesday, and it was only the first of many long days. Blitzkrieg had finally come to England.

Spires of smoke slowly rose across the city as fires began to rage out of control. Damage spotters on rooftops called in locations where German bombs had fallen, where fires had broken out, and where they could see explosions going off. A father hunkering down in his basement with his family around him switched on the wireless. The sound of a man's voice came over the BBC, reading out a steady stream of announcements, declaring which parts of the city were being hit. A fire crew fought to put out the flames at a six-hundred-year-old church in Barking after the structure had been directly hit by a falling bomb. A cat in Wapping, startled by the thunderous explosions, ran home and squeezed itself through the half-open window in the bedroom of the little girl who loved him. Both would die when the roof of the home collapsed on top of them. All over London, the story repeated itself. Thousands would die before the end of it.

The attack went on for hour after agonizing hour. The sounds of a broken siren wailing, and resounding explosions going on for so long were enough to drive anyone mad.

Fires were still burning the following morning. Smoke still rose above the city. Everywhere there was ruin and destruction. Buildings and homes had been hit by explosives, roads were destroyed, and schoolhouses and churches used as shelters were cordoned off in order to let rescue workers sift through the ruins. The bodies of Londoners were carried away in stretchers by the dozens. It had been like something out of the Bible when Churchill made his way through the city streets of the East End. Like a picture of some post-apocalyptic world, filled with ruin and chaos. Thousands of people emerged from tube stations and basements as the prime minister walked solemnly down the road. He waved to as many of them as he could have, shook some hands, and offered words of comfort to those within the sound of his voice. But more than anything else he made sure that the people could see him. He could feel their pain as he made his way through the rubble.

He'd been in a bunker underneath Westminster when the bombing had begun last night, along with most of the government. And it had been a long night indeed. He was used to being up until very late in the night, but he hadn't gotten any sleep whatsoever after the first bombs dropped. For two hours the explosions had gone off just feet above him, and in that time all he thought about was the safety of the people. It had been a relief when the last explosions went off, and a strange silence seemed to settle on the bunker complex.

He'd wanted to go out then, to see the damage above, but his staff wouldn't allow him to, for fear of some unexploded ordinance going off. They'd had to wait for the police and Army to secure the areas, and bring in special units to search for unexploded devices. But when dawn came, and they'd still insisted that he remained underground, he'd directly over-rode his people. Even Jock Colville, ever his most trusted advisor, had attempted to keep him safely locked away underground but had reluctantly conceded when Churchill had threatened to fire his entire senior staff.

But as he'd walked through the city streets, and met with the victims, anyone who saw the reaction in their eyes to their prime minister being seen publicly just hours after such destruction had taken place, knew that Churchill had made the right decision. He could not, as both head of the government and as a national symbol, stay stuffed away in some bunker somewhere. Some of his aides even muttered that Chamberlain never would have gone to see the damage so soon. Maybe that was the biggest difference between the two men. Churchill wasn't afraid of seeing the truth behind things.

It was just before noon when he and his entourage returned to 10 Downing. The house staff was busy cleaning up the residence when Winston got back. Though Westminster had not been hit, the rocking tremors caused by the bombing had dropped items off shelves and shattered glass. The door to his private office was already open, and Winston found a single lady already there, picking up pieces of broken glass from the floor.

He cleared his throat as he entered.

"Oh," the lady said as she stooped down to brush the broken glass into a bin. "Prime Minister Churchill." She stood back up and wiped her eyes, which were red from where she'd been crying.

"My dear Miss Robinson," he greeted her warmly. She smiled at him when he remembered her name. Their first meeting last year had not gone well.

"I... I found some broken glass on the ground. I thought I'd clean it before you came back." Her voice trembled and her hands shook nervously.

Winston crossed the room and took her by the hand. As he touched her, she broke down instantly and began sobbing.

"I'm sorry," she squeaked.

"There, there, my dear," he told her and put his hand gently on her arm. Tommy Thompson was right behind him, and Winston tossed a nod over toward his liquor collection. Thompson opened the Johnnie Walker and poured two glasses. Winston took one and gave the other to Miss Robinson. She wiped the tears from her cheeks and took the glass. "Now you'll have two stories to tell your children and grandchildren."

She smiled back at him. "Sir?"

"You survived two great bombings in one day," he replied cheerfully and lifted his glass up in toast. The two clinked their glasses together before downing them both. "Now, I want you to take it easy for the rest of the day. Don't worry about the mess, we'll deal with it later."

"Thank you, sir," she said to him. She put her glass down and exited the room.

"Whew." Winston blew out an exhausting breath. "Only seven-fifteen in the morning. That might be a record, even for me," he told Thompson. "I want a full meeting with Dowding today. And his top people. What do I have on my schedule?"

"You're supposed to meet with your outer cabinet just before lunch, the American ambassador just after lunch, and the address to Parliament is on for this afternoon. Shall I cancel them for you, sir?"

Winston opened up his desk drawer to pull out a Havana and snipped the end of it off. "Tell the cabinet members, I won't be able to meet with them today. The American ambassador too for that matter." He lit his cigar up, and began puffing away as he sat down behind his desk. He still hadn't had any sleep, and he knew that would catch up to him later on in the day. "After the RAF boys get here, I should probably meet with the king to let him know the situation. Keep Parliament on my schedule. They should be fully informed. Besides, it wouldn't hurt for the BBC to cover it, to let the nation know that we're still standing."

"I'll move your schedule immediately, sir."

Winston sat alone for a good while, putting his only slightly disheveled office back into place. He could hear the voices of people working around the residence and in the streets outside. A house servant arrived at some point with his breakfast tray. Two hard-boiled eggs, some toast, jam, and a thick slice of cooked ham. He'd barely touched any of it by the time that his private secretary knocked on the door again, announcing the arrival of Air Marshal Dowding.

"Good morning, Prime Minister," Dowding said as he entered the room, followed immediately by Vice Air Marshal Park and another man whom Churchill was not familiar with. He was dressed in an RAF uniform, and his red hair was thick and shaggy.

"Not exactly what I might call a good morning," Winston said back. The door shut behind the line of men. Churchill offered them chairs to sit in. "Breakfast for anyone?"

"Uh, no thank you, sir," was the general reply.

Winston let out his cigar smoke and threw a look toward the window. "Bloody mess last night. We've joined in the unlucky circle of great cities that have now become targets for indiscriminate bombing."

"Quite so," Dowding reluctantly replied.

"Hmm. Until now the enemy has reserved itself for our military bases and installations. But, I supposed looking back on things, we should have probably expected this."

"I'm afraid, Prime Minister, that this may well become a nightly occurrence," Vice Marshal Park told him, to which Dowding and the third man seemed to concur.

"Who is this man you've brought with you today?" Winston asked Dowding.

"Sir, this is Air Commodore Maitland," Dowding introduced. "He was at my headquarters first thing this morning and I thought he might do well to tag along with Park and me."

"Oh?"

"Yes. I've been toying around with a notion in recent days. Ever since we activated the foreign squadrons we spoke about at our last meeting."

"Yes," Winston cut in before Dowding could go on. "What of those squadrons?"

"Three have been completely activated. Two French squadrons, one of which is serving with Number Ten Group, and a Polish Squadron. That squadron and the other French have been posted with Twelve Group in the north. I plan to cycle squadrons between groups to rest them whenever possible."

"Very well." Churchill relit his cigar to life. "Continue on."

"Commodore Maitland is just recently promoted to his position. Air Marshal Newall, before he leaves to take on his new post in New Zealand, planned to put him in charge of a new command that we're looking at establishing. One that deals directly with those very foreign units that we're employing. We both feel that having a direct commander in the field to lead those squadrons would be the best route to take. All responsibilities for training and support would go through Maitland."

"I see," Winston replied, giving the red-haired commodore an appraising look. "Your qualifications, sir?"

Maitland cleared his throat. "Eton, class of '29. Officer training in '32, followed by flight school right after. My most recent charge was as logistical officer for Two-Oh-Two Air Group in the Mid-East."

"Maitland also has extensive experience as a squadron commander," Dowding quickly added. "He knows what the men in the cockpits are up against, and he knows how to get them organized. Arthur

Tedder was his previous commanding officer, and gave him top recommendations."

"Number Eleven Group is getting hammered pretty hard, sir," VM Park stated, and his voice was blunt. "We've given out as good as we possibly can, but I would be lying if I said that we're not spreading ourselves thin. A quarter of my pilots are listed on the casualty boards. I can't afford to furlough too many for more than a couple of days at a time, but they need a break. Seven weeks is a long time to keep going up."

Churchill nodded with him. Park was unusually undiplomatically sounding today. Perhaps last night's air raid had been the proverbial straw, or perhaps just a contributing factor. He knew that Park's command was the main line of defense around London, and they took the heaviest hits. Particularly as of late.

"Gentlemen, I would be remiss if I didn't tell you just how sorry of a shape we're all in, but I'm sure that's self-evident." Winston gestured a hand to the scene of smoke off in the distance. "Bad enough we were dealing with Hitler in the middle of the day, against overwhelming odds, but now we're having to contend with night raids as well. As you said, this will no doubt be but the beginning of these types of attacks. I'll also level with you personally, Hugh. I believe that last night's event will fall on your shoulders." He looked Dowding square in the eye with as much dead seriousness as he could put into it. "I'll be in Parliament this evening, and I'm quite sure that there will be those who will call for your removal." He paused ever so slightly. "If not your head on a platter."

Dowding didn't so much as move. His old professionalism kicked in, and he sat in the chair, straight-faced as ever.

"I understand, Prime Minister," he said courteously.

"I'll do all in my power to protect you, but I wanted you to know exactly what my old political instincts tell me." Dowding nodded in understanding. "Good. Now, tell me about this new command you're giving this man."

"We have three squadrons active right now, and five more in the coming days. That'll give us the basis for the new command. I have to say, things are moving along quicker than I had expected, sir. Foreign volunteers are remarkably well educated, and take instructions quickly. There's a sense, by most of them, that they're eager to get into the fight. We've really denied them that opportunity, much to my regret." Dowding bit his lip and cocked his eyebrows in a moment of self-remorse. "We've got more than enough fighter craft, between Spitfires, Hurricanes, and those planes we bought from the Americans earlier this year. Some of them have never been flown. Maitland here can organize them into fighting units. By the beginning of July, we could potentially have seven or eight new combat-ready squadrons."

"All made up of foreigners," Park added.

Churchill leaned against his desk and gave a gesture of approval. In fact, he found himself in an oddly enthusiastic mood after hearing that. Notwithstanding the fact that London had just been bombed, and probably would be again, he was quietly optimistic at the news that the RAF would have an additional seven or eight fighter squadrons available for combat in the days ahead.

"You did give me the authority to do whatever was necessary, Prime Minister," Dowding reminded him.

"I certainly did. And under that authority, my next question, and I'm sure the one that the king will ask me when I see him next, is: what do you plan to do about repeats of last night?"

Dowding and Park gave one another brief looks before replying. "Honestly, sir, I'm not sure just yet. I'm pulling in my entire staff this morning to discuss the subject. This isn't the first night attack on us, but fighting in the air at night is much different than daytime. We've made significant developments in our RDF detection in the last year, but that's only good when it comes to detecting groups from the ground. It's one thing when a ground station can direct our fighters to within a few miles of a German formation during daytime when the pilots can see their targets miles off. It's quite another, to send up a squadron to engage with an enemy they cannot see. The Germans do have an edge over us in that regard. Truth be told, very few in our fighter arsenal are equipped for nighttime combat."

"We can deploy some of Bristol Beaufighters at bases around London," Park suggested. "They have a limited air-to-air radar capability. But, as the air chief marshal has said, we don't have many in number."

"We have been working on getting the newer Spitfires equipped with radar," Dowding then added. "But we won't see the fruits of that labor for at least another month, I'm afraid. And our even newer de Havilland Mosquitoes will not be rolling off the assembly line until September. We were so concerned with getting our daytime defenses prepared, that we were neglecting what happens at night."

A muffled grumble came from behind Dowding and Park. Churchill took his cigar out of his mouth.

"Did you have something to add to that?" Winston asked.

"Me sir?" Maitland asked.

"You, sir."

Park and Dowding half turned to look at the man, who gave them both looks in return.

"No, sir. Well, actually, yes, sir. It just dawned on me as you were speaking of nighttime engagement." He paused, half waiting for someone to dismiss him, then went on when it seemed that wasn't going to happen. "Putting some of our night fighters in with squadrons that don't have any would seem to be a good idea." In front of him, VM Park nodded an agreement. "Better to have some eyes in the sky, who can guide others into combat. Also – well I'm sure this has been thought of – but it seems to me that we might consider that the enemy is using some sort of navigational system of their own, to steer their bombers toward their target. Night bombing should be a rather inaccurate business, but what they managed to do last night would seem to counter that belief. As an aviator myself, it's difficult enough for one plane to find its destination, much less three or four hundred planes, in the middle of the night, with no lights to guide them."

"I'm not following," Winston said.

"Radio navigation, sir," Park explained. "They've been used to guide pilots in on designated points. A pilot follows a pre-directed flight path given to him via a transmitter tower. Once they reach a certain point along that path, they drop their bombs." He shook his head. "But nothing I've heard of would be strong enough to reach more than a few miles. Certainly not enough to reach London."

"Perhaps we need to assume otherwise," Winston retorted. "I can't say that I'm following all of what you're telling me. But it seems to me that we must start to broaden our horizons some." He pointed toward the smoke in the distance through the window. "We can't have this go on night after night. Hugh, do what you must. Call in whomever you need. Experts, scientists, whatever. Just get the situation under control."

"Yes, sir."

"If I thought letting that bastard drop bombs on London would give your squadrons the time they need to replenish their strength, then I'd do it. But the Nazis have the strength to do two great things at the same time. Whereas we seem to only have the capacity to do one. I'll expect your recommendations." He nodded and the men got up. Winston looked at Maitland and gave him an approving grin. "So far as I'm concerned, you're hired, Maitland. Do what you must to get your command underway. Those squadrons will be needed."

"Prime Minister," he said before they exited the room.

Winston looked quickly at the clock on his desk. It was just half-past eight o'clock, and he'd gotten no sleep last night and was expected to meet with the king at some point today. He was scruffy looking and needed to refreshen and change his clothes before then.

He also knew that he'd need to get at least a little bit of rest. Between the king, parliament, and potentially another bombing tonight, it was looking as if it was going to be a very enduring day. He also knew that he didn't have the luxury of having what he wanted. Not today anyhow.

He picked up his telephone.

"Get me the chief of the air staff," he told his secretary on the other end. "Tell him that I wish to speak with both himself and the head of Bomber Command."

CHAPTER TWENTY-FOUR

A night attack against a fortified position was never a sure thing. In fact, in most cases, they tended to end in total and utter failure. There were just too many variables, things that could go wrong in the dark of the night. But they did have one advantage over a daylight attack, in that the defenders seldom saw it coming. That statement was even more true when the two countries in question were not currently at war with one another. In that case, the defenders would be caught even more unaware of an impending attack. If the element of surprise meant anything at all then it was most effective against a non-belligerent nation.

The biggest foreseeable problem right now for the attacker was that the great Rock of Gibraltar was both heavily fortified and lit up like a giant beacon in the night, seen from miles and miles away. Spotlights from all over the small British territory scanned the night sky back and forth repetitiously, and it was nearly impossible for any aircraft nearby to go unobserved or for a sea vessel to approach unnoticed.

A daylight assault on such a position would have been both impossible and suicidal to undertake. During normal times, Spain would never have undertaken such a venture. Not even under the most favorable of circumstances. But these were not normal times. With their own island under attack, and the Royal Navy engaged heavily at sea, the British were stretched far too thin to adequately defend their vast empire.

Along with an impressive arsenal of field guns sent from Berlin, the Spanish forces had also been equipped with several more modern aircraft supplied by the new French government in Vichy. But most important of all, Madrid had been informed by the Germans, guaranteed even, that the British garrison at Gibraltar was at its weakest point. Spanish listening stations, both in the Mediterranean and Atlantic, had assured them of no Royal Navy activity.

General Yagüe, commander of all Spanish forces going in on the assault, had scoffed at those reports. Their own intelligence sources could scarcely be called reliable, and the Germans had their own agenda. Whether or not a Spanish assault on Gibraltar succeeded or not was almost irrelevant. The attack alone would be its declaration of war on Great Britain, and the cost that Spain would pay would be a high one. Despite his personal hatred for the British, he knew that London would retaliate, and that Spain would suffer for it. But he was only a general, who followed his orders to the letter.

The Mirador Hotel, just across the bay from the British enclave, made for an excellent headquarters. From its rooftop, he could see the entire western side of Gibraltar, the huge mountain that jutted up from the sea and guarded the British naval base. The sight of it made him both sick and anxious to retake the long-lost territory once again.

He checked his watch. It was just after zero-two-hundred, and it was going to be starting soon.

His mind raced with thoughts, calculations, and probabilities. Behind him, his staff officers were chatting among themselves. The plan was not the best. It was quite possibly one of the worst battleplans that he'd ever seen on paper. The main assault would go in the most direct way possible: across the main Anglo-Spanish border. Two lighter assaults would come by way of the sea, around the eastern and western sides of Gibraltar. It was going to be bloody, and victory would only come after the attacking forces simply overwhelmed the defenders. Given the sheer number of Spanish troops that had been assembled for this operation, everyone expected victory.

The British had taken extra measures to fortify the territory following Germany's invasion of Poland. Additional defenses had been built at the northern end, along its border with Spain. Sea mines and anti-torpedo nets had been placed strategically on the eastern and western seas where great coastal artillery covered the approaches. But those defenses were built around the notion that large enemy capital ships would be spotted well before any attack. The British didn't seem to consider the possibility of small boats being used in an assault.

That had been one of the challenges for Spain as well. The Spanish Navy paled in comparison to its British counterpart. Only a small handful of ships were in active service, and those squadrons were deliberately stationed away from Gibraltar. If they moved, then the British would have almost certainly known about it. So they'd been kept at anchor until the operation began. Instead, hundreds of small boats had been assembled in secret, and stored away out of prying eyes. Each boat would carry only a few soldiers, and those were just enough to keep the enemy flanks occupied while the main attack unfurled.

Neutralizing the web of chain nets on the eastern side of Gibraltar had proved to be a bit more challenging. Sea mines and other defenses just offshore could cause a big problem for the armada of small boats that would come around from Spain via the coast. To get around this obstacle, they would have had to nullify those defenses so the boats could get all the way to shore.

At first, the thought of abandoning a seaborne attack was considered but rejected after someone had recalled hearing about some salvage operation that had occurred by a team of Frenchmen a couple of years earlier. So they'd rigged up a floating contraption that allowed their divers to move about on their own underwater, far away from any ship. The diver would descend to the sea floor, tugging a tiny bundle that floated along the ocean top, which pumped oxygen down to the diver. They would then weigh down whatever obstacles the boats above might get caught up in, and allow them to pass safely by.

There had been a lack of volunteers for just such an assignment, which had forced General Yagüe to employ crews of civilian divers. Their cost had come high, but should the plan succeed it would be well worth it. If it happened to fail… well, a bullet would be far cheaper than the compensation would have otherwise been.

The British warships parked offshore were as few in number as there had been since their war with Germany had begun. Only a handful of destroyers and a single cruiser were anchored presently. Yagüe had assigned enough of his own artillery to sink those ships that he expected it to be a short exchange. Even now, his guns had been pulled into positions all along the Spanish shore. Just yesterday those positions would have appeared as nothing more than open parks, and empty outcroppings of land by some observer looking across the bay with binoculars. But now they hosted batteries of heavy guns, each trained on British positions.

He stood and watched in the dark of the night. Waiting. It would only be a matter of minutes now.

* * *

Lance Corporal Burrett flicked open his lighter and ignited the end of his cigarette. The cramped space of his concrete fortification didn't allow for much airflow and the short ceiling left nowhere for the smoke to go. He scribbled watch notes onto a pad of paper sitting on the tiny metal desk. From outside he could hear talk going on between other soldiers standing post. Overlapping battlements ran along the eastern shore overlooking the Mediterranean, just above a line of small huts and buildings that faced the beaches below. Offshore a dozen or so small vessels swinging at anchor toward the southern end of Gibraltar. But from Catalan Bay north, there was nothing but empty seas.

He leaned back in the small metal chair and yawned. It was another slow-moving night shift. Even with the steaming cup of coffee sitting next to him, these nights drew the energy straight out of him. Gibraltar was about as far away from the war as Hong Kong was at this moment, and sitting around on garrison duty was about the least exciting post that a soldier could pull. Right now he'd give anything to be back in England.

Burrett relaxed, and took a long sip of coffee, and a drag from his cheap Spanish cigarette. His eyelids had just barely closed when one of the voices from outside the concrete bunker shouted out.

"Hey, Corp! Come have a look at this."

His forehead creased in wonder and the metal chair dragged across the concrete floor as he pushed himself away from the desk. Hanging the cigarette on the side of the small ashtray, he stepped outside into the dark night. Two other men, both privates, were huddled around a small parapet, gazing out at the approach to the bay.

"What is it?" he asked them.

"Right there," one of them answered, pointing his finger out to the center of Catalan Bay.

Burrett squinted, and looked out at the waves crashing against the rocks and sand. His eyes adjusted in the darkness of a waning crescent moon. Far above, at the top of the Rock, spotlights beamed outward, scanning the night sky. He stared out from his position, looking beyond the outer markers. His pupils widened, and he could observe several objects bobbing up and down in the water. They inched slowly across the ocean surface, moving only slightly with each wave. It was as if giant sacks had been dropped off a ship and were slowly washing ashore.

"What is that?" the second private quietly asked.

"Looks like sea turtles," the first private remarked.

Burrett watched them move for a minute, bobbing around on the surface, getting closer and closer with each wave. There must have been close to fifty of them, spread out across a hundred meters.

Maybe some ship dumped its garbage supply overboard, he thought.

He tapped the first private on the shoulder. "Run up the causeway, will ya'. Tell 'em to shine a –" His words were instantly drowned out by the sound of a loud, shuddering boom coming from the north, beyond the airfield. His instincts instantly awoke. He'd served in the British Army long enough and knew very well the sound of heavy artillery firing. Within seconds a series of explosions erupted on the eastern side of the Rock. Chunks of stone flew in every direction, eruptions rose from along the defensive fortifications higher along the eastern parapets.

A second round of distant booms followed immediately, then a third. Men ran for cover as shells suddenly began exploding. The ground reverberated with each detonation, and fireballs began to light up the night. One of the coastal guns burst apart on impact, and in a matter of seconds, the entire Rock of Gibraltar erupted in flames. The giant spotlights flickered off, then on again as power was interrupted, and backups took over.

Further explosions went off from the crown of the Rock above. They were high explosive rounds, sending up great bursts of fire when they exploded. The great explosion was followed by the wailing sounds of alarms being cranked to life.

"Get to cover!" Burrett shouted. He grabbed the nearest man and threw him hard toward the bunker. He tried to get the second private, but the kid had taken off running. He stopped about fifteen feet away and dropped down behind a high wall.

The spotlights settled in on a search pattern. The shafts of light scanned the night skies above and the seas below. Burrett ducked down behind the rock wall rampart overlooking Catalan Bay. In the dark seas below he could see the floating objects he'd been looking at before beginning to take form. They were coming in a long and wide line. There was something about it. He looked back at the private hunkered behind the wall.

"Get up there! Tell 'em to shine some bloody light down there!" He shouted. He pointed up with his thumb, and the private was quick to take off, moving like a marathon runner in the dark. The shelling continued. From above, an artillery round took out a radar array, which toppled over. It was sheer panic. "Dammit."

"What the hell's going on, Corp?"

Burrett didn't even bother to look back at the other private. "What the hell does it look like? Just be ready. Grab your rifle you damn fool!"

He wasn't a great military tactician by any means, but he was smart enough to know that it wasn't some German battleship that was shelling them. Some Italian ships perhaps, that had gone unobserved by air patrols. Burrett's mind raced. Garrison duty in Gibraltar wasn't supposed to be a dangerous assignment.

More incoming shells exploded, and the spotlights dimmed momentarily. He crouched backward into the bunker, grabbed his rifle from the side of the desk, and pulled the lever back to chamber a round. His helmet was sitting on an empty chair, he grabbed it and went back to the wall as more guns fired in the distance.

* * *

General Yagüe watched from the hotel rooftop as the explosions went off one after another in the distance. He didn't need his field glasses to see what was happening across the bay. Though it was close to five miles away, the huge Rock of Gibraltar could have just as easily been right across the road from him. Shell after shell fell on it. Heavy mortar shells rained down on the north end, where the airbase was located, and a battery of howitzers from his side of Gibraltar Bay fired volleys at the line of defenses.

From positions closer to the beach, the batteries that he'd moved into place during the night, as well as some of his larger German-built guns in the hills behind him, opened with a terrifying bang. Seconds later those Royal Navy ships in the harbor began to receive their own treatment.

There was a scream coming from down below. The general leaned his head over the side of the building. He could see civilians running through the city streets. As part of the deception, and simply because he didn't care, he hadn't evacuated the civilian population beforehand. Thousands of them would have had no idea about what was to unfold this night and were now running through the streets in a desperate attempt to flee. Despite possible losses among the city residents he'd had no intention of tipping his hand to the British.

He brought his attention back to the Rock, sitting there defiantly across the water. Grabbing his binoculars off a table, he focused in on the action.

The north airfield was out of commission. Fires around it were burning out of control. The silhouettes of men running every which way could be seen against the fiery backdrop. A cacophony of explosions went off all across the enclave simultaneously, and in the distant background, there was still the sound of heavy artillery thundering.

Finally, after long minutes the British batteries opened up in reply. From the Princess Caroline battery on the north end to the Genista battery on the south, rounds were loaded, fired off at the enemy in the shadows, then paused to reload. It would be very difficult for those batteries to zero in on the Spanish positions, but he knew the defenders simply couldn't sit there and do nothing.

In Gibraltar Bay, one shell after another fell. Their shots mostly fell into empty water, but for every four shells that missed, a fifth would hit one of the British vessels at bay. A tanker swinging at anchor exploded like a volcano. Its tanks, half full, spilled burning petrol into the bay when the hull broke open. Two destroyers, both having taken hits during the opening salvo, were sitting ducks as more guns from the Spanish coast opened up on them. Burning sailors jumped frantically from the ships into the sea even as boiling fuel spread throughout the enclosed bay. The propellers of a third destroyer churned up the waters behind it as it alone started towards the open water. Off in the distance, a fleet of small motorboats sped off toward yet another enemy ship. A lone British light cruiser had been on approach when the shelling began. Now its triple six-inch guns began to reply to the artillery flashes on the Spanish side of the bay. Her gunfire was like bolts of lightning in the darkness, followed moments later by explosions in Spanish territory.

He watched as the tanker in the harbor beyond burned out of control, lighting up the entire western side of the huge mountain. British spotlights on the Rock were trying to zero in on his artillery units, but one after another, they too winked out as Spanish shells hit them or the power lines feeding them. He was pleasantly impressed with the accuracy with which some of his batteries were landing hits. He had not planned on knocking out so many targets in such a short period of time. It had only been twenty-six minutes since the operation had begun, and it was going mostly as planned. His heavy guns were doing a good job of battering the defenders, and his lighter pieces picking apart the line of defenses and barricades on the north front. And any moment now he expected to hear the bombing from his air forces.

"Captain," Yagüe called, and one of his subordinates stepped forward. "I expect the Air Force bombing to begin any minute. Go down to the Santa Maria Battery. As soon as the bombing begins, shift artillery fire to those Royal Navy ships. Especially that bigger cruiser. Major!" The captain bowed and ran off to be replaced by a major. "Get me an update on the eastern landing. Then I want you to report directly to General Ramos' headquarters. As soon as the landing forces hit the ground, make sure Ramos sends his troops in. He has a habit of delaying. I want you there. Understood?"

"Understood."

Yagüe waved him off and raised his binoculars. He could see plumes of sand and rock exploding all over Gibraltar and caught small glimpses of people running across the burning north airfield and trucks racing to put out the flames. He smiled at the chaos. If things went even half according to plan, the troops crossing the water would be reaching the enemy shore in minutes. After that, when the British defenders were fully engaged, General Ramos would lead the full force of his division across the border from the north and simply swamp the remainder of the defending soldiers there.

It was early, not yet three in the morning, and it was going to be a bloody day. A very, very bloody day.

* * *

"There!" a voice yelled over the sound of explosions. "Down there!"

Along the raised battlements, soldiers shouted and pointed down at the bay. A single spotlight cut through the night and settled in on a watercraft making its way toward the beach. Some flares fired in that direction, illuminating the water. Small boats began to emerge out of the dark. They passed right through where the mines should have prevented them from going. Not a single mine went off, and not a single boat seemed to get caught in the chained nets.

"Damn!" Burrett shouted. "Man the guns! Stay at your posts. Fight!" He lifted his rifle and fired down on the approaching boats. They were still two hundred yards or more out, but he couldn't sit and do nothing. More men began firing on the rows of boats as they drew closer. Some of their occupants began firing back, but the ramparts didn't have lights beaming down on them, giving away their positions, and the men standing on them were as safe as they could be.

A sergeant buzzed past behind him, with a dozen others right behind. They reached a circular flanking tower along the wall where they set up a pair of Browning machine guns. As the lead boats came ashore the dual guns opened up on them, strafing the shoreline with bullets. Dozens of bodies fell at the edge of the beach.

To his left and right men were firing away with their Enfield rifles, dropping down only to reload. There were close to a hundred of them along the fortifications, and a battery atop the Rock added to it. A single mortar kept sending explosive shells down to meet the attack. In the sea below, geysers of water exploded up.

"Bloody bastards!" The private next to him hollered. He fired off the last of his clip then knelt down to reload. "We'll send 'em back to Mussolini in a damn box!"

"I don't think they're Italian," Burrett said but the other didn't seem to hear. Burrett wasn't stupid. He may only have been a lowly lance corporal, but he suspected who it was that was attacking, and it wasn't the Italians.

He spared a quick look up to the north end of the line. It was burning bright where the airfield was located, and there was the sound of explosions going off that way. He hadn't seen a single one of their planes take off since the attack began, and he assumed from the explosions that the airfield, and everything on it, had been taken out. He thought about what was going on up there and on the opposite side of the Rock. Any attack that was going to come with a real chance of breaking through would come from the north.

More flares fired off into the night, slowly descending toward the beach below. A dozen boats had made it to shore, disgorging dark uniformed soldiers onto the beach. A few fell at the waterline, others ran straight toward a row of small houses and fishing huts at the top of the beach, between the shore and the ramparts. He hoped that the residents who lived there had gotten out before the shooting had begun. All the same, the British riflemen tried to avoid shooting up the tiny huts.

A larger shell landed out to sea, sending up a spray of water illuminated by the red flares. Another shell followed, hitting a small boat, and cutting it neatly in half. But it didn't stop more troops from landing. Scores of them kept emerging out of the sea, some manned by soldiers paddling to shore. Within minutes there were forty or fifty of them hitting the sand, with half a dozen soldiers in each. Burrett could hear the shouts of the attackers between gunshots. One of them flung a loud curse at the defenders, and he could hear it clearly. Spanish.

Volleys of rifle fire kept the attackers pinned on the beach, and the machine gunners unloaded as fast as they could on the approaching boats. But more boats were hitting the beach every moment, and the two gunners couldn't keep up. Then came another sound. It was a low humming sound. Above the echoes of gunfire Burrett could hear the winding sounds of airplane propellers. For one brief second he was hopeful that some of their own planes may have gotten airborne. His hopes dimmed as it was followed immediately by the shrieking sound of bombs falling straight on top of them.

* * *

Admiral Somerville stood on the observation deck of the battleship *HMS Rodney*, unconsciously tapping his right foot anxiously as he stood there. Below him, the crew had all manned their action stations, and he could hear the call of officers shouting orders and the splashing of the waves hitting the hull.

It had been nearly an hour now since the first message arrived from Gibraltar Station. It had been a brief and uninformative one: **Enemy attack underway. Request any and all immediate assistance.**

He cursed inwardly. That had been the extent of it, and he'd ordered the task force to come to flank and move straight for the Rock with all due haste. Either someone had not been properly trained in their job or else the message had been cut short. Since the transmission had been received, and no further one had come in, his gut told him that the second option was most likely.

If the damn Germans had sent a bomber force and taken out communications...

He hated the thought of it. The idea that the Luftwaffe could strike so unknowingly at the important British naval base was unnerving enough. But now that the French had thrown in with them, anything was possible. However, Somerville had briefly considered another possibility as well. Since the garrison at Malta had reported no activity, he wondered whether any attack might have originated from somewhere else, then pushed away at the notion.

In the darkness, the lone Royal Navy task force glided across the ocean. Ahead his escorting destroyers had taken point, and five hundred meters astern, the carrier *HMS Argus* was gearing up to go into battle. He'd ordered her captain to have his planes fueled up and ready.

Somerville had been senior officer on sight, and he knew Gibraltar's defenses well. He also knew that, despite the Rock's fortifications, the Royal Navy presence was at the lowest it had been in months. A ripe time for an attack. With most RN and RAF resources tied up back home, a German bombing raid could be disastrous for Gibraltar.

He gripped the rail tightly, squeezing with anxious anticipation. He hated not knowing, as any military commander did. It dawned on him for a brief moment that his task force was sailing beyond Trafalgar at that very moment. The distant lights of Cadiz Spain were tiny pinpricks on the horizon.

"Sir," a voice said from his side. Somerville turned his head to Commander Garfield, *Rodney's* first officer. "ASV has unknowns on approach."

Somerville's face scowled in confusion. "What?"

"Pilots reporting at least eight large ships closing on our position, sir. Bearing three-two-five degrees."

The admiral's expression turned blank, and he stared out in that general direction. *Three-two-five?* That didn't make any sense to him. For a few moments, he ran through the possibilities. There were no other Royal Navy ships in this area, and certainly no task forces. He would've known about that. *Italians?* He thought, then mentally dismissed that notion. They were far too distant from any Italian naval base for that to be true.

"Good Lord," he muttered as a different possibility struck him. "Signal the fleet, Commander. Bring up *Sheffield* and *Abdiel* immediately! Notify *Argus* that we need her planes in the air."

"Now, sir?" It was just after zero-three-hundred.

"Now dammit!" Somerville replied. The words had barely escaped his mouth when in the distance just off the port horizon, there was a series of brief flashing lights. Moments later there was the low hum of airplanes flying overhead, and the shells began to fall.

* * *

The whole of the Rock of Gibraltar was bright with fire, from one end to the other. The harbor where the Royal Navy vessels had been stationed, as well as the airfield on the north end, were both burning uncontrollably. One of the enemy destroyers was listing heavily to one side. One had escaped the harbor but had taken so many hits by Spanish guns, that it was smoking black. A few of her smaller guns were still firing back but to little effect.

A staff sergeant had just handed him a note a few minutes earlier that the attack against the eastern shore was underway, and that hundreds of his men were pushing in from the beach. Add to that, the fact that waves of boats were now heading across the Bay of Gibraltar, with hundreds more men who'd attack from the west. They'd land on the western shore, hitting the British defenders on two sides.

Anti-aircraft guns were shooting upwards at the planes dropping their bombs. Most of the explosions were on the Rock itself, but a few fell onto the defenders around the shore as well. The heavier bombers hadn't even started their attack yet.

Everything seemed to be going right. Any minute now he expected to be told that General Ramos' brigades were beginning their charge across the border. That was the plan anyway. He'd sent one of his staffers to make sure Ramos, who was known to be cautious, sent his men in at a specific time. The only real resistance thus far had come from the Royal Navy cruiser maneuvering about out there. His big guns had opened up on it almost immediately, and gotten in a couple of hits. But the cruiser was still afloat, and fighting on. He was no navy man, but he quietly congratulated the commander of that vessel for some neat little maneuvers. The torpedo motorboats he'd sent to neutralize it, appeared to have failed, and no torpedo impact had gone off. But now that his bombers were hitting the Rock, he could shift more guns to dealing with the nuisance.

"General." A lieutenant stepped into the light of the hotel balcony, holding up a message.

"What does it say?" Yagüe asked him, not taking his sight off the fight.

"Admiral Flores reports engagement with a Royal Navy task force southwest of Cadiz," the lieutenant told him. "He's pushing forward with his attack, and will advise."

Yagüe sneered and shook his head. *So much for intelligence reports. Good thing Flores sortied when he did.* The admiral would have air support as well, and hopefully, with some luck and skill, they could turn back the RN task force. It might be too much for him to hope that they could sink those ships on the same night they took Gibraltar. Such a feat would certainly boost Spanish standing.

"Very well. Keep me informed." The lieutenant was just about to walk away when the general stopped him. "Also, find out where the hell the Italian squadron is. They should've been on sight by now." The lieutenant nodded.

He put his field glasses up and watched the north for signs of the attack wave. It was all in Ramos' hands now.

* * *

"Ah, shit," Burrett cursed. The fingers of his right hand dug into his stomach, just below the left rib, and latched onto a sharp object. With an effort, he pulled it out of his body and held up the blood-slick pointed rock that had got him during the bombing. He tossed it away, clutching the small wound with his left hand. It wasn't bad. Had it been a bullet no doubt it would've been far worse.

"You alright, Corp?"

He nodded at the private hunched over him. The kid was dirty-faced, but didn't seem to have any injuries. Other men weren't so lucky. Half a dozen that had been closer to the explosion were lying in bloody pieces now, including the sergeant who'd been commanding the machine guns. But mortars were still dropping on the beach below, and men were still fighting. He grabbed his rifle, using its butt to get back on his feet.

"Medic!" he shouted, hoping there was one around to hear him calling. He steadied himself against the stone wall. Spanish troops were taking shelter all around the homes on the beach, some had even made it as far as the single-lane road that hugged the coast, between the beach and the rampart wall. From the water, there were yet more boats coming ashore.

"I got you, Corp," a voice said, and Burrett turned to see a medic arrive. "Nasty cut is all," he said after probing the wound. He pulled some bandages out of his pack and went to work.

More men were arriving from out of the tunnels that ran throughout the mountain. They'd been constructed to allow the free movement of troops in case of an attack. A platoon of riflemen took positions up and down the line, filling gaps caused by the bombing attack, and medics and hospitallers carried away the severely wounded on stretchers. The medic double-taped some gauze around the wound sight, then gave him a tap on the shoulder before he moved on to the next man.

"I need a report!" A voice shouted. Burrett turned to find a captain leading a second platoon out from the tunnel.

"You in charge here?" the captain asked him.

Burrett nodded. "Yes, sir. Sergeant there is dead." The captain looked at the shredded body lying on the ground.

"No time for that right now," the captain said. "Situation?"

"At least a battalion down there, sir," Burrett informed him, nodding to the beach. "More coming in. Not sure how they got passed the nets. We've got them pinned down there though. I can't see how they're going to get up that cliffside."

The officer nodded. He looked down at the brown-clad men trying to cross the road.

"You can hold here?" the captain asked after seeing his wound.

Burrett nodded. "Give me four machine guns and I'll hold them, sir."

The captain gave him an appraising look, then grinned and nodded. He barked an order to a corporal standing nearby, who passed the word along for machine gunners to set up on the line.

"You'll need to keep them from gaining a foothold, Corporal. We're heading north."

"What's the situation, sir?" Burrett asked him.

"The situation is the Dons are hitting us everywhere at once. We're heading to the north front. General Richardson expects an attack up there at any moment. I need you to hold here, Lance Corporal...?"

"Burrett, sir."

"Well Burrett, I'll give you whatever I can, but it won't be much. Hold here, no matter the cost. Maybe you'll be Colonel Burrett before the end of the day."

With only a single nod the captain took off down the line, heading north with a platoon following behind him. Machine guns set up twenty yards apart, and a flurry of flares fired off just seconds before the line of men opened up on the enemy once again.

* * *

Winston tossed in his sleep, rolling from one side of the bed to the other. His eyes flung open at the sound of the knocking. He threw the covers off just as the door opened, letting in a shaft of light from outside his room in the bunker below Westminster. It was a bright light, and he instinctively held up a hand to shield his eyes.

"Sir," a voice said.

His vision adapted to the bright light, and he could see three men setting foot in his room. One of them was Tommy Thompson.

"What is it?" he replied gruffly. They'd been hit by the Germans again earlier in the night. Perhaps there'd been a second wave approaching.

"I'm sorry, sir," Thompson apologized. He switched on the small light next to the bed, which made Winston wince. Thankfully, he'd been alone when they'd arrived. Clementine had gone back to Chartwell for the time being. "We've just gotten a priority message."

"What about?" Winston sat up and rubbed his eyes. He searched the tabletop for his glasses.

"Just came in," Thompson said, handing him a slip of paper. "Gibraltar, sir."

"What?!" Winston grabbed the paper, put his feet in his slippers, and stood up. He read through the message, reading off certain parts audibly. "Enemy forces… heavy fire from batteries… Spanish soldiers!" He huffed heavily. "Make the calls, Tom. I want the war cabinet downstairs in –" he looked at the clock, "–one hour."

CHAPTER TWENTY-FIVE

Firefighters had completely given up on trying to put out most of the flames around the airfield that marked the border between Spain and Gibraltar. They'd switched to putting out the ones around more explosive material. Whatever was left of the gate between the two territories was now gone, destroyed by the constant shelling. The hedgehogs and other defenses that marked the dividing line were being chiseled away at by the howitzers on the Spanish side of the border. British artillery was returning fire, but it was clear that the enemy vastly outpowered them.

Brigadier Richardson looked out between the narrow slits of the bunker overlooking the North Front. The bright light of the blazing fires illuminated everything north of the Rock, and there seemed to be no end to the Spanish artillery coming down on them. He'd been with the Royal Welsh Fusiliers in France before being given this assignment. He'd seen artillery fire there, but he never imagined that the Spaniards would have such firepower. It was generally accepted that their military had slipped into a second-rate status. If he got out of here, he planned on setting the record straight.

Gunners in pillboxes traded fire with their counterparts across the empty space between the borderline and the Rock itself. The burning wrecks of what had been their air force were sitting out there as plain as day. Dozens of planes had been lost, hangars still burned, and bodies lie out in the open. God himself only knew how many were already dead.

Grabbing his field glasses, he stepped over to look out at the western-facing view slits. The harbor was in complete chaos. He could see the bow of *HMS Diana* sticking out of the water. *HMS Duncan* had taken damage but was still afloat. Sporadic anti-aircraft fire from her guns shot away at the planes circling above. Merchant vessels and civilian boats were being caught up in the wave of burning petrol from the tanker. Further out he caught brief glimpses of the lone destroyer which had made it out of the harbor. *HMS Mohawk* had gotten her fires under control and her guns were back in action. Along with the cruiser *Nigeria*, the two ships were thundering away at the Spanish town of Algeciras.

Double lines of brief lights were flashing from across the bay. Those would have been the Spanish gun batteries. They'd fire in unison at the Royal Navy vessels. Long lines of zipping tracer bullets skipped across the water from positions on the west side. He couldn't see what they were shooting at, but his gut instinct was that more boats were approaching out of the west, just as they'd done from the east.

Before they'd lost their transmitting tower, they'd gotten off a signal. There'd been some interference on the receiving end, but several reports had come in from a Royal Navy task force that was supposedly on the way. He hoped that the radios aboard either *Nigeria* or *Mohawk* were still in working order and that some form of communication was taking place with the outside world.

The general put his glasses down. Though they'd been caught off-guard, the garrison was completely mobilized. But it had taken the better part of an hour to get it that way. The Spaniards had been quite precise in their timetables.

The North Front was rapidly being hammered away at. Defenses that it had taken months to put together, were now being methodically taken apart with each shell that fell on it. But it would take a miracle for an attacker to just come straight through without taking uncounted casualties of their own.

Richardson stood, waited, and watched. All he could do now was watch things play out and pray for dawn to come.

* * *

Guillermo Ramos tapped the back of his left hand nervously. The general had been tasked with securing the northern entrance into British Gibraltar. To send his troops storming through the breach they'd created, and to overwhelm the defenders beyond. He looked up at the enormous Rock, fires burning at its base, and couldn't help but feel only inches tall at that moment.

General Yagüe had personally sent one of his staff officers to ensure that the attack kicked off at precisely the correct moment. Which had been ten minutes ago. He'd hesitated briefly at first. He was supposed to coordinate the attack with the arrival of an Italian naval squadron, which was supposed to materialize from the east and add supporting fire for his soldiers. So far, no naval support had come. But he'd been forced to give the order anyway. Now, having done just that, he could only watch as the first of his brigades started their charge.

From points all across the border, the troops assembled. With artillery support carving a path ahead of them, the men of the *Ostras Brigade* launched their attack, storming across the burning fields by the thousands, maneuvering around the wreckage and the barrier of obstacles the British had put up. They crossed into the British enclave and kept charging. The burnt-out buildings of the airfield didn't slow them down a bit. Hundreds of them stopped briefly as they ran by the airstrip, firing their rifles at the enemy, but the British positions were far out of range for any sort of accuracy.

General Ramos shook his head at the stupidity of it. But what did he expect? They were, after all, just cannon fodder. Half-trained recruits who'd been taken, given a rifle, and told to charge into the fray. *Ostras*, the Spanish word for Oyster, betrayed the fact that most of them had been conscripted from small fishing villages. Their job was simple: let the enemy mow them down by the score, and deplete their resources for when the real attack came.

But they charged in anyhow, not knowing the role they were playing. Amateur officers lead their men toward the enemy defenses just beyond the airstrip. As the first lines of them made it passed the airstrip, the first enemy mortars and field guns fired on them. Whole sections were cut down in only a few seconds. That's when the forward lines stopped. Some of them returned fire with their pathetic rifles, but many others simply put their heads down. But that didn't stop the mortars from landing right on top of them.

Officers shouted, urging them forward. Few did. Even as Spanish shells flew by overhead, giving them some cover, most of them barely moved an inch. Eventually, a few units moved forward, disappearing into the shadow of the Rock. Enemy pillboxes built into the ground opened up as they approached, cutting even more of them to pieces. To the British defenders, it must've seemed as if the attack had already stalled out.

Of the nearly five thousand men of the conscripted *Ostras Brigade*, a thousand had fallen in those opening minutes. The rest of them just seemed to sit there, taking their punishment.

General Ramos watched the scene and breathed deeply at the sight of those men dying. And in the darkness around him, the next wave moved into position.

* * *

Eight of the German-made Henschel Hs 123s came skimming in at just about a thousand feet. The biplanes, which the Vichy government had given to them, moved slowly through the air, coming down on the center of the town just west of the Rock. Machine guns fired on the streets below, and there was the distinctive popping sound of rifles firing back. The first plane dropped all of its 50-kilogram bombs onto the town below. Loud booming followed.

AA guns from *HMS Duncan* fired up at the approach, hitting the second plane, causing it to spin out of control. It crashed into the mountainside. But the third and fourth biplanes were able to drop their bombs on the town. Anti-aircraft gunners on the ground managed to break up the rest of the flight before they could add to the damage.

The lead boats from the Algeciras side of Gibraltar Bay coasted toward the western arm of the North Mole of the harbor. As the occupants launched out they were met by British riflemen who gunned them down before they could get far. More boats emerged, their occupants firing back as their prows hit the concrete wall, and began to unload. Machine gun nests and pillboxes on the western side cut down many of them. But a surprise element gave the Spaniards an advantage.

Flame throwers spewed to life. Several boats unloaded troops with heavy packs on. Long lines of fire gushed out onto the British positions. Machine gunners abandoned their positions, and a bunker that was coordinating the defense was set ablaze. The men inside burned to death.

"General." A sergeant handed Yagüe a report.

The eastern landings were hung up on the rock face, unable to progress further. The British there had them pinned to the beaches and were picking them off. The northern assault had sent in the first of its waves and was preparing to send the next. Ten minutes late as circumstances would have it. But the bombers had hit their targets, and the artillery barrage had achieved some real measures of success.

No mention of any Italian support, however. He half-crumpled the message.

Damn Italians.

If he'd had the support that they'd promised, his eastern landings might be going better than they were. All in all, however, things seemed to be progressing about like he'd expected. Though it was still early, and dawn was three hours away, anything could very well happen. There were over ten thousand British defenders at Gibraltar. Though he outnumbered them six to one, he had no intention of misjudging them.

He gave the young lieutenant a hard look and pointed his finger at the battle across the bay.

"Get on the phone. Have Colonel Nadal send in the next wave. The heavy bombers will be coming in shortly. Have them drop their bombs on top of that north road. At the base of the Rock. Do you understand me?"

The sergeant looked uncertain. "Sir? The road? Won't they hit our own soldiers?"

The general gave him back a cold, hard stare. The other man bowed his head in understanding and left him.

* * *

There was a brief pause in artillery fire from the positions just north of the town of La Línea de la Concepción, just north of Gibraltar. General Ramos had ordered the second phase of the main attack to commence. From points all along the border, the soldiers of the 32nd Division stood ready to move at a moment's notice. Up ahead there was still the staccato of guns firing, but it had died down noticeably in the past few minutes.

The general stood on a sharp hill, overlooking the battle. The men of the *Ostras Brigade* were still down there, but they'd taken quite the beating. Enemy mortars were hitting them left, right, and center. He couldn't tell quite clearly, but the general had to assume that the brigade had taken heavy casualties. But better them than his professional soldiers. The men of the 32nd Division were quality troops, veterans of the war with the Republicans. They knew their business, and killing was second nature.

The general waited. After a minute he finally heard the sound he'd been waiting for. Even with no lights on he could see the dark shapes of the bombing flight flying in. Six twin-engine bombers came in from both east and north, flying only a couple thousand feet in the air. The men had been given strict orders not to threaten to give away their positions with unruly cheers, but a few let go with screams of victory and vengeance.

The three planes out of the east were the first to move into attack position. AA guns from Gibraltar streamed upwards. Bullets hit the first bomber, but not before it released its bomb load. Six 150-kilogram projectiles came diving downward, and a line exploded across the front, where a single road rounded the northern end of the Rock. The next two followed, turning the entire front for a thousand yards into mushrooming earth.

Ramos let out a brief chuckle as he watched the destruction. Some of those bombs had fallen short of their target, killing the men of the *Ostras Brigade* as well. The second flight came across from the north, pouring their own destruction down on the defenses. Secondary explosions went off in the distance as ammunition dumps exploded, taking a pillbox or two with it. The entire front of the Rock of Gibraltar shook furiously, and for a brief moment, the general didn't know if the whole thing was simply going to come down.

"Send them!" Ramos ordered.

The word was passed. Even as the bomb explosions were still rising off in the distance, the first soldiers began their movement toward their objective. One of the attacking bombers fell into the Bay of Gibraltar, but the other five escaped with little harm. It was at that moment that his guns, which had been silent, opened back up. Scores of projectiles flew a hundred meters above the heads of the advancing soldiers, landing in the burning stretch of landing between what was left of the airstrip, and the battered enemy defenses.

But instead of explosions going off, the canisters fired began to release thick smoke. Dozens of them landed and released, just yards in front of the enemy line. Before the first of the 32nd Division even reached the border, smoke was already spreading out. There was a good wind tonight, but Ramos had fired enough to hopefully cloak their approach for a few minutes. A few minutes was all they would need.

The division moved straight in, advancing in a regiment-wide front. Close to eight thousand men in all. The gun batteries in the rear, having dropped the smoke screen, turned back to a general barrage, but this time it was much more methodical. Rather than flinging large amounts of shells in the general direction of the enemy, now the fire came slower as gun crews aimed, fired, re-aimed, adjusting for the movement of the advancing infantry, and fired again.

Through the smoke, there were bright flashes of light coming from the British defensive line. Machine gunners fired blindly into the smoke. The defensive fire was much slower now, following the great bombing. He had to think that there was a lot of shock over on that side of the fight. They'd taken a lot of punishment after that last, and with any luck, the second wave would break them.

* * *

A heavy blast of hot air went down the length of the mountain, over the line of men still firing down on the attack against the eastern flank. For a moment it seemed overpowering, but it passed with most of the men not taking any lengthy note of it. What had been a single battalion, just a while ago, had turned into at least a regiment of

Spanish soldiers assaulting them from out of the sea. For the company-sized unit holding those ramparts, things had gotten quite desperate. Ammunition, for instance, was running low. Mortar support had died off, and the flares which had lit up the beach below were becoming fewer and fewer.

A lieutenant had shown up a few minutes earlier with another platoon, and taken charge. From the maze of tunnels running through the Rock, medics arrived to care for the wounded, but no amount of medics would save them if the ammo ran dry. And in the dark, it was damned impossible to shoot a man with a single shot from a hundred yards.

"Fix your bayonets!" Lance Corporal Burrett called out as he knelt to fix his own to the end of his rifle. The Spaniards were crawling their way to the roadway, and from there they'd scale up the rockface in droves. Once they got a toehold on the ramparts, that would be it. Unless more reinforcements came out to assist, then their positions would simply be overrun.

One man launched a grenade over the side, caught a bullet to the throat, and fell back. Machine gunners ran out of ammo, and switched to their rifles. Some resorted to picking up rocks and throwing them down the side.

"Jesus Christ!" Burrett popped his head over the side, and fired at two men who were climbing up the side of the mountain only twenty feet away. He got one in the chest, missed the other, then fell back. "They're getting damn close!"

The young lieutenant looked at him but said nothing. Realistically, what could he say? The officer had sent a runner already, begging for relief, but none had yet emerged. Should the ramparts fall, the enemy would sweep through the tunnels, and then they'd have a real problem on their hand. Burrett left his position on the left end of the line and made his way up to the lieutenant.

"Sir!" The officer gave him a look that said he knew what Burrett was going to say, but was already shaking his head. "I'll go. Jesus. We can't hold here if we don't have anything to shoot at them with."

The lieutenant grimaced, then reluctantly nodded his head. "Go!"

Burrett turned to move toward the tunnel. He was just about to take the first step when a head stuck itself over the opposite side of the wall. He brought his rifle back over him just in time to shoot the man's head. As he did, the first of those who'd climbed the rocky hillside jumped up and over the wall. Instead of running toward the tunnel to ask for assistance, he pushed the lieutenant aside and rushed the Spaniard with his bayonet. He stuck the fat man once, then pushed in hard. The man died staring at him.

"Defend yourselves!" The lieutenant cried, blowing his whistle. He pulled his Colt 1911 out and leveled it at the next head that came over the wall.

The men in the center of the line wavered. Some of them had run dry of ammo, turning to use the butts of their rifles to club the Spaniards to death. Others used bayonets or hand-held knives. Whatever they could. One after another Spanish soldiers pushed themselves up the side of the hill from the road below, scaling over the rock wall, like armies of old besieging some castle.

Burrett fired off the last round from his rifle, turned it around, and dealt a crushing blow to the head of a Spaniard. It was a general melee. The lieutenant fired his final shots before picking up a discarded rifled and making use of it. Burrett heard something that made him think of a car horn honking coming from up the line. It sounded again. He turned to look.

Out of the tunnel, some fifty paces away, a group of civilian-garbed men was running out and down the wall. The riflemen still firing away outside the tunnel, saw them and gave a cheer. The lead man held up a hunting horn and blew on it enthusiastically. They rushed down the battlement wall handing out clips of ammo to the men on it. Some had rifles slung across their arms, and those took up positions of their own.

"Holy Christ!" a private cried out joyfully, taking a handful of ammo.

"Civvies?" the lieutenant asked, to which Burrett shook his head.

"Merchant marines."

The white trousers of the merchant crews made for a happy sight. Men cheered as they arrived. The few Spaniards who had made it over the wall saw what had happened, and threw up their arms in surrender. The seamen didn't stop for a moment. Those that didn't fill gaps in the line handed out ammo, or helped get wounded men off the wall. There was no more mortar support, and no flares lit up the beaches. They were still outnumbered, but they'd held. Just paces below them, crossing the road twenty feet down the side of the mountain, more and more Spanish troops came.

* * *

Captain Mora stood in front of General Yague with his head hanging, his arms limp at his side.

"Why is that ship still afloat?" Yagüe asked him, pointing with two fingers at the cruiser in the distance. She was still maneuvering about, absent any signs of damage. Yagüe had turned an inordinate number of guns onto that ship after the bombers had struck the Rock, but still, they hadn't ended the confrontation. "I asked you a question."

Mora breathed heavily. "I'm sorry, General," was all he could get out.

Yagüe pursed his lips. He was seething with anger right now. That cruiser and the destroyer that had escaped the harbor were causing a real inconvenience right now. It had upended a couple of his heavy guns in a return fire and was forcing him to commit more resources to sink it than he would have liked. The situation had to be dealt with.

"I ordered all fire to be placed on it. Did I not?"

"Yes, sir."

"And yet, there it is. Explain."

"We shifted all the batteries, as you ordered, sir. But… we just couldn't get clear shots, sir." Mora shook his head desperately. Other officers on the hotel rooftop stood by quietly. "The darkness… we couldn't get a clear shot."

"I see." Yagüe gave the man an almost sympathetic look. He nodded, and in one fluid motion, he pulled out his sidearm and shot the man in the head. He then turned around and chose another officer. "Captain Lopez. You just took over his command. I want that damn ship sunk. Do you understand me?"

"Yes, sir," Lopez answered. He gave Mora's dead body a quick look then made off.

"Someone get this God damn body out of here," Yagüe ordered.

* * *

The forward line of the 32nd Division advanced in a five-hundred-yard wide front. They drove through what was left of the *Ostras* and on toward the enemy lines. These men were professional soldiers. They knew how to fight, and how to move. Fire and advance, fire and advance. Machine gunners would set up, cover advancing infantry, then uproot and move ten paces.

General Ramos peered through his glasses. It was very dark under the Rock, and the smoke didn't allow him to see what was beyond. Barb wire and other obstacles had been successively shelled until there was little left in the way. The men advanced, and he saw them go right up until they disappeared into the haze of smoke.

His shelling had slackened as well. The batteries were running low on ammunition, and what was left had been turned to the mountaintop. The searchlights that had so casually scanned the night sky just hours before, were now motionless. The crews must have abandoned them at some point. Reports were still coming in of the fighting on other fronts. General Yagüe's batteries in Algeciras had shifted their fire to a pair of Royal Navy ships, and his waterborne assault on the harbor was still being fought out. What was happening on the eastern flank was just about anyone's guess. Reports of breaches along the fortifications were countered by others saying the assault wave was still fighting on the beach.

But worst of all, absolutely zero news had arrived concerning the Italian fleet that was supposed to materialize out of the east. Those guns could have made the difference between a successful landing, or a disaster. Ramos didn't know what deal had been made with Mussolini for that support, but the bald man had made no friends here today.

The second attack wave of troops had reached the airstrip, pivoted left, then charged off into the fray. The next battalions moved up, ready to strike to the right. They too advanced until the smoke enveloped the last of them. A few wounded could be seen limping or crawling back to their lines.

So long as his men were down there, and he could hear gunfire, he knew that every moment that went by they were wearing down the British defenders. He looked off to the side roads that led down to the town below. Men of the 31st Division, the *Argonese*, filed through the streets. They were his best. They were also his last chance. Once the 32nd made a breakthrough, he'd send them in. The nail on the coffin.

Beyond the line of smoke, all one could see was the dull flash of guns firing. But you could hear the sound of death coming from everywhere. The Spaniards rushed through the haze, firing at only what moved in front of them. The British didn't have the problem of caution, and were firing into the smoke, albeit blindly. Grenades were thrown, and explosives had been detonated ahead of the attacking line, but it didn't stop them.

The first of the Spanish troops came out of the opposite side of the smoke firing their rifles at the British fortifications. Their bullets pelted uselessly against concrete bunkers, while gunners inside shot them on sight. Combat engineers moved forward after the first of the infantry, tossing their explosives back in return. A forward bunker erupted in flame as an incendiary landed on it, killing the men inside.

The second wave thrust left, toward the eastern side of the Rock. They ran smack into the defenders with only yards to spare. They stopped only to trade point-blank rifle fire with the British soldiers. The right flank, despite heavy bombing damage, met considerable resistance as they drove toward the main town to link up with the men storming the harbor.

At that point, General Richardson had deployed his reserve force, which had been kept in the vast tunnels dug under the Rock. Men of the King's Regiment and the Somerset Light Infantry came rushing out in a counterattack on the center. Just north of the Rock ran the Devil's Tower Road, which ran around the length of the mountain. Just beyond that road was a fenced-off cemetery. The counterattack pressed into the Spanish force crossing through that cemetery. Men with Enfield rifles, Bren light machine guns, and any vehicles that could get through drove right through the line, cleaving a hole that separated the center from the Spanish left flank.

They forced the middle of the attacking force to stall out. The Spaniards there settled in, trading shots with the British. But they would advance no more. As minutes ticked by, the smoke began to clear in the night breeze. General Ramos could get faint pictures of the stalled-out second attack. They'd pinned the enemy to the wall, but they hadn't broken them.

"Send them all in," he ordered quietly to his staff officers.

The men of the *Argonese Division* started their attack. But they didn't go in line, as the first two had. Instead, they've advanced in columns. Three of them moved in like a three-fingered hand. It wasn't until the first units were beyond the line where the *Ostras* had stopped that they unfolded into battle line.

By this time the smoke screen had almost completely blown away, and one could see just about everything on the North Front. It was a wasteland, full of scorched earth, charred remains of airplanes, and death. Spanish bodies littered the ground for a hundred yards. The final remnants of the British garrison were holding to a small area to the front of and the two sides of the great Rock of Gibraltar. The town and the harbor were burning uncontrollably.

The Spanish troops advanced in three enormous phalanxes. The *Argonese* was ten thousand strong, most were veterans. The advanced companies fanned out and joined the men of the 32nd that were still holding the British down. They pinned down enemy positions on the right, trying to link up with those troops storming the town, but the defenders were more resilient than anticipated.

Ramos watched the action. He even found himself praying to God to let his men push through. If they could just push through on the right...

He scanned the horizon, watching the men approaching the front line. If the British should have another reserve, then he should still have more than enough troops to deal with it, though it would be costly. If the enemy had committed their entire force, then his boys would be within sight of victory. Not that it would be easy, but he much preferred to have some semblance of his army left after this action.

As the lead units of the *Argonese Division* approached the rear of the 32nd, there was a great lurch forward by the entire army. There must have been close to fifteen thousand of them, all squeezed into this tiny strip of land no wider than a kilometer and a half, firing away with all that they had. He almost felt sorry for the British down there. Almost.

"We have aircraft," a voice said. Ramos looked around and saw a man holding his finger to the sky. "I think they're our Henschels."

The flight of biplanes came down out of the western skies, right toward the town. At first, Ramos thought they were going to go for the two Royal Navy ships still putting up a fight, but they didn't even aim for it. In fact… Ramos brought his binoculars up and looked at the two ships down there. Both of them were still trading shots with General Yagüe's batteries in Algeciras. He looked back at the biplanes.

"Why aren't they shooting at each other?" Ramos said aloud.

The lead plane broke away from its approach on the town, shifted north and dropped out of the sky like a vulture. His guns opened fire on the line of Spanish troops, strafing right through the formation, then dropping a single bomb on them before pulling up and away. The bomb tore right through the Spanish line, followed by a second plane that released its own on the center. As it pulled away a rear gunner opened fire on the men below.

There were eight of them in total. Each dropped their bombs right on top of the Spanish lines like precision marksmen. The infantry caught out in the open with no air support became victims of machine gun fire from the air and ground. The planes each made second runs on the enemy below, who were already fleeing backward. Their main guns cut hundreds of them down in the cramped space. One pilot brought his plane around right over Ramos's position, half rolled, and the general could quite clearly see the distinctive blue, white, and red roundel of the Royal Navy Air Arm.

Guillermo Ramos stood petrified. He watched as the flight of planes sent the Spanish Army scattering back north, strafing them as they fled. He scrunched his cap up in his hand and threw it angrily on the ground. The officers around him all ran, and the men around the artillery positions ducked for cover as the planes buzzed by them as well. The very last thing that General Ramos remembered before being dragged away by his men, was the sound of a gigantic cheer that went up from across the distance.

* * *

It was morning but you wouldn't have known it. Smoke from the fires that were still burning had blotted out most of the sun. Much of it was dark, thick smoke from oil fires. There was an unnerving silence in the air. Something about the silence might have been terrifying considering the intense fighting that had gone on throughout the night. The artillery and gunfire had been so extreme that some were quite certain that they'd wake up this morning to find the Rock itself little more than a pile of rubble.

Under the darkened skies one could hear the call of seagulls flying above the thick smoke and gentle waves smacking against the beaches. A swift breeze picked up, and after a few minutes, the great Rock of Gibraltar became visible to all who looked toward it. It was quiet. Those who were going to die had done so already and only the cries of the wounded and the hushed voices of the survivors were heard.

Somewhere a distant ship's bell rang. The morning breeze blew away the smoke, exposing the great Rock, and then all could see it. Atop the Rock the Union Jack waved in the wind. Ripped, torn, and a bit worse for the wear, but it flew intact.

Offshore, Admiral Somerville gazed through his binoculars on the deck of the damaged battleship *Rodney*, his sights set on the flag fluttering in the breeze. His eyes welled up, and a single tear streamed down his cheek. They'd survived the night.

To the soldiers, airmen and civilians huddled around the base of the huge Rock, and from all around Gibraltar that could see it, the first sight of the flag sent up a tremendous cheer.

And across the dividing bay, at the roof of the Mirador Hotel, in the city of Algeciras, General Juan Yagüe stared through his own set of binoculars. His mouth dangled open and the aides around him stood silently by. It was unbelievable. It couldn't be. It just couldn't have happened this way. It had started so well. How could it all have gone so wrong? Through his lens, he watched as the breeze blew the smoke away. The tattered-looking flag flapped about defiantly.

His own eyes welled up, and a different sort of tear began to stream down his face. Slowly he lowered the field glasses, then turned hesitantly back to his staff officers, none of whom could bring themselves to look at the general. From one hand he let the binoculars slip from his grip and fall away. With the other hand, he tore open the top of his uniform. Buttons snapped off, dinging on the rooftop.

He had one duty now. He had the unfortunate business of informing Madrid of the failure. As he began to walk toward the stairwell door, he wondered which one of his officers would be the one who volunteered to put the bullet into the back of his head.

CHAPTER TWENTY-SIX

Carl Goerdeler made sure that the curtains overlapped one another, preventing any unwanted eyes from seeing into the third-story window of the Leipzig apartment. He ran his fingers down the thick, black velvet to make sure they were straight. The wide apartment belonged to an old acquaintance of his, from his days as mayor of the city. The building itself was half empty. Many of its former residents had been deported to the occupied zones as enemies of the state. As a result, the building was as quiet a place as any was going to be in the city. Under the cover of the dark of night, it became an ideal place for a group gathering.

There were twelve people in the room, including him. Some were military, or formerly so, but most were civilians. Some of them still worked in government sectors under the guise of being good and obedient members of Hitler's government.

Goerdeler exhaled noisily. Feeling irritated, he fished into his pocket for his cigarettes. He fell back into a cushioned, leather chair and lit up.

"Where the hell is he?" he whispered under his breath.

"Patience," another man said. He was an older man, well dressed, with an air of upper-class gentry. Ludwig Beck had been chief of the general staff before his abrupt resignation three years earlier, in protest of the planned invasion of Czechoslovakia. Since his retirement, however, the general had wasted little time in gathering together a cadre of like-minded people to his side. People, Germans mostly, who felt that the Nazis represented a serious danger. Not just to Europe, but to Germany as well.

"Yes," Goerdeler replied facetiously. "Patience."

"Look, Carl, he'll be here," Beck told him. "He has responsibilities, and he can't afford to just drop them in order to run off to some secret meeting. Be patient. He'll be here shortly."

Goerdeler nodded. His left leg was dangling over his right knee, and he began to swing it about anxiously.

"We might as well get started before he gets here," another man suggested.

"Yes!" Goerdeler said. "Wonderful idea."

"Very well," Beck replied, his tone steady, and showing no outward sign of concern over the lateness of their colleague. "Since we're here. I'd like you to hear from Hellmuth first if you don't mind."

"Fine. Whatever," Goerdeler replied anxiously.

Eyes shifted to a man in uniform, sitting in a chair in the dimly lit corner of the room. The rank on his uniform said that he was a Wehrmacht colonel. This was only his second or third meeting with the men in the room. His face was familiar to any who frequented Army High Command in Berlin, and he'd been specifically vouched for by Beck himself as a man who could be trusted.

"Where to begin?" the man said.

"Why don't you just give us a rundown of what you told me earlier, Hellmuth," Beck told him. Colonel Hellmuth Stieff was an adjutant to General Halder, the Army Chief of Staff. His position gave him great insight into the goings-on at High Command. He'd been an aide to Beck when he'd occupied that role, and the two men had been quietly disdainful of Hitler and his party well before any fighting had started. When Beck had left, he'd convinced Stieff to stay on under Halder.

"Well," Stieff began, "Hitler has approved of a plan by Himmler. I had some paperwork cross my desk yesterday evening. The SS have temporarily commandeered some trains between our factories and Vichy. Our men have been told to stand down, and allow Himmler's people to move about as they wish."

"Trains for what?" another man asked.

"Probably moving some of the so-called undesirables out of France," Goerdeler suggested. "Now that they've got a new ally there, Himmler's probably convinced Vichy to turn over their Jewish minorities. Not the first time we've seen that. The trains are probably taking them right to the factories. Used as slave labor." He spat the last words and shook his head.

"I don't think so, Carl," Beck replied. "Go on, Hellmuth. Tell them what you told me."

"Part of my responsibilities include ensuring that war production gets to the right places," Stieff went on. "We purchase from the factories and have them shipped directly to where we need. Tanks, planes, bombs, etc. Everything must be accounted for. I had a memorandum handed to me by Halder himself. We were expecting a new shipment of armored vehicles, even tanks, to go toward outfitting our divisions. We're phasing out most of our older tanks, as most of you know. Handing them off to the Hungarians and Romanians. Anyways. A shipment for approximately a hundred of the Panzer Threes has been diverted from use by the Wehrmacht."

"Threes?" Goerdeler asked. "Aren't those obsolete anyhow?"

"Not obsolete. But the new Fours are coming off the assembly line in great quantity now," Stieff replied. "Threes are still quite effective in the field. At any rate, the order from Halder came straight down from Hitler himself. Signed by him."

"They're shipping them directly from the factories to unoccupied France," Beck said. "Listen to what Hellmuth is telling us. Orders from Hitler, the Army is to have no part in this."

"An SS operation?" someone suggested. It was Erich Kordt, a member of the diplomatic service who worked for Joachim von Ribbentrop.

"Exactly," Beck responded.

Goerdeler shrank back in his cushioned chair, confused at what he'd just been told. "I'm not sure I follow."

Colonel Stieff answered. "The SS have requested, and Hitler approved, of a large number of weapons be transported via railway, to be handed over to the French in the south." Goerdeler still wasn't putting it together.

"The SS are arming the French, under Laval," Beck told him. "From what Hellmuth has told me, this is just the first of several shipments. There'll undoubtedly be more to come in days ahead."

"Are you saying what I think you are, Beck?"

"Yes, Carl. I am. The SS engineered that overthrow, it's no secret. Now Hitler has an ally in France. One that he can prop up."

"There's only one reason why that much equipment will be going to France. I suspect, they'll be used to form the nucleus of a new French Army. One whose first loyalty will be to Pierre Laval." Stieff's words cut like a knife. Even Goerdeler, not a military man, understood the meaning.

"And by default, Himmler," Goerdeler said, and Beck nodded.

The SOL, the new collaborationist regime in France, had quickly positioned itself closely with Himmler following the coup. The head of the SS had spent an excessive amount of time and resources propping up his new ally. That was now showing signs of a blossoming relationship. Pierre Laval had just recently signed an order rounding up religious and other minorities from all over France. Thousands of his new national police had taken to arresting anyone even vaguely suspected of disloyalty to the new regime.

"I thought Hitler didn't trust those people?" Goerdeler asked. "That's a lot of guns to give to people who just surrendered not three months ago."

"But it lines up with some things that have come to my attention," Erich Kordt added, and faces turned to him. Kordt was nominally a part of the German diplomatic mission to Switzerland. Though Ribbentrop's intense dislike for him had meant he was a junior member of the embassy, he still kept his ears to the ground. "Money transfers through Zurich. Some of the old MEFO accounts that have been sitting in Swiss banks have seen considerable transfers of money. I didn't think anything of it when I learned about it. But now it makes sense. The franc is practically worthless nowadays. Reichsmarks would give Vichy a real –"

The front door creaked open, and everyone went suddenly still. A uniformed man entered, taking off his hat and closing the door quietly behind him. Everyone relaxed when it was realized that it was Oster, the man they'd been waiting on.

"Apologies for my lateness," he said to them all.

"Come in Hans," Beck greeted him. "You know Hellmuth Stieff. He was just giving us a rundown of things. Go on Erich. Swiss bank accounts?"

"Yes. I was just finishing. Millions of marks are being quietly transferred out of Switzerland. They coincide with Himmler's visits to France. After hearing the colonel here speak, it dawned on me the connection. The SS give our marks to the French, who in turn, use it to purchase weapons from our factories."

"The French?" Oster asked. He looked around at them. "I know I only just arrived. But am I to assume that the Laval regime has been receiving aid secretly from the SS?" Beck nodded. "Huh. That's quite interesting. At a state function a few weeks ago I spoke with Reich Minister Speer. He asked me what I knew of private communications between Berlin and Vichy. He was quite insistent actually."

"Speer, you say?" Beck asked. "The minister of war production was asking you about talks between Hitler and Laval? Strange." He rubbed his lower lip as he pondered on it. "Possible that Speer's been kept out of the loop on something."

Oster shrugged. "Possible. Time may tell what comes of it. I apologize that I ran late, but it was a busy day at the Bendlerblock." He made an interesting expression. "Some intelligence reports came through the office this morning. Signals intelligence out of Brittany have indicated that the British are assembling an expeditionary force in Wales. I had to brief Brauchitsch on it before I left. We don't have its end destination figured out just yet, but it seems likely that they'd be sent to Spain in retaliation for the attack on Gibraltar."

Beck leaned forward in his chair. "Are you certain? About the troops being assembled, I mean?"

"We know they're there," Oster replied. "Aerial flyovers confirm that, and a Royal Navy squadron is assembling in the Bristol Channel. There are enough transports to move a couple divisions."

"Has there been a declaration of war yet?" Goerdeler inquired.

"Not yet. It looked as if there was to be one, but, there's some intelligence to suggest that there are some backroom pleas being made. Some of our assets in Madrid and Lisbon are of the mind that there's some back-channel discussions going on between certain people in Spain's military and London. We're not sure what about, but something is stirring in Madrid."

Beck took it all in. There was a lot of information to absorb, and a lot of secrets to unravel. His old military thinking took over. The Spanish attack had come as a surprise to everyone who'd heard about it, which weren't that many. The news certainly hadn't been made public. It failed, but should it have succeeded Doctor Goebbels would even now be playing it up over the radio as a great triumph.

"Sounds to me like things didn't go according to plan, and now parties in Spain are quietly trying to make gestures," Kordt said, to which both Beck and Oster nodded. "I'll make a few quiet inquiries when I return to the ministry. Nothing too deep."

"Be careful, old friend," Beck told him. "Paranoia runs through the foreign ministry these days."

"It'll all be in the briefing for Hitler tomorrow," Oster stated. "I've got the staff working up the details now. But I'll tell you this; should the British send an expedition down to Spain, Hitler could well see that as the opportune time to launch the invasion."

In the dim corner, Colonel Stieff shook his head. "I don't think Hitler wants to invade England."

Oster looked over at him with interest. "What makes you say that?"

"Halder. Every day he gives Hitler an update on preparations, he comes back huffing and puffing. You know how Halder is, talks when he shouldn't. Every indication that he's given me is that Hitler balks at the mere mention of Sea Lion. He seems to have lost his confidence recently."

"Hmm. Maybe he's getting tired of war," Goerdeler sarcastically commented.

"Getting back to Spain," Beck began, looking at Oster. "What do you plan to say tomorrow?"

Oster shrugged. "Just what we have to go on. If some new intelligence comes in between now and tomorrow's meeting that can paint a clearer picture for us, then we'll brief Hitler on it. Right now there's nothing definitive to suggest anything one way or another. They could go to Spain, or they could not. Why?"

"I was just thinking," Beck replied. "If there are behind-the-scenes talks going on, without Franco's knowledge presumably, it could mean some in Madrid are not happy with recent events. We can't know for sure. But assume there is. Then Churchill sends a force to land on the peninsula, with the aim of eliminating the threat of Spain. If even a couple of divisions set sail it could make Britain's position even more tenuous at home. If Hitler believes that to be the case, as you said, he may launch Sea Lion." His eyes floated around the room, only to turn back to Oster in the end. "So long as Britain remains, the war will never truly be won. Not in Hitler's eyes."

"I see." Oster nodded, understanding what Beck was saying. "Well... we can't make any conclusions about British intentions, can we? A training exercise in Wales perhaps."

"What about Himmler's office?" Stieff asked. "If Reich Security has intelligence of their own...?"

Oster thought about the question, then reluctantly shrugged. "I can't do anything about the Reich Security Office. Though if they had something definitive, then it would've been given to Hitler already I believe."

"I don't believe that it'll matter," Kordt told them. "If Spain and Britain go to war or not, one of three things will happen. The first: Britain will be successful in a short time. The Royal Navy can pound Spanish ports into dust in no time. The second outcome: they're locked together in a prolonged ground war, in which case Spain will ask for German assistance. But I don't believe that will be the case. London doesn't need another war right now. I also don't believe most Spaniards want German intervention."

"The third option?" Goerdeler asked him.

"The third option would be what Oster and Beck are eluding to. Spain is in a very fragile position. They've attacked one of the great powers of the world, without a declaration of war. Also without Hitler's aid. Why?" He shook his head, confused at any potential reasoning behind it. "It doesn't make any sense. His countrymen don't want an alliance with Germany. If Franco acted independently then he'll suffer the consequences alone."

Goerdeler signaled he agreed with that. "Well, it'll be awfully hard to disguise things if a British expeditionary force lands in Spain. Even if the Spanish people turn on Franco, London will have a serious problem on their hands for a good while." He exhaled noisily in agitation. "Anyway. Aren't we getting a bit off point here? The object of this group is to bring an end to the Nazi regime, not sit around and speculate on what may or may not happen in another country." He jumped forward again, waving his finger straight up in the air. "We need to take action now!"

"We agree, Carl," Beck said to him. "There are many ways we can take action. We're not in a position right now where we can just march into the Reich Chancellery and order the Army to put down their guns and go home."

Goerdeler sighed. "He should've been overthrown when we had the people in place." Beck gave him an offended look, and he immediately waved his hand in apology at the remark. "I didn't mean to suggest you, Ludwig. I just get so frustrated at times. Two years ago we had all the pieces neatly in place, then... Czechoslovakia, then Poland, then Denmark. All those who thought the Nazis were a threat to the nation just fell right in line."

"Not all of them, Carl."

"Carl's right, though," Oster said. "The time has come. We've been blowing around in the wind for too long. We're going to need to take action. Otherwise, I truly fear for the future of Germany."

CHAPTER TWENTY-SEVEN

General Asensio Cabanillas was already on the phone when Foreign Minister Suñer walked into Franco's palace office. Franco wasn't there, but several of the nation's highest-ranking military commanders were. All of them look tired, all looked grim. Asensio Cabanillas had the receiver pressed to his ear as the foreign minister arrived. He gave Suñer a silent nod in greeting.

The other officers present were mostly Army, but there were a few from the Navy and the state police service also. Nobody looked happy. It was just after four o'clock in the afternoon. Madrid had been locked down for two days now, but there were reports of mass gatherings, and protests coming in from all over the capital region. Thousands, maybe tens of thousands of people had taken to the streets. The police had become overwhelmed almost immediately as they'd been unprepared for the civil disruption. Worse yet, there'd been radio reports of similar things taking place in other major cities. Andalusia had been almost completely cut off from the capital. There'd been some sporadic reports of fighting in that region. Scarier still, were the dispatches of British naval vessels shelling positions around Cadiz, followed by even more disturbing rumors.

"Is it true? Suñer demanded to know. The general held up a single finger at him as he finished up his phone call.

Around the room, the other officers and officials stood quietly by, speaking in small groups to each other. They averted their eyes as the foreign minister scanned around, taking note of who was present and who was not.

Finally, the general hung up the phone. There was a very serious look on his face.

"Is it true?" Suñer repeated his question.

"About Cadiz?" he asked, and Suñer nodded. Asensio Cabanillas reached into his pocket, pulling out what was left of his cigarette pouch. There was only a single smoke left. He lit it up and crumpled the pack up and tossed it in the basket. "I'm afraid so."

The foreign minister's expression turned from shock to terror in mere seconds. He looked absently around the room, running his fingers through his hair. His eyes went blank, and looked at the general as if he wanted the other man to simply revise the information, and tell him that everything was alright.

"Where is the generalissimo?" Suñer asked him.

"He's on his way."

"So what is the situation?"

The general blew out a stream of cigarette smoke, then craned his head toward the map of Spain propped against the bookcase.

"The British have shelled our naval bases at Rota and Ferrol," he told him. "Contact has been lost with our main airbases around the region as well. We've sent couriers and pilots to reconnoiter the situation. We haven't heard back yet."

The foreign minister's expression got even worse, and beads of sweat formed on his forehead. The man looked like he was having some sort of breakdown. Asensio Cabanillas studied him.

"Are you alright, Minister?" Suñer shot him a panicked look. His eyes were dark, and his hands were moving around erratically.

"You... you said that victory was assured," Suñer finally stuttered out. "You said weeks ago that victory was assured. That we would –"

"I said no such thing!" the general snapped back. The foreign minister took a step back as he flinched. "I said we stand a better than even chance. There are no certainties in war, Ramon. None. Our intelligence was accurate about British defenses at Gibraltar, but your so-called allies never materialized. The Italians promised a naval force in support, and not one ship ever showed up!" His voice carried, and other heads began to turn toward the two men.

Foreign Minister Suñer stood there in shock. He pulled a handkerchief from his back pocket and dabbed his sweaty forehead with it. At that moment, another aide entered the large room. His boots were muddy, and he reeked of body sweat. In his hand, he carried a folded brown paper, which he handed to a heavy-set colonel.

"General. We have received a message from our command at Sevilla." Colonel Diaz ran through the message quickly, then looked at the aide who'd brought it with him. "Is this confirmed?" The aide nodded, and Diaz's face went strangely blank. "The British have landed a force just outside of Cadiz." There was a ripple of concerned voices that went around the room.

Asensio Cabanillas walked up, snatching the message out of the colonel's hand. He continued reading.

"What does it say?" Suñer asked him when the general just stood there quietly.

"At least two divisions have landed, including armored." More chatter went around the room. "Our garrison there..." he hesitated, not wanting to believe the news, "...surrendered."

The room erupted into a scene of panic. Army and Navy officers alike began to suggest what the enemy's next move would most likely be. And everyone was equally shocked at the news. Asensio Cabanillas let his arms drop to his sides. Even he was unable to contain his shock. He looked at Suñer with rage in his eyes.

"You," he said accusingly. "You and your foolish dreams of glory have caused this!"

"Caused what?" The room stopped and turned their attention to Franco and his entourage entering through the tall double doors. His voice boomed over all of the chatter going and everyone quickly fell silent. "Caused what?"

"Excellency. I've just been given this message. It's from our command in Andalusia." The general held up the message for Franco's review. "The British landed a force outside of Cadiz." Franco took the message. "Once they establish a beachhead, they'll move inland.'

Franco's eyes read through the words. His mouth gaped open at a loss for words. He reread the message and looked at General Asensio Cabanillas.

"Well, we must stop them. What are you doing about this?"

"Excellency, this message just arrived moments ago. The garrison has reportedly surrendered already." He shook his head. "There won't be any resistance to stop the landings."

"Then we need to move our forces south!" Franco snapped angrily. He looked around, and found the officer he wanted. "General Villegas, what's the condition of the troops in Andalusia?"

The heavy-set Villegas hesitated briefly, then shook his head. "I don't know, Excellency." Franco's eyes went wide.

"What do you mean you don't know?"

"I'm sorry, Excellency," the general replied, trepidation in his voice. "I have been unable to contact our command in Seville."

"There have been reports of sporadic communications from all regions," Asensio Cabanillas stated. "We've had to rely upon aerial surveillance just to get confirmation on this." He pointed to the message clasped in Franco's hand. "I've sent couriers to all major military commands. I expect word shortly."

Franco looked at him with wild eyes. "Why was I not informed of this?!" he asked angrily.

"I'm sure it's only temporary," Suñer told him, but his tone of voice said that he was full of doubt. "Between the protesting going on, and this reported landing, I'm sure that lines all over the country are being sabotaged. The general here has ordered all available troops into the streets to put down the riots. We'll reestablish the telephone lines very shortly."

Just as he finished his sentence, the telephone at the other end of the room rang loudly.

"It seems that not all the lines are down, Ramon," Franco told his brother-in-law. An aide picked up the receiver and took the call. Franco turned back to Asensio Cabanillas. "Get your senior commanders together, Carlos. I want a general order to go out to every one of their headquarters immediately. All troops need to mobilize. Not later today, not tomorrow, now!"

"Of course," Asensio Cabanillas replied bowing his head slightly.

"Villegas. I want you to go to Andalusia immediately," Franco barked, pointing a finger at the fat general. "Find out what the hell is happening. Take command if you must, but get those soldiers –" His words were cut short.

"Excellency," the aide's sharp voice cut over him. "I'm sorry." He was holding the telephone receiver up in the air. His face was red, and he seemed to be out of breath. "It's... it's Minister Tovar." Tovar was the interior minister. He held the phone outward. "I think you'll want to take this."

Franco gave sour looks to both Asensio Cabanillas and his brother-in-law, then stomped over to the phone, snatching it out of the aide's hand.

"Antonio?"

"Excellency. I have some very dire news to give you. We've received news out of Burgos. It came in by way of courier pilot. I don't know quite how to say this, but the entire city has risen up. Tens of thousands of people have mobbed the streets there. The police have lost control."

Franco's eyes blinked rapidly, his heart began to pound heavier.

"What?" he replied in disbelief. "I'll have Asensio Cabanillas get in touch with Alvara. His troops will move in and crush them."

"*Excellency,*" Tovar's voice came back. It seemed strained. "*I think that will be quite impossible. I've also received word that –*"

"Yes, yes. We know that the lines are down," Franco cut him off. "There are reports that lines are down all over the country. British saboteurs no doubt. They've landed a force near Cadiz. I'm sending out couriers to all commands. We'll mobilize to meet this threat."

There was a long-drawn-out silence on the other end of the telephone line. For a few moments, Franco thought that he'd lost the minister. Then his voice came back, and it seemed to Franco as if the man were weeping on the other end.

"*Excellency,*" Tovar began, then paused a moment. His voice came back as silent as the grave. "*Excellency, none of the lines have gone down. I have confirmation that our communications are working fine.*"

"You're not making any sense, Antonio," Franco told him. He was being stared at by every person in the room. A sudden chill went straight down his spine. "None of our military commands are responding to orders."

"*I know,*" Tovar replied. "*This is not an act of sabotage, Excellency. This is a coup.*"

"What?" Franco replied, not believing what the other was saying could possibly be true. Tovar's voice came back on, but he wasn't listening. He felt his breath go shallow, and his blood seemed to stop coursing through his veins. "Rubio? Alvara? Saliquet?" he whispered back.

"*They've all turned on you. Excellency, you must escape Madrid now, before it's too late.*"

Franco dropped the phone and staggered back toward the gathering. Everyone was watching him. His mouth hung open, his eyes shifted furiously around the great room. He spat some curses out silently.

"Are you alright?" Asensio Cabanillas asked him, reaching out his hand when it appeared like Franco was going to stumble.

"They've... they've turned." Franco gripped the general by both shoulders and stared into his eyes like a man gone crazy. He shook the general furiously. Asensio Cabanillas pushed himself away. "They've turned on me!"

Outside the giant window came the sound of light gunfire. Rifles at first, then the staccato of a machine gun off in the distance. The room went deadly silent. So silent that one could quite nearly hear the sounds of a loud commotion coming from outside. Military officers and civilian officials rushed toward the windows to see what was happening. But Franco didn't move. His legs seemed to be stuck, and he couldn't make himself move.

"There's a crowd forming outside the gates," someone said aloud.

"Franco gave General Asensio Cabanillas a look of sheer panic and terror, who returned the look in kind. It was the first time he'd ever seen the general look so petrified. Despite all the killings they both took part in over the years, all the executions during the civil war, neither man had ever seemed so horrified. Finally, Franco turned his gaze toward his brother-in-law, Suñer. The man was back-stepping foot by foot toward the doorway.

"You!" Franco barked at him. "You're to blame for all of this! I should never have listened to you!"

Suñer held up both hands in a gesture of innocence as he continued to back away. He shook his head vigorously.

"No," he said. "No."

In a mad rage, Franco grabbed the general's belt and clumsily unbuttoned his holster. He dug inside and retrieved the man's pistol. Asensio Cabanillas was too shocked to resist him. He leveled the gun at Suñer, whose eyes were as wide as the sun, staring in horrified shock.

"No!" He screamed mercifully. "Francisco, no!"

Frothing at the mouth in anger, Franco hesitated, then almost uncontrollably, squeezed the trigger. The first bullet missed and struck the wall. The aides that were standing near the doorway ran out of the path of his outstretched hand.

"Excellency!" Someone yelled, in a half-hearted attempt to stop him.

"You did this to me!" Franco screamed and squeezed the trigger again. This time he found his mark. Suñer dropped to his knees, grabbing his stomach as the bullet penetrated. A second shot went through his clasped hands, and the man cried out in pain.

"Francisco," Suñer begged. He tried to hold up a single hand, but couldn't find the strength. "Please."

He squeezed the trigger a third time. This time the bullet went right through his brother-in-law's forehead. The man was dead seconds before his body crumpled to the ground. His eyes were wide open, and a single dark hole drilled right through his skull. Others in the room began to panic. Some of them even ran out into the hallway.

Franco brought his gaze back to the general, who had raised his own hands as if he were surrendering. But Franco had no intention of shooting him. Outside, the sounds of rifle fire grew closer, and inside the palace, he heard someone call for a general surrender. Like a cornered animal the generalissimo looked in every direction as if looking for one last way out. But there wasn't one.

He stared Asensio Cabanillas in the eyes one last time before he opened his mouth, jammed the pistol inside, and squeezed the trigger.

* * *

Churchill flipped through the pages outlining just what happened yesterday in Madrid. MI6 had been quick to receive the information from the Spanish authorities. A day that had begun with an amphibious landing on Spanish soil; the first invasion Spain had suffered in over one hundred years, and ended with a military coup d'état, and the suicide of the Spanish head of state. The report ended with clear photos of the deceased dictator's corpse lying face up in the center of a large, bloody carpet.

He shook his head at the image. He'd never met Franco, but he had spoken with him on occasion. Though he personally found the Spanish government, and Franco's actions particularly during their civil war to be utterly repulsive, he understood well the role that Spain still played in European affairs. He never wanted Spain to enter the war, at least not on Germany's side, but he also knew neutrality was almost never an option for them. But, in the end, he was glad that the assault on Gibraltar had failed, and that the fighting in Spain had been brought to a swift end before it got out of control for everyone. Britain was spread thin enough as it was.

"We dodged a real bullet," Eden commented. Winston folded up the report and sent it coasting over his desk toward him.

"Mmm. We did indeed. So, what's the situation there like?"

"Still tenuous," Eden replied. Winston knew that they'd received a flurry of diplomatic cables today. "The Spanish Army is in the streets in nearly every major city. But the unrest died down shortly after Franco did. Seems that he didn't take into account the people's desire to not have another war."

"He didn't take a lot of things into account," Winston said. "Who's in charge?"

"Well, right now there's a ruling council made up of military and civilian officials. The mayor of Madrid is the provisional head of government right now. There's some talk of bringing the Count of Barcelona in as head of state."

Winston coughed on his cigar smoke at the news. His eyes opened wide, and his belly chuckled.

"Really? Bring back the monarchy? Haha. Well, Infante Juan is a well-known Anglophile. We'd find an ally in him. Probably why they're choosing to restore the House of Bourbon. Keep your fingers on the pulse over there. Order might be restored now, but anything could happen." Eden nodded. "General Dill. What about the military situation over there? Any chance of Germany intervening?"

Dill sat with his legs crossed on a sofa across the office from Churchill.

"There's always that chance, Prime Minister," he answered, and Winston instantly agreed. "I've had the opportunity to communicate with their chief of staff today. General Saliquet, I believe is how you say it. He's got his hands full at the moment, still dealing with the civil unrest and all that. But he's assured me that he has made his position quite clear to foreign governments, including Germany. No foreign invasion will be tolerated."

"Warnings don't seem to work with Hitler. Doesn't he know that?"

"He understands that, sir. But I have reliable intelligence of our own that they've still got quite a sizeable number of troops along the Pyrenees. I wouldn't doubt his warning. Should the Germans try to invade, they might find it much harder than they think."

"And Monty?"

"Yes. I've also spoken with him. His corps has established a toehold on the peninsula. The Spaniards are giving his force a wide berth. But truthfully, I doubt they have anything that could match up to him. A few beat-up old French tankettes, but nothing heavy. And, tomorrow we'll have the first engineer units arriving at Gibraltar to reconstruct the defenses." He sighed noisily. "And take away the killed in action. Over a thousand."

Winston sorrowfully nodded. It had been a long list of dead. Not just the defenders at the Rock, but there'd been plenty of naval casualties as well as the loss of two destroyers and a number of merchant vessels. Quick action on behalf of Admiral Somerville had also saved the day. After fighting his way through a Spanish attack of his own, he'd gotten some air support off to the besieged Gibraltar. But still, the Spanish had come within a hair of succeeding. In that case, Britain would now be cut off from North Africa. Which brought Winston to his next point.

"What about North Africa?" he asked grimly.

"News from there isn't much better than before, sir. The Seventh Indian and Fourth Armored have arrived in Egypt. I expect additional forces to arrive in the next week. ANZACS mostly. But the Italians have greatly reinforced their positions in Egypt. If General Wilson is pressed from the west, he may not be able to hold the line. But we have everything we can going to that theatre. Including half the troops we had in Singapore."

"Yes. And it can't get there fast enough," Winston said.

CHAPTER TWENTY-EIGHT

"Mind if I join you?" a voice asked. Sharp, shaken from his thoughts, looked up from his breakfast tray and grinned at Harkins.

"Not at all," he replied, lifting an inviting hand for him to sit. The mess was nearly empty by now. Breakfast was just about over, and most everyone had left. Harkins pulled out the chair across from Sharp and sat down. "Is that coffee?"

"Yep," Harkins replied with a smile. "I like tea, but Jesus, I don't know how you people can drink it all the time. I had a guy I know bring me a can of this on a flight back from the States a couple days ago. Care for some?"

Sharp grinned and shook his head. "Another time maybe. Coffee always made me wheezy in the cockpit. Doesn't settle right."

Harkins began eating his breakfast. Sharp was almost finished with his. Outside, the morning sun was beginning to shine across the field. Johnny cut into a sausage with his fork and knife, then looked up at Sharp. The other man seemed to be drifting off into his own thoughts.

"So?" Johnny prompted him.

"So what?" Sharp asked.

"Don't be humble, Chris," Harkins said to him, using his first name. An informal relationship had unexpectedly sprung up between the two men. To Sharp, who never really mingled much with the other pilots, even his own, it was a refreshing experience. The younger man was you're a-typical American; brash, maybe a bit reckless at times, and full of himself. He had a leap-without-looking attitude that Sharp liked. "Your promotion."

Sharp sighed and rolled his eyes. "Oh, yes. Finally came through officially."

Johnny looked at him and squinted. Only Sharp could be so modest. The man was like a rock who never showed any outward sign of... well, anything really. He flew his missions, he did his job, and at the end of the day, he wrote his reports. But that was about it. Johnny, by contrast, was much more of a socialite, not afraid to unbutton his tunic now and again.

"Most people would be pretty happy with that kind of news," Johnny said to him, and Sharp shrugged modestly.

"Just another day on the firing line. When I was still in the ranks it didn't matter who did what, or what your rank was. One stripe or three, it didn't matter. You just do your job and get things done." He threw his chin over toward a group of other officers sitting together at the long table. "Some officers, the ones that came from Oxford or some such place, have a different view. They believe in leadership by some sort of divine right." He scoffed into his napkin.

"What about you?"

"Me?" He shrugged and took a drink of his morning tea. "Rank be damned. I got my commission because I got tired of watching some prim and proper officer using my mates like their household servants." He shook his head at the memory of it. "In India, they'd show up in their finest uniform, custom made for them, waving their crops around, shouting out orders, then retreating to the officer's clubs for afternoon tea. Some of those men are leading this war now."

Johnny chuckled a little. "Not all of them seem that bad. But I understand what you're saying."

"What about you? You've been here a while now, we've spoken many times. You've never told me what drove you into the uniform."

Johnny swallowed a bite of the egg and wiped his mouth with his napkin. "Hell, I just needed a job. My little corner of Pennsylvania was about as small a place as you could find on a map. I was just a kid when the market crashed and the economy went to hell, but I can remember my dad freezing his rear off cutting firewood in the middle of winter to sell off because we needed the money. When I was fifteen maybe, or sixteen, I saw a Howard Hughes picture about pilots during the Great War. You know, the Red Baron and all that. I was enamored. Signed up right out of high school. Never looked back."

Sharp smiled. "Do you look back now?"

"Nope," Johnny replied immediately. "Dad's gone, mom gets a portion of my paycheck each month. Won't leave Perry Township for her life. I've got a girl in New York. What's not to like?"

"Yes. Gwendoline," Sharp said, taking another drink of his tea. "What did she say about you being posted over here?"

"She was happier about it than the alternative. We both thought the Army was sending me to China." He laughed. "They didn't tell me until I was packing up to leave. When I called her, she was glad that I was coming to England. Though... still concerned. But better here than Shanghai or wherever."

Sharp gave an agreeing look. He'd been in India when the Japanese had invaded China, bombing places like Shanghai and Nanking. News from that part of the world had seemed so savage back then. Indiscriminate murder really. Now, he felt that way about their situation. Having been in places like Poland, and a Soviet prison camp.

"I can certainly understand that. I was –" Sharp's words were abruptly cut short at the wail of an air raid siren cranking. Everyone in the mess jumped into action. Sharp ran out the flapping door, followed by Harkins. The whole airfield screamed with the mechanical noise.

"Not a moment's rest," Johnny yelled to Sharp as they jogged across the compound.

It was just after sunrise. There was still morning fog hanging low across the treetops. But men were running every way to get to their duty stations. Sharp ran into the squadron hut, where men were already gearing up and running back out to the field. He kicked off his shoes and grabbed his boots quickly, then reached for his headgear. Just as he reemerged the first of 308 Squadron was taking off from the end of the airstrip. He started toward the line of Hurricanes, then stopped suddenly when he saw Harkins following.

"Where are you going?" he asked him.

Harkins looked like he was about to say something, then fell silent. Sharp only nodded at him, then sprinted off, leaving him behind. Group Leader Bushwell was standing out in the field, giving orders when he saw Sharp approach.

"Sharp!" He ran over to Bushwell. "You're bringing up the rear. The Poles are up now, and two squadrons from Eleven Group are coming from the east."

"Eleven Group?" Sharp muttered, shocked by that. Eleven Group had been taking the brunt of the losses in recent weeks.

Bushwell pointed up with his thumb. "Get up there! We've got a large formation coming in."

His Hurricane was spinning up when he got to it, and he taxied into position. The rest of 239 followed right behind. Half the squadron was out of action for one reason or another. That left only six to go up, and he didn't like those odds.

At the other end of the airfield, Johnny Harkins could barely control himself. As an American officer and a neutral one at that, he technically could take no part in the fighting going on in the skies.

But as a fighter pilot, his instincts were to jump into the first available cockpit and get up there. Bombs would be dropping like rain, and people were dying. Good people. He knew that he shouldn't, but he wanted desperately to show those German sons-of-bitches just what an American fighter pilot could do. But all he could do right now is watch as the line of Hurricanes and Spitfires took off from the end of the grassy runway. As the last one lifted up he watched it go, and it made him sick.

"Form up," Sharp called into his mike. The rest of his planes fell into position. The flight held steady at eighteen thousand feet. There were six of them, four on his left and one on his right. On the horizon ahead, he could see the tails of the Polish 308 Squadron. The Poles had an almost insatiable thirst for fighting. Hard to blame them. He could hear some cross-talk going on between them, and he understood basic Polish, be damned if he could speak it though.

"Enemy flight ahead," Sharp relayed. His Polish was rusty but that's what he thought he understood.

Miles away the dots that indicated 308 Squadron broke into smaller formations as another group appeared on the horizon. The new planes, Germans, came in three wings, and the Poles broke to engage them. Sharp strapped his mask on and propped himself in his seat. Above him and to the left he could see another flight moving in from the northeast on the same heading. They were Spitfires flying at higher altitudes. A choppy voice came in over the earpiece identifying themselves as Mary Flight.

Along the skyline, the large bomber group began to appear. Sharp was shocked to see so many planes in one large formation. The pattern stretched out for miles. The German advantage was always numbers, and the enemy bomber group directly ahead had to be two hundred and fifty strong. Mixed in with them would be the fighters; Messerschmitts and Focke-Wulfs.

The Germans were getting quite good at anticipating RAF tactics and kept some fighters back as a reserve. Meanwhile, they'd be sending in waves of their fighters to engage, keeping the RAF busy while the bombers hit their targets. But that tactic had been used time and again, and Allied pilots had learned a thing or two as well.

"Get ready!" he ordered. The Polish squadron broke up the first attack, but it was just a feint, and they knew it. Designed to keep them away from vulnerable bombers.

The opposing Hurricanes and Messerschmitts closed in with each other. The Poles were the first to open fire, then the Germans, but nobody got in a kill shot. Nobody ever did in the first go around. But the Polish pilots did get the upper hand, breaking the Luftwaffe flight up, and sending the gray-painted planes scattering. Anyone's first instinct would be to give chase and go after them. And that is exactly what the Germans would want them to do.

"Stay in formation," Sharp ordered, though not one of his pilots had broken off to go chasing after them. Beyond the first squadron, there was a second one, waiting to chase after any RAF pilot that broke off to go after the first group. "Here they come!"

He gave the scattering German planes one final look to make sure that none of them were going to double back any moment now. But the Poles were right on their tails. Ahead, ten thousand meters, was a second wave of fighters. Their bright yellow noses pointed straight at them, and this time they were the first to open up when they reached firing range. Their machine guns flashed brightly as each flight came within two thousand meters of each other.

"Break and attack!" Sharp pulled his fighter into a wide turn, firing off a volley as a single Focke-Wulf flew briefly into his sights.

The six Hurricanes broke off and dispersed in pairs. Each pair chased after a German fighter. The odds were about even as the two waves of Germans began to weave in the skies with the British. 308

Squadron dueled with the first group, flying in some pretty tight maneuvers, never getting too far away from one another, and allowing the enemy to pick them off individually as they so frequently did. The second group, Focke-Wulfs, engaged with 239 Squadron. The newer German fighters were nimble and highly deadly. Their appearance in the skies over England had come as a shock to the RAF pilots, who'd been used to the Bf 109. But the Fw 190 was just as good, if not better than anything the RAF currently had. Encounters with them seldom went well.

He reached up and squeezed his mike.

"Fox Leader to Mary Flight. The door is open. Repeat: the door is open."

Ten thousand feet higher above, holding on a perpendicular course, the flight of Spitfires moved forward, avoiding the German fighters entirely. Twelve of them sped in toward the giant bomber group. The more heavily armed Spitfire could tear even a Henkel into pieces in little time. Even as enemy fighters rose to meet them, the Spitfires came dropping down like eagles, picking up speed and firing their guns into the thick of the bombers.

Turning to his left, Sharp saw two Messerschmitts turn straight in on him. Beyond them, two of his own were pinning down a pair of Germans.

"Fox Six, here they come. Give them just enough then peel off."

"Yes, sir," came the reply.

The targets were no less than five thousand meters and turned their noses right in on them. Sharp braced himself. He was looking forward to getting back to Chilbolton and finishing his chat with his American friend. With one eye shut, he zeroed his sights in on the nose of the attacking plane, then squeezed off ranging shot. Tracers let loose but fell short. Neither of the Messerschmitt pilots flinched as he had hoped. Veterans.

"Steady, Fox Six, steady." He tried to keep his voice calm for the other pilot. Jacobsen was a good pilot and had good chops for flying. But it had been no different for those Polish airmen he'd served with a year ago. They were good pilots also but had succumbed to the overwhelming numbers of the Luftwaffe.

The Messerschmitts opened fire. Bullets saturated the air ahead and around him. Bits of metal pinged against his craft, and he rolled his wing over, still firing all his guns on the German plane. Fox Six kept on for another couple of seconds then followed the maneuver, turning his plane over and away from the attack. The two Germans whizzed by and kept on going.

Sharp didn't waste a moment. He banked his Hurricane around until the closest slow-moving bomber fell into his view. From above the Spitfires of Mary Flight dropped into range, cutting the center of the bomber phalanx into fiery bits. The machine guns tore into them, blowing five of them out of the sky in just seconds. Sharp and Jacobsen sped in toward the lead Heinkel, adding a sixth kill. The cockpit of the Heinkel blew apart almost instantly. Bullets hissed past them as the two planes flew by.

"Stay with me," Sharp told Jacobsen. He could catch glimpses of his wingman in the rearview. Jacobsen was a good pilot and kept right on Sharp's tail. Machine guns from the bombers opened fire when they could get clear shots of him. He tried to keep his Hurricane right in the thick to prevent that from happening, but the Germans weren't going to just let him go by.

He squeezed the trigger, his guns blowing a hole into the side of a passing Dornier. They both rolled their planes over and turned right into a third bomber. All of a sudden the bomber broke apart into pieces. He hadn't fired a shot. The wreck fell from the sky like a brick, and a single fighter plane flew almost straight up through the smoke. It wasn't a Hurricane or a Spitfire that had done the job either. Sharp squinted his eyes at the plane. It was one of the Aircobras, an

American plane. The dark brown fighter climbed swiftly, much better than a Hurricane could have.

"Good shot Aircobra!" Sharp said into his mike. The Americans had supplied them with a number of them. Sharp didn't care for them himself. Found they lacked firepower.

"You bet," a voice garbled back. Sharp heard the voice and recognized it instantly. He knew who the other pilot was, and shook his head.

"Best not to say a word," Sharp warned. He watched the Aircobra turn away. A certain American could potentially get into a lot of trouble should he be found out. Staying off the airwaves could save him from a skinning later on. But still, Sharp was grateful for whatever assistance he could get.

The Spitfires of Mary Flight, having blown through the enemy, were now circling back around for a second set of runs. One plane was missing, and a single parachute was descending to the earth. The line of Heinkels and Dorniers began to turn westward, showing their sides to the British planes, letting their guns fire on the attackers. But the Spitfires came speeding back in on a half dozen different vectors. Their guns flashed furiously, cutting the ranks of bombers to smoking hulks. Two of them burst apart in midair, two more broke formation as they were hit and began smoking.

Sharp, with Jacobsen, made pass after pass on the enemy. The lead bomber wedge went unprotected for a time, and the two swooped in, taking the opportunity to break them up. It was the Spitfires that could do the most damage, and their pilots kept hitting the center formation. The huge enemy attack spread itself out, letting their machine gunners defend themselves without risking hitting their own aircraft, and getting some help from their fighters. But the German fighter protection could only fly so long in British airspace.

The general aerial melee continued for the better part of half an hour. Another squadron of Hurricanes, the second backup from

Eleven Group finally showed up on the scene. They came straight in on the German rear flank, knocking a dozen planes out of the air. German fighters who'd accompanied the bomber group fell out and headed back to France as their fuel tanks waned, only to be replaced with additional squadrons of Messerschmitts from airfields in Normandy.

"I got one!" a voice called out joyfully. Sharp could recognize the voice. Norton had flown eight combat sorties and had never so much as claimed a single kill. He now roared victoriously at the death of a single 109 as it death spiraled down to the earth below.

Sharp got in a third kill that morning, and a certain unnamed pilot, who Sharp was content to leave out of his report, downed a second bomber. Though the lighter P-39 Aircobra could bob and weave well in the air, it lacked punch when it came to shooting down another aircraft. Nevertheless, he'd performed well and assisted in keeping German fighters off the tails of RAF planes.

The enormous bombing group, under fire from all sides, released their loads short of their intended target: the airfield at Middle Wallop. A raid, which should have annihilated the RAF base below, instead ended in failure for the Luftwaffe. As 239 and the other squadrons made their way back to their separate home fields, they'd counted forty-eight bombers and seven fighters killed. In return, the four squadrons that had intercepted, had taken a mere nine planes as casualties and two pilots unaccounted for.

Sharp settled his plane in on the left of the single Aircobra mixed in with 239 Squadron. He looked across the empty air at Harkins and simply nodded. He couldn't see the other's face, but he could almost picture him over there with a big grin on.

* * *

General Ernst Udet nibbled slowly on a plate of cheese. He was sitting at the long table in his office, and carefully skimming through the end-of-the-day reports from his squadron commanders. It was an enlightening reading. Besides the raid on Middle Wallop, everything else had gone off well. Bombers had successfully reached their targets over eighty percent of the time, and the fighters had provided excellent support. His chief of staff, General Ritter, had noted at the bottom of the last page that air superiority over the southern coast of England had tentatively been achieved. Intelligence had confirmed the movement of enemy fighter squadrons further north. It was a great achievement. This meant there was now a window of opportunity. A wedge had formed which would finally give the Luftwaffe the opening that they needed.

He grabbed his cold cup of tea, and read through the final lines. It struck him at that moment just how truly brave those enemy pilots must be. They flew every day, day after day, against an enemy that was four or five times its strength. But still, they'd put up a valiant fight. For one brief moment, as he finished the last sentence, he felt a great swell of consternation.

Udet had come from a time and age when besting your enemy in the skies was a reward in itself. When even enemies could show some form of respect for one another. But that was another time. Perhaps Udet really was a relic from a forgotten age. He knew well the next step that Hitler would take. He'd fought against the bombing of civilian population centers, yet every night for two weeks now they'd bombed London indiscriminately. That would only be a taste of what would ultimately be unleashed upon the British people. Already there were those who were planning for the next step: the occupation of Great Britain.

He couldn't help but feel guilt. If places like Poland were any clue, then he shuddered at the thought of what awaited that country once any invasion had proved successful. Men like Himmler and the SS had already stated their intentions. For a people, and a nation, that valued liberty so much, he could hardly think of it as some outlying region of the Greater Reich chopped up into smaller pieces under a Reichskommissariat. But he knew that was exactly what would happen.

Putting down the empty teacup and file, he stood up. The office was completely empty, and only a few lights were on in the hallways outside. It was well past two in the morning, and he hadn't realized it until now. Udet walked out onto the open-air balcony and stood there with his hands in his pockets. In the darkness, nature seemed to be wide awake. He listened to the sound of the crickets. He closed his eyes, and for a heartbeat or two, he could swear he heard the sound of distant explosions. But it was just his mind playing tricks.

After what was a long period, Udet stepped back in. Grabbing a pen off his desk he scribbled a note, folded it in half, and left it for General Ritter in the morning.

Tell Göring – He has what he wants!

CHAPTER TWENTY-NINE

Churchill stood outside the closed doors of the king's private office with his hands clasped behind his back, just waiting to be received. A lone footman stood like an immovable statue in the corner, staring straight ahead. Winston could not help but stare back, wondering what thoughts might be running through the man's mind at this moment. Working in Buckingham Palace put one close to the heart of British society, but was no guarantee of safety either.

Last night's raid on the city had come close to hitting the palace. The bombs had only narrowly missed, and fallen on Hyde Park instead, but the message was quite clear. It seemed nothing would be off limits to Nazi bombers. Had their bombardiers been a little bit quicker, they may well have cut the head off the British monarchy, as well as a half dozen other heads of state who'd been granted the use of St. James Palace. Even now preparations were being made to remove most of the staff workers to safer locations. Only those people necessary for the king's day-to-day schedule would be asked to remain behind. King George himself had made up his mind to remain. To be, what he called, a pillar of normalcy.

The room remained utterly silent right up until the wide double doors swung open, and Churchill was welcomed in. King George stood in the center of the room, dressed in his British Army uniform. Winston approached halfway and gave a half bow as the door closed behind him. When they were alone he walked over to him, the two shaking hands.

"Please." The king lifted his hand, offering for Winston to sit across from him. They both plopped down into opposing sofas, the king immediately reaching into his breast pocket for his silver cigarette case. "Busy evening again."

Winston nodded grimly, running his fingers down the buttons of his undervest. "Quite. And, I fear things will become much busier."

The king took a modest drag on his Benson and Hedges then coughed into a closed fist. It was a Friday, and the two men usually met on Monday for lunch, so that the prime minister could provide a weekly update. But this was no ordinary visit. Only a fool needed to be told of the dire situation that the nation now faced. That was something that King George was not.

"Your Majesty," Winston began. His lips curled at the thought of what he was about to say. "Under the circumstances, I'm going to come straight to the point of things."

"I would not have it any other way." The king stared back at him, squinting his eyes with interest.

"I've conferred with the General Staff, Your Majesty. It's their consensus that we will very shortly find ourselves attacked on our southern coast." He bit his lip after the words came out. The king's nostrils flared, and his eyes seemed to dim at the news. "I believe that the long-awaited invasion is all but imminent."

The words rang out in the still air of the room. The king coughed again, nervously this time it seemed, then pinched the end of his nose. His hand ran down the front of his face, and he gave a repetitious nod, followed by another long drag of his cigarette, which had only been lit moments ago, and drew it down almost halfway. Churchill could plainly see the impact the news had on him. The monarch ran his hand through his thick hair. He sucked in the air of his next breath loudly.

"I.. I see," he stuttered. He inhaled sharply. "Are you... you, sure about this?"

"Our listening stations have picked up increased traffic from German Army commands in France. Bletchley's deciphered parts of it. They confirm information we already had concerning enemy troop movement and make reference to landing grounds. We're quite certain that the German Navy has made a large sortie from their bases in the Baltic. They wouldn't do that unless there was a strategic purpose behind it. Coastal observation posts have also reported spotting large numbers of barges and seagoing vessels assembling along the French coast. These things, combined with the fact the RAF has been forced to concede the skies along the south, have the General Staff convinced of the situation. I wouldn't say these things, Your Majesty, if there wasn't a high certainty about it."

His cigarette now quickly finished, King George crushed the butt into his ashtray. Winston had noted that the monarch's smoking habit had quickened in recent weeks. He was now smoking more than he had in the past. But the same could be said of himself as well.

"No," he replied. "I don't suppose you would. What is our situation?"

"All of our defenses are as prepared as they can be, given the time we've had. All Home Guard units are deployed to support our regular forces. But, given the current status of our troops, the fact that we're down to one-eighth of our artillery strength, our armored units are few in number, and the lack of fighter support, we don't have much to hang our hats on right now."

That was a widespread overview if ever there was one. He'd kept the king as informed as he could have since the retreat from the continent. The monarch had been as understanding as anyone could have been in his position. He had an acute comprehension of the situation, and of things in general. The rocky start that the two men had begun with, had seemed to evaporate over time.

"But we aren't defenseless by any means," the king replied.

"No. Aside from the fortifications that we've erected, we've managed to refit roughly forty percent of the divisions we rescued for combat. Though, I will say that their strength is not what it once was. Some of them are at or below half-strength. Most of our allies that escaped with us are in even worse condition. The Commonwealth forces that have arrived recently are in fighting shape, but there aren't many of them. Two Canadian divisions and a couple of ANZAC brigades are well equipped enough, though very little armor between them. Some Indians." He waved a dismissive hand.

"What about the troops we sent to Spain?" the king asked him. "Could they be brought back in time?"

"In all honesty, Your Majesty, I don't think they'd make a difference one way or the other. While the Spaniards don't have anything that can match General Montgomery, the Germans certainly do. We kept our best equipment and tanks in England. Besides that, Gibraltar is still vulnerable, even with Franco gone from this Earth. Should the absolute worst happen here, it'll serve in the defense of other parts of the empire."

"And the fleet?"

"Kept in reserve," Winston replied. "The Home Fleet is out of range of the German Air Force. Only a few ships will be kept in the Channel for the time being. We're going to barricade vital ports with block ships. Reinforce a few potential landing grounds. But until we determine where the main enemy thrusts will come from, we'll have to hold back a substantial reserve. I should also mention that I've been forced to remove Dowding."

"Oh?"

"I'm afraid it couldn't be helped. Between the London bombing and our losses in the air, the political footing simply wasn't there anymore. A good man, but just not the right one. Trafford Leigh-Mallory will take temporary charge of Fighter Command. He's working up a new defense strategy as we speak."

Dowding had gone, offering to remain on as a reserve advisor, but the animosity between him and Leigh-Mallory seemed to be too much for either man to overcome. In the end, Keith Park had retained command of Number Eleven Group, but Leigh-Mallory was calling the overall shots. His tactics would now be the order of the day. Hopefully, it would be enough to meet whatever else could conceivably come at them. Although, Winston could hardly begin to speculate as to what the Germans could possibly have in their arsenal they hadn't thrown at them already.

"Things are sounding quite dismal," the king said. Winston, almost unconsciously, nodded in agreement. "What do you place our chances at?"

He looked the king square in the eye, then reluctantly shrugged. "Perhaps one in four. The way things stand right now, Your Majesty, should the Germans successfully land a hundred thousand troops on our shores, fully armed and equipped, we'd most likely be unable to dislodge them. If tanks make it ashore, well, London would most likely be moved upon immediately. I'm having the Army assist in evacuations of towns in the south." He leaned forward, crossing his fingers in his lap. "We do have one card that we could potentially play. It was the one that I was hoping we wouldn't need to play. And I needed to seek your permission for."

As the king listened to the suggestion, his face went from slightly nervous to outrightly appalled. Without averting his eyes, he dug into his pocket again, popping open his silver case, and drawing another cigarette. His hand seemed to shake as he tried to light it up.

* * *

Miles Creech looked proudly down at the single stripe sewn on the arm of his uniform. He gave a smug grin as he felt the fabric of it with his fingers. Private no more, Creech had gotten the papers first thing this morning, and he had wasted no time whatsoever in sewing the symbol of his new rank on. Now Lance Corporal Creech proudly displayed his new status to any that came through the makeshift barracks. Some just looked at him and rolled their eyes, others congratulated him on the promotion.

But to most of his mates in 1st Platoon, B Company, they couldn't have given a shit less who was a whatever. Most of the lads he'd served with during the Norway Campaign had gotten one of their own anyhow. Truth be told Creech was one of the last to receive his. That would bump well over half the company up from the glamorous rank of private. They'd earned it after all. The heroes of Narvik.

B Company was posted to the town of Royal Tunbridge Wells in the south of England. It was a nice, quiet town. Out of the way. Following last year's retreat from Norway, the entire brigade had been scattered around Scotland initially. Scotland had been dreary, the winter weather harsh. Southern England had been a welcoming reprieve following that. A nice cushy posting, where the entire 1st Battalion could rest, and recuperate. There'd been some fear that after Norway the Irish Guards might be sent to the continent. But France had fallen so damn quickly that never happened. More Frenchies had come to Kent than had gone the other way.

For a good while, following Boulogne and Dunkirk, the countryside here had been crawling with the blue uniforms of the French Army. For a time it seemed as if French might become the second language of these parts. But most of them had departed in the weeks following the surrender. Swedish transports had been pulling out of port left and right, taking the repatriated back with them. Little by little, fewer of their continental allies had remained, until there were few left but a handful of French who had decided to fight on. The locals certainly weren't missing them any. It was difficult enough to squeeze forty-thousand British soldiers into local area camps, let alone another hundred-thousand Froggies.

Rumors were swirling about now, however. Talk of another fight coming. Right now, given the circumstances, if you spoke to any of the locals they'd have said that they wished for those hundred-thousand Frenchmen to still be around.

The so-called barracks they occupied was nothing more than an old brick textile mill on the outskirts of town that had been gutted, and a couple hundred cots thrown in. Two wooden outbuildings in the small rear courtyard of the building served as privy, and a separate brick structure that had once been the mill oven was the new armory. Company drills were held daily in the yard at an unused rail depot. The days and nights were pleasant here. Much nicer than either Scotland and certainly Norway, had been. But nobody had any illusions that this was their last stop.

The planked wooden door swung open. A couple of the other lads filed out, and a single man came back in. Miles looked up at the man.

"Lookie here, Flanagan," he said with a smile.

Lance Corporal Flanagan looked up sharply at Miles showing off the badge of his new rank. The Irishman saw him sticking out his left arm, and the smile on his face then rolled his eyes.

"Jesus Christ," Flanagan said in jest. "Bad enough we've got Englishmen in this regiment as it were. Now they're making them lance corporals." He shook his head, sitting down in the bunk across from Miles. "Must be hitting the bottom of the barrel."

"No more calling you lance corporal to your face," Miles told him.

Flanagan reached down under the bunk, pulling a small flask out of his personals. He unscrewed it, took a swig then let out a refreshing breath. Drills were over, and there was no sense in letting good downtime go to waste.

"Nope there isn't," he told Miles. "Got my papers last night. Corporal Flanagan. Better ring to it. That reminds me, I need to sew my own stripes."

The smile on Miles's face melted away, and he scowled. "Corporal? You didn't tell me that yesterday."

Flanagan kicked his feet up and laid back on his bunk. "You're not my wife." He held out his flask. "Want some?" Miles shook his head. "Have it your way."

Since moving down to England the Irishman's normal sour demeanor had improved. One way to know he was in a better mood was when his language wasn't so foul. When he was swearing the man could be quite taxing. Despite his views on English society and his Irish republican upbringing, English summers seemed to agree with the man.

"Wonder what's for supper," Flanagan muttered, running his tongue around in his mouth.

"I've got some coin. I was thinking 'bout going down to Abercromby's," Miles said to him. "Woman there's got some pot pies. Nice hot pot pies. Mmm."

"Oh, is that why you're going down there?" Flanagan asked facetiously. "Pot pies, my arse."

Miles smiled, shrugging at the humor. "She's got a nice bum too."

He had been going down to the small tavern maybe a bit too much to escape notice. The locals were an inviting bunch of people, and standing orders allowed for men in the ranks to go into town during off hours. So long as they returned before the night watch began, and weren't inebriated. A couple of privates who had broken the second rule had found themselves up to their waists in trouble shortly after their arrival. They'd gotten back to quarters in time alright, drunk as lords and unable to walk in a straight line. Marched off to the stockade for the night, the two had been placed on latrine duty early the following morning before the effects had worn off. Neither man had lasted long before retching themselves to a point they couldn't stand on their wobbly legs. That and the loss of weekend privileges had been enough to send a message that such behavior was not to repeat itself.

"Well, I suppose," Miles said. He reached down to lace his boots up when the hand whistle sounded. Everyone knew the sound instantly and jumped to it. Miles let out a depressed sigh.

"Fuck me," Flanagan swore. "Just when I lay down."

The whistle sounded again. Colour Sergeant Lowell, the newly promoted company sergeant, had made studious use of it in recent days. He'd stand out in the yard outside the barracks, blowing on it for everything from mail call to major announcements. Miles sighed. Grabbing his tunic off the corner of his bunk he followed the others in quarters as they filed out, buttoning down as he went. The whistle blew a third time.

"Jesus, I'd like to shove that whistle right up his –" Flanagan fell silent as soon as they walked outside. Colour Sergeant Lowell stood in the dirt roadway between the old mill building and the outer brick wall. He was as bellowing as ever, shouting for the company to form up. The man's deep baritone voice could shake that brick wall down to the ground if he wanted.

One hundred forty-seven men. That's how many had remained of B Company following Narvik, or had joined up since. And they were one of the better-off companies of 1st Battalion. Other companies had taken terrible casualties, to a point they'd almost been written off.

"Fall in!" Lowell bawled. Every man within earshot, which in Lowell's case had to be everyone, fell into place, Miles in the third row. The group dressed right, then brought their arms down in clapping unison, and stood at attention. "At ease!"

The company relaxed its stance, putting their hands behind their backs. Colour Sergeant Lowell peeled back the pages on a clipboard. The battalion had been put on reserve status, and aside from daily drills, had for weeks been performing mainly fetch and carry duties. They only assembled before drill or mail call typically. And mail had already been handed out today.

"Listen up. We'll be moving off at dawn." Miles could hear his mates around him let out tiny, almost inaudible sighs. "First thing tomorrow we're moving south. We're to assist with evacuating civilians. Getting them out of the way of the damn Jerry bombers. Pack your gear up tonight. The trucks'll be here first thing in the morning." He looked left and right, then dropped the bomb. "No leaving the barracks this afternoon. No trips into town."

Miles growled through his teeth. He'd been looking forward to going to Abercromby's.

"When are we comin' back, Sarge?" It was Higgins.

"You'll God-damn come back when they God-damn say you come back, Higgins!" Lowell snapped. His eyes flared at Higgins. The fool-headed private's back straightened up, and his face turned flush in embarrassment. He was always talking out of turn. "Now, since we're all here anyways, and if it's alright with Private Higgins, I'd like to call the role." The sergeant's deep voice boomed. There was a wave of laughter from the men. The sergeant looked down at his clipboard and began reading off names. "Aiden..."

WHATEVER THE COST

CHAPTER THIRTY

"I understand, sir." General Köhler held the telephone up to his ear, but his eyes looked around at the troops passing through the center of town. The eyes of his staff officers casually glanced at him from time to time, waiting for him to finish with his phone call, and give them the final yes or no. "Yes, Field Marshal Rundstedt. I shall carry out my orders to the letter."

The general hung up the phone. He strut slowly through the center of the courtyard, pumping his gloved fist into the cup of his left hand over and over. The staff was looking at him in between conducting their work. He knew what they were waiting on. If Field Marshal Rundstedt had called off the operation, if Hitler had decided to not go through with it, well, that would've been the final opportunity to say so. General Köhler had over twelve-thousand men, half of which were loaded up onto a motley collection of sea vessels, barges, rivercraft, whatever could haul them across the choppy English Channel.

"Sir." Out of the corner of his eye, another general approached. Köhler waited for the other man, watching as columns of troops marched through the town streets toward the harbor below. Major General Hartmann came to a swift stop, snapping off a crisp salute, which Köhler casually returned. "If I may ask, General?"

Köhler gave him a short nod. "We go," he told his second in command. General Hartmann hid a subtle grin by biting the end of his lip.

He growled anxiously. The man was not shy in expressing his eagerness for the operation to begin. For weeks he'd howled in support of it, begging in fact. Now he would be getting his wish. "Your command is ready?"

"It is."

The question was foolish. Of course, they were ready. Wehrmacht soldiers did not just sit around idly on their hands. They weren't the French after all. Since the defeat of France had come, the men and officers of the Twenty-second Division had done nothing but drill and drill and were anxious to add a battle ribbon to their guidons. Perhaps earn a small sentence or two in the history books. After all, the division had seen no action during the charge across the Western Front. Having been one of the last divisions out of Germany, they'd been content to escort Allied prisoners of war into camps. But it also meant that they were one of the better-organized divisions. Instead of getting fat off buttery croissants and French cheese, as some other units were doing, General Köhler had ordered a strict drill routine amongst the regiments. They were as prepared as any division in the German Army could be. Now he intended to prove it. While other generals and units were being decorated lavishly with Iron Crosses, his men were training on the banks of the Somme. Practicing the very amphibious techniques that would become useful when this day came.

"Do you have any last-minute orders for me?" Hartmann asked him.

"No," General Köhler shook his head. "You know the objectives." Hartmann nodded. "Just reinforce to the men that we're soldiers. That means we act as soldiers."

"I understand," Hartmann replied. He'd given that instruction to his battalion commanders half a dozen times in the last few days. When battle commenced, men had an almost primal drive to shoot everything in sight that wasn't waving the German flag. They'd seen quite enough death bringing up the rear of the German column back in April. Many of the dead had been soldiers, but there had been tens of thousands of civilians killed as well. Some of them had simply been caught in the middle of the fighting. But there'd been plenty of others as well, dead by reprisal. Everyone knew who'd done most of it. The SS made no bones about their methods. But Wehrmacht soldiers could sometimes get out of control as well if not reined in by their officers.

"When do we go?" Hartmann asked him.

"They'll give us the word," he told him. He looked up at the midday sun to the south. It wouldn't be too long before that order came down. Already word was spreading about sighting one of their heavy battleships cruising in from the east. That alone had been an encouraging sign. Their heavy firepower would be what picked apart British defenses along the shore. Intelligence had little to no clue about what those defenses might be, but everyone with a brain would have to assume they'd be formidable.

General Köhler tapped Hartmann on the chest and curled a finger. The two generals walked over to a large wooden table. There were layers of maps and geographical charts strewn across it. He picked through them, found the one he wanted, and spread it out on top of the others. The southeast coast of England and the Pas-de-Calais were enlarged on the map. Every hill, every major roadway, canal, railroad track, village, and town between there and here were marked.

"Here." General Köhler tapped his finger on Hastings, on the English coast. "The bombardment will begin shortly." He checked his watch and looked around as if he was expecting an artillery barrage to open up on his words. "We have an added surprise. The field marshal wanted all the support he could give us when we cross. Two railroad guns, one here, the other here."

"Railroad guns!" The other general excitedly exclaimed.

The enormous guns had been used with devastating effects during the trench warfare of the First World War. Their barrels were so long that shells fired from one could hit a town fifty miles away. They were so powerful that their recoil alone meant they could only be brought in via railroads. It took days, and hundreds of people to put the gun together. On top of that, it took over half an hour to reload after firing. But those 4800-kilogram high explosive rounds they fired would be like getting hit by a locomotive.

"I know you know this, Oskar, but as soon as you hit the beach you need to move inland as quickly as possible." The general ran his fingers out to the hamlets and villages that dotted the area. "A thousand boats need to make the turnaround as rapidly as possible. You'll be on that beach for the better part of an hour by yourself. Wish I could do more for you, but..."

"We'll hold, General." Just as soon as he said that, there was a gust of wind, carrying the sound of heavy guns firing off in the distance. The wave washed over them, drawing the attention of all.

"Our battleships," Köhler said. Another distant boom went off, then another. "Twenty-eight-centimeter guns. Couldn't ask for better support." He looked up at the partly cloudy skies. The weather was cooperative and was supposed to hold. But who the hell could really say for sure? The Channel had a mind of its own. "Anyway. Push inland where you can, as quickly as you can. I wish I could give you more tanks than what you're taking with you."

He said it, but he hid the fact that nobody knew for sure whether the Panzer Twos would even be able to traverse the beaches. They'd damned sure make the crossing though. Scores of them were crammed onto retrofitted river barges, taken from Parisians whose need for them was not as dire as the German Army's was. They'd been gutted down to the bolts, and heavy outboard engines welded onto them. They'd make the crossing alright, slowly. Whether or not the English beaches could support their weight was anyone's guess.

Köhler disliked sending any of his men off with such a lack of information. Invading an island was very different from crossing over some marker drawn on a sign stuck in the ground. Terrain between Germany and France didn't change at the language barrier. But across that stretch of choppy sea, the rule changed. Even the damn sea itself seemed to have a mind of its own.

"Strange, isn't it?" Hartmann asked. "We've come so far, so fast. One more obstacle to go." He threw his chin toward the distant shore in the north. "We get there, then the war is over."

"Perhaps," General Köhler quietly replied. He looked around and dropped his voice so that only Hartmann could hear. "Remember, we're not the SS. Our men are soldiers, not murderers."

The two generals exchanged nods at the same moment that a wave of bombers flew by far overhead. It wasn't the first flight to go by, and it wouldn't be the last one before the day was out. So far the operation was moving along as Command had planned it. That meant that the airborne elements would be flying out shortly.

"Well. I suppose that I should be going," General Hartmann said. "I don't wish to keep Churchill waiting."

"Good hunting, Oskar." The two generals shook hands, then saluted one another. Hartmann turned and marched off toward the harbor where the boats awaited him. He disappeared out of view, falling in with the thousands who were still filing toward the waterfront.

Just then a mighty blast went off to the south, that could be felt as well as heard. The ground tremored, and the whistling sound of a projectile the size of an automobile passed overhead.

* * *

Winston entered the main briefing room as he had a hundred times before. Only this time was different. The battles he'd been used to receiving updates on were typically at sea or in the air. Up until this point, the few land engagements they'd fought had been across the Channel, in France and Gibraltar. As he stood there, the fact dawned on him that he was watching the first major invasion of the British Isles since William the Conqueror landed his army almost nine hundred years earlier. Despite this, he offered up no emotion whatsoever.

"Prime Minister," General Dill greeted him. The general hung up the phone that he'd been speaking on and went back to handing out orders to the small army of people in the room.

The room was twice as busy as he'd ever seen it before. Uniformed men and women were on telephones, passing on a constant stream of information that was pouring in over the wires. The large table map at the center of the room was the focal point of activity. Two women in blue uniforms, headsets over their ears, were busy pushing markers around the map with long sticks. Those charts were not painting a very good picture right now either.

Red markers had been placed at points off the southeast coast, and yellow ones at airfields that had been taken out of commission. The red markers off the coast represented confirmed German warship positions. The list of abandoned airfields was a lengthy one. Most of the main bases north and east of London had been hit. A line of German submarines had taken up picket positions to the east of Dover and were doing a good job of keeping the destroyers and cruisers of the Channel Squadron from moving into those waters. The situation looked grim, but Churchill couldn't let it show. One problem at a time.

"What do we have, General Dill?" he asked.

Dill glanced at him and shook his head.

"Where do we start?" Dill replied with exasperation. "We have confirmation of a German battleship, probably *Bismarck*, sneaking into the Channel with no less than five escorts. Most likely headed toward Portsmouth. The Luftwaffe is hitting all the major crossroads between London and Crawley."

"What about the Royal Navy?" Churchill asked. He knew Admiral Pound was still on his way over from his headquarters.

"The Third Destroyer and Eighteenth Cruiser Squadrons are pushing in from the east. I'm not the naval man, but from what I've been told is that the Jerries have enough picket subs to give our boys serious problems. At least one of our squadrons is making its way from Cornwall right now. But they won't be much use against a battleship like *Bismarck*."

"Not to mention the air support the Germans will have from Northern France," Air Marshal Leigh-Mallory added. "Even a flight of Stukas could hinder our ships from coming to the rescue."

"What about our Number Ten Group?" Churchill asked. "Aren't they covering the Western Approaches?"

Leigh-Mallory nodded. "They are. But we can't risk sending them into combat over the Channel. If the Germans do as I suspect they will start operations around Portsmouth, we'll need to shift those planes to the east to support Number Eleven Group. As it is we're still short of pilots. If we lose even a fraction of them over the water, we'll effectively give up control of the skies in the southwest."

Churchill grumbled a disparaging reply. The board was set, and the pieces were now all in play. Fighter Command was already hanging on by their fingernails. They'd performed admirably, and he was proud of all his pilots, of course, but the damn Germans simply outmatched them at nearly every turn. It didn't help either that intelligence estimates of Luftwaffe strength had grossly miscalculated the number of aircraft they'd employed. The RAF had defended their airfields valiantly for weeks and weeks at first. But when the bombing of the major cities and industrial areas had started they'd also been forced to defend those skies as well. And as good as they were they were now stretched far too thin.

"Excuse me, Prime Minister," Dill said. "I've just been given this, sir." He held up a handwritten note. Churchill waited for the general. "Reports of German Army coded transmissions. Our field units picked this up just minutes ago."

"Coded transmissions?" Churchill asked hesitantly.

"Yes, sir. Field units picked them up coming out of the South Downs." Air Marshal Leigh-Mallory motioned for the report, Dill handed it to him, and he read the note for himself. Leigh-Mallory blinked in concern at the report. That was a mere fifty miles away from London.

"Lord," Leigh-Mallory muttered. "Most likely glider troops, sir. We have no reports of landings yet. If they came in low, under our radar..." he just shook his head.

"Even a few units holding key points along those roads could be costly," Dill told him.

Churchill studied the ever-changing map. New markers had been added. A thin line of blue was holding the coast from Eastbourne to Portsmouth. That was where it was going to come ashore from. If the Germans controlled those beaches for an hour, they'd control them for a week, and getting enough troops down there might prove to be next to impossible.

"I'd highly recommend we mobilize the Third Infantry and move them south to meet this threat," Dill told him, and Churchill eyed the general. "General Horrocks can move fast enough if we send his division in now. We have to neutralize any potential landings quickly. We can't risk having our frontline units getting cut off from behind."

Churchill studied the great map and the pieces moving around it. The open stretches of land on the southern shores of England that ran for over a hundred kilometers from east to west was the perfect place for an airborne drop, and Winston was disturbed that the possibility had not been discussed. The sloping landscape and woodlands of the Downs were ideal for German infantry. No doubt a carpet laid down before the land invasion. Seizing that area would effectively cut London off from the port cities of the southern coast.

"Yes," he finally replied. "Very well, General Dill. Give the order." He hesitated a moment before adding, "And contact all commands immediately. Codeword is Julius Caesar."

All eyes within earshot of the Prime Minister suddenly looked over at him. Dill, telephone already in hand, stopped, and stared at Churchill for a disbelieving moment, before finally accepting the order. Everyone present knew exactly what those words meant.

"This is General Dill. Send a message to all commands. Julius Caesar. I repeat. Julius Caesar. Invasion of the British Isles is imminent!"

Winston patted his coat down, realized that he had no cigar on him, then frowned in frustration. He knew the others around him hated the smoke, but he wished more than anything that he'd had another stogie right now. If they could get even a handful of ships passed those Germans, they could cut any potential invasion force to pieces. But the Luftwaffe had done its job well in the last few days and sealed off a wide stretch of the English Channel. Even a few heavy cruisers, or a battleship, could shell a city like Portsmouth into ruin, and there would be damn little they'd be able to do to stop it.

"I have to inform the king of the situation," he told the others. The royals had been moved out of Buckingham to Windsor for their safety. He knew King George wouldn't be getting any sleep tonight. No one would this night. The clock on the wall was just after six o'clock. Teatime.

"I have an open line to the palace already, sir," Tommy Thompson said from behind. The naval commander had been standing silently near the doorway.

Winston gave a slow double nod in reply.

"I'll leave you to things here," he told Dill and Leigh-Mallory. "I suspect the king will have me on for quite a while. When I return, hopefully, we'll have better news. But I believe, gentlemen, that this day will mark the beginning of the end for either us or the Germans. Do what you must."

* * *

Bess turned on the kitchen faucet, letting the cool water run over her hands. The wireless was on in the other room, and she could make out broken sentences of the BBC announcer coming over it. It was weak, often filled with long moments of static. The announcer was steadily reading off the names of places where the bombardment was falling heaviest, or where enemy ships had been sighted off the coast. Areas around London were being hit by the Germans again, and a general evacuation had been ordered from all areas along the coast.

She cupped her hands together, then leaned over the sink and placed her face between them. The water was refreshingly cool. She could feel tension running through her system. Or was it panic? The water made her feel a little bit better, and she released a reaffirming breath. The faucet handle squeaked as she shut it off, and she stood there for a minute or two wiping her eyes.

She was scared of course. Who wouldn't be in days such as these? She thought about the people in those other places. Countries that the Nazis had already taken. The people living under the thumb of occupation. Would London become the next Paris? Or worse. Warsaw and Rotterdam had been all but wiped away from the surface of the Earth. Like Sodom and Gomorrah.

Is that to be our fate as well?

"Bess," Simon called from the front room. His voice was gentle, as always.

She wiped her eyes again, then grabbed the towel from off the counter and dabbed her face dry with it. She thought about her aunt and uncle down in Dover. They'd removed to Canterbury a few days earlier, but she couldn't help but worry anyway. Half of everyone she knew, half the town of Maidstone, her neighbors, had fled. But how far could one go? You couldn't remove the entire population of England.

"Bess," Simon repeated himself, a little less gently this time.

"I'll be right there," she answered.

"*... German warships had been sighted near the Isle of Wight...*" She strode through the dining room. Even the announcer's voice was becoming tense. She could hear the change in his tone. "*The government is asking that any civilians still in the area, please take shelter.*"

She wanted to turn it off. To just shut the whole world off. Things were bad enough without having to listen to every single detail going on. She stopped at the radio, put her hand on the knob as if she were about to shut it off, then thought otherwise. Her fingers slipped away. It was bad, but turning it all off wouldn't change anything about it.

"Bess!" Simon shouted.

"Coming," she replied. His voice was hard, and it took her by surprise. Simon was always such a sweet boy. She walked through the living room, gazing around for him. "Where are you?"

"Here," he answered. She walked toward the voice. He was standing in the middle of the doorway, his back turned to her. He was still holding onto the small planting tools he'd been using earlier, and his trousers were smeared in dirt and potting soil.

"Are you alright?" she asked him, putting a gentle hand on his shoulder. He didn't answer. She shook him gently. "Simon?"

He half turned to her, his eyes were red, and tears were running down his cheeks. She squinted, her heart seemed to come to a stop.

"What...?" she half asked, then saw him point his finger.

Bess stepped out the doorway, half the town of Maidstone must've been out on the street. People were everywhere up and down the neighborhood. A car flew by, a man at the wheel, the backseat packed with children, luggage dangling out of the open trunk. She watched it go, alarmed that someone would go speeding off through the streets like that.

"Look," Simon whispered.

She followed his finger, saw what he was pointing at, and gasped. Her eyes bulged, and her breath left her. The skies to the south were filled with something that she'd only ever seen pictures of in a newspaper. She could see the faded outlines of planes flying north, and out of them the sight of parachutes descending slowly to the earth. There were hundreds of them, perhaps more. Every moment that went by more and more of them fell out of the sky. Her eyes welled up instantly. She cupped her hands over her mouth.

"Oh my God," she breathed in horror. Her mind went blank, all she could do was stand and stare. In the background, the voice of the BBC announcer still came through the tiny speaker.

"We're getting reports of landing craft approaching the beaches now... The Army is fighting in the South Downs, and I've just been handed... handed a report of paratroopers dropping in areas around the High Weald. Good Lord. We'll stay on the air for as long as we can. If you're still hearing this broadcast, please stay safe. Lock your doors, hide in the cellars. And God be with you all..."

EPILOGUE

Moscow

Stalin sipped slowly on a glass of diluted red wine in his private office of the Kremlin, staring out of the window that provided him with a full view of Ivanovskaya Square. Outside he observed the bodies of another dozen traitors, who'd been hanged just this morning, dangling from the makeshift gallows that had been set up in the center of the wide courtyard. Their lifeless bodies hung there, swinging ever so slightly in the summer breeze. The victims of yet another purge by the Soviet leader following the disastrous campaign in Finland.

And it wasn't over. For nearly a month now, the NKVD had systematically gone down the lists of Red Army officers that had failed to successfully prosecute that campaign. Hundreds of them had so far been sentenced to death by the tribunals. Thousands more were still awaiting their turn, and many, many more had been deported off to the Far East, to isolated gulags that dotted Siberia.

The failure in Finland had been nothing short of disastrous, both to the Red Army and to Stalin himself. The humiliating defeat had portrayed the Soviet Secretary General as a weak figure internationally. Despite overwhelming numbers, his armies failed to overcome the Finnish defensive lines and had been routed by the Finns during a devastating counterattack. The result had been the capture of an entire Soviet Army corps, and the collapse of morale among the Russian soldiers.

Now someone had to pay the price, lest Stalin himself look weak. Some would no doubt already be whispering in the hallways about replacing the Soviet leader, and he could not – would not – permit that. The trials had been brief, the verdicts returned had been harsh, and punishment swift. The guilty had to pay, along with their families.

Behind him, sitting in utter silence, the Council of People's Commissars waited patiently. He took another long sip of the wine. Outside the window, the first raindrops were beginning to fall on Moscow. In the distance, dark clouds began to form. There was nobody in the square today. Nobody except the guilty that was. He thought he'd been done with this business years ago. Thought that he'd cured his country of the disloyalty that existed within it. But, now he understood that the purging would never end. Not truly. The Soviet Union, his nation, the one he had created and pulled out of the dark ages from the old Tsar, would require a sterner hand than the one that he had governed with before. He understood that now. That the old would constantly need to be swept away in a never-ending revolution.

Those that could not or would not conform, would be dealt with. Those that did not work for the total betterment of the state would not be missed. Those that were victorious for Mother Russia, would be part of the new order. Those that did not, would be done away with.

Slowly, the man turned back around, walking unhurriedly toward the group seated. The wooden chair squeaked as he sat down at the head of the table.

"We've suffered humiliation," he told them. His voice was blunt, and ice-cold. His gaze was iron hard. The man had dark eyes that just seemed to get darker when his mood worsened. "In the eyes of the world we've suffered a national embarrassment." His voice became sterner. He looked into the face of each and every man sitting. Then he took a long sip of his wine. The quiet room practically echoed with the sound of the single clinking of his glass on the table. "What is being done?"

Faces turned as the ministers looked at one another.

"Arrests are up," a voice answered. Heads turned toward Beria, Minister of Internal Affairs. The chief of the notorious NKVD was responsible for policing the country, seeking out and dealing with internal disloyalty and security matters. "As you can see, Comrade Stalin, executions are also up. We feel that we've rounded up all of those whose disloyalty led us to this disaster."

"YOU FEEL!" Stalin shouted, pounding the table with a closed fist, causing those around to jump in sudden dread. There was an unnerving silence that followed. "You feel?" Stalin repeated coldly. "If you feel that your department has rounded up all of those responsible for this betrayal, then perhaps new leadership is needed at your ministry." Beria swallowed hard and slowly nodded his head at Stalin.

"Apologies, Comrade Stalin," he choked out. "I meant to say that we will weed out all of those who are disloyal."

"Disloyalty led to this disaster," Stalin told them. "Disloyalty will lead to the next one. I want it weeded out! I will not tolerate anything less than absolute devotion to the state. We will have order!" He gave them all a hard stare. "What's the state of our armed forces?" he asked, his eyes settling on Timoshenko.

"I've compiled a complete report," the People's Commissar for Defence licked his dried lips as he spoke. "The Finns inflicted heavy casualties on us during the war. The collapse of the 8th Army has sent shockwaves through the Red Army. With the arrest of so many officers and traitors, we're recommending a full reorganization of our forces."

"Double the number of political commissars in every unit," Stalin said icily. "And for every political commissar who is also found in dereliction of his duties, they are to be shot immediately! No trials for them. Their bodies should be put on display in Red Square for all to see. Whatever comforts were given to their families should be stripped of them. Betrayal starts at home. If we do not root it out, it'll only be allowed to spread." No one argued.

"What do we do about the Finns?" Foreign Minister Molotov asked. "They've asked again whether or not we wish to ratify their proposed treaty."

Stalin let his gaze drift absently down to his half-empty wine glass, and he seemed to stare off into nothingness for several long moments. His fingers rhythmically tapped at the tabletop. His first inclination was to tear the proposed treaty in half and send it back to Helsinki, along with the head of the Finnish ambassador. But he knew, despite himself, that his first inclinations could sometimes be wrong. As far as he was concerned the Finnish demand for territorial concessions was outrageous, though not altogether strategically important. Most of it was empty land, inhabited scantily by farmers. He didn't care anything about the territory, nor did he care for the Russian families who lived there. Though, he might be able to make a case, later on, to justify some future military action against Finland again. Just as Hitler had done with Czechoslovakia, when he'd claimed that German minorities were being suppressed. Yes. That could make for an excellent casus belli at some point.

Right now, both the country and the Red Army needed to be reorganized. Both needed to be built back from the ground up. And first, that would mean getting rid of all of the traitors within the Army that had failed him.

"We are not ready for another war," Timoshenko bluntly stated. Hard words, but he knew hard words didn't frighten Stalin. The man only wanted what all dictators did: Victory. "Six months from now, perhaps. We need time now to rebuild our armies." He swallowed hard at the next words. "To deal with those whose patriotism was not strong enough. Give us time, Comrade Stalin, give us time. We will have our forces ready."

Stalin's eyes were glossy, and his stare was unnerving. He pointed a single finger at Timoshenko, and a strange grin graced his face. "You will be held to those words, Comrade. If you fail..." his finger waved towards the large window, "... it'll be your neck in the noose. Your best men will be on the task. Understood?"

Timoshenko, visibly shaken at the threat, cautiously nodded. "Understood. I will have Zhukov himself take personal charge of the matter."

Stalin leaned back in his wooden chair and took a sip of his wine. Outside, the sound of large raindrops pelting against the huge windows filled the room. Dark clouds began to move in over the city, and in the courtyard below, at the far end of the square, a pair of tall double doors opened, and a line of handcuffed prisoners garbed in black were led out toward the gallows. It was only now noon, and there was still plenty of time left in the day.

Printed in Great Britain
by Amazon